WITHDRAWN

Britta Röstlund has lived in Paris for fifteen years. She is a freelance journalist covering everything from the Paris Fashion Week to French politics.

BRITTA RÖSTLUND

Translated from the Swedish by Alice Menzies

WEIDENFELD & NICOLSON

First published in Great Britain in 2017
by Weidenfeld & Nicolson
an imprint of the Orion Publishing Group Ltd
Carmelite House, 50 Victoria Embankment
London EC4Y 0DZ

An Hachette UK Company

1 3 5 7 9 10 8 6 4 2

Vid foten av Montmartre © Britta Röstlund,
first published by Norstedts, Sweden, in 2016.
Published by agreement with Norstedts Agency.

English translation © Alice Menzies 2017

ISBN (Hardback) 978 1 4746 0545 8
ISBN (Export Trade Paperback) 978 1 4746 0546 5
ISBN (eBook) 978 1 4746 0548 9

Typeset by Input Data Services Ltd, Somerset

Printed and bound in Great Britain by Clays Ltd, St Ives plc

MIX
Paper from
responsible sources
FSC® C104740

www.orionbooks.co.uk

At 73 Boulevard des Batignolles, there is a small grocer's shop. The type of place English-speaking tourists tend to call an 'Arabic shop'. Mancebo, the owner of the shop, doesn't like that, but he holds his tongue. In any case, they don't get all that many tourists on the boulevard. Most visitors stick to the Champs-Élysées, the Eiffel Tower, the Louvre or the Arc de Triomphe. Tourists who want to discover the 'real' Paris will go somewhere like Château Rouge, feeling bold and cosmopolitan as they stroll at a reassuring distance from the metro entrance. The fact is, there's no such thing as one real Paris. The city has many faces. If you want to discover Paris, it's better to sit on one of the city's benches. From there you can watch several million people trying to find their place in life.

Mancebo discovers Paris every day, sitting on his stool outside the shop at 73 Boulevard des Batignolles.

It doesn't occur to Mancebo that he discovers Paris every day. He unconsciously registers everything that goes on on the street. The smell of cooking causes him to interrupt his observations. The first time it happens is at lunchtime, when he knows that a meal prepared by his wife, Fatima, will be waiting for him in the apartment upstairs. But before the clatter of china even has time to reach him, Mancebo's cousin, Tariq, comes rushing into the shop. He works not far away, just across the boulevard in fact, in his cobbler's shop. The very shop he claims he is about to shut up and sell in order to move to Saudi Arabia and open a school for parachutists. Not that he knows anything about skydiving, but one day about five years ago a man had come in to get his shoes reheeled and in the time it took the glue to dry, he told Tariq how he had changed profession, giving up work as an IT consultant in Paris to open a bungee-jumping school in Jordan. And later that same day a young man came in and happened to mention that he and his wife had moved to Dubai. They had been getting by in ordinary jobs in Paris, but now they lived like kings. That was how Tariq got the idea for his skydiving school. 'The Saudis are gagging to get airborne,' he often says. As long as the oil keeps on flowing, they'll pay, Tariq is sure of it. He's even gone to the library to borrow books on Saudi Arabia. But Fatima thinks he would be better off mastering the parachute jumping part first.

Tariq doesn't discover Paris the same way Mancebo does; he keeps to his cobbler's shop, often having a cigarette in the office. Mancebo is only allowed one cigarette a day, even though he feels like smoking more. Fatima has decreed her husband will smoke only after dinner. 'Just imagine if a food shop smelled of smoke!' she likes to say. She also claims to be allergic to cigarette smoke, so Mancebo can't smoke at home. Mancebo isn't afraid of his wife, not really. While he works seven days a week she stays at home. Beyond cooking, he's not really sure how she passes the time, and he doesn't ask.

The cousins not only work close by, but live close by. Tariq and his wife, Adèle, live in the apartment above the shop, and Mancebo, Fatima and their son, Amir, live in the one above that. It should be the other way round, Mancebo often argues. It would be much more natural for him to have Tariq's apartment, because then he'd only need to go down one flight of stairs to open the shop, and up one flight after he closed it. But Fatima doesn't agree. 'It's the only exercise you get.'

A few years ago, when Mancebo had more energy, he'd mustered every argument he could think of to engineer an exchange. The first, and most persuasive, was that he is much older than Tariq, and in a few years' time the stairs could become a problem for him. Secondly, he gets up earlier than the others and sometimes wakes them when he goes downstairs. And, thirdly, Fatima always cooks on the first floor because the stove there is better. It was as clear as day, at least to Mancebo, that his family ought to have the first-floor apartment.

He diligently assembled his arguments and presented them over a grilled chicken one evening. But to his surprise, no one backed him up, not even his wife, which still today strikes him as odd. In fact, she made a joke at his expense, asked if he'd been round the neighbours collecting signatures for his petition. Tariq had laughed, as he always did, Adèle had said nothing, as she usually did, and Amir probably hadn't been listening.

If anyone asks Mancebo what his job is, he says that he works in the service industry. If anyone asks for further details, he says he owns a grocer's shop. All this is true. And if anyone asks where this shop is, he replies that it's at the foot of Montmartre. That point is debatable.

Mancebo likes the idea of living and working at the foot of the white, pointy confection that is the Sacré-Cœur. But his answer leaves many with the impression they can find Mancebo and his shop on the little square called Parvis du Sacré-Cœur, or squeezed into one of Montmartre's alleyways. That is not the case. You can see the basilica from his address, but it's far off on the horizon, high up on the hill. Fatima thinks it's childish of him to say he lives at the foot of Montmartre and snorts every single time he does. Sometimes she tugs his ear and Mancebo protests that no one knows the size of Montmartre. He's right, of course.

Mancebo's daily life is governed by the scents and signs of the city.

He has no need of a watch. But he does have an alarm clock, which rings just after five o'clock every morning. Fifteen minutes later he's in his white van on the way to Rungis, to the south of Paris, to buy fresh fruit and vegetables. By eight, he's back in Paris, and a few minutes after that he drops in on François at Le Soleil for a quick coffee, which he calls breakfast.

Along with Mancebo's shop and Tariq's cobbler's, the cousins' local café, Le Soleil, forms a triangle in their neighbourhood. 'The Golden Triangle', the bar owner likes to joke, alluding to the more famous triangle between three well-known old cafés: Café de Flore, Les Deux Magots and Brasserie Lipp. 'Bermuda Triangle, more like,' Tariq always says. Neither François nor Mancebo really understands what he means by this.

At nine on the dot he pulls up the grille and the shop breathes in the morning air. Then he works until the smell of cooking intensifies. Down with the grille and time for lunch. Once he's finished his meal, he makes his way downstairs to pull up the grille for the second time that day. It comes back down late in the afternoon, when the time comes for a pastis with Tariq at Le Soleil. After that, it's back to work until the smell of cooking again lies heavy in the air, at around nine. The grille comes down for the last time.

Another day is over. He counts the day's takings, twisting rubber bands around the notes and putting them into a plastic bag. He'll take those to the bank. The aroma of a rich bean stew wafts through the chink between the door and its frame, a pair of slightly parted lips. The very breath of the building lets Mancebo know when it's time to bring in the stands, which in turn signals to Tariq that it's time to shut for the day. In the mornings, when Mancebo opens up the shop, yesterday's breath is always lingering in the air, but only for a few minutes, or as long as it takes to pull the fruit and vegetable stands outside. Then it blends with the dubious freshness of the Paris air.

Mancebo finishes counting the money. It hasn't been a good day. Heat has paralysed the city, but now a storm seems to be brewing. He starts shutting the little green doors on the vegetable stand. Mancebo adjusts the small black cap he wears all year round. He feels naked without it. Just as Adèle does without her headscarf. He remembers the dinner when they discussed the similarities between his cap and Adèle's headscarf. Both have become a part of them. Fatima thinks neither the cap nor the headscarf serve any purpose. She would never wear a headscarf, it would only get in the way of her chores. Whenever she's fed up with Adèle for not helping with the housework, she chides that headscarves were invented for people who sit around listening to the radio all day. Adèle claims she can't do anything more because of her back. Fatima thinks it's this back problem that has prevented Tariq and Adèle from producing children. Not the condition in itself, but the fact that they might not be able to do it in the 'baby position', as Fatima puts it.

Sometimes Tariq closes only an hour after his pastis, and spends the rest of the afternoon in the office behind the workshop. But he never leaves the shop until it's time to eat. 'What would I do up there with the womenfolk?' he always says. Mancebo doesn't really know what he does in the office when he shuts up early. Tariq claims he has financial matters to attend to, but Mancebo can see him, reading the paper as he smokes.

A middle-aged lady comes in, and Mancebo greets her politely. He knows who she is, she often comes in to buy a little something in the evening. She probably does her big shop somewhere else and only comes to him when she's forgotten something. Today it's biscuits and a Coca-Cola. She pays, Mancebo wishes her a good evening and accompanies her to the door. She leaves just as Tariq comes in, pats his cousin on the shoulder, opens the door to the stairwell and vanishes upstairs. The scent of food grows stronger now that the lips of the shop have been flung open.

It's been a thoroughly ordinary day. A day that started like all others and passed like all others, and Mancebo assumes, understandably enough, that it will also end like all others. But in actual fact, he assumes nothing. It's only once a day becomes extraordinary that the time leading up to it seems ordinary. Mancebo has nothing but food on his mind right now, food and his daily cigarette. Maybe Fatima is right when she says Mancebo's reptile brain takes over as the day progresses. The morning demands that he be bright and alert for the drive to Rungis, working out the quantities of everything he needs to buy. But as the day wears on, he becomes more and more passive. The gateway to the slower tempo is his afternoon pastis at Le Soleil.

'Hi there,' he calls to announce his arrival.

Fatima vigorously stirs the orange-coloured stew, and Tariq lights his sixteenth cigarette of the day as he grumbles about not having had time to smoke.

'You hear that!' Fatima cries, 'Tariq hasn't even had time for a smoke.'

She laughs and tastes the stew.

'Hi there, you lazy devil,' Mancebo calls out to Tariq before he ruffles Amir's hair and kisses Fatima on the cheek.

The heat in the room is unbearable. Everything is quickly laid out on the low table and they sit down on the rugs, everyone except Fatima, who is still pottering around them. Tariq gestures with one hand that she should sit down. She does so, immediately, as though she had been waiting for his signal. They start helping themselves to the food. Tariq puts out his cigarette and Adèle removes her veil from her face.

'We'll all die of passive smoking in here,' grunts Mancebo, mainly to placate Fatima.

They sing the praises of Fatima's cooking. But Adèle is unusually quiet tonight.

Suddenly, she jumps up, as though something had startled her, and glances around the table.

6

'Didn't you hear that?'

Fatima shakes her head, causing her double chin to tremble, and licks the last of the dressing from the spatula. Amir's mobile rings and Fatima tells him in extravagant gestures that he needs to leave the table.

'Relax, darling. It was only the mobile,' Tariq says.

'No, it was before that, there was someone knocking . . . banging . . .'

She hardly gets to the end of her sentence before they all hear it. Yes, there's definitely someone down there, banging on the bars of the grille. Tariq gets up, takes the chance to light another cigarette and looks out of the window. A light drizzle has started to fall, and the boulevard is empty.

'I can't see anything, but there could be somebody down there.'

They hear more banging, and without a word Mancebo puts on his black cap and hurries downstairs. He doesn't really think about who it could be, doesn't even try to guess. He's too tired to think. He's only going down, really, so he'll be able to eat in peace afterwards, to have his smoke and then go to bed.

There's a woman standing outside the shop, and once Mancebo unlocks the door and pushes up the grille she comes sweeping in. Mancebo thinks that the bread will be gone by the time he gets back up. But at the same time, he knows that his survival depends on good, personal service in the shop, and that includes flexible opening hours. Otherwise his customers may just as well buy their food at Monoprix, or at the Franprix nearby. Many of his lines are available there for half the price. But that doesn't change the fact it's highly likely all the bread will be gone. The woman looks around, as though she's surprised that she has entered a shop. Then she smiles. Mancebo doesn't return the gesture. The woman smiles again, and this time he smiles back.

7

'What can I do for you, madame?'

She looks around the shop, as though she can't quite believe where she is. As though someone had dragged her in there, blind-folded. She smiles again, but Mancebo pretends not to see. He's starting to feel weary and wonders if he'll miss the tea and cakes as well.

Suddenly, the woman takes an interest in his wares, as though she has finally realised that Mancebo's patience is running out. The woman sweeps around, there's no better way to describe her progress through the shop. Mancebo scratches his head beneath his cap and yawns. She stops, but this time she doesn't smile. Instead, she looks earnestly at Mancebo, grabs one of the jars of olives and heads towards the till. She holds out the jar as though she wants to show him what she has found, as though Mancebo should exclaim, 'Wherever did you find a thing like that?' When he doesn't, she lifts the jar a few centimetres from the counter then heavily sets it back down.

'Anything else?'

He doesn't know quite what to make of this woman. She picks up the olive jar for the third time and again puts it down on the counter. It's as though she's trying to make Mancebo understand something. She shakes her head conspiratorially, her gaze now directed at the street. She pays, thanks him and walks off carrying the jar as though it were a relay baton. Mancebo locks up and shakes his head.

'I had a real nutcase down there,' he pants when he reaches the top of the stairs.

'As I always say, if you locked up the population of Paris and only let out the sane ones, we'd be down to less than a million,' Tariq replies.

Fatima laughs and shows Mancebo the bread she's saved for him. It's her way of showing love. He is just tucking in to the warm pitta when the banging starts up again. They glance at each other. Are they hearing right? Fatima frowns and goes into the kitchen.

The banging resumes, and this time it's more desperate. But Mancebo doesn't budge. When the knocking starts yet again, everyone around the table stares at him. It's his job to do something about it. Mancebo takes his bread in one hand and trudges back down the stairs he had hoped not to see again that day. Halfway down, he realises he's forgotten his black cap. It would never have occurred to him to greet a stranger like that, so he walks back into the babble of voices. It seldom stays quiet for long in his family. Adèle casts a quick glance at Mancebo but the others don't notice his return.

Back downstairs, Mancebo switches on the light above the till and squints towards the grille. He can't see anyone and starts to doubt whether someone really was knocking on his door this time. His fingers drum against the door frame, waiting the few seconds he has decided to let elapse. Then he stops drumming and strains to hear anything unusual. He hears nothing, other than the gentle patter of rain.

Mancebo yawns and switches off the light. The requisite time has passed and he has almost forgotten what he's doing down in the shop. But the instant he turns his back, there's more knocking, even harder this time, as though his visitor is banging something hard against the grille. Bloody hell, what now? He realises that it's the same woman, the one who bought the olives a few minutes earlier. Her smile suggests that she finds the whole situation embarrassing, but that she has no choice in the matter.

The rain beats down on Mancebo's fingers as he opens the door, keeping the grille down just to be on the safe side. He looks at the woman in her long black coat and black shoes. Her hair, which looks black now that it's wet, contrasts vividly with her pale face. She holds up the jar of olives, as if the mere sight of it will make Mancebo raise the grille. Rain is splashing into the shop now, and all Mancebo wants is for this strange encounter to be over.

'What do you want now, madame? Can I help you with anything?'

9

Mancebo is surprised at his own patience. The woman starts nodding hysterically.

'Yes, you can help me, monsieur . . .'

She falls silent, as though she wants Mancebo to supply his name. He doesn't have the slightest urge to do so.

'Yes, you can help me, monsieur, but you'll have to let me in.'

'The shop is closed, madame. Can't it wait until tomorrow?'

The woman shakes her head. 'No, it can't wait until tomorrow.'

She sounds desperate. Mancebo looks to check there's no one with her, but sees only a couple caught out by the rain, hurrying along the boulevard. The woman is clutching the olives tightly, and it dawns on him that she must have been banging the jar on the door. She looks him straight in the eye.

'I promise not to stay long, monsieur.'

In the end, Mancebo raises the grille and the woman sweeps in like a wet cat, quick and gracious. She pushes back her hood and shakes her head. And then she smiles, a calm and easy smile, and takes in the shop, as though she has forgotten her urgent business now she's safely inside.

Mancebo starts to feel a certain tension in the air. He's never experienced anything like this before. This scene doesn't fit in his humdrum life, and perhaps it will give him a story to tell. Usually Tariq is the one making the jokes and telling the stories. He's read most of them on the Internet, but even so. Mancebo always says that if you run a cobbler's shop you have time to read any old rubbish, but Mancebo feels his silence acutely.

The rain had stopped the moment the woman entered the shop, as though the weather gods were after her and her alone. Mancebo doesn't throw her out straight away, instead he observes her from a distance. She laughs and drops the jar on the counter, even though she's paid for it.

'Just so you don't think I've stolen it.'

She's playing for time, maybe she doesn't want to go back onto the street. But if she's scared of something out there, why would she seek refuge here, Mancebo thinks. Plenty of bars and restaurants are still open, there's even a McDonald's not far away. Mancebo's shop is shut and she couldn't have even been sure he would hear her knocking and come downstairs. She runs her long white fingers over the tins and jars, as though she's checking them for dust.

'How can I help you, madame?'

She looks disappointed, as though his question has come too soon. As though there was something she wanted to do before the question arose.

'You can call me Cat,' she whispers, holding out her hand.

Mancebo instinctively shakes her hand. 'Madame Cat?'

'Cat will do fine.'

'Like the animal?'

She nods. Mancebo nods back, and decides the story is getting better and better. By now he has forgotten the cakes and tea upstairs.

'So how can I help you . . . Madame . . . Cat?'

The woman suddenly looks uncertain.

'So how can I help you?'

'You're the only one who can help me, Monsieur . . .'

'Mancebo.'

'Can we talk in peace here?'

Mancebo nods and straightens his back. He likes this feeling of importance. Never before has he been the only one who could help somebody. He might have been the one to save a party when all the other food shops were shut, or to supply an item for a half-mixed cake or a spontaneous picnic. But no one has ever told him that he is the only one who can help them.

'I want to ask you a favour. Or rather, I want to offer you a job.'

'I've got a job.'

'And it's precisely because you've got this job that I want to offer you another.'

Mancebo gives her a sceptical look.

'No one could do this job better than you, Monsieur Mancebo.'

The rain resumes and a couple of happy teenagers dash across the boulevard, hand in hand. Their laughter makes Madame Cat jump.

'I want you to spy on my husband.'

For the first time, Mancebo starts to wonder whether this is all a joke. But when he looks into Madame Cat's eyes, he realises this woman isn't joking. She looks as earnest as any woman could possibly look.

'What, me, spy on your husband? Why? And why on earth me, of all people? I haven't got time to tail a stranger all day long. Can't you see how much I have to do here? I get up at five in the morning to go to the market, and I don't turn off my light until midnight.'

'Exactly,' she says, 'you've answered all your questions. See that building over there?'

She points across the street and Mancebo looks at the building above Tariq's cobbler's. It's identical to the building they are standing in. It has a shop on the ground floor and two apartments on the floors above. The only difference is that the building opposite is free-standing, and there's a fire escape running down one side.

'My husband and I live in the apartment on the top floor. The apartment beneath us is empty. For a while now, I've suspected that he's cheating on me. I work away a lot, travelling, I'm an air hostess, and since he's a writer he works from home. Or he used to work at home, but he's suddenly changed his habits. He doesn't write as much . . . And my friend has seen him out and about during the day.'

'But what makes you think he's cheating on you?'

'A woman can feel these things.'

Mancebo's back is starting to feel stiff, but his brain has perked up, not to mention his heart, which isn't used to pumping red excitement round his body. He puts up one hand to indicate that she's not to go anywhere, and disappears behind the counter. He quickly returns with two stools. She takes a seat and unbuttons her raincoat. Mancebo takes it as a sign that she trusts him and he feels honoured. He puffs himself up like a proud toad before he sits on his stool.

Madame Cat's hair has started to dry and Mancebo can see that its true colour is more of a chocolate brown. Even though he has asked her to sit, Mancebo has no intention of taking on the job. But he very much wants to hear more of her story. He gets to hear gossip about his neighbours every day, but he's never heard anything like this.

'But you surely must have more proof that he's having an affair than the fact that he sometimes goes out during the day?'

'I do. He seems stressed.'

Madame Cat goes quiet, as though she's trying to think of something else that has changed recently.

'And he brings books home.'

'So? I thought you said your husband was a writer, surely there's nothing odd about that?'

'You're right . . . he writes crime fiction and it's the only thing he likes reading, but he's been coming home with all kinds of books lately. One day, I found a book about pruning fruit trees.'

'So?'

Madame Cat looks at Mancebo.

'We live in an apartment.'

Shame washes over Mancebo. He doesn't feel like the most quick-witted of detectives, but the fact that her husband has stopped writing surely doesn't have to mean that he's unfaithful? There is such a thing as writer's block, Mancebo thinks. And he can't be accused of marital infidelity just because he has been seen out and about during the day.

'And how would I recognise your husband?' Mancebo asks, mostly to show that he can be capable of clear thinking.

Madame Cat gives Mancebo a questioning look.

'We're the only people living in the building opposite, and he usually wears a brown cap. I was thinking of hiring a private detective. I even called a few. Did you know that there are two thousand and thirty-seven private detectives in Paris?'

Mancebo shakes his head and eagerly absorbs this fact. He likes short, pithy gobbets of information that he can show off later at Le Soleil.

'But then last Saturday, around lunchtime, when he went out to buy cigarettes, I looked through his computer, and that was when I caught sight of you, sitting on your stool outside the shop. I must have seen you there a thousand times, but that was when the idea first came to me. I realised there was no one who could carry out the task better than you! Nobody would suspect a thing because you're always sitting there, from morning until night. And you wouldn't have to do much.'

Madame Cat lowers her voice and moves closer to Mancebo.

'All I want is for you to give me written reports of what goes on during the day and in the evening. When he goes out, when he comes back, who goes into the apartment, or anything else you think might be of interest. You'll be paid handsomely, let's say the same rate as a professional private detective. The money will be in one of these, every Tuesday morning.'

She holds up the olive jar. Mancebo scratches his head and is about to take off his cap when he changes his mind.

'The money will be in a jar of olives?'

Madame Cat nods.

'I've lived here long enough to know that every Sunday evening you put out the glass for collection, don't you? So you'll put the week's report into an empty olive jar, and I'll make sure to collect it early the next morning, before seven. The week's new delivery of bottles arrives early on Tuesday mornings, usually before you've had time to open the shop. That's where you'll find your payment.'

Mancebo scratches his head again.

'I need your answer right away, if you don't mind, Monsieur Mancebo. I've waited long enough.'

It didn't feel particularly special to be back in the café, oddly enough. The last time I'd been there, I was being interviewed about the revelation that HSBC had helped its clients to place their capital in Switzerland, evading hundreds of millions of dollars in tax.

I hadn't been the only one to investigate HSBC. There were 140 of us, journalists from forty-five countries, but the work itself was solitary. Towards the end, I was working day and night because *Le Monde* had set a strict publication date. Our research also showed that the bank had been doing business with arms dealers who supplied weapons to child soldiers in Africa. The affair grew, and with it the pressure.

I was back at square one, the café, looking for new commissions. The tablets were in my bag. Just in case. I hadn't really been taking them for long enough to have seen the promised benefits. During the months I was working on the HSBC case, I had been hoping the result and eventual revelations would be appreciated. But when it finally came around, the whole thing felt meaningless. And with that meaninglessness came the collapse.

I'd seen the warning signs, the trouble sleeping and strange physical ailments. Depression caused by exhaustion, that was the diagnosis, but I didn't feel depressed, just indifferent. The medicine I was prescribed was for anxiety. And that was the knotty equation which made me wait before starting the tablets. Though with the wait came the anxiety, as though on command, which made it easier to start the medication.

There was nothing strange about the way he entered the café, but then he paused in the middle of the room as though he was some kind of chosen one. His eyes darted from person to person. I glanced up at him. In the man's eyes there was an unusual but very attractive blend of uncertainty, hope and tenacity. Once he had scanned the customers nearest the till, he moved on to the group sitting closer to him. Then he looked directly at me and I held his gaze, while not exactly returning it. The man continued to peer around intently and I had the feeling he was looking for a woman. I lowered my eyes and went back to my work.

'Are you waiting for Monsieur Bellivier, madame?'

His tone was formal, and implied the answer itself was unnecessary. It was more like a greeting, a message or code. There was no hope in it, nothing personal, his voice expressed no emotion whatsoever. I shook my head, almost instinctively. The man looked at me as though he was giving me time to change my mind. He took several steps back and returned to his spot in the middle of the café. Then he began scanning the customers again.

I studied him and became increasingly convinced that it had to be a woman who was waiting for Monsieur Bellivier. The man was paying no attention to the male clientele.

He turned to another woman, and though I couldn't make out what he said, I was sure he was asking her the same question. She shook her head. I put a full stop at the end of my sentence and studied the woman. She had brown hair in a pageboy cut, just like me. The man was beginning to look a little desperate. Was he Monsieur Bellivier? Or was he his representative?

The man was still standing in the middle of the café, resolute. That was when I had the idea. It was a banal act in and of itself, but it both frightened and appealed to me. The woman was meant to be there. I waved him over. The first step. A slight movement of the hand. He didn't seem surprised, more embarrassed that I hadn't waved him over sooner. I whispered:

'Yes, I'm waiting for Monsieur Bellivier.'

He extended his hand and I shook it, but we didn't exchange names. For a moment, I found it strange that he didn't introduce himself, but I decided it must be because he was, in fact, Monsieur Bellivier. And introducing myself was unnecessary, since he clearly ought to know who was waiting for him. A silent handshake was therefore the most appropriate greeting. The fact he shook my hand told me that we didn't have any sort of personal connection. If we had, he would have kissed me on the cheek. So, this was a professional encounter.

That was it, wasn't it? I'd satisfied my sudden urge. But the thought of playing along for a little bit longer was tempting. I could just as well take a few more steps. He would realise I wasn't the right person as soon as we started talking.

I closed my laptop. It could give the game away about who I was. If he was angry when he realised I wasn't the right woman, it would be better that he didn't know my real identity. The man suddenly looked around, as though to check whether we were being watched. He sat down in the armchair opposite mine and smoothed his trousers a little, while I took the opportunity to drop my phone into my bag. I was shedding as much of myself as I could.

He got to his feet and asked whether I wanted anything. I shook my head because I was afraid to use my voice. Could we have spoken on the phone? He went over to the counter. The green armchair I was sitting in seemed to grow when he left me. The seat that normally felt so safe, so enveloping, suddenly felt far too big for me.

The man added sugar to his coffee and stirred it. I stayed silent. I tried to work out a way of calling the whole thing off, but my fantasies about who the man was and what sort of person might be waiting for Monsieur Bellivier took over. Maybe he thought I was an escort? Wasn't that how it worked? You agreed on a public meeting place and then went to a fancy hotel afterwards?

'Have you been waiting long?'

Perhaps he was simply being polite, but it could also have been a trick question. Maybe he was an hour late, or an hour early.

'I wanted to be in good time,' I replied. My voice had returned.

It seemed like he wanted to smile, but he resisted, his face remaining neutral.

'Let me explain that Monsieur Bellivier sent me. He couldn't come himself, unfortunately, but I'm sure you'll get the chance to meet him.'

So, the man opposite me wasn't Monsieur Bellivier. Not that this information was much help. He could be absolutely anyone, which meant I knew as little as I had before.

'We're glad that you wanted to do it, and I hope you'll be happy.'

That you wanted to do it. So there was a task to be performed. My mind turned back to escorts.

'Tired?'

I shook my head and smiled.

'Well, I don't suppose I ought to tell you too much more right now, we'd be better off taking a look at the place. I can explain everything when we get there and you can settle in.'

He held open the café door and we stepped out into the wall of heat. My decision to work in that particular café in the Paris business district was based largely on the quality of its air conditioning. Working in a café also meant that I got out into the real world, which made me feel normal.

I stole a glance at the man as we took the escalator down to the plaza and wondered how to find a natural opening that would enable me to extract myself. I could pretend to get a text from the person I'd actually been waiting for and apologise – it was all a misunderstanding. I could pretend I felt ill . . .

'It's not far,' the man said with a smile.

Suddenly, we were in front of Areva, the tallest tower in La Dé-fense. I abandoned the escort idea. Areva was one of France's leading energy companies, and it had recently been in the news for question-able business practices. I had often come across the company's name in my work on HSBC's dealings in Africa.

Was this where Monsieur Bellivier worked? Would I be given access to confidential documents? Could this be a scoop? My inter-est had been piqued and my fear abated a little. I wanted to know more. The man went through the swing doors and over to the vast reception desk to exchange a few words with the receptionist. Sud-denly, a little more rapidly than I'd expected, he came back with a pass.

'Don't lose it.'

I turned it over to see who I was, apprehensive I might read my own name. But I hadn't been given a name, only a title. 'Sales Man-ager', the blue pass said. The man studied my face and then said something more cryptic than anything he'd said before:

'He's got a sense of humour.'

I couldn't be sure, but I imagined he must mean Monsieur Belli-vier. Which meant I wasn't actually a sales manager. My idea about being shown documents started to seem more likely.

The man had a pass of his own, and I tried to read it but I couldn't. He placed it gently on the barrier, there was a beep, and he was through to the other side. I needed to do the same. I'd missed my chance to extract myself naturally, or as naturally as I could in the circumstances.

We stopped to wait for the lift. A few people were already queuing, which meant I wouldn't have to be alone with the man. That very moment, in front of the lift, my appetite for work returned. It was a long time since I had felt that way.

We entered the lift with men in suits and a woman in a red dress.

Her beautiful legs looked surreal against the bright red colour. I saw the man press the button for the top floor. It merely strengthened my theory about confidential documents, which would probably be stored well out of the way. The two men wished us a good afternoon before they got out of the lift. We continued on up. The shapely legs also left us. I kept a firm grip on my pass.

For the first time, we were alone together, and I sensed that he was nervous. Maybe I wasn't the only one being forced to play someone I wasn't. Time seemed to stretch. But all lifts stop eventually, and this one was no exception. The doors opened and the man gestured theatrically for me to get out first. The floor was silent. I couldn't see another soul.

There was an emergency exit sign on one of the doors. It wasn't far from the lift. But what would I do if the door was locked? A feeling of panic washed over me and I started running towards the emergency exit. I grabbed the door, which swung open, and heard the buzz of people. I turned around. The man had made no attempt to stop me. He was still by the lift, watching with dismay. I was breathing heavily. I looked down, took a few steps downstairs and caught sight of a suited man hurrying past with a cup of coffee.

I went back up. Several hundred people were working right beneath me. I could reach them easily, and they could reach me.

'Sorry. It happens sometimes. I'm claustrophobic. The lift was an ordeal. Excuse me.'

'Don't worry. You should have told me. As you see, there are stairs.'

I followed the man along the corridor. There were windowed doors on either side, and I could make out huge conference rooms through the blinds.

'Here we are,' he said with a wave of his hand.

I stopped. He produced two identical keys and unlocked the door with one of them. This time he strode in first. I loitered in the doorway. It was a large room with a boardroom table in the centre. Over by the window there was a low desk with a computer, and there was a shabby old swivel chair in one corner. The few items of furniture had a forlorn look to them. Even the computer looked second hand.

The man glanced out of the window.

'Rather spartan, I'm afraid, but it's neat and tidy. A woman comes in to clean every day. Even if it's only you here, the wastepaper bin will need to be emptied and the floor vacuumed from time to time.'

Was I supposed to thank him at this point? I said nothing. He took one of the keys from the key ring and walked back to hand it to me. I took the key and he suddenly looked relieved. Like I had shouldered some of his burden.

'Well then, I suppose I'd better explain.' He spread his arms wide. 'You certainly can't complain about the view. You can see all the way to the foot of Montmartre from here. Can you see the Sacré-Cœur over there?'

This talk of the basilica was clearly a way to entice me into the room. I accepted the invitation. The view was magnificent. We both looked out at Paris, and for a few seconds, our eyes met in the pane of glass. He turned around and I continued to study the unfamiliar woman reflected in the window.

'Well. Where shall I start . . . ?' He put his briefcase on the desk, opened it and took out a document. 'I'll let you read it yourself, and then you can ask me any questions you have, I think that'll be best. I'll go and get us some coffee. There's a machine on the floor below, by the way. You can use it whenever you want.'

Just a few minutes earlier I had been sitting in the café, worried about revealing the slightest thing that could give away my identity. Now I was about to read what looked like a contract while my unknown employer went to fetch coffee. He left the door open, for which I felt a certain gratitude. I took out my mobile. Suddenly, it was no longer a threat but a source of security, not that I knew who I would ring if the need arose. But I checked I had reception all the same, and then I started to read.

The contract was well written and comprehensive, but it didn't answer any of my questions. My working hours were given, modest in length, and maybe there was some logic to them. They meant I would arrive later than most other people in the building, leaving before the standard working day was over.

The contract was for three weeks. For obvious reasons there was nothing about a period of notice, but it did say what my task would be. The salary would be paid after the final working day. The amount was stated in bold type. A large sum of money. This couldn't be a standard journalism job.

I could do my ordinary work here just as well as in the café down below, and maybe I would also be given access to some interesting material. Though I doubted I would ever receive the promised sum, I decided that if I did, my son and I would go away on holiday. Otherwise he would be stuck in the city all summer.

My eyes were resting on the Sacré-Cœur when I heard a knock at the door. I jumped.

'Sorry if I frightened you, but you'll have to get used to this being your office.'

The man had returned with two plastic cups of coffee. In some strange way it was good to see him again, he was at least a real, living human. He wasn't just a name, a signature or a shadowy figure. He suddenly seemed more real than I did. I had no idea who I was, and even less now I had read the contract.

'So, as you've probably realised, there's going to be a lot of dead time. Unfortunately, this isn't a job in which a great deal happens. Maybe not all that intellectually demanding, either, but as I said, it's stress-free. You'll have plenty of time for other things.'

He pointed to a brown cardboard box under the table. I hadn't

23

noticed it before now. I started to doubt it had even been in the room when we first came in.

'Mr Bellivier said you loved reading, so he's left you a whole box of books. So, are we agreed?'

I made my signature illegible. It hadn't occurred to me that contracts often demand you print your name underneath. The man took the contract and I made some other comment about the view, to distract him from the signature.

'Good, so that's that. In case we don't meet again, I'd like to wish you the best of luck. But I'm sure it's all going to be fine.'

I nodded.

'Take the afternoon off, you can start properly tomorrow.'

'If I have any questions, I mean, if anything happens, if the computer stops working, is there anyone I can ask, anyone I can get in touch with?'

For the first time, he lost his way in the script. He changed tack. Now we were in a different play.

'Nothing's going to go wrong, everything will work. But if anything should happen, it's important that you don't contact any . . . outsiders. If something isn't working I'm sure Monsieur Bellivier will soon notice and contact you personally.'

We walked to the lift together. What was I supposed to say if some Areva employee came up and asked me what I was doing there? I didn't ask the question out loud, but I knew what the man would have answered: 'Nobody's going to come up here.' And maybe he was right. The lift arrived and we got in.

'Do you know who once lived up here? This whole floor was his apartment.'

I shook my head, I didn't dare guess it had been Monsieur Bellivier.

'Before Areva, Framatome owned the building, and before that, Fiat. And the CEO, Giovanni Agnelli, took this floor as his private residence.'

It was a good lift anecdote, both in length and form. It could even have been written for that purpose.

'It's best for you not to have any contact with the people who work here. How shall I put it . . . it's important that you're as discreet as possible. But I'm sure you understand that.'

I understood.

Mancebo is woken by Fatima shaking him. This is only the third time in twenty-eight years that he has overslept. He looks at the alarm clock, 6.59, swears once and swears again.

Fatima gets up, slots her feet into her slippers and shuffles around, looking for her husband's trousers.

'Where on earth did you get undressed, husband?'

Mancebo eventually finds his trousers on the sofa, then turns the apartment upside down looking for his van keys. They've never sneakily vanished like this before.

'Take it easy, husband dear. You don't run a sushi restaurant.'

As Mancebo always told his wife, the sushi restaurants had to be first in line at Rungis. The best fish sells fast. Especially the fat-rich tuna.

He casts a quick glance over to the apartment opposite, but its windows are all dark. Amir passes the bedroom and looks at his father with tired eyes.

Down at the van at last, Mancebo puts the key into the ignition then stops himself. If he goes to Rungis now, he won't be able to open the shop before ten o'clock, maybe even later, depending on the traffic. He can't be late starting his new job. He looks into the mirror as though to remind himself what he looks like, and runs his hand over his stubble. He quickly debates the matter. He could go to Rungis for fresh supplies, but that would mean opening at least an hour late. How would it look if Madame Cat discovered he was cutting corners on his first day? She knows his opening times, after all. But if he doesn't go to Rungis, it'll be the first time in his long career that he hasn't had fresh fruit and vegetables midweek. What eventually makes him leave the van is the memory of Madame Cat's green eyes and the thought of being able to tell his family about his mission – once it's complete.

He unlocks the door. He hauls up the grille. He drags out the fruit and vegetables and says good morning to Madame Brunette as she passes with her badly groomed white poodle. These are the things he does every day. But nothing is being done with his usual energy or concentration. Because this is not a usual day. He is focused on the building opposite.

The city is still slumbering. The smell of rain casts Mancebo back to the night before, and he smiles to himself. Whatever happens, this has happened. He has met a woman by the name of Madame Cat, and she has asked him to be her private detective and spy on her husband. No one can take that away from him. Even if he's sacked from his new job on the very first day, or if no writer in a cap ever appears, he'll still have a story to tell.

Right, off we go, he thinks, wheeling out the slightly wizened apples and freshening them with a spritz of water. The city is starting to wake, in the way big cities do. Slowly, as though preparing to welcome millions of people. The sun is now glittering on the rooftops; a lovely day is dawning after all that rain.

Many of the carrots go straight into the bin, and the tomatoes don't look that great either. As Mancebo starts sorting through the peppers, something catches his attention. This early in the day he can still keep on top of everything, even if it's only a leaf drifting to the ground. It's going to get harder as the day wears on.

A bulky woman in black shuffles across the street. She distracts him from the vivid colours of the vegetables, and it takes him a few seconds to realise that it's Fatima. Mancebo didn't realise she ever went out before lunch. He isn't sure why he assumed she stayed at home in the mornings, but maybe it's because she never mentions going out. Maybe because he thought she told him everything she did each day. He goes out onto the pavement and watches his wife cross the boulevard. But then something strange happens. As though she has eyes in the back of her head, she turns around and stares at her husband, who is standing at a loss, a pepper in each hand.

'What are you doing here now?' she shouts, turning back towards the shop.

For a moment or two, Mancebo forgets that under no circumstances is he meant to be in the shop yet. It's only eight. He's supposed to be on the motorway back from Rungis, his van full of fresh fruit and vegetables. But Mancebo quickly regains his wits, as any good private detective should.

'That rust bucket wouldn't start. It coughed and it spluttered and then it just died on me. This is no good. What'll the customers say? Come and look at the veg!'

He pretends to wipe a tear from his cheek, just to be on the safe side. Fatima inspects the vegetables and angrily evicts a few carrots.

'I told you that heap of scrap would conk out. What're you going to do tomorrow?'

'Tomorrow?'

'Yes, how are you going to get to Rungis tomorrow?'

'Well, yes, er . . . I've got the rest of the day to sort something out.'

Mancebo is so focused on getting out of his corner that he forgets to ask why she is out and about so early.

'Those apples don't look too pretty either. You can't sell those,' Fatima declares, confiscating the spray.

Mancebo suddenly loses his temper, because if it were true, if the van really had broken down and he hadn't been able to get to

Rungis, then she shouldn't be angry with him. She should feel sorry for him – shouldn't she?

'And what are you doing out so early?'

Fatima looks up and shakes her head.

'Early? I heard the van, it was coughing its head off, you said so yourself. I was shaking rugs on the balcony and I thought I should come down and help you sort out the fruit. What's so strange about that?'

Mancebo notices that she is carrying her handbag. And why was she crossing the boulevard? Because she was, wasn't she?

He holds his tongue, not only because he is afraid of Fatima but also because, from now on, he'll have to be careful.

People start fighting for space on the pavements, making it harder for Mancebo to keep track of all the passers-by. There isn't a brown cap in sight. It isn't ten yet, but his stomach has already started to rumble. He thinks it must be because he was deprived of his usual coffee that morning. The hot drink seems to have the ability to keep his stomach quiet right up until lunch. He looks over to the other building again, but it's completely dark. Mancebo hears sounds on the staircase and then Tariq comes dashing in.

'I heard about the van. What a pain. Do you want me to ask Raphaël if he can drop round and take a look at it?'

Raphaël is Tariq's best friend. He works as an electrician, but he can repair anything. His latest trick was to fix Fatima's foot spa, which had been gathering dust in a corner, in the belief it would never work again.

'Thanks, but I can ring him. I'll try fixing it myself first. It's bound to be a quiet day seeing as the shop looks like a compost heap.'

'Bloody bad luck.'

'Yep.'

Tariq lights a cigarette, almost certainly not his first of the day, and sets off across the boulevard. It strikes Mancebo that Tariq might know the writer; he lives above the shop, after all. Maybe he's a good customer. But Mancebo can't remember hearing Tariq talk about a customer who lives above the shop, nor of a writer who pops in from time to time. It's strange, because everyone needs to get their shoes resoled or have a key cut every now and then. And people go to the nearest cobbler which, in the writer's case, would be Tariq.

If nothing happens, what will he report to Madame Cat? The morning is passing without drama, with no visible action from across the road. The smell of cooking slowly penetrates the shop. Mancebo is so hungry he feels queasy. Reluctantly, he shuts up the fruit and vegetable stands, his eyes fixed on the building opposite. Still nothing to report. Tariq ambles across and helps to pull down the grille. They go upstairs in silence, towards the smell of cooking, towards the lunch that is served as usual, on a day that is anything but.

As he sits at the low dining table, Mancebo angles his head so he won't miss a thing. He can't afford to, not on the first day. One by one his family members sit down without saying a word, and Mancebo wonders whether it's usually like this. They all have set places. His is with his back to the window, in the corner beside Tariq.

He can't remember why he was allocated that seat, years before, nor why the others were allocated theirs. But, for as long as he can remember, this is the way it's been. Adèle sits at one end, Amir opposite Tariq, and Fatima opposite Mancebo. But perhaps there is a logic to their seating plan. Fatima's place is nearest the kitchen, meaning she doesn't have to disturb anybody when she dashes in and out to fetch the delicacies she has prepared. Amir sits next to her. Maybe that's because he often gets home later, and can sit down without having to squeeze past the others.

From her seat at the end of the table, Adèle can survey everyone and everything, though why she should need to do so Mancebo has no idea, beyond the fact that she is, after all, their hostess – this is her home, even if she isn't responsible for the cooking. Mancebo mops the sweat from his forehead and studies his family. They're strangers to him. He's never felt that way before. But he has never had a secret to keep before. Mancebo can't really follow the rapidly changing topics of conversation, but he knows that he must. It's part of his assignment – to behave as normal. And that's the hard part. On top of the fact that his right eyelid has started to uncontrollably twitch, he has also spilled water from his glass and failed to hear Adèle ask, repeatedly, if they're going to Tunisia this summer.

I can't sit with my back to my work, I have a job to do, Mancebo thinks, and decides to act. He gets to his feet and, since Amir hasn't arrived yet, sits in his place. It's as though he's committed a crime or moved to a different continent. The table becomes an ocean. A few seconds earlier, his natural place was on the opposite shore. Tariq looks up wearily and lights a cigarette.

'What are you doing?' he asks.

'What am I doing?'

'Yeah, why are you over there now?'

Fatima comes in with a steaming bowl of rice.

'What are you doing there? Move, man, so you don't burn yourself.'

Risky behaviour demands focus, and Mancebo is more focused than ever before. Adèle casts a glance at Mancebo, but she says nothing.

'Why are you over here now?' Fatima repeats the question, sitting down beside her husband.

'Maybe he wants to see more of me,' Tariq laughs. 'Staring at me all day long isn't enough.'

'What have you done to your seat?'

Fatima peers at the rug by Mancebo's official place to see if she can detect a spillage or some other explanation.

'Feng shung.'

Tariq stubs out his cigarette and grins at the others.

'It's called feng shui,' Adèle laughs.

Fatima glares at her husband.

'The way we were sitting, or the way I was, it was no good. Two old men over there and nobody here because Amir hasn't arrived, and then the window there and . . . no, it's very bad feng shui.'

'What makes this any better?' Adèle asks. She sounds genuinely interested.

'I'm here, man and woman, on the same side, and it should be the same over there, man and woman. So you should move next to Tariq and let Amir sit at the end when he gets here.'

He has no idea where these words are coming from, but a few weeks earlier Adèle had been explaining feng shui to a clearly uninterested Fatima. Fatima had been so obvious in her indifference that Mancebo had felt sorry for Adèle and feigned an interest himself. But even if you're only pretending, you have to actually listen so that you can ask polite questions. His act of mercy is now bearing fruit.

'What do you know about it?' asks Fatima.

'After Adèle introduced us to it, I got interested. And I happened to hear something about it on the radio, in the van. The way we've been doing things isn't good feng shui. We'll have to change. Then things might go better for all of us. The shop might do better. Fortune follows good feng shui. Balance, harmony, success. It's a whole way of living.'

Mancebo throws out all the words he can remember from Adèle's sermon. Adèle sniggers. Fatima shakes her head. Tariq starts eating.

'And where is our son supposed to sit when he comes in?'

'The light comes from here . . . and the room is rectangular . . . the kitchen's there, the rug is red . . . that's where he's got to sit,' he exclaims, pointing to the corner where the TV is. 'That's where I want my son to sit when he comes home.'

Adèle hoots with laughter. Even Tariq laughs, and Mancebo can't help but smile.

'What are you saying, husband? Are you OK? How did you come up with all that? Are you crazy?'

Mancebo realises he must now calm Fatima down and reassure

her that everything's fine, so he kisses his wife's perspiring brow.

'No, I'm joking. Amir can sit wherever he wants, but a bit of a change doesn't hurt. I mean, if Adèle's into feng shui, I don't see why we shouldn't give it a try. It came to me when I overslept this morning. I started thinking about what Adèle said last week, when she told us feng shui could do wonders for a business, and I thought: why not give it a go?'

Mancebo is impressed with himself.

'Sit down, you idiot, so we can eat before the food gets cold. Luckily for you, Amir isn't coming for lunch today, so we can deal with this later.'

Mancebo would never have believed that such a seemingly pointless conversation with Adèle could have helped him out of this difficult situation. They start to eat.

'You want me to ring Raphaël, then?' Tariq asks, letting out a sound somewhere between a belch and a sigh.

'No, I'll do it.'

Mancebo gets up, dons his cap and is on his way out of the apartment when he remembers that he usually washes his hands after a meal. He can't change his ways or they'll suspect something. He remembers that he usually hums while he washes his hands. But what comes out of his mouth is a sound he's never heard before. He's forgotten what he usually hums, but he continues the tune he's started. As he goes down the stairs, he feels the eyes of the others upon him.

An old man with a large red mobile phone is waiting outside the shop. Mancebo generally recognises his customers, unless they're tourists, of course. This man seems at home in the city but not in the shop, perhaps not even in the neighbourhood. Mancebo greets him cheerily and switches on the little fan beside the till. He normally likes to chat with new customers, but today he feels only irritation. All he wants is to get on with his new job.

The man picks up a bottle of wine, some bread, cheese, olives and some little lemon cakes. An impromptu picnic, Mancebo guesses aloud, and the man nods. Maybe he isn't such a bad detective after all. Of course, he's spent his whole life around people. And how many hours has he spent on his stool, watching how they behave? That's excellent groundwork for a detective. When the man places the olives on the counter the gesture reminds Mancebo of Madame Cat.

It feels like weeks since she came into the shop. The till jangles and as soon as the man leaves, Mancebo takes up his position again. He has spent years sitting on this stool. But now his intentions are very different.

The hours pass slowly, the sun drags itself across the sky. The radio tells the old and the young to stay indoors and drink water. No one has entered or left the building opposite, or not that Mancebo has noticed. He starts to despair. Maybe he'll never get to begin the task that, in just a few short hours, has become the spice in his otherwise tasteless life.

As he pulls down his grille he realises he should hurry. He sees signs that he has delayed his afternoon break. Madame Brunette has already taken her poodle for its afternoon walk. The restaurant further down the boulevard has already bought its bread for the evening, and the light tells him he's definitely half an hour late for his pastis. Tariq shambles over the road, picks out a wizened apple and pulls a face, and they set off for Le Soleil. The Sun, there's no better name for a bar on a day like this.

'This bloody heat,' Tariq mutters between gulps.

'No one should spend the summer in Paris.'

'You're right there. Did you know that in Saudi Arabia people have air conditioning in every room, even the tiny ones?'

They turn onto Rue Clapeyron, where tall buildings block the sun.

'Well then, brother, did you call Raphaël?' Tariq asks

'No, I think the van's working again now. Maybe it just had heatstroke.'

'You sure? A van can't just repair itself. You better take it for a test drive.'

'Yes, OK, you're right. I'll do it after our drink.'

The last thing Mancebo wants is to take the van out, but he knows he has to stick to his story.

François shakes the cousins' hands, and turns the fan in their direction.

'For my VIPs,' he says, setting down two glasses of pastis in front of them, one with ice and one without.

'Mancebo's van broke down,' Tariq tells the bartender.

Mancebo is getting really fed up with this now. How can such a petty problem, a broken-down van that hasn't even broken down, take on such proportions? Why can't his cousin just drop it? Mancebo wonders why Tariq always tries to shoulder his burdens. Of course he's grateful that Tariq fixes the grille when it jams, or helps him with his tax return, but this time the help is unwelcome.

'Yeah, I couldn't get out to Rungis this morning, but one day without fresh fruit and veg won't ruin my reputation, will it?'

'Give Raphaël a ring,' is François' suggestion.

'That's what I told him,' says Tariq, draining his glass.

Tariq can't stop talking on the way back. Mancebo says nothing. He feels slightly disappointed. Virtually a whole day has passed and there's been no sign of the writer. Maybe he'll never have anything to tell stories about. Mancebo feels deflated as he trudges back to the shop with Tariq, who is telling him about a tramp who handed in a pair of shoes for repair that morning.

The van splutters to life straight away, but he starts it a few more times, in case anyone should hear his clumsy attempts to check the engine. Mancebo sighs and pulls out into the heavy traffic. The air is still. It's total madness to drive around for the sake of appearances when the radio is telling them all to leave their cars at home. Mancebo drives around the block. As he passes Le Soleil, François looks up from the bar. He waves and raises an eyebrow. Mancebo gives him a thumbs up and forces a big smile.

Though he is only a few hundred metres from his shop, he feels as though he's discovering the neighbourhood for the very first time. For thirty years now, he has walked the block around his shop, but he's never driven it in the van. There's never been any reason to. Lost in thoughts of how different things look from behind the wheel, he takes a wrong turn up a one-way street. His fellow Parisians waste no time in alerting him to his mistake.

Mancebo raises a hand to acknowledge his error, mutters something and looks around for road signs which can lead him back to the safety of his boulevard. Sweat trickles from beneath his black cap. It's as though that, too, has been waiting for the right moment to make an appearance. The tourists, maps in hand, are moving slowly.

Mancebo studies a group of pigeons relieving themselves on a balcony. Maybe they can't fly and shit at the same time. He turns right, and to his relief sees the boulevard straight ahead. Then he sees the writer. He's going down the fire escape with a sheaf of papers in his hand. Though he knows it achieves nothing, Mancebo toots his horn; it's just a way of channelling his stress. He indicates to turn left into the boulevard, but swiftly turns right instead.

He has to seize this opportunity. The dense traffic now works to his advantage, it's moving at a snail's pace, which allows Mancebo to keep pace with the writer on the other side of the boulevard. He grips the steering wheel more tightly. The writer turns in to Rue de Chéroy and Mancebo whizzes around the roundabout to catch him up. This street is narrower, and Mancebo is now nearer to the man. He can study the writer as he goes on his way, oblivious to the pursuit. Nothing in his face suggests a lover. Though exactly what would, Mancebo has no idea. A lipstick mark, perhaps? But that would be too obvious. Mancebo is trying to search for some other sign of infidelity when, suddenly, he hears a bang.

The steering wheel slams into Mancebo's chest. He hadn't even considered putting on his seat belt, he was only pretending to check the van was OK. Everything stops. Silence fills the van. Mancebo feels like he is looking straight into the writer's eyes. He is one of the many people who have stopped in their tracks. The taxi driver Mancebo has rammed into, a smallish young man with a lot of tattoos, is already on the pavement.

Mancebo knows he has to get out and take responsibility. His chest hurts. He snatches the prayer beads hanging from the rear-view mirror but holds them behind his back. He does not want to be mistaken for a terrorist. He pushes the wooden beads along the string with his sweaty fingers. That was what his father always did when he was under pressure.

Suddenly, two traffic officers have appeared. Mancebo has no idea how they got there so quickly, but maybe they were already on the boulevard, giving out parking tickets. Both are standing at the ready with their notepads in their hands.

The left headlight of the van is smashed, but the taxi is in worse shape. It has a substantial dent. Before the police officers come over to Mancebo, they urge only those who actually saw the accident to remain and the rest to disperse.

Mancebo quickly glances up at the writer, who is still standing there after the officers' appeal. Mancebo's hands are now so sweaty that he finds it hard to move the wooden beads. Is my mission going to come to an end now, before it's even begun, he wonders. If the writer comes forward as a witness, it's all over. Then we'll have a relationship, albeit a superficial one. He wouldn't under any circumstances be able to continue observing the writer. He would no longer be just an anonymous man over the road, he would become the man who rammed into the taxi.

The taxi driver gives his version of events to the police and

Mancebo is grateful for that, because he's sure it's correct. As for him, he has no idea what happened. The writer slowly starts to move away from the scene of the crime. The police advance on Mancebo.

My duties consisted of forwarding emails to Monsieur Bellivier. Every time a message came in, there would be a little *pling*. The log-in details were provided in the so-called contract of employment. I'd been allocated the email address tout.mon.monde@free.fr and was to forward any emails that arrived to monsieur.bellivier@free.fr. Nothing was said about why these emails couldn't be sent straight to Monsieur Bellivier. What was made very plain, however, was that I wasn't to add, amend or delete anything from the emails; my only job was to forward them.

Strangely enough, I slept well the night before my first day at work, despite the heat which was paralysing the city. What I didn't know was that it would be the last good night's sleep I'd enjoy in a very long time, something that would have nothing to do with the heatwave. I shoved an extension lead in my laptop bag, even though I wouldn't be needing it at my new job. Part of me was convinced I would be spending the day at the café after all.

There were a number of hurdles to negotiate on the way to my assignment. The first was the swing door into Areva, you could never trust those things, followed by a critical stage: reception. Maybe the receptionist would stop me. Maybe rumour had reached her that someone was trying to move in at the very top of the building. Using CCTV footage, they might have been able to identify the two people who ascended the tower block yesterday using fake passes. And in front of her on her impeccable desk she might now have the photos of the wanted individuals. A man and a woman. But only the woman would walk into the trap. Only she was stupid enough to return to the scene of the crime. And if the receptionist didn't abort my mission, maybe my pass card would. Would it make the light go green? The fact that it had worked the day before didn't really mean a thing. It could have a best-before date.

The last hurdle was the door to the office. Would the key fit? There was also no guarantee that the computer would work, that the log-in details would be correct, that any emails would arrive. It was all those critical stages, plus my own doubts, that made me pack my extension lead that morning. It seemed fairly likely that I would end up being a cyber nomad again that day, just like every other. I deliberated for a long time about whether to take one of my anti-anxiety tablets. In the end, I put them in my bag.

By the time I had changed my outfit twice, I realised that I really did care how I looked. It was a long time since that had happened. It was a long time since I had cared about anything at all. It would be an exaggeration to say I felt expectant, but I did care, and that was enough. For months I had dressed and packed my things without sparing a single thought to either my clothes or the contents of my bag. But today I did.

It's hard to get dressed when you don't know who you are. Nothing seemed right for who I was meant to be. The most logical thing might have been to wear the outfit I felt most comfortable in, something that was me, but that was what scared me most. It was like going on stage without a costume.

An unmanageable sense of insecurity came creeping over me, and I stole a glance at the tablets in my bag. The only way to handle the situation, maybe even make it pleasant, was to simply decide who I was. I made the rules, no one else. The others, whoever they were, would have to fit in with me. Or so I told myself, anyway. My pass became my identity card, and it said sales manager, so in the end I opted for a black skirt with a short-sleeved white blouse and red shoes. I looked at myself in the mirror and saw someone who looked just like me.

In a big city, you're never really alone, and I was far from alone in walking towards the black skyscraper that morning. Despite that, I was probably the only one in that specific set of circumstances, I thought, clutching my laptop bag more tightly. Or was I? Maybe there were lots of people acting as pawns in a game they knew nothing about. Lots of people playing roles, carrying out apparently meaningless tasks.

The swing door hit me right in the face. No harm done, but it was like it had heard my fears. Maybe it was offended that I had doubted its competence. A dark-skinned man in a suit quickly asked if I was all right. I nodded and smiled. My heart began to pound. It was the same receptionist as the day before. She was on the phone, her eyes staring into the distance. Maybe she had the police on the line.

There were barriers on both sides of the reception desk. There might even be two lift systems, leading up to different sections of the tower block. I followed the stream of people to the left. If it hadn't been for the incident with the door, I wouldn't have felt so nervous. It was time to use my pass. I calmed myself down with the thought that if it didn't work, if the light went red, all I could do was calmly turn round, leave the building and go back to the café. Nobody would notice a non-functioning pass. But the light flashed green and I hurried for the lift, not giving it the chance to change colour.

From day one, the lift became the place where I felt most secure. A limited amount of space, four walls, and everyone who entered it nodded and said good morning. They fascinated me. The women in all their femininity and the men in all their masculinity. Perfectionism reigned supreme, and I felt pleased with my choice of outfit. Finally alone in the lift, I was carried up towards my destination. The first thing I noticed when I stepped out into the corridor was that the lights were on. Maybe the skyscraper had an automatic lighting system. I decided that must be it. The top floor was silent as the grave. The lift began its downward journey and I walked towards my door. My red shoes were an attractive sight against the dark red carpet. Key in the lock. There was no one there, but I had already assured myself of that by peering in through the blinds. I left the door open. Everything looked different from yesterday. Maybe it was the light. I took my contract out of my bag as though doing so gave me permission to switch on the big computer. It took some time to start up, and I gazed out at the Sacré-Cœur while I waited.

I logged in. My inbox was empty. Not even a welcome email from the operator. That meant someone else had used the account before me. I switched on my own computer. If this was all just a joke, I wasn't going to lose any working time. I decided that if nothing happened by lunchtime, I would leave, and I started an article I should have tackled earlier. Devoting a few hours to something as banal as the tourist attractions of Paris felt good. It was like keeping one foot in the real world. And that was what I did, for a while, before that foot was dislodged by a loud *pling*. An email. I opened and read it, and a small smile played on my lips. I was happy that it was all true, that there really had been a *pling*.

I got straight up and closed the door. This was my office now. And though I knew what I had to do with the incoming email, I read the contract again, slowly, word by word. As though I'd suddenly lost confidence in my own abilities, I spelled out the address the email had to be forwarded to. The email itself consisted of a combination of numbers. An account number, perhaps. The sender was laposte.92800@free.fr.

I pressed send as though performing some kind of ritual. Done. And before I stepped back into the real world I just sat there for a while, staring at the screen. Then I returned to writing about the most popular tourist attractions in Paris with a new-found energy.

There were a total of three *plings* before lunch that first day. It was as much fun every time. I had been living in a sort of haze for months, breathing in an atmosphere that felt impenetrable. It had been such hard going that I'd even sought help. Therapy and tablets, guilt and emptiness had filled my days. So how on earth could a totally meaningless task suddenly give me a sense of purpose? But it did. The work amused me. I'd been hoping for the chance of an exposé, a way of uncovering Areva's dirty dealings in North Africa. But the more *plings* that came in, the more I realised it wasn't going to be anything of the kind. There was never anything in the subject line, no title to the emails. The sender was always laposte.92800@free.fr, and I worked out almost immediately that the numbers in the address were the postcode of the business district.

I read every email carefully, but they said nothing to me. They usually contained a string of numbers, sometimes some capital letters, and they were never more than three lines long. I had plenty of time for thinking between *plings*. One terrifying thought which struck me on the very first day, and which made the whole thing feel a lot less fun, was that I might be a pawn in some kind of terrorist network. A network that had chosen La Défense as its next target. The area seemed quite plausible as a target: the largest business district in Paris, where many French and international companies had their head offices.

I started to google how terrorist organisations operated, which just fuelled my sense of dread. They frequently make use of isolated cells, which are both independent and often unaware of each other; the individual typically doesn't even know why he or she is carrying out a particular task. I tried to keep a cool head. Tried to tell myself that these were just innocent emails I was forwarding. It would have been different if I was running between suburban basement storerooms with various liquids or tubes of gas. I don't know how many times I had to force myself to see the situation as it really was. One thing was clear: Monsieur Bellivier didn't want anyone to know where he was, and that was why the emails were being forwarded.

Emails can easily be traced, and if I'd had more computer expertise I might have been able to find out who laposte92800 and Monsieur Bellivier were, or at least where they were. If laposte92800 wished Monsieur Bellivier ill and I was the intermediary, that meant I was also in the firing line. If that was the case, and I was being drawn into a terrorist organisation, surely the identity of the person forwarding the emails would never come out? Not even the man who had shown me to the office knew my name. But on the other hand, maybe that was how they worked. Maybe even they didn't know who their colleagues were. Areva was one of the tallest buildings in the business district, which could mean it was an attractive target. But then why put the person forwarding the mail at the very top of that target?

Eventually, I calmed down enough to go for the first lunch of my new job, at McDonald's. I knew I wouldn't see any of my colleagues there – old or new. I kept an eye on the time as I sat there with my fish burger, as though someone were expecting me back at the office. No one was, but I had a job to do all the same. The contract specified that lunch was from 12.00 to 13.30. Five minutes before the end of my lunch break, I was back in my room. I closed the door and locked it behind me. The terrorist idea had evaporated a bit while I was at McDonald's. No emails had come in during lunch.

I had almost finished the Paris article, but I wasn't particularly happy with it. I had more exciting things to do than write articles about tourist attractions. I heard the first *pling* of the afternoon. This time, it was a short string of numbers, plus the words 'inc VAT'. That was easy enough to work out, but surely terrorists didn't bother with VAT or tax returns, I thought. Only a few more emails came in that afternoon, which gave me a chance to make the final revisions to a piece on the political situation in the country. I spent the last hour at my desk looking out at the Sacré-Cœur.

The last *pling* of the day arrived. Two letters, AF, followed by a string of ten letters and numbers. Something about the combination seemed familiar to me, but then I started to doubt myself. Though I didn't quite know why, I noted them down on my phone. A quarter of an hour to go. In a few minutes' time, I would face up to reality. Sit alongside the living dead in the metro. And in an hour, I would collect my son from holiday club. All those things that make us human beings feel secure, but which also make us so incredibly vulnerable. No more *plings* arrived. I switched off the computer, locked the door and walked to the lift.

I thought that I had overcome all the obstacles by then. That any difficulties would arise when I arrived at the office, not when I left. My pass behaved itself, the green light lit up. The foyer was almost empty. Nobody was coming to work at that time of day, nor leaving, unless they had a meeting somewhere.

'Madame!'

I immediately knew it was me the receptionist was shouting after, but I didn't want to believe it. Everything had started so well. Was it about to come to an abrupt end? I stopped and looked down at my shoes. The white marble floor made them seem a different shade of red. I turned. The receptionist smiled.

'Don't forget these, madame.'

She handed me a beautiful bouquet of flowers.

'For me?'

I instantly knew I had made a mistake. I shouldn't have seemed surprised, but I shouldn't be so hard on myself. Sometimes we react instinctively.

'Yes, they're lovely, aren't they?' she said.

There was a cold breeze blowing through the foyer. The café wasn't the only place with efficient air conditioning.

The stems made my hands feel wet and sticky. They were red, carnation-like blooms with delicate green foliage for decoration. The flowers made me feel like I was under surveillance, as though Monsieur Bellivier had decided to follow me home. I didn't want

45

that. There was no card, no sender's name on the bouquet. Just a label announcing the florist they had come from. Everything had felt so good on my first day in the new job, until the flowers came into the picture.

My feet were sticking to my high-heeled shoes as I turned off the avenue. The flowers were upsetting me so much that I just had to get rid of them. The easiest thing would have been to dump them straight in the nearest bin, but that felt wrong somehow. It wasn't just the idea of throwing away beautiful, fresh flowers, I also felt like doing so would come back to haunt me in some way.

A paranoid thought had taken root. The bunch of flowers was like an anonymous relay baton. I had been given it by the receptionist, who in turn had doubtless received it from Monsieur Bellivier, and now it was my turn to hand it on. A bit like the emails. But it wasn't just the thought of giving flowers to the dead that made me turn off the avenue and into the cemetery; it was also the prospect of a little breathing space before I went to pick up my son. A way of coming back to reality. Death reminded me of life.

The woman in the security hut gave me a nod as I walked into the Jewish cemetery. Over the past year, guards had been introduced to all Jewish cemeteries in the city after a number of graves were vandalised following the terrorist attacks. The bouquet transformed me from an anonymous visitor into a plausible relative.

I walked aimlessly among the graves. The dry leaves crunched beneath my feet, a sound otherwise associated with autumn. The heat seemed to recede the deeper I walked into the cemetery; the cold gravestones were worthy adversaries of the heat. I had wandered through the cemetery so many times before, but I had never paid so much attention to the detail. If the dead person was a Jewish woman who had married a non-Jew, her maiden name was also given on the headstone, a reminder of her origins. But there were no Jewish symbols. No Stars of David or menorahs on the gravestones. Nor was there any Hebrew script, just crosses of all kinds, plus dates of birth and death.

The large family tombs towered up like small, uninviting playhouses of stone. Many of the graves seemed abandoned, and a dignified covering of moss had grown over them. Others boasted flowers, fresh that day. There was nothing sad about the abandoned graves, in fact it was the opposite: they looked beautiful in the attire nature had given them. It was the graves adorned with plastic flowers that made me feel uncomfortable. They looked both abandoned and false. Someone had remembered the dead purely out of duty, taken action only to ease their own guilty conscience. Plastic flowers never withered or decayed, making them as dead as an object can be. When I left the cemetery that day, there was a beautiful red bouquet on the grave of a certain Judith Goldenberg.

My mornings differed, depending on whether I had my son or not. My ex-husband couldn't take any leave that summer and I couldn't go on holiday straight after I had been off sick, so my son had to spend his summer at holiday club. I think he liked it there, or at any rate that was what I convinced myself; I lacked the energy to consider anything else. If I asked him what he thought of his summer days, he just shrugged. It was during the mornings that my questions came. I was too busy to ask them during the day, and by the evening I was too tired. That was when my emotions welled up instead.

The next morning, I asked myself whether I had done the right thing by taking on the assignment. My son gave me a funny look every time I came into the kitchen, wearing a dress one moment and a pair of trousers the next. I don't know if he gave much thought to all these changes of outfit, but if he told his father about my new morning routine, my ex would assume I'd met someone. But that was neither here nor there.

The swing doors didn't cause any problems on my second morning.

The receptionist gave me a smile. What did she know about my work? What did she know about me, or about Monsieur Bellivier? I decided not to dwell on it. I would never be able to find a natural, risk-free way to broach the subject with her. The minute I entered the office I could see someone had been in there after me. I couldn't say exactly how I knew until I hung up my coat and sat down at my desk. The wastepaper bin had been emptied, the chair set unnaturally straight. Even the window had an extra gleam to it. Someone had come in to clean.

Despite being interrupted by *plings* several times an hour, I got more done than usual. I polished off an article and gazed out of the window. There were a couple of military vehicles out there, driving back and forth. From where I was sitting, they looked like my son's toy cars. They were most likely there to lull people into a false sense of security, a belief that they were keeping tabs on the terrorists.

'Madame!'

Yesterday's finale to the working day was repeated. I turned and took the bunch of flowers with a smile and managed to utter a thanks. Today's bouquet contained some delicate blue flowers, fighting for space with a few yellow ones. The only thing that really troubled me about my assignment was this daily conclusion. And the thought that every day would end in this way made me feel a little sick. I suddenly felt as if I'd been running too fast. Was there something I'd missed here? Something I should have realised or noticed? Who did people usually give flowers to? The winner of a competition, someone whose birthday it was, someone they loved, someone who'd died . . .

I sat down on the edge of the fountain by the entrance to the metro and then the thought struck me: I was the only one coming out of Areva carrying a bunch of flowers. I stuck out from the crowd. Anyone armed with the knowledge that I was carrying a bouquet would be able to spot me easily. The flowers were to identify me. I looked all around. Paranoia began its gentle caress and then quickly took over my entire body. Without really thinking it through, I climbed up onto the slippery, wet rim of the fountain. It would do as a platform. I held up the bouquet as high as I could. It was my only means of giving myself some kind of advantage. Demonstrating that I'd worked it out; that I knew what the flowers were for. Hopefully the ritual could end now, and with it the paranoia might also subside.

The blue and yellow flowers found a new owner, too. This time, a living one. A heavily pregnant woman was engrossed in a phone call. She had a pained look on her face. I waited until she finished the call. She glanced at her watch and seemed to be thinking.

'Hello, excuse me, would you like these?'

I held out the flowers. She looked at them and then straight at me.

'No,' she eventually said. 'Why would I?'

'My lover gave them to me, but my husband's going to be here any minute and I thought I'd give them to somebody rather than just shoving them in a bin.'

'Yeah, that'd be a shame. They're beautiful.'

'Take them. Always nice to have flowers on a day like this.'

'Well, thanks. And good luck . . . with your husband.'

When I looked back over my shoulder a few moments later, I saw she had nonchalantly put down the flowers beside her. Maybe she didn't appreciate them after all. Not that it mattered. The vital thing was for me to get rid of them, without throwing them away. Where they ended up was less important. What mattered was to convince myself that they'd ended up in good hands.

The next morning, I woke with a start. I thought I knew why I had recognised the combination of letters and figures in one of the emails. I went into the kitchen and found my purse. The man in the apartment opposite was awake. He had cancer, the concierge had told me. It probably wasn't the cancer itself keeping him awake, but his fear of it. I watched him pacing to and fro between his kitchen table and the radio. Nervously, I compared my Air France frequent flyer's card with the string of numbers and letters I had noted down on my phone. There was no doubt. It was probably a membership number from the Air France loyalty programme.

I felt sick. Why couldn't it at least be a members' number from a supermarket chain? Air France, an airline company, caused the terrorist associations to come flooding back. Though it was perfectly possible, of course, to take a flight without planning to blow the plane from the sky. My neighbour moved over to the window with his cat in his arms, stroking it gently on the head. His fear, his anxiety soothed my own. What were a few matching numbers compared to looking death in the eye every night?

It takes Mancebo a while to work out why his chest hurts. The memory of the accident is all mixed up with Madame Cat's green eyes as he hauls himself out of bed. He has woken before the alarm goes off, but even so he feels rested and ready to face the day and his two jobs. Before he goes into the bathroom he turns the clock forward fifteen minutes so that it won't ring. He's never woken of his own accord before, and Fatima would think it was very strange if the alarm clock rang and her husband was already up.

Pleased with his solution for the clock, Mancebo tramps into the bathroom and pulls up his white nightshirt in front of the mirror to see if the crash has left any mark. There's no sign of it on his skin. It's all inside me, Mancebo thinks.

Before leaving the apartment, he stands in the middle of the room and studies his wife, who is still sleeping deeply. He quietly wonders why she was out so early the previous morning. But he has neither the time nor the inclination to spend any longer thinking about it, he has a lot to get done today. He can't let a single minute go to waste if everything is to go to plan. His white lie has left him with a bashed-up van, but it still runs and that's the main thing. He checked yesterday after filling in all the insurance papers with the police and the taxi driver. The problem now is making sure no one in his family sees the broken headlight.

God wanted to punish me, Mancebo thinks. The Almighty gave me the lie I created. He pulls on his cap. Now he really does need Raphaël's help.

The air is heavy. It's going to be another hot day, he can feel it as he loads his wares into the van at Rungis. Mancebo sets off back towards Paris. The traffic hasn't built up yet, and he puts his foot down a bit further than usual so he can get to his first task. It's a one-off, but still vital for his ongoing work. It will help him do his new job in a correct and professional way. He's going to buy a notebook.

He turns onto Avenue d'Italie and drives deeper into the 13th arrondissement. He knows the area, but not anyone who lives there, and that's exactly why he has chosen it for the purchase of his notebook. The 13th arrondissement is home to lots of Chinese people, people that Mancebo doesn't like doing business with because he finds it hard to understand what they say. Their French sounds like a foreign language to his ears, but on this occasion he has no choice.

Mancebo gets out of the van. In the few minutes he saved by driving faster than usual he now needs to find a notebook. He walks down the street. Chinese banks, clothes shops, grocery shops, and a video-rental place, its front window cluttered with Chinese martial-arts films. But they're all shut. The Chinese aren't awake yet. He's on the verge of giving up when he sees a man and a woman dragging boxes in front of an open door. He moves closer and sees red and black bags in the window. Towards the rear of the shop, he glimpses some porcelain hares and a picture of an electric waterfall.

'Good morning, I wondered whether you have any notebooks?'

The Chinese couple look at Mancebo in alarm, and then at each other in the same way. They're not used to seeing an Arab in their neighbourhood at this time of day, particularly not one asking for notebooks.

'We not open yet.'

'No, I can see that, madame, but I need to buy a notebook, don't you sell them? It doesn't matter what it looks like, but one with hard covers, if possible?'

'It's not allowed,' the woman replies, since the man seems unable to speak at all, or not in French anyway.

I knew it, Mancebo thinks, I shouldn't have got mixed up with others.

'Not even a little notepad?'

'It's not allowed.'

'It's not allowed? What do you mean, madame?'

Mancebo is starting to feel indignant. In all his years in the shop trade he's never told a customer that something isn't allowed. What service!

'I mean, it's not allowed. We only sell to companies, wholesale, not like you, monsieur, private person, only large quantities, not retail. Not one little book, many.'

Mancebo pulls up outside Le Soleil for his usual morning coffee, but he's not alone in the van. He's accompanied by three boxes of lettuce, two boxes of green and red apples, several kilos of carrots, five small trays of raspberries and seventy Chinese notebooks. The old clock behind the bar reads 08.36. Mission completed.

It's Friday, which means that the Paris streets take on a faster tempo. The city's inhabitants want to get everything done before the weekend, and they hurry everywhere they go. The streets fill with people who have to get everything done after work but before dinner. That includes an aperitif with the friend they didn't find time to see during the week. Tariq always tries to do business with the authorities on Friday afternoons. His theory is that the bureaucrats, otherwise dry and strict, loosen their ties after the glass of wine they enjoy with their Friday lunch. Meaning that things generally go his way.

Tariq has just opened his cobbler's shop for the day, and Mancebo has taken a moment to jot down his observations from the previous day in one of his many Chinese notebooks. But not for a single second has he neglected to observe whether anything is happening across the street. At one point, he jumped and thought something was about to happen, but it was only Tariq coming out to let down his sun awning. Mancebo proudly adds a final full stop to Thursday's report, writes today's date on a new, blank page, closes the gaudy notebook and stashes it under the cash box where it has to jostle for space with invoices, important receipts and a couple of till rolls. The other sixty-nine notebooks are stacked up at the very back of a shelf beneath the till. He has no idea what he's going to use them for. He might just as well throw them away, but something tells him that doing so would be a waste of the earth's scarce natural resources.

Just as he is hiding the notebook under the cash box, a man in a brown hat comes down the fire escape of the building opposite. Mancebo's first thought is to dash outside so that he doesn't miss a thing, doesn't miss a single movement or sound that could indicate a possible lover, but he restrains himself. Behave like normal, he tells himself, and he calmly and level-headedly picks up a rag and a piece of chalk and trots outside into the morning sun.

The writer lithely makes his way down the steps and looks up at the sky as though to work out what the weather will do today, then he turns left, past the cobbler's, and carries on along the pavement. He is carrying a small suitcase in one hand. The writer walks briskly, which means the suitcase can't be heavy. That, in turn, suggests he won't be away for long, which means he might only be going away for the weekend.

Mancebo quickly comes up with a number of plausible explanations and alternatives. Maybe he's going up to Normandy to spend a weekend by the sea with his lover? The thought takes root and gives Mancebo the energy he needs to carry out his task.

He imagines himself following the writer to Gare Saint-Lazare, where he will watch him meet the woman he loves beneath the huge board showing trains departing to Normandy. They take their seats in first class and can't keep their hands off each other. They kiss tenderly and, just as the train pulls away to start its journey towards the coast, Mancebo jumps on board. There he sits, behind them and across the aisle, with a newspaper covering his face, able to hear every word they say.

From time to time the writer reads a chapter of his new book aloud. His lover listens. She's beautiful, like a rose in bloom. For the moment, Mancebo can't think of any better way of describing her face, anything less banal. When they go to the restaurant car to order two glasses of champagne, he writes it all down in his red Chinese notebook. When they come back, Mancebo discreetly puts down his notebook and returns to his paper.

Mancebo suddenly realises that he needs to check what time it is and stop daydreaming. The writer could just as easily be meeting up with his wife so that they can spend the weekend together. He looks up at the clock tower to check the time for his report, but it stares back disdainfully, like a human face with no eyes or mouth, dumb and blind. The clock has stopped. Time has long since thrown in the towel. An old couple come into the shop.

'Good morning, madame. Good morning, monsieur.'

'Good morning, Monsieur Mancebo,' the old lady replies.

The man gives him a nod. The couple live a stone's throw from the boulevard, and they have been Mancebo's customers ever since he opened the shop.

'How can I be of service this lovely morning?'

'I want a packet of biscuits, dark ones if you've got them, with plenty of fibre. I'm having such trouble going to the toilet. Can't get it out, if you know what I mean. The doctor prescribed high-fibre biscuits.'

'Then I'll need to see the prescription, please.'

The old couple laugh, the man in a rather forced way. Mancebo checks to see what he's got. Eventually, he spots a packet that has been there as long as he can remember. At least as long as the clock on the tower has been out of action. Wholemeal, it says on the packet.

'I think this is what you want.'

The woman scrutinises the packet carefully and spends a long time rummaging for her glasses in her big red cloth bag. The man snatches the biscuits from her hand and starts to read the ingredients aloud.

'We'll try them,' the woman says after a while, mainly so she doesn't have to listen to her husband read the entire list.

Mancebo takes the packet and goes over to the till.

'Is the van all right?' the woman suddenly asks.

'Perhaps you should ask Monsieur Mancebo if he's all right,' the man sighs with a shake of his head.

'The van?'

Mancebo pretends to be unperturbed and uncomprehending, though he's anything but.

'Yes, we saw the accident, it was just outside our window, you see. A front-row seat, you might say.'

The woman laughs and the man sighs.

'Oh yes, the accident . . .'

Mancebo wants to dismiss it with a joke, but he can't think of anything amusing to say.

'No, well yes, it's all right, just a broken headlight. These things happen. I expect it was the hot weather that did it.'

'Yes, that's what your wife said, too.'

'My wife?'

'Yes, Fatima.'

'Perhaps we ought to be going,' the man urges.

'My wife, she saw the accident?'

'No, but we saw her later that morning and asked her how you were.'

'You saw her? Where?'

'In the tobacconist's below our apartment.'

The woman is starting to seem confused, and the man just wants to take the biscuits and go.

'What was she doing there?'

The woman gives Mancebo a quizzical look.

'Well, I don't know. She's often in there, having a coffee with the monsieur who works there. They're usually behind the curtain, in his office. I thought you knew . . .'

'Chérie, perhaps you should leave Monsieur Mancebo's private affairs in peace. Let's take these home and solve your problems.'

The sun is high in the sky and the exhaust fumes find their way into every pore. Millions of people trying to survive in a red-hot cauldron that doesn't stop boiling even at night. Mancebo wipes the sweat from his forehead and briefly considers taking off his cap. He dismisses the idea as quickly as it arrived. For the first time, he starts to doubt that he'll be able to see this through. It's all just too much. He can't quite process this new information about Fatima. The words 'behind the curtain' are problematic. What is Fatima doing behind the curtain in a tobacconist's shop? And if she knows about the van incident, why hasn't she confronted him about it? She's usually the first to have a go at him whenever he does anything stupid.

The heat makes it impossible for Mancebo to think clearly. He gets up to fetch a bottle of water and quickly returns to his stool. It's his safe place. The tarmac beneath the legs of the stool bears a clear imprint of its usual position, and every time he sets down the stool he unconsciously matches it precisely to the indentations in the pavement. The other shopkeepers have also carried chairs and stools outside to get a breath of air, though it could hardly be called fresh.

Other than the Picard, which sells nothing but frozen goods, the shops are doing poorly in the hot weather. Many people go there just to cool off, and the rough sleepers crowd around its vents. But for someone who owns a tiny grocer's shop, the heat is a curse. Mancebo hasn't even got air conditioning to tempt the punters in.

He spends the afternoon noting down the observations he made at lunchtime. He also writes a short shopping list of things he needs in order to continue his work. The only problem is that he doesn't know when he'll be able to get out and buy them. He would usually give that kind of task to Fatima, but how would he explain the sudden need for a wristwatch and pair of binoculars? He's not entirely sure about the binoculars. After all, the aim is to act like normal, to behave like usual, but he also needs to adapt to the situation. There might be occasions on which he has to spy in a more professional way, albeit discreetly.

Huge black clouds stack up on the horizon, making the heat easier to bear. A respite is on its way. Tariq whistles to signal that it's time for their daily stroll to Le Soleil. Mancebo gives him a thumbs up. Since Tariq doesn't have anything to bring inside, he can shut up his shop quickly, and he comes across to give Mancebo a hand, helping himself to an apple in the process.

'Did you get a touch of sunstroke, brother?' he suddenly asks, pointing to the apples.

With all his attention on the writer that morning, Mancebo had rubbed out the old price and written in a new one. He is now selling apples for forty-nine euros a kilo.

'They can't be that tasty.'

Mancebo scratches his head when he realises how it happened. I'll learn, he thinks. I've got to develop my capacity for multitasking. He rubs off the price with his sleeve. They walk down the boulevard, Tariq with a red apple in his hand and Mancebo with white chalk on the right arm of his jacket.

Tariq and François are talking about the weather. Mancebo tries to keep up with their chatter, but finds his imagination running away with him. In his mind, he isn't in a smoky bar in Paris, he's on a beach in Normandy. The sun is shining there, too, but the sea breeze prevents any sweaty brows. There's nothing romantic about sweaty brows. The writer has it all planned. They've been talking about the trip for weeks, but they hadn't really fixed the date. This is the first time the lover's husband and the writer's wife have both been away at the same time.

The waves roll compassionately towards the shore as they take an aperitif to celebrate their weekend of love. Though are they really having a drink at the beach? Didn't they order champagne on the train? Maybe they've already checked into their picturesque little hotel in the fishing village, or . . .

Mancebo interrupts his thoughts with a theatrical clearing of the throat. He has to give the young lovers a bit of privacy. He can't be too inquisitive. Be professional, my friend, Mancebo tells himself, downing his pastis. The last break of the day is over, time to get back to work.

Since he is convinced the writer has gone away for the weekend, or at least for the night, he doesn't feel in a hurry to get back to the shop. He's perfectly justified in allowing himself a slight diversion on a private matter.

'I'm just going to get cigarettes,' Mancebo says apologetically as they emerge onto Boulevard des Batignolles.

'You can have one of mine, brother. If you like, I can sponsor you for cigarettes for the rest of your life. It only comes to about a packet a month, seeing as you've got a wife who cares about your health.'

If there's one thing that amuses Tariq it's Fatima's rationing of her husband's cigarettes. Mancebo doesn't know why, but every time the subject comes up he feels humiliated.

'Maybe it's Fatima who sponsors your cigarettes?'

The words leave Mancebo's mouth before he knows it, questions about his wife's relationship with the tobacconist are playing on his mind.

'What the hell's that supposed to mean?'

Tariq grabs Mancebo by the sleeve then thinks better of it and tries to calm down.

'Sorry, but what do you mean by that?'

Tariq's eyes are black. They've never been blacker. Mancebo doesn't recognise his cousin. Tariq is scaring him. The two men glare at one another. Mancebo knows he needs to get Tariq back onside. He can't cope with having him as an enemy, not at the moment.

'What? What did I say? Can't even remember. Why so angry, brother?'

Tariq studies him for a few moments, and then his face softens and he laughs.

'Ah, sorry. Must be this heat making me crazy.'

'It's making us all feel that way,' Mancebo says with a smile.

Mancebo shouldn't really have to conceal the fact that he's decided to go to the tobacconist's on Rue de Chéroy rather than his usual one on the boulevard. But he feels obliged to after his cousin's outburst, and so he turns left, as he always does, towards the tobacconist's where he usually buys his cigarettes. He wants to turn around to see whether his cousin is watching him, but doesn't have the nerve.

He steps inside the tobacconist's, waits a second or two and then comes back out. He turns into Place Prosper-Goubaux and carries on around the block to get to Rue de Chéroy. Memories of the crash come flooding back to him as he passes the scene of the accident. No broken glass or skid marks. There's nothing to suggest that any kind of collision took place at that spot. Mancebo feels grateful to the street cleaners of Paris and their long green brooms.

What if Fatima's behind the curtain, Mancebo thinks. He has

only set foot inside the tobacconist's once before. He was with Amir, who needed a daily paper for school. Mancebo has no idea why he never buys his cigarettes here. He has his ways.

A bell rings as he steps through the door, and a glorious coolness hits him. Some shopkeepers have it easy, Mancebo thinks. The hugely fat tobacconist turns and raises his eyebrows at Mancebo, as though he's surprised to see him in the shop. Odd, Mancebo thinks; to him, the tobacconist is a stranger. It's probably just the heat making people act oddly, he reassures himself. But now that he's here, Mancebo wonders why he really came. He hasn't the faintest idea what he's going to do, but he casts a furtive glance at the curtain.

'Good day.'

'Good day, monsieur, how can I help?'

'It's lovely in here.'

The man gives Mancebo a nonplussed look.

'Nice and cold.'

'Ah, right, yes,' the man says in relief.

How can I bring things round to my wife in a natural way, Mancebo wonders desperately.

'Well, I came in here because I'm looking for my wife.'

'Your wife? Here?'

'Yes. She told me she was coming here.'

'Aha . . . And who is your wife?'

'Fatima.'

The man starts shuffling the newspapers on the counter.

'No, it's just me here.'

'I can see that, monsieur, but doesn't she come here sometimes?'

'No. Sorry, but I don't know who you're talking about. I don't know a Fatima. Maybe you've got the wrong shop? There's another tobacconist's further up the street.'

'Yes, maybe that's it.'

Mancebo realises he'll have to employ the same tactic here as he did with Tariq a few minutes earlier. Best to throw in the towel. Give up. Play dead the way animals do.

'Well then, monsieur, have a good day.'

'You too,' the fat man says with a false smile.

Mancebo goes back along the street at a virtual jog. His jacket flies out behind him as he dashes round the block, and finally he's back on Boulevard des Batignolles, where he flings himself into his usual tobacconist's.

'Afternoon, Mancebo. Out running on a day like this?'

'I need to get back to the shop.'

'Business is brisk, then?'

Mancebo smiles and puts the exact change on the counter. On his way back across the boulevard he casts a glance at the cobbler's shop. Tariq is standing in the doorway, watching him. There's nothing odd about his cigarette purchase taking a long time; he often stops for a chat.

Mancebo holds up the cigarette packet, proof that he hasn't been doing anything stupid. Tariq nods and goes back behind his counter.

The eagerly awaited rain finally arrives during the night, accompanied by its good friend thunder. The storm is rolling in over the city and Mancebo throws off the covers and gets up. He looks out at the empty boulevard and the equally empty apartment opposite. He wants a cigarette so badly, but he's already smoked his evening's allowance. Plus, what would Fatima say if she found him smoking in the middle of the night?

He shudders. A flash of lightning and a loud crash make him jump. Even Fatima, who normally sleeps like a log, sits up in alarm. She drags her lumbering body over to the window as quickly as she can, and they stand there, looking out. Fatima's eyes scan the boulevard to see where the lightning struck. Mancebo's gaze is fixed on the apartment opposite. Not even the thunderstorm can tear him away from his assignment.

'It must be the church spire,' Fatima mutters.

Mancebo looks at his wife. Studies her in profile. Her and the fat tobacconist? The thought is impossible. Mancebo tries to imagine the two of them behind the curtain, but he can't. And why hasn't she confronted him about smashing up the van? If you only knew, Mancebo thinks. I have my secrets, too.

I googled Monsieur Bellivier's name for the first time. The search brought up quite a few hits, but by the time I had weeded out the ones I considered irrelevant, a farmer in Belgium for example, there were only a handful left. One of them, a gynaecologist called Bertrand Bellivier, had a clinic in Pont de Neuilly, just a few stops away from the business district. I checked there was no one outside before I called.

'Hello, I'd like to make an appointment with Doctor Bellivier.'

'Are you an existing patient?'

'No.'

'I'm sorry, but I'm afraid Doctor Bellivier isn't taking on new patients at the moment.'

'It's a bit of an emergency, my own gynaecologist is away, so it would only be this once, just to check something . . .'

'OK. I can give you an appointment next week.'

'It'll have to be between twelve and one-thirty . . .'

That morning, between *plings*, I also had time to look into booking a flight to the Maldives in the name of Monsieur Bellivier, using the code from the Air France card. Just to see whether the code matched the name. But before the booking could move on to the next stage, I had to provide a forename and telephone number. Back to square one. I tried another roll of the dice and called the airline's customer service desk.

'Hello, I've got an Air France membership card here and I'd like to know who it belongs to.'

'Oh yes, why's that?'

'I found it, at work, and I just wanted to know who lost it.'

'But all the cards have names on them.'

'Yes, but it's gone . . . rubbed off. I have the numbers, though.'

'I'm sorry, madame, but I can't give out any information about our customers. Please send the card to us and we'll contact the person in question.'

'Thank you.'

Back to square one. The dice would have to go unrolled, for the time being at least. There was a *pling*.

Feelingly slightly dejected, I took the lift downstairs for lunch. It wasn't just that I was alone in my work, I was alone in everything. My son felt like a stranger, even after just a few days in the job. He was starting to look indistinct, and that upset me.

The thing that made me go on, and not lose my grip, was that my days here were numbered. I would hear the *plings* for three weeks, and then it would all be over. I'd be back where I normally was. What would I have gained from the experience? A fair amount of money, perhaps; memories, a bit of excitement. That was what I thought, at any rate, as I sat on the bench outside my building. It really was too hot to eat outside, but for some strange reason I felt like sweating, suffering.

An aeroplane roared past the skyscrapers and I instinctively looked up. In the wrong hands, it could be a weapon of mass destruction. Ironically enough, it was an Air France plane. Events on the far side of the globe more than a decade before had changed everything. I got to my feet. Duty called.

I decided not to do any more digging into Air France, nor into strings of numbers and letters, nor gynaecologists who happened to have the same name as my employer. I would focus on my work instead. I had a few articles to finish. They were my salvation. Not even the *plings* could impinge on my new-found focus. I kept a perfect check on the time and knew that I was now working overtime, only a few minutes, but I wanted to get an article sent off. As long as I didn't leave the office or the building while everybody else was leaving, I doubted it would be a problem.

I heard a sound, one unlike all the other sounds that reached me at the top of the building. Someone was taking the lift up to the forgotten floor. What would I do if it was a security guard? The pass hanging around my neck said sales manager, I reminded myself, feeling a little safer. I put the phone to my ear. If anyone came in, I would just pretend to be talking about some sensitive subject, which was why I had come up here. I could pack away my computer in an instant. There would be no trace of me left behind. Eventually, I caught sight of someone through the blinds, and before I had time to guess who it could be, she was standing there in front of me. I put down the phone.

'Good afternoon.'

'Good afternoon.'

'I was just leaving.'

The woman didn't reply, she just pulled the big vacuum cleaner into the room and then went out into the corridor to fetch the cleaning trolley. I remembered the man had said something about a cleaner. Maybe she knew all about this game, or maybe she was completely unaware of what was going on. Maybe she, too, was a living, breathing, oblivious terrorist cell. The vacuum cleaner was horribly loud and I felt like switching it off and telling her someone down there might hear us.

I had caught myself creeping about on tiptoe for fear of being discovered. But maybe she had always cleaned up here, and the people down in Areva were used to hearing noise from the empty floor during the late afternoon. Or perhaps the sound was simply inaudible down there. It was a frightening thought. I logged out and switched off my computer.

'Goodbye, madame.'

'Goodbye, madame.'

She didn't even look at me as I left the room. But then, why should she?

The man seemed to be deep in thought, leaning heavily against the doors of the metro. He was trying to make a call, but there was no signal down there. I was only a few metres away from him. His amber eyes were filled with a spark that was struggling not to go out.

I immediately started to fantasise about him. This was someone with a *joie de vivre*, who loved cooking and the good things in life. I based this on the fact that he was slightly overweight. But now his work had taken over and he was worried that he wouldn't cope with the project he'd been dragged into. No, that wasn't right. The spark wasn't being stifled by anything work-related. He looked up at me. I lowered my eyes.

It was planned, of course, even if it looked like an impulsive gesture. The metro stopped at Saint-Paul. He stepped back from the doors as they opened. I got off, waited for other passengers to board the train and then held out the bouquet to him. He took it automatically, to stop it falling to the floor, and looked at me with a question in his eyes. The doors closed and I walked off towards the exit.

Before I took on the assignment, I'd thought I was quite a lonely person. I now realised I hadn't been lonely at all. But I was now. I didn't talk to anyone, and I lowered my gaze whenever anyone addressed me. I caught myself looking at the floor when the supervisor at my son's holiday club asked if he would be going with them to the swimming pool next week. I didn't know who I was. I had taken on a role, and one which I played well, but I was lonely all the same.

My anonymity had gone so far that I was giving away bunches of flowers to total strangers, including dead ones. By the end of the first week, Judith Goldenberg had already received several bouquets. Maybe I'd chosen her grave because it was so anonymous. Because it reminded me of myself. And also because it was one of the few graves without either fresh flowers or plastic ones. That reassured me that Judith's relatives wouldn't complain or be upset by my putting flowers on the grave. If she had any relatives, that was.

I had reconciled myself to my security pass, but not the flowers. I was only given roses once, but the flowers all felt spiky, hostile. They were an infringement, arriving after working hours. They became an inescapable link between the assignment and my private life.

To vary things a little, and so as not to just give them to dead people and strangers on the metro, I had once been on the verge of handing a bouquet to my ex-husband when he came to pick up my son. I managed to stop myself at the last moment. He would have taken it as a sign that I wasn't entirely well. Otherwise, I was fairly dull company; I didn't dare get into conversation, not even with my neighbours, for fear of revealing what I was working on. Those who knew how my past six months had been took my silence as a sign of depression. But I wasn't depressed, just in unknown territory.

The young man smiled at me. He didn't look like someone who worked in a florist. I wasn't sure exactly where he would have looked right, but it wasn't there. Actually, the florist itself looked quite out of place above the metro, next to a refuse collection area. Amidst all that concrete, the flowers of every colour and shape were dazzling. I'd thought of going to the shop sooner, but I hadn't found the courage. I explained that I wanted to know who had arranged for the flowers to be delivered to the Areva reception desk every afternoon. The young man seemed slightly suspicious, and with every right.

'Why do you want to know?' he asked.

'I'm just interested.'

'I'm afraid I can't tell you that. Who are you?'

The man wasn't really interested in my name, of course, it was a routine question, but my body reacted by making my heart race. To avoid saying anything, I held out that day's bouquet.

'Do you like them? I made up that one. Beautiful, eh?' he said with a smile.

I nodded. 'I like them all. And that's why I want to find out who's sending them.'

He hesitated, and it dawned on me that he thought there was a man trying to win my heart. I studied him. Part of him wanted to be the link between us, but at the same time he was afraid to reveal the customer's name.

'I'm sorry, madame, but I can't help you with that. If there's no card with the sender's name, then he – or she – wants to remain anonymous.'

'Monsieur Bellivier?'

The flower seller's face revealed nothing.

The metro carriage jolted and I could see my fellow passengers wondering why I was being so careless with my bouquet. It got crushed between other passengers and knocked about every time anyone elbowed their way out of the carriage. There were little green leaves all around me, as though I was marking my territory.

An old lady smiled at me; maybe she had once mistreated a bouquet of her own. She looked as if she knew what I was going through, at any rate. The state the flowers were in after the metro journey made them unfit even for Judith Goldenberg's grave. One has to respect the dead.

I thrust the flowers into the cold bronze arms of Michel de Montaigne. The statue with the well-polished shoes looked pleased. I heard clapping. Some students from the Sorbonne approved of my action. I stepped away and studied the installation from a distance.

Michel de Montaigne looked made for carrying a bouquet. I was free. My hands were free. I hurried home.

The door was open and there was no one at the reception desk, if you could call the little white table and chair a reception desk. I went straight through to the waiting room. There was a young woman sitting next to her boyfriend. Presumably the man who got her pregnant. I guessed she must be six or seven months gone. We said hello, as people do in a waiting room. Quietly, discreetly, but politely. They were holding hands. They were here for love. I was here because I was paranoid. They were here to assure themselves that the thing they held dearest was doing fine. I was here to see the gynaecologist because of his name.

I knew that this gynaecologist idea was a long shot, really. Like when I stood up and brandished the bouquet above my head. Both actions were an attempt to suppress my feeling of powerlessness, the idea that someone was controlling me. Making an appointment with a gynaecologist who happened to have the same name as the man I worked for was desperate. And even if the gynaecologist turned out, against all odds, to be the Monsieur Bellivier who had come into my life, would that actually mean a thing? It wouldn't change anything other than that he'd know what my vagina looked like.

I heard voices and realised that a patient must be leaving. Sure enough, a woman around my age walked through the waiting room. She was accompanied by a slim, grey-haired man. They stopped to shake hands, just as the receptionist returned with a flustered smile. The gynaecologist, the man with the grey hair, turned around. He didn't give me a single glance, which was disappointing, but I felt a little thrill nonetheless, because now, for the first time, I actually was waiting for Monsieur Bellivier. For the first and last time, I promised myself. Monsieur Bellivier nodded to the young couple. They stood up, and the man steered the woman ahead of him as though she was incapable of walking on her own. She seemed to appreciate the gesture. Maybe it made her feel like she was being taken care of.

A sudden cold sweat came over me and I started to feel queasy. For a while, I thought I was going to be sick, but I managed to calm myself down with the thought that I probably wouldn't be the first person to throw up in a waiting room for pregnant women.

'Madame.'

The receptionist was trying to attract my attention. Just as I was about to get up and go over to her austere little desk, she appeared beside me with a form.

'Since it's your first visit,' she explained, and she was soon back behind her desk, filing her nails.

I started to fill in my personal details and my medical history. I gave a made-up name, address and date of birth, something I'd never done before. I could say I had left my hospital card at home, it would only cost me a few euros extra. I read through all the information to check I hadn't made any mistakes, though it hardly mattered considering not a single letter or number was really right.

The strangest thing of all was that I chose an address only a stone's throw from where I actually lived. There were over a thousand streets in Paris, so why choose the one that intersected my own? Maybe it was so I felt I'd almost told the truth, or maybe it was just a lack of imagination. It didn't matter. Nothing seemed to matter any more. One child, I wrote, a son. I couldn't lie about that. I didn't know what a gynaecologist could tell by looking at a vagina. Maybe there were year rings, like you see in trees, which showed the number rather than the age of any children. What did I know? Eventually, I changed my mind, rubbed out 'son' and wrote 'daughter' instead.

I didn't know if I should hand the form to the receptionist or Dr Bellivier, but before I had time to decide, she came over and took the form and pen from me. Time was running out. I had to be back at the office in twenty minutes. It surely wouldn't be the end of the world if I was a bit late, so long as any emails were forwarded within a few minutes. I heard voices again. The young couple and the doctor were approaching his door. I don't really know why I felt so nervous. Whether it was the fact that I would soon be face to face with a Monsieur Bellivier, or because I was at the doctor's for no reason and had provided false information.

For the first time, I saw Dr Bellivier's face. I don't really know how I had imagined him, but he felt familiar somehow. He gestured for me to go into his room. He brought the form I had filled in with him. He hadn't done that with the young couple, but on the other hand, it almost certainly wasn't their first time there. My body was poised for flight. From the person I had claimed to be, from myself and this whole crazy situation I had got myself into. The doctor might be a psychopath who lured in young women by putting them at the top of a skyscraper and then calling them down to the ground to slice them open.

My queasiness intensified and I looked around for a wastepaper bin in case I really did throw up. I didn't know if I was allowed to sit down, so I remained on my feet, staring at a picture, an anatomical chart of a pregnant woman. Not that it made me feel any less sick. My head was spinning and I heard the door close behind me.

'Take a seat, madame.'

Why did his face seem so familiar? He sat down opposite me, not looking in my direction. He started copying the information from my form to his computer. He took his time. No sense of urgency.

'And what gives me the honour of having you here today?'

The room, which was white, suddenly felt very dark. Could a doctor say things like that? 'What gives me the honour of having you here today?' Was it meant to be a way of lightening the mood?

'I . . . I'd like a smear test,' I managed to stammer.

'Aha. When was your last one?'

'A few years ago, I suppose.'

72

'Do you have a regular gynaecologist?'

'Yes, but I've just moved here, temporarily.'

He didn't ask for the gynaecologist's name, merely indicated with his hand that it was time for the examination chair. A small trickle of sweat ran slowly down my leg.

The results of my smear test would be sent from pillar to post around the city. If I had any cell changes, the news would never reach me. Monsieur Bellivier would find out, or in this case Dr Bellivier. It's important to distinguish between them, after all.

The doctor said he would get in touch if the test showed up 'anything funny', and that the results would also be posted to my home address. But I would never see them. And he wouldn't be able to contact me. The test results would presumably be returned to the postal service and be kept there for a while, alongside all the other falsified, misspelled or mistaken addresses.

I couldn't get to sleep that night, so I installed myself at the kitchen table and opened the window, only to quickly close it again. It was still hotter outside than in.

The light went on across the courtyard. My neighbour with cancer started to pace his kitchen. That made me feel sick. Again. What if I had cancer, and yet there I was feeling sorry for the man opposite. Why had I chosen a smear test as my pretext for seeing the gynaecologist? Maybe I would be punished for playing games and develop the problems I feared. I promised to go for a smear test soon, under my own name. And I promised to go and say sorry somewhere. All to compensate for what I had done to all those poor people who really did have the disease.

The hours I spent in the kitchen were insightful and necessary. I was coping brilliantly with my assignment forwarding cryptic emails up in the skyscraper. It was my own thoughts and eccentricities that I couldn't control. This innocent assignment had allowed them free rein. They seemed to be stimulated by banal things and events, flowers, doctor's appointments, numbers . . . It was only going to be for a short while, and I promised myself to try to focus on my work and my son. To attempt to see the assignment for what it was, just a job forwarding a few meaningless emails for three weeks. Nothing more.

Amir usually helps his father in the shop at weekends, but Mancebo explains that he only needs him for an hour or two that Saturday. No more. Mancebo has used his sleepless night to think everything through.

Amir accepts the new schedule without questioning why he isn't needed at all on Sunday. Mancebo is sure he doesn't suspect a thing, and he'll probably never discuss his weekend shifts with Fatima. And since she spends every Sunday with Adèle at the hammam, she won't be wondering why Amir isn't in the shop.

The air feels fresh. There's nothing happening in the apartment opposite. Mancebo has things under control. He swings back on his stool and, despite his sleepless night, feels exceptionally good. He can't allow himself to be impatient.

Just two days have passed since he started his task, but things need to pick up. Mostly for Mancebo himself. Ever since the writer disappeared with his suitcase, Mancebo's developed a real appetite for detective work. He watches Tariq move through the shop in his usual boorish way. His cousin has time to pat Mancebo on the shoulder before he rushes out onto the boulevard, where he almost manages to get himself run over. The baker shouts as the car brakes, and the driver holds up his hands to show he wasn't in the wrong. Sure enough, he has the law on his side. Mancebo saw the whole thing. Tariq and the baker exchange a few words. Mancebo guesses he's joking about the lie-in Tariq gave himself. His ability to perceive details has come on leaps and bounds in just a few short days. Or maybe he has just discovered his talent for observation.

He remembers that his mother always used to say that the only hurdle to good observational skills was vanity, and Mancebo certainly isn't vain, far from it. If he really makes an effort, he can read from the baker's lips that the man is now saying something about last night's weather, that it's an odd climate we've got nowadays, monsoon rain one day and a desert sun hanging over the city the next. Tariq says something about climate change. What does he know about that, Mancebo wonders, juggling a couple of plums as he greets two passers-by.

Mancebo continues to swing on his stool, and amuses himself by placing it right on top of the marks it has made in the tarmac. What was it that made me put the stool here, of all places, he asks himself as Amir comes down and rests a hand on his father's shoulder.

'Everything OK, Dad?'

'Yep, all good. When it's too hot, no one feels like shopping, and now that it's cooler, people want to seize the moment. Running to the shops is the last thing on their minds. I'll be back in an hour or two. If you need help with anything, you know you can close up and ask Tariq. OK?'

Amir nods.

'I'll be back in an hour or two, did I say that?'

Amir nods again, sits down on his father's stool and starts leafing through a comic.

'Don't forget to smile, my son. That's the only thing we give away for free.'

Mancebo pats his son on the cheek then makes his way towards the garage. He calls Raphaël from the road. First, the van needs seeing to.

*

Today is my day, Mancebo thinks, accelerating gently. It feels like the van has more energy now that Raphaël has fixed it up. Mancebo had mumbled something incomprehensible about how he broke the headlight, but Raphaël didn't seem to care, he was more concerned with how to fix it.

Mancebo isn't familiar with this area of Paris and has never set foot in the place he is now heading towards. He drives into the garage. He can't afford to lose any time looking for a space. The barrier goes up and he spirals down into the depths of the garage. His decision to pay a visit to Galeries Lafayette department store is based on three things: he needs a shop which sells everything on his list; it's not far from Raphaël's; and Mancebo is sure that in this area of town he won't bump into anyone he knows.

He shares a lift with a young couple carrying a number of huge shopping bags. It's the bags that make Mancebo feel uncomfortable, and he clasps his hands in front of him. But if he feels uncomfortable in the lift, it's nothing compared to what will happen when the doors open. He's met by glitter, noise, perfumes, a fast pace, money quickly changing hands, mirrors, crystal chandeliers, lights and crowds of beautiful people chasing after it all. He stands there in his blue coat and black cap, not knowing quite where to turn. It feels like everyone is staring at him, and he can't remember ever having felt so like a fish out of water before.

The fragrant, lovely people crowd past him and he feels like a ghost, an invisible ghost, one who has a job to do. He is suddenly struck by the thought that he might bump into Madame Cat. She probably comes to places like this all the time. She's just as lovely as the other women here.

Mancebo pulls the sheet of paper from his inner pocket. First on his list: a watch. He glances around for an information desk. In an attempt to get a better overview of this newly discovered world, he moves towards the middle, but all he can see are colours, lights and glitter. If Fatima only knew that I was in Galeries Lafayette, he thinks, which makes him smile. He dares to take a step into the inferno. And there, in the distance, he finally spots the information desk and reluctantly makes his way towards it.

Small watches, big watches, glittery watches, matte watches, expensive watches, eye-wateringly expensive watches, colourful watches, discreet watches, ladies' watches, men's watches, diving watches, watches with inbuilt alarms, ugly watches, beautiful watches, loud watches and silent watches.

'How can I help, monsieur?'

'I'd like a watch.'

'Mmm, what did you have in mind?'

'A watch, a wristwatch.'

'OK, any particular brand?'

Mancebo isn't aware of any watch brands, but he does know a country which makes them.

'I'd like a Swiss watch, one which is discreet and not too expensive.'

The young shop assistant smiles and goes away to fetch the perfect watch for a private detective.

He crosses the word 'watch' from his shopping list. He knows exactly what he needs, but it feels more professional to have a list. The second, and therefore last, word on his list is 'binoculars'. He decides to go back to the information desk. The helpful woman managed to send him the right way to the watches, so she can probably also tell him how to find the binoculars.

Mancebo's progress to the information desk is hindered by a crowd of Japanese tourists. Their guide is keeping them together like they are a flock of sheep, and it's practically impossible for him to make his way through the homogeneous group. Mancebo has to wait patiently until they pass.

There aren't as many binoculars to choose between as there were watches. There are plastic binoculars, for hunting, he guesses, a couple of ordinary black types, and then two kinds of opera glasses.

'Good afternoon. How can I help you, monsieur?'

'Are these all the binoculars you have?'

'Yes, what were you planning to use them for?'

Mancebo cautiously glances around before he answers:

'Espionage.'

He regrets his choice of word the minute it leaves his mouth. He could at least have said detective work. But the word 'espionage' was probably the right one for showing that he wasn't just an old man who owned a grocer's shop; he was a genuine detective, albeit in disguise, someone who demanded respect. Mancebo stands up straight. No one is perfect. No one is completely free of suspicion. No one is completely in the clear. Not to Mancebo.

'Oh, that sounds interesting. In that case I'd recommend these, if it's from a distance, if you're sitting in a car or something.'

The sales assistant takes out a big, classic-looking pair.

'But if you're closer to your person, or your object, or . . . well, then I would recommend one of these pairs of opera glasses. They're more . . . discreet.'

He places the two smaller pairs next to the bigger one.

'I'll take the more expensive of the opera glasses.'

Choosing the most expensive pair is also a way of commanding respect in this new world in which Mancebo feels so uncertain. He crosses 'binoculars' from his short list. Mission completed.

He puts on his watch, high up on his wrist so that it isn't visible from beneath his coat, and stretches his arm to double-check. Maybe buying a Swiss watch from Galeries Lafayette was unnecessary if it's not going to be visible to anyone. The watch shows 12.45 as he leaves the parking garage.

He throws the parking ticket and the two receipts out of the window and pulls out into the traffic. Seventeen minutes later, he parks his van, shoves the binoculars into one of his coat pockets and waves to Amir, who is still engrossed in his comic. Mancebo heads over to Tariq's shop and steps inside. Tariq has a customer, and Mancebo starts absent-mindedly playing with a flashing key ring as

79

he studies his own shop. How much can you see from the cobbler's? Can you see what Amir is doing? Where can you hide in the shop, without being seen from over here? Where does the light fall? He has time to observe and memorise all this before Tariq says goodbye to his customer.

'You been out running?' Tariq asks.

'I was at Raphaël's with the van.'

'I thought you said it was going.'

'It was, but then one of the headlights . . . it wasn't sitting right, so I thought I might as well get it sorted today.'

'Good idea. How's he doing?'

Mancebo wants to cut off the discussion, like he had earlier at Raphaël's. He still hasn't realised that he can relax. His work is done for the day. He no longer needs an alibi.

'Yeah, fine. And his wife, Camille, was as lovely as ever. The kind of woman you'd be glad to have. Always happy and young-looking.'

'Not like ours, you mean?'

Both men laugh, shake hands and tell one another to have a good afternoon. Mancebo crosses the boulevard with the watch strapped high on his wrist.

'Everything OK?'

Amir nods in reply and then slopes off. He probably has better things to do, Mancebo thinks, stashing the binoculars behind the sixty-nine Chinese notebooks.

The sun will soon be setting, and since it's early summer the swarms of German and English tourists have not yet arrived. A couple of horses appear in the distance. They're training ahead of tomorrow's race. There are a few children testing out their newly bought kites, but otherwise the only people left are the day's swimmers, who are now packing up their towels, sun lotions and picnic baskets to head home for a shower before dinner.

The writer and his lover have probably already showered and

got ready for the evening. They walk along the beach, both have taken off their shoes and she has her arm linked through his. Maybe they're talking about something serious, about how their love is an impossible card that no one would want to be dealt in a game of poker. But as in many games, their love is down to chance. Neither of them chose to love the other. They know that their time together is precious, rare, and that makes them melancholy. Mancebo tastes the word 'melancholy'. He can't remember ever having used it before, not even in his thoughts. But he does so now.

Mancebo is sitting on the stool outside his shop as usual. Things have been quiet all day, and he's grateful for that. It was just what he needed after a sleepless night and those hectic hours in Galeries Lafayette. His thoughts return to the writer and the beaches of Normandy, to Cabourg in particular. The young lovers are just passing the Grand Hôtel, which looms over the beach, impressive and stylish. The same hotel in which Marcel Proust, the writer's great idol, used to stay. Cabourg was the only place where the famous author was able to get any respite from his terrible asthma. The writer tells his lover all of this, and she listens intently. The fact that Mancebo knows of an author like Proust is purely down to Amir having done a school project on him. He had practised his presentation on his family. Tariq kept the time and Fatima had said that maybe she should check in to the hotel in Cabourg to get away from the asthma she suffered as a result of everyone smoking around her. Mancebo remembers that part particularly clearly.

The more Mancebo thinks about the sinful couple, the stronger his feelings of empathy for them grow. He suffers with them. That might seem strange considering everything Madame Cat has woken within him, but Mancebo can't for anything in the world connect Madame Cat's despair to the writer's infidelity. It's as though they're elements from two different stories, and Mancebo is beginning to take the side of the villain in this tale.

He wonders whether his feelings might affect his work. Shouldn't a private detective stay on his client's side, both practically and emotionally? Otherwise, it's like a defence lawyer turning up for closing statements with a heart that beats for the prosecution. Their weighty words would fall flat, not even the prosecution would manage to catch them, because they weren't directly aimed at them. Mancebo spends some time thinking about this similarity, and misses the moment when a Vespa and a car crash outside the bakery. People stream out into the road to find out what happened. Mancebo stands up to get a better look, and that gives him an idea. This is the perfect moment to try out his binoculars.

He points them in the direction of the crowd, but all he can see is a grey haze. It's the first time he has ever used binoculars, but he knows how to adjust the focus. Suddenly, he recoils and tears them from his eyes. The people had become so sharp that it makes him gasp. He hadn't realised that binoculars could be so powerful. He carefully studies every person around the accident scene and then points the binoculars at the building opposite. Everything becomes blurry again and it takes him a moment to adjust the focus to the new distance. He studies Tariq. His cousin seems unreal through the binoculars, it's almost as though Mancebo is seeing him for the first time. Is he really so dark, Mancebo wonders, casting one last glance up at the fire escape before he carefully puts the opera glasses back into their case and hides them beneath the till. He returns to his stool and notices the rich scent of food making its way down into the shop.

Alongside his exhilaration about his new job, a feeling of loneliness has also reared its head. The room is dark, and Mancebo knows that he needs to get a few hours' sleep. If he's going to manage to look after the shop and get his detective work done, he needs to sleep. But since the evening Madame Cat came into his life, nothing has been the same. Even though very little has actually changed.

Mancebo is lying on his back with his arms crossed over his

stomach, but he suddenly realises that in that position he looks like he has started his eternal rest. He quickly moves. He hears the sound of a car every now and then, the occasional siren, but otherwise the night is unusually quiet. The feeling of alienation had come over him during dinner, about the same time as he sat down in his new seat.

For the first time in his life, he knows and is doing something that he hasn't mentioned to his family. Or not intentionally, anyway. He doesn't know, as he lies with his arms behind his head, staring up at the white ceiling and its worryingly large cracks, whether that change is good or bad. But one thing he does know: he has to keep going, he has to go the distance.

Sacré-Cœur rose up like a shapely marshmallow above a hazy Paris. On the TV and the radio, presenters urged the population to leave their cars at home. My eyes were brimming with tears, but it wasn't because of the pollution. My lack of sleep must finally have been catching up with me. There had to be some kind of punishment for staying up all night.

The first email of the day arrived, '3A 3B 27E 27F'. It took a certain amount of energy just to forward it on. Ordinarily, I had impressive difficulty remembering numbers, but I started memorising all the strings of numbers and letters that I could.

I spent the afternoon working on personal things, like making an appointment for a smear test with my actual gynaecologist, cancelling a place on a seminar and ordering a pair of shoes. I even had time to do some research into holidays before I started packing up to leave.

The lift stopped on my floor, and though I was sure it was the cleaner, my body got ready to run. Maybe I would be able to make it out to the corridor before she came into the room. I did. She was holding open the lift doors while she hauled the cleaning trolley and vacuum into the corridor.

'Afternoon.'

She jumped, as though her mind had been somewhere else entirely.

'Afternoon,' she replied.

The man hadn't said anything about talking to the cleaner, just that I should try to be brief with the people who worked here.

'Are you off?' she asked.

Maybe she had been given the same instructions. She pulled the vacuum cleaner into the office. I was still standing outside, debating whether to try to start a conversation.

'Have you worked here long? Do you work in other buildings too?' I asked.

She looked up at me, and for the first time I realised that she was very cross-eyed. I didn't know which eye I should focus on. She was a stout little woman in her fifties, probably with Arab heritage.

'I clean here during the afternoon, and another building in the morning.'

I had no idea what I was going to do with that information. Our conversation, if you could call it that, fell flat.

'Goodbye,' I said, heading for the lift.

I mentally prepared myself to collect the day's flowers.

Lately, a new idea had taken root. I don't know if it was any easier to handle than the thought that I was an isolated terrorist cell. I now suspected I was part of a study. Into what, I had no idea, but it started with finding a carefully chosen individual to carry out the experiment. A depressed woman was perfect. That would then be followed by a study into how a person adapts to their environment and role. How someone reacts when faced with an indecipherable, completely meaningless task. A bit like a modern version of Pavlov's dogs. Where his dogs were given food, I got flowers. If that was the case, it wasn't the work which made me suffer but the reward.

If the sole purpose of the flowers was to distinguish me from the crowd, then it was just as well I came face to face with whoever was looking for me. I sat down on a bench outside Areva with the flowers in full view in my lap. Though today's bunch was one of the most beautiful I had received – they looked like they had come from a summer meadow – it still disgusted me. My cheeks were aching and I was fighting back tears. Feeling so alone and degraded and still having to be brave; I didn't know if I had it in me.

I was being watched. It wasn't just a vague feeling, no paranoia this time; from the corner of my eye, I noticed a man studying me from ten or so metres away. I looked down before I had time to register his face.

Had he been there every day when I left? Without looking up, I left the bench and calmly started walking towards the metro. If he followed me, I would have no trouble shaking him off. I knew the area well, better than most people. And if I managed to shake him off, we could swap roles. I could watch him. The idea gave me courage, but at the same time I realised that exposure could be the end of everything. And I wasn't sure I wanted that.

I slowly made my way up the stairs to the open plaza. I didn't turn around to see if he was following me, I knew I would be able to discreetly check whether he was behind me in the huge windows of the HSBC building. As I continued around the old carousel where children were laughing, a surreal feeling came over me. I was being followed, in broad daylight, through the Paris business district, carrying a bunch of summer blooms in one hand, the whole thing soundtracked by the laughter of children.

The minute I passed the entrance to the bank, I glanced into one of the windows and saw that he was close behind me. There was no way it was a coincidence that he was going the same way. I turned off towards the Cnit building, already knowing which way this cat and mouse game was going to go.

At every corner of the Cnit building there are small glass lifts running up to the next level. The floor above was shaped like a glass tunnel which looped around the edge of the building. There wasn't room for more than a few people in each of the tiny lifts, and I found it hard to imagine that if you were tailing someone – and wanted to remain anonymous – you would dare get into the same lift. The man following me probably wanted to retain his faceless identity for a while longer. If one of the lifts was on the ground floor, I would be able to quickly jump in and head up to the glass tunnel. From there, I could study him more closely. He wouldn't have time to get away. That was my plan as I headed towards the Cnit building.

The moment I stepped inside, I noticed that the lift in the far left corner was heading down, and I slowly made my way over to it. The doors opened and a handsome couple stepped out. With my eyes on the floor, I pressed the button. The doors started to close, but then someone suddenly squeezed between them, and they opened wide to welcome another passenger.

'Hi again,' said the man.

I didn't reply, though I recognised him immediately. It was the man to whom I had given the flowers on the metro a few days earlier.

My new bouquet was past its best. The flowers had lost their freshness during the walk, and my hands were covered in a mix of sweat and sap. My fingers clutched the slender stalks. We left solid ground and were carried above the people down below. Nothing was forcing me to reply to his greeting, maybe he would just give up if he didn't get any response. Maybe he would leave me in peace once the lift came to a stop, just head back downstairs again. I'd never talked to the man, so why start now?

I stared down at my black shoes, which were now embellished with a number of tiny blue petals. The lift stopped with a jolt and the curved doors opened to let us out into the glass tunnel, which I had previously thought would be my place of refuge, my vantage point.

Though I hadn't really had time to reflect on my next move, I still managed to think logically. The man couldn't be involved in my task, for the simple reason that I was the one who had made first contact. I was the one who had climbed on board the metro carriage, who had chosen him. I left the lift first and took a few aimless steps into the glass tunnel.

'Maybe we could introduce ourselves?' I heard him say behind me.

I kept walking, but I wasn't sure I was doing the right thing. If I was confident he had nothing to do with Monsieur Bellivier, then maybe it was best not to chase him off. I kept walking anyway, but then I did something surprising. He was the first person who had appealed to me in a long time. And there was something about his eyes. They made me want to know what was going on.

His arms were slumped to his sides, as though his shoulders couldn't hold them up. He wasn't prepared to take a single step towards me. Maybe he thought he had done that already. And so I walked over to him instead. Before I reached him, I held out my hand as a peace offering. There, in the glass tunnel, above the heads of hundreds of people, we shook hands.

'Christophe,' he said in a gentle voice.

'Afternoon,' I replied.

He smiled.

'Can I take you for a coffee?'

I realised we were still holding hands.

'Thanks, but no thanks.'

I pulled my hand away and caught a flash of disappointment in his hard-to-read eyes.

'In that case, let me say thank you for the flowers you gave me. They're still looking beautiful.'

'You're welcome,' I replied and swallowed.

I wanted to get far away from this man. I could see that he was looking at my bouquet and that he was about to comment on it, but he decided not to. Instead, he insisted on standing in silence, and so eventually I just turned my back on him and continued down the glass tunnel towards the Hilton hotel. It was my only option.

'Good afternoon, can I help you?' the receptionist asked.

'No, I'm just waiting for someone.'

'A hotel guest? Would you like me to call up to their room?'

'No, he'll probably be here soon.'

The receptionist smiled and continued tapping away at her computer. The place smelled clean, almost like a dentist's surgery. I sat down on a firm, uncomfortable seat. My flight from Christophe had raised my adrenaline levels, but that high had now started to recede and I could feel the melancholy creeping back in. The receptionist looked up and smiled. I smiled. The time passed.

'Would you be able to give this to the man in room seven?' I eventually asked.

'Yes . . . but are you sure? I only have a lady in that room.'

'Ah, sorry, yes. They're for her.'

'Who shall I say they're from?'

'She'll know who they're from.'

It felt good to turn my back on the receptionist. On my way back to the metro, I walked with my head bowed. I had no interest in finding out whether anyone was watching me, mostly because I knew no one was. I was alone.

Gradually, my feeling of melancholy was replaced by a welcome calm. After twisting and turning in bed, I got up and made some tea. My neighbour had been pacing back and forth in his kitchen, but he went to sit at the table. Though I watched him quite often, I never had the feeling that he'd noticed me. But why would he, really? He probably had other things on his mind.

With my new feeling of calm came a sense of guilt over the fact I had been so self-pitying. I wasn't alone. My son was sleeping deeply in the room next door. I had a choice. Before I went back to bed, I pushed the door to his room ajar. Nights can cloud a person's thoughts. The darkness can discolour reality. I couldn't lose my nerve now.

Sundays are different to the other days of the week. The cobbler's shop is closed. The grocer's shop is open, but Mancebo doesn't go to Rungis and he doesn't pull up the grille until after lunch. But this particular Sunday is also different to all of the others. Mancebo opens up at ten, right after Fatima and Adèle leave for the hammam, and he reminds Amir that he doesn't need his help today.

Mancebo is meant to submit his first report that evening, putting it into an olive jar which he will leave in the recycling container outside his shop. The green plastic container is far from full, just a couple of juice bottles and an empty Nescafé jar, but by the end of the day, it'll contain something of a different nature.

The delivery of the report won't, in itself, give Mancebo any answers as to whether he can take his new job seriously, whether the whole thing will end here or whether more pages will be written. The olive jar is just one step on the way to the truth. The definitive proof of whether he has done his job properly will depend on another jar, with very different contents. Mancebo's compensation, or wage if you prefer.

Families with small children crowd the streets. Sunday is a family day, and on Sunday mornings, the fathers are often in charge of the kids. Mancebo likes Sundays. The people who come into his shop are grateful to find somewhere that's actually open. And no one ever complains about his high prices on a Sunday. They're all just happy to get hold of whatever they forgot to buy earlier. A couple of tourists from Sweden come in and ask for cigarettes, but otherwise his customers are people from the neighbourhood popping in to buy milk, bread or a bottle of wine. The day passes at a Sunday pace. As it should.

Nothing of note happens, nothing worth jotting down. Not until the afternoon, when Mancebo finally spots something he can use to round off his report. At exactly 14.56 – Mancebo knows this because he checks his watch – a taxi pulls up outside the cobbler's shop and deposits the writer. He is wearing the same clothes he had on when he left, something Mancebo finds noteworthy.

The writer is carrying the same bag as before, but Mancebo has the impression that it's heavier now, or is it just that the writer is no longer carrying it with the same ease? Mancebo feels closer to the answer as he studies the writer making his way up the fire escape. Before, there had been a lightness, an energy, a sense of freedom to the way the writer moved through space. But now the world seems to be weighing on his narrow shoulders.

The taxi driver pulls away and Mancebo lifts the binoculars to his eyes. The writer's face looms before him, and it's now perfectly clear to Mancebo: the writer is suffering. He can't remember having seen such silent anguish on a person's face before. Not that he has ever studied a stranger so closely. It feels like he has all the world's suffering under a magnifying glass.

Before the writer makes it into his apartment, Mancebo shifts his attention to the bag, to check whether he can spot a label. If so, that would suggest it had been on a plane journey, rather than just a train. But the old-fashioned bag lacks any such marker. Mancebo feels proud that he thought of that detail. He can't allow himself to forget that he actually has no idea where the writer spent the weekend. Not yet, anyway, but one day he'll find out that and so much more. Right now, however, he has nothing but his fantasies to go on. All due deference to the truth, but he wouldn't want to be without his new-found imagination.

Though what is happening on the other side of the boulevard isn't particularly remarkable, Mancebo still gets excited. The possibilities opened up by the binoculars make him forget both his shop and himself. All that exists are espionage, the binoculars and the writer.

Mancebo moves behind the till and positions himself in the corner, by the tissues and matches. No one can see him there, he knows that for a fact, he's checked it out. But the problem with this spot is that he can only see the writer's hallway. There's a shadow in the window, but it's too dark to make out anything else. The shadow moves from the hallway, and Mancebo quickly and smoothly makes his way to the entrance so that he can watch what happens next. He really hopes no one will pay a visit to the shop.

Mancebo has put the binoculars into his coat pocket, and his eyes sweep over the three rooms: the hallway, the bathroom, the office. Suddenly, the writer appears in the office window, he's standing with his hands on his hips. The whole thing looks a bit theatrical to Mancebo, and he starts to worry that the writer suspects he has an audience, that he's overacting as a result. Maybe he knows that his wife hired a detective, and he's acting as though he is in a play. If so, that would mean he has absolute power, reducing Mancebo to a marionette, with the writer holding the strings.

Mancebo becomes convinced of this when the writer sits down in his chair and stares straight towards him. Mancebo's eyes dart back to the street, and he raises his hand in a wave to no one to demonstrate his complete lack of interest in whatever is going on in the building over the road. No one returns his greeting, it ebbs out into a city in which no one cares about an anonymous wave. In Paris, there are countless messages with diffuse addresses and senders.

After his awkward wave, Mancebo starts to sort the apples with his back towards Madame Cat's building. When he turns around, he sees that the writer is still staring straight ahead. If his gaze is resting on the shopkeeper or the boulevard, or even on the building opposite, it's impossible to tell, and to avoid taking any unnecessary risks, Mancebo continues to weed out the carrots which can no longer be sold. Maybe the writer has realised that the man who crashed his van on Rue de Chéroy and the greengrocer over the road from his building are the same person.

When he next turns around, the writer has disappeared and, since he can't see him, he decides he must be in the kitchen. Mancebo pulls his stool outside, automatically places it on top of the marks on the tarmac, scratches his head and waves. This time, his greeting is aimed at someone. Madame Cannava is rushing past on high heels. The writer is back and Mancebo watches an odd spectacle as he moves from room to room with a glass in his hand. He could be listening to music, Mancebo thinks.

Suddenly, the writer disappears into the bedroom, and Mancebo imagines that he has flopped down onto the bed. This gives him the opportunity to document everything that happened between 14.56 and 15.48.

From the point of view of a private detective, Sunday has been quite eventful. Mancebo glances at his watch and smiles. He likes his new watch and wonders why he didn't buy one earlier. But he knows the answer to that. Until now, he hasn't needed to live his life by the hour, minute, or second. And no one has ever needed him the way Madame Cat needs him. The fate of two people lies in his hands. It could even be more than two. The choices people make send rings across the water. Many different people will be affected by the wake of a bellyflop, which is, after all, precisely what infidelity is. Never before has Mancebo thought of himself as a cog in the machine, a ring on the water, someone who is contributing to something. He can't even remember what he used to do before he started this task.

Since nothing of interest is happening over the boulevard and he doesn't have any customers in the shop, Mancebo has trouble keeping himself busy. What did I used to do, he thinks, scratching his head beneath his cap. But he doesn't have to wonder for very long, because at 18.04 his subject reappears in the window. Mancebo goes back to work.

Then he decides to close up for the day. If he's any later than usual, suspicions might be aroused. He rarely works past seven on a Sunday. Though there are still plenty of people out on the streets, very few of them pay his shop a visit.

It's as though the Parisians are taking the chance to get some exercise after the heatwave, before the next one arrives. Because it will. The inhabitants of the city have been given the five-day forecast. A warm front is approaching from Eastern Europe, where many people have already died.

Mancebo pulls the fruit and vegetable stands inside and chases away a small bird hopping towards the shop. He still hasn't quite worked out what he's going to do with the olive jar. Should he empty a full jar and wash it out? Or should he save a few olives in the bottom and push the report between them?

He decides to let the question simmer and starts by tearing out the five pages from his notebook and folding them carefully. Should he write some kind of personal greeting? In the end, he decides not to – what if the jar fell into the wrong hands?

It's now 19.12, and Mancebo is starting to feel tense. He picks up a jar of olives, empties the contents into the bin and rinses it clean in the handbasin behind the door. There is still an oily residue on the inside of the jar, but Mancebo is happy enough with the result: a half-clean, fully empty olive jar. He pushes his report inside.

With a steady grip, he takes his modern-day message in a bottle, his message in a jar, and casts a quick glance over to the building opposite. The writer is hunched behind his computer screen. Mancebo places the jar on top of the glass for recycling and leaves the green plastic tray outside the door. Suddenly, he can't remember where he usually puts it. Right by the door, or a little way out onto the pavement? Old habits feel strange when he thinks of them. He moves the green tray a couple of times, a few centimetres here and there, before he eventually pulls down the grille and locks up.

On his way up the stairs, Mancebo hears a thud. He turns on the light and looks over to the window, but he can't see anything. He takes a few steps towards the door and realises he is staring straight into Madame Cat's green eyes on the other side of the boulevard.

For a fraction of a second, he thinks about raising his hand in greeting, but he changes his mind. She is just about to make her way up the fire escape when a taxi's tyres screech. Her face is expressionless, without a trace of recognition when she sees Mancebo. Though there is an entire street between them, there's no doubt that she is looking straight into his eyes. Mancebo doesn't move an inch until Madame Cat closes the door behind her, and then he makes his way to the front of the shop and stands there with his eyes fixed on the fire escape. Not to watch anything in particular, it's mostly to calm his thoughts before he makes his way upstairs. Right then, he notices a tiny sparrow lying motionless on the ground by the door. There is a small, red mark on the windowpane. Mancebo studies the bird's tiny, beautiful body for a moment. It's the same bird he shooed from his shop.

If the tiny bird hadn't flown into the window, sacrificing itself, I would never have had those sacred seconds with Madame Cat, Mancebo thinks later in bed. During those few seconds when their eyes met, Madame Cat managed not only to show that she had faith in Mancebo, but also to convince him of something else. Though what that was, he still doesn't know.

He had almost forgotten her green, catlike eyes. Eyes which absorbed some light, but emitted even less. Eyes which, in that briefest of moments, had managed to convey sorrow, desperation, relief and joy. If that little bird hadn't . . .

Fatima turns in her sleep and stretches out an arm, which hits

Mancebo on the forehead. He rolls over and closes his eyes. He knows he needs to get some sleep. Tomorrow is the start of a new week, and he can't remember when he last slept through the night. He hears footsteps from the floor below and listens intently. His detective's instinct now never seems to leave him. Who could be up so late? The footsteps seem light, so he guesses it must be Adèle. She's probably up to take some painkillers or to read another chapter of her feng shui book. Mancebo smiles at the thought of their new seating arrangements.

The sound of the footsteps dies out and he hears someone flush the toilet. If that little bird hadn't . . . Its delicate, lifeless body refuses to leave his thoughts. Mancebo doesn't normally feel any particular affection for animals. To him, animals are animals, there to be eaten. He doesn't have much time for pets, either.

Tonight, though, he can't sleep for thinking about a small, dead bird. It's already dead, there's nothing I can do for it, he tries to tell himself. He can't go out and bury all the dead birds in Paris. That would be a third full-time job.

Eventually, he gives up any thought of sleep. The sky has started to brighten. The bird should be given a worthy funeral. Maybe I'm going crazy, Mancebo thinks as he swings his feet to the floor and gets out of bed. Fatima is still sleeping deeply. Just as well, because he's sure she wouldn't want to play any part in a nocturnal bird funeral.

He catches the soapy scent of the hammam as he passes her side of the bed. They always use a rose-scented soap after the scrub massage. He automatically glances out of the window and notices a light glowing in the office across the boulevard. But then it goes out and a shadow vanishes. Who it might have been, he has no idea.

Mancebo wonders whether he should write this down, and decides he probably should. The fact he's alert even at night might mean an extra gold star for him. And maybe he'll need one spare if he misses anything crucial going forward. But he can't let working at night

97

become a habit. He doesn't want Madame Cat to take it for granted that he'll work nights. I can offer a bit of extra time and energy every once in a while, Mancebo thinks, rifling through the plastic tubs in the kitchen to find a suitable bird coffin.

The friends of the dead hold court. It's the first time Mancebo has heard such twittering, but then again he doesn't tend to be down in the shop in the middle of the night. He opens the door and pushes up the grille far enough for him to get outside and search for the cadaver.

There's a full moon in the sky, and he looks up at the white ball illuminating the near-empty boulevard. In truth, there is no such thing as a completely empty street in Paris. The city is a living being in that sense, Mancebo thinks, but one with many dead souls. Broken people sucked up into the world of the living. Maybe they seek out the big city in the hope of being able to share some of the energy. Paris, a complex city which refuses to admit its faults. It lives as though its past never happened, as though it were all just made up, lies. In any case, it's forgotten. In Paris, it's tomorrow that counts.

For the little bird, there is no tomorrow, and that might be the thing that bothers Mancebo most. He doesn't know why. Tomorrow has never felt as important as it does now. But nor has it felt so uncertain. That fact doesn't scare him. Quite the opposite. Mancebo searches for the bird. He is clutching the plastic box Fatima keeps cheese in. He's sure the bird was right beneath the red mark, which is glowing brightly in the light of the moon. But that's the only trace left. The only evidence that the bird incident ever actually happened.

He steps further out onto the pavement, but he can't see any birds, or no dead sparrows anyway. A living pigeon takes the trouble to jump up onto the pavement. He looks at the white plastic tub, which will go on being a cheese box rather than a coffin, and then up at the equally white moon. Could the bird have blown away? But there isn't a breath of air. Maybe it's been swept away already? But the city's cleaners don't arrive until later, Mancebo knows that. Maybe a cat?

He leaves the near-empty street and goes back upstairs to get the sleep which will help him to confront an uncertain tomorrow. Dead and missing, Mancebo thinks with a slight shudder. 'Let the little bird be the first and only victim in this tale,' he mumbles to himself as he pulls on his white nightshirt. He goes out into the kitchen to fill a glass of water, and as he steps into the bedroom, he sees Fatima's eyes snap shut when she spots him.

'Are you awake?' Mancebo asks.

Fatima doesn't reply. It's not enough that she spends time behind the curtain in the tobacconist's shop; now she's pretending to sleep, Mancebo thinks, lying down next to her.

The military police paced solemnly back and forth across the plaza between the skyscrapers. Their huge guns stuck out in front of them like divining rods. They were there to keep the tourists calm, to reassure them that their holiday wasn't about to be blown to pieces. Nothing more.

I walked past them and took the escalator down to the metro, waving to the florist as I passed. It had become a habit. He was convinced he was the link between two lovers; I could see it in his eyes. In a way, I felt sorry for him, and I wondered how I would react to flowers in the future. I would probably forever associate them with this task. A shame, really.

I held up the day's bouquet, three simple peonies wrapped in a thick, dusty pink velvet ribbon, and the florist gave me a thumbs up. The minute I saw them, I knew they were for Judith, even though she had been spoiled lately. The dusty pink ribbon suited someone with that name.

I cast a quick glance up at the church clock before I stepped into the cemetery. I had half an hour before I needed to leave to pick up my son. It was unusually quiet that warm afternoon. There was an old couple sitting on one of the benches by the entrance, each fanning themselves with a newspaper, and I smiled at them. Though I had only been to the cemetery a handful of times before, I would have been able to find my way to Judith's grave blindfolded.

As I reached her discreet grey headstone, I had the feeling that something wasn't right. I glanced around and then down at the grave, as though something there might have changed. But Judith Goldenberg had still been born in 1916 and died in 1992. It was only when I noticed the lifeless bouquet on the neighbouring grave that I realised what it was. In the past, I'd always had to remove the old flowers before I could put the new ones down. But this time, there was no need. The bouquet was already gone. Maybe there was nothing strange about that. It could have blown away or been cleared up by one of the wardens. Graves were desecrated from time to time, so there was nothing particularly unusual about a bunch of decaying flowers disappearing.

I looked over to the compost heap, but the bouquet wasn't there either. There was a trace of the flowers, however. The petals looked like small pieces of confetti, the remains of a lifeless party on the path leading into the labyrinth of graves.

I didn't place the bouquet as carefully as usual, and instead just dropped the flowers nonchalantly onto the grave. It was like I wanted to prove to myself that I wasn't a slave to the flowers, that they didn't have the power that they did, in fact, have over me. That I had taken a serious detour to make my way to the graveyard was something I decided to ignore.

The flowers had left marks on my hands, white ones, pallor mortis. Marks which showed I had been clutching them tight. I rubbed at my palms to try to get them back to some kind of living colour. A man was approaching the grave. I didn't notice his appearance at first, he was more like a shadow. All the caution and guardedness I suffered during the day vanished the moment I entered the graveyard. The dead couldn't attack me. It was a free zone. Maybe that was why I only noticed him once it was too late. Too late to defend myself.

If anyone had been watching us, they probably would have thought that he was a gentleman inviting me if not to dance, then at least for a walk. The man grabbed my arm and made it very clear which direction we would be going in. I tried to pull away, but despite his age he had a tight grip on me. I could have kicked and shouted, but there was something vulnerable about him. It struck me that the old man had the wrong person. These things happened. Maybe he was blind. Maybe he had Alzheimer's. And so I let him steer me for a few metres, until we reached the spot where you can fill vases with fresh water. We came to a stop.

'Excuse me?' was all I said.

He didn't even look at me before he slapped me, and hard.

Life had taken its toll on his face, though he couldn't be much older than seventy. Despite the heat, he was wearing a long black coat, grey trousers and a pair of well-polished shoes. He had a black hat on his head. This man who, in my mind, had been a poor, confused pensioner, had transformed into a madman in the space of a second. A lawless person, someone I should be wary of. I backed away from him.

I wasn't scared, just shocked. Fear often allows us to act logically, intuitively. Shock doesn't allow for that. And so I just stood there, staring at him. I could have overpowered him easily, despite his height and gender. He seemed weak. He might be able to slap, but that was where it stopped. I could have given him a push, and that would have been the death of him. I could have made a run for it. It would have been my escape. But I didn't. Anger took over, and though that isn't particularly logical either, it did make me act.

'What was that?! What the hell are you doing?' I shouted. I used the informal form of address.

'Polite.'

'What?'

'I'm at least worth the polite form of address.'

He wasn't blind. His hand had struck the middle of my cheek. He didn't have the wrong person. He was a madman. Big cities were full of them. All I could do was leave. There was no point trying to reason with someone like him. And it's always a good sign if you don't understand a crazy person's answers, it means you haven't reached that point yourself.

'If you touch me again, I'm calling the police. Leave, now,' I said.

He didn't move. His icy blue eyes were looking straight at me, and though he wasn't blind, his eyes did seem to have some kind of film over them. He wasn't quite present. Part of me wanted to shove him so that he fell back onto a grave, hit his head and died. There were many before him who should have been spared. I thought of my neighbour. I didn't want to turn my back on this man, I didn't dare. And so I asked him to leave. Even a weak old madman might have a weapon.

We stared at one another. He was like a wild animal, calm for the moment, but you never knew. I backed away. His hands were hanging in a strange position. He looked like a marionette going through some kind of cramped death throes. I turned and walked away, but glanced back frequently. The dying doll was now shaking all over, but I didn't care. He could stand there and shake until he belonged to those who had finished shaking, I thought.

But then I heard a sound. It was a strange mixture of a scream and a sigh. The old man lay down, his shakes had become more like spasms, and his face twisted beyond recognition. He was about to die.

I looked around for someone who could take over. Someone who could guide him over to the other side, if that was what was needed, or who could try to keep him here. It didn't really matter which. I also needed someone to witness what was about to happen. Someone who could give evidence in my favour. I hadn't put my morbid thoughts into action. He had caused all of this himself. But there was no one in sight.

Should I shout for someone? The man was about to die before my eyes, and no sane person could watch that without trying to help. I dialled 112 for the first time in my life. I explained that I had found an old man who seemed to be dying in Cimetière de Grenelle. They told me to ask for his name, presumably to check whether he was conscious. I moved closer to him, but couldn't bring myself to ask. I was afraid.

'He's not responding.'

The ambulance arrived quickly after that.

My hands were shaking as I went over what had happened. The young ambulance driver listened. I didn't mention that the man had hit me, out of fear that I would end up being drawn into something. I explained how he had come over to me and then collapsed. If I had mentioned the slap, they probably would have thought I was hiding something. They took my name and number.

People started to gather. They were like hyenas around us. None of them had been there when I needed them. That was always the way. A living dead man in a churchyard will draw attention. The ambulance staff had placed a mask on the man's face.

Someone who hadn't heard my chain of events asked if I wanted to go with them in the ambulance. He thought we knew one another. I could have explained that I didn't know him, that I had to go and pick my son up from summer club. But the man might have been about to die. Was I meant to let him do that alone in the ambulance? What eventually convinced me was that if I didn't go, I would always be left wondering who had hit me, and not least why.

I called my ex-husband and said that an old man I had met on the way home was probably having a heart attack, and that the ambulance staff needed my account of what had happened. That was my excuse.

The man seemed stable as we pulled up at the hospital entrance. That's what I assumed anyway, because the ambulance staff were chit-chatting about everything else. But maybe they also did that when they had someone on the verge of death in their ambulance. It's their everyday, after all.

A nurse came over and asked whether I wanted a coffee while I sat in the waiting room. Waiting for what, I thought, and shook my head. My ex-husband called to ask if he should come and pick me up, and I said yes. Unless anyone needed me, I could probably leave with my conscience clear. A doctor came through the swinging doors just as I ended the call.

'Madame. You were the one with Monsieur Caro?'

'Yes, if that's his name.'

'You don't know his name? You don't know one another?'

'No, no, I . . . we bumped into one another and he collapsed. I just wanted to check he was OK. It was the ambulance staff who asked me to come along.'

'I see. He was suffering from poisoning.'

'Poisoning?'

I had assumed it was a heart attack or something similar. Poisoning sounded like a crime had been committed.

'Yes. We think he probably poisoned himself. A suicide attempt.'

'Oh. But he's going to be OK?'

'Complete recovery. Thanks to your quick thinking.'

'Good . . . Thanks.'

I turned around and left without looking back. I trusted doctors. I could turn my back on them. And I thought I could trust this particular doctor, too, until I heard him shout. His words cut straight through me.

'Monsieur Caro would like to see you.'

The doctor showed me into his room. To my surprise and horror, he didn't follow me in, he just closed the door behind me. Being shown into a strange room by a strange man was starting to feel familiar.

I looked down at the man who, just a few hours earlier, had given me a slap. He was lying beneath two blankets and there was a wire coming from his nose. It was the kind of thing I had only ever seen on TV. I doubted he had asked to see me. Maybe the doctor had made it up. Maybe he thought we had some kind of relationship after all.

I thought about my son. I didn't want him to have to come to the hospital. I didn't want him to have to see anything that scared him. Despite everything, I was still a mother, and I would protect him. Even if he would discover all this misery himself, sooner or later. I could have just left. I had done what I had to. I had saved the man's life and found out his name.

Monsieur Caro was sleeping. The yellow curtain brushed against his hand. If he had died, his last act in this life would have been hitting one of his fellow humans. My imagination had taken over again, and so I stayed in his room. Maybe he had been a devout believer his entire life and never so much as hurt a fly. Maybe people had always kicked and trodden on him, and now that he knew he was about to leave his earthly life, he wanted payback. I spotted a tattoo on his forearm. Without really thinking about why, I pulled out my phone, took a photo of it, and then nodded goodbye to the seemingly sleeping man.

'We can use the informal address with one another if you'd like.'

Coming from someone who had been wandering between life and death just a few minutes earlier, his voice was unusually clear. I moved closer so that he wouldn't need to exert himself unnec-essarily. He opened his eyes. They seemed clearer now. The film which had been clouding them earlier must have been the blanket which moves across them before death. As though to suffocate their owner.

'Why honour her?'

'Sorry?'

'Why honour her?'

'Who?'

'My mother!'

I glanced over to the door, convinced it was about to open. Despite his condition, the man could shout.

'I'm sorry, but I don't understand. Who's your mother? And what have I done to honour her?' I addressed him formally.

'I've already told you, you can use the informal. We seem to have the same interests, after all. My mother was Judith Goldenberg. You've been putting flowers on her grave. Don't you call that honouring her, woman?'

In the car on the way home, I sat and watched my son. Waiting in the hospital entrance didn't seem to have done him any harm. The Paris night passed by outside the window. There was unusually little traffic. The outdoor seats at all of the cafés and bars, however, were full to bursting.

It was cold in the car. Maybe my ex-husband wanted to show off his new car's air conditioning. Oddly enough, he didn't ask what had happened. Not because he thought that accompanying strangers to hospital was an everyday occurrence, he likely just assumed he already had all the details. And he probably did. Or maybe he just had other things on his mind. I squeezed my son's small, cool hand.

'Are you cold?'

An ambulance pulled up in the inner courtyard. Right up to the door. I had a ringside seat from my kitchen table, where I was sitting with a cup of lukewarm tea. I knew why it was there. Something in the way he had been moving earlier that evening suggested what was about to happen. Now I understood why he had let the cat out. He'd never done that before, and the cat didn't seem to appreciate its new-found freedom on the balcony. After clawing at the door for a while, it had jumped up onto the warm railing and then climbed the drainpipe, before disappearing over the roof of the bin room. Sorrow welled up inside me, and I didn't know who I felt most sorry for: my neighbour or the cat. If not dead already, both were surely at least sentenced to death. A house cat wouldn't last long on the Paris streets. The ambulance staff jumped out, and that seemed to be a good sign, a hint that my neighbour was still alive. I heard a sound from my son's room. Maybe the ambulance had woken him? But had it even had the sirens on? As the lights came on in my neighbour's apartment, I got up and turned on the light in the bathroom, using the glow to check on my son. I pushed his door ajar. He was sleeping deeply, his hands clasped beneath his chin. I went back to the window to follow the drama.

It took quite a long time. I knew I should be trying to sleep, but I couldn't miss the end. The lights in the apartment opposite went out. After that, it wasn't long before they came out carrying a stretcher, on it my neighbour. He raised a hand to his face. The ambulance left the courtyard, and this time I noticed that its lights were flashing in silence, there were no sirens. Perhaps they were showing some consideration to the sleeping Parisians. In a way, I was relieved. Now I wouldn't have to see him any more, wouldn't have to watch the suffering going on outside my window. Recently, I had started to imagine that he was nothing but a ghost in my sick brain. Someone only I could see.

I had once asked my son if he'd seen the man opposite, the man who always seemed to be home. But he hadn't, and I regretted drawing him in to it. And now my neighbour was among people who were used to meeting the dying. I didn't want to see it. Though having a dark apartment opposite wasn't much better. I hoped a family would move in, one with a baby suffering colic, or a teenager who played the latest hits with the volume turned up high. Anything but a silent cancer patient who stayed up all night.

Curiosity bubbles through Mancebo like a fizzy drink as he drives back from Rungis. His excitement at seeing whether he will find the money among the jars has grown bigger than Mancebo himself. He's about to explode, and feels such an urge to kiss François when he serves him his freshly brewed coffee. For the first time, Mancebo realises how much he appreciates the bar owner. He's a good man, one who has never broken his unspoken promise of fresh coffee every morning.

Though both Tariq and Mancebo know François equally well and see him equally often, Mancebo has a feeling that he himself is closer to the bartender than his cousin is. Despite the fact that he rarely sees François other than from his side of the bar. He could have a wooden leg for all I know, Mancebo thinks. François doesn't even live in their quarter, he lives in the 7th arrondissement with his four women: one wife and three daughters.

'I saw Amir the other day. Good boy you've got there.'

'Yeah, he is, maybe a bit too good.'

'What do you mean?'

'Well, he's just so kind. And you know how Fatima can be . . . pretty blunt.'

'Yes, there's always something. For me, I can't say the same. At my place, we've got slamming doors, "hag" and "old bastard" being

flung about. Three daughters in their teens, at the same time . . .
well, they're definitely not too nice.'

'Sounds like how it should be.'

'And Nadia?'

'I heard from her last week, we got a postcard from . . . Brighton,
I think it was. They're on holiday there, her and her husband.'

'No kids yet?'

'No.'

'It'll happen.'

'Yes, a few grandkids would be nice.'

François pats Mancebo on the shoulder.

'I won't keep you any longer, I can see you're on tenterhooks.
You're a dedicated man, Mancebo.'

Mancebo smiles, slightly disappointed. He had thought he'd
managed to hide his eagerness to get back to the boxes waiting
for him outside his shop. Mancebo feels such a strong urge to hug
the great François, standing with his shirtsleeves rolled up so that
his faded tattoos are visible. But it'll have to be another time. He's
worried about doing anything he might come to regret, the energy
he feels is hard to keep on top of. If given free rein, it could have
unforeseen consequences. Mancebo thanks François and goes off at
a half-run, like a trotting horse whose only desire is to gallop. But
if it does, there's a risk it'll be disqualified, he knows that, and so he
slows down on the way back to his van. François watches him as he
cleans a glass.

The boxes are there, on the pavement outside the shop. Mancebo
can't remember what he ordered this week. He made the order in his
former life, before this new task came along. All that is history. Back
then, he was completely unaware of what the future would have in
store for him. Mancebo is more and more convinced that there won't
be a single olive jar in any of them.

He unlocks the grille and notices that the key is starting to get a little bent. Need to ask Tariq to make a new one, he thinks, feeling the lactic acid in his legs. The grille rolls up slowly. The key for the door slips easily into the lock, the door swings open and he is met by the scent of yesterday's dinner. His heart is beating fiercely, unevenly, he can't remember when he last felt like this. Maybe he's too old for this after all, he thinks. Though on the other hand, he's convinced that with time, as he gains more experience, he'll learn to keep a cool head in situations like this. Mancebo calms himself by thinking that eventually imaginative methods of handing over the money will come to feel as undramatic as getting a payslip in the post.

Mancebo turns on the lights behind the counter, props open the door using the little handmade loop and hook. The scent of cooking mixes with the fresh morning air. It probably has no choice. The laws of physics see to that. He has already planned how he's going to tackle his Christmas presents. First, he brings in the three white boxes. They're heavier than he expected, and he remembers that he ordered a lot of mineral water. He did that after seeing the ten-day forecast. He remembers more of the order now. He puts down the boxes in front of the till.

Then he carries in the two brown boxes. These are lighter, but he can't remember what might be inside them. Mancebo jumps. A stressed man with a dog trying to go in the opposite direction comes into the shop. Maybe the dog is on to a scent, or maybe it just doesn't like the smell of yesterday's bean stew. Professionalism, Mancebo manages to think before he greets the customer.

'Good morning, monsieur. How can I help?'

'Good morning. Do you know where I can buy cigarettes?'

'There's a tobacconist's to the left here on the boulevard, on the other side.'

'Is it far?'

'A hundred metres, up by the metro.'

'Thank you.'

The man is about to follow his little white dog, which is already halfway out onto the pavement, but he feels compelled to buy something and pulls it back. Please, you don't need to buy anything, I won't be angry if you just leave, please, just leave me in peace, Mancebo thinks.

'Looks like it's going to be warm again today. Do you have any small bottles of mineral water?'

Mancebo looks up again and smiles, or attempts to smile. He's suffering. Holding back his curiosity is hard work. Mancebo knows the small bottles are in one of the new boxes, but he doesn't want to start opening his presents with a spectator. That wasn't the plan. Or he hadn't planned it that way, anyway. He reluctantly starts to cut open one of the boxes, dearly hoping, with all of his heart, that he won't find any jars of olives inside. Madame Cat probably chose a box which wasn't taped shut.

'We're in luck, Sherlock,' the man chuckles to his dog, pulling on the lead.

Fitting name, Mancebo thinks. The dog doesn't seem to think they're in luck at all, it's still struggling to leave. Mancebo has picked the right box. The one containing the mineral water that is, and only that. Nothing else, no jars of olives. Mancebo's face lights up and he is probably thinking that he really is in luck today.

The man pays with the correct change and practically flies out of the shop; Sherlock has clearly had enough. Mancebo takes the opportunity to lift up the cash box, where he just placed the money, to pull out his watch. As usual, he straps it high on his wrist. Just as he is straightening his jacket sleeve over the top of it, the door swings open and Tariq stomps in in his own particular, brusque way. Mancebo was so deep in thought that his cousin's appearance gives him a shock. Tariq's entrance doesn't usually scare him, but then he's never normally so far away from the business of his shop. Out of sheer fright, Mancebo drops the cash box onto his fingers, and he yelps.

'That's what I call being caught with your hand in the cookie jar,' Tariq chuckles.

'You scared me.'

Mancebo casts a quick glance at his arm to double-check that his jacket is covering his watch.

'Look at this!'

Tariq waves a lotto ticket in the air. Mancebo sighs, mostly to get rid of the last of his shock.

'A thousand euros! It was just lying there! I got Adèle to check it this morning. I didn't believe her at first. You know, Adèle has a wild imagination and always wants to interpret everything to her own advantage. But crikey, it was just there! This calls for a celebration!'

'Congratulations.'

Mancebo can't quite bring himself to feel overjoyed about his cousin's win, and he wonders why. He likes Tariq, and he would wish him and Adèle all the money in the world. They don't have an easy life. Childless, plus her back pain. He decides that his lack of joy must be down to wanting to focus on the boxes. As luck would have it, Tariq leaves fairly quickly, clutching his lotto ticket as though it might blow away or someone might snatch it from his hand.

But once Tariq is gone, it's as though Mancebo's excitement has vanished. His bubbling expectation has run off with its tail between its legs, having been put off one too many times. As a plaster on the wound, Mancebo pushes the door closed. He hadn't planned on doing it, but things are different now. He stacks the white boxes behind the till, they can wait, and then he carefully lifts one of the brown ones onto the counter.

Wonder which is most likely, winning the lotto or there being an olive jar full of money in this box, Mancebo thinks, folding back the lid. He casts a glance at the other boxes to reassure himself that he still has a chance if he isn't lucky this time. The box contains a couple of tins of tomatoes, seven of celery, ten cans of sweetcorn and there – bingo! Mancebo's legs practically give way. He grabs the olive jar, which stands out among its friends thanks to its more valuable content. He can see that immediately. A number of 50 euro notes.

Gripping the jar tightly, Mancebo sits down behind the till. He slowly unscrews the lid. He's prepared for anything. Nothing can surprise him now. If a customer comes in, he'll put the jar on the shelf beneath the till. If anyone comes down from the apartment, he's sitting with his back to them and they won't be able to see what he has in his hands. Not that anyone would raise an eyebrow at him counting a few banknotes. Mancebo pulls the wad of money from the jar and quickly notes that the glass has been washed thoroughly. He counts them. Twenty 50 euro notes, a thousand euros. He counts them again and realises that he is holding his breath. One thousand euros for one week's work. Suddenly, he feels nervous. Is this legal? Do I need to declare it? What if someone attacks me? Where should I hide the money?

The questions send Mancebo's mind into a panic, but he eventually calms down. I'm almost sixty and haven't done a single dodgy deal in my life, he thinks. Who cares about a few thousand undeclared euros here and there? Besides, who knows how long this is going to last. Maybe it's a one-off. No point assuming the worst.

There was no message inside the jar, but when Mancebo screws on the lid, he notices that someone has written three letters on the top in black marker. C.A.T. He shudders and stashes the jar of money in the same place as the sixty-nine Chinese notebooks and the binoculars. Keeping his valuables out in the open, among the rubbish beneath his counter, is a smart move. No one searching for anything important would ever think to look there.

We'll celebrate tonight, Mancebo thinks, opening the door wide and looking out to the apartment opposite. A new working day has begun.

*

The cork pops. Just like a champagne cork should. Fatima laughs and picks up the phone. Even Amir seems to be in a cheerful mood tonight. After his drink at Le Soleil, Mancebo had stopped off at the wine shop, Nicolas, to buy two bottles of champagne. This was something worth celebrating. All day long, he's been in a great mood. Mancebo is like a child who has been given the Christmas present he wanted above all else, and now he just wants to enjoy it. Like a gift from above, Tariq's lotto win has given him a reason to live out his own joy.

'Yes! Didn't you hear me, a thousand euros, just like that!'

Everyone knows that Fatima is talking to her old aunt. The woman is the only one of her relatives still alive.

'Come on, let's drink to it,' Tariq laughs.

Fatima tries to end the call, not so that she can drink but because it costs a lot to ring Tunisia. Everyone raises their glass. Adèle is the only one without any alcohol in hers. She never drinks, and claims never to have even tasted it. Mancebo raises his glass to eye level and studies reality, his family, through a sea of golden bubbles. His thoughts drift to the binoculars, which makes him even more cheery. He likes them. Tariq's white smile appears through the champagne glass. He seems happy, Mancebo thinks, wondering whether he has ever seen his cousin in such a good mood. He doesn't think so. Not even at his own wedding. In fact, Mancebo doesn't know whether Tariq is a happy man. There's so much to suggest otherwise: a sick wife, no children and no real dreams for the future.

Mancebo takes a sip of champagne and then raises his glass again. This time, it's Adèle he studies through the bubbling golden liquid. She has taken off her veil tonight. Mancebo has seen her without it any number of times, but she looks different today. There's something naked, cheerful and relaxed about her. Mancebo has the feeling that it's something other than the lotto win which is making her so happy. She's beautiful, he thinks, studying her almond-shaped brown eyes. His glass sweeps across to Amir, who is leaving the room, as though he knows he would otherwise be under observation. Mancebo's eyes move on to Fatima, who is laughing and talking about this and that. The shock of seeing her after Adèle's elegant face makes Mancebo jump. He puts down his glass so that he can study his wife without the distortion of the light through the glass and the champagne, and he hopes that was all that distorted her nose. But champagne tends to have the opposite effect: it beautifies both people and the world.

Tariq goes out into the hall and then quickly returns with a brown box. Fatima is in the kitchen making tea. Adèle has vanished, Mancebo doesn't know where. He himself is clutching his third glass of champagne, looking out at the apartment over the boulevard. He is daydreaming about the writer's double life.

'You look like you're dreaming, brother.'

Tariq sits down next to his cousin and opens the brown box.

'Here, you bought the champagne, I bought the cigars.'

The brown box contains five fat cigars on crisp brown paper which looks like baking parchment. Mancebo is just about to take one when Fatima, who has returned with the tea, snaps the lid of the box shut on his fingers.

'If I'm not mistaken, you've already smoked your cigarette for the day?'

Mancebo's fingers hurt. The lid is heavy. It might not have been her intention to hurt him, but she does. And it isn't the pain which bothers Mancebo most, it's being so abruptly torn from his fantasies. It's like brutally shaking someone who was sleeping deeply. He hates her. Fatima's nose grows with the hate.

'Tough wife you've got,' Tariq says, lighting a cigar and gently closing the lid.

Mancebo's bubbling joy has curled up into a subdued foetal position. It's no longer fizzing in time with the champagne, it has been dulled considerably. Adèle comes back just in time for the tea. Even Amir turns up, not for the tea but for the sweet biscuits. Mancebo grabs the champagne bottle and empties the last few drops into his glass. He isn't used to drinking any more than his usual afternoon tipple at Le Soleil, and he feels slightly woozy as a result. Fatima glances at him, but he pretends not to notice.

When he spots the writer locking the front door, he instantly sobers up. Mancebo's eyes move discreetly to the clock above the TV. Quarter to eleven. Where is he off to at this time of night? The apartment is completely dark, meaning that Madame Cat is either sleeping or already gone. It doesn't matter which, since the person who gave him his task knows the answer herself, Mancebo thinks. A strong urge to get up, go out and follow his subject washes over him. The Paris night is just stirring into life. The anxious take themselves out onto its streets

During the morning, I couldn't think of anything but Monsieur Caro, and between the *plings* I managed to come up with a handful of theories. There were few facts. Judith Goldenberg was Monsieur Caro's mother, and she had been a woman who didn't deserve to be honoured. That was her son's opinion, anyway. What could she have done?

Judith had died twenty years earlier. The gravestone had provided me with that information. Monsieur Caro had seen me placing flowers on his mother's grave. Could it be that I, or the flowers, was the cause of his suicide attempt? Had my actions been too much for an old man who hated his mother?

Monsieur Caro had also informed me that I was like Judith. I didn't quite understand why he said that. He had wanted an explanation, but I'd just left him alone in the hospital room. He shouted helplessly after me. The young doctor had appeared and wondered what was going on. I explained that Monsieur Caro had got it into his head that I knew his dead mother. Despite everything, that was true. The doctor had nodded and said that it might be best if they did further tests before sending him home.

After a bit of googling, I realised that the tattoo Monsieur Caro had on his arm could be the type of number the Jews were branded with in the concentration camps. I spent the afternoon reading about the concentration camps of the Second World War. The *plings* felt almost disruptive. I delved into how the Nazis had used different coloured triangles to divide the Jews into groups: political, criminal, emigrants, biblical researchers, homosexuals, asocial elements . . . and how they were then given their numbers in the camps.

The sun had started to set, and it was drizzling nicely outside. Just to be on the safe side, I checked the church gate to see whether it mentioned anything about closing times. Even if no one would miss me, I had no desire to get locked in a cemetery. My ex-husband had our son that weekend. They were going up to Normandy. It was a long time since I had last experienced the kind of freedom I felt as I crossed the cemetery. Maybe I was even a little happy.

I saw Judith Goldenberg's grave from a distance. The three peonies were no longer there. Had Monsieur Caro already been released from hospital? I approached the grave and then turned away. One of the benches by the compost heap had been spared from the rain, which was strange considering it wasn't beneath a tree or anything else that could have stopped the raindrops. As I sat down on the dry bench, I noticed a handkerchief at one end. Someone had wiped it down, and since it was still drizzling, it must have been very recently. Had someone been sitting there when I came into the graveyard?

The flowers came home with me that evening. I hadn't been able to bring myself to leave them on Judith's grave. They were now standing in a chipped crystal vase on the kitchen table. If I'm honest, I hate broken things. Glasses which have cracked, even if it's barely visible, I throw away. But with this crystal vase, it was different. It was like it had been made to look broken. In my melancholy, I had convinced myself that the flowers could be beautiful on a night like this. That they could be something for me to look at in my loneliness. But it felt more like they were mocking me. They had finally been allowed in. Like a missionary, one minute they had rung the bell and the next they were sitting at the table. Shown in but still not quite welcome. I had even given them a glass of water.

Eventually, you had to ask the redeemed one to leave the table. I opened the balcony door. The rain would do them good, I convinced myself. Police sirens worked their way into the room. To begin with, I carried the vase outside and closed the doors. But then I changed my mind and swapped the vase for a mug. The vase would probably just blow over, and I wasn't going to give the flowers the satisfaction of taking the life of such a beautiful object. A mug would be more or less fine. I locked the balcony doors and drew the too-long beige curtains which I needed to shorten, turned on the TV and slumped onto the sofa. I was alone in my apartment at last. My neighbour had let out the cat. I had let out the flowers.

I poured myself a glass of champagne. Though it was only four in the afternoon, and though I had nothing to celebrate. I had spent the whole day doing ordinary things like washing, ironing and reading the newspaper. With a freshly topped-up champagne glass in front of me, I sat down at my computer to look up all of the Caros in Paris. There were a few. One of them lived not far from the cemetery, but he was listed as being an IT co-ordinator. I had trouble picturing Monsieur Caro in that role.

Another Monsieur Caro lived in the Jewish Marais district. The fact that I dialled his number was more out of boredom and curios- ity than it was concern. I wasn't responsible for his suicide attempt, it was the flowers' fault. They had a life of their own. Old people went to bed early, and suicidal old people might go even earlier, so I thought I may as well get it over and done with. As I dialled his number, I tried to think about something else so that I wouldn't change my mind. I don't know what I had expected, maybe that the ringing signal would die out in a dark, smoky room, or that a hoarse voice would hiss a 'Hello' down the line. Anything but a lively female voice, laughter and music in the background. I hung up.

If I had found the right number, that meant Monsieur Caro must be back home and doing well, otherwise you wouldn't invite people over and play music. Or maybe it meant he was dead, and his nearest and dearest had gathered in his apartment. Maybe his death had come as a liberation for them. But it was probably just the wrong Caro, I told myself, pouring more champagne.

The phone call hadn't brought me any closer to the truth, but nor had it taken me further away. I put the bottle of champagne in the fridge and tidied up after the weekend. Not because my son would soon be coming home, but because my ex-husband would likely take the liberty of coming in.

My son hugged me. He seemed to be glad to be back. My ex-husband went around the apartment turning on all of the lights, as though he didn't dare leave our son if there was any darkness around me. I sat with my son on my lap at the kitchen table, the man I had spent years with opposite us. My son smelled different. He would smell like mine again soon enough. My ex-husband talked about the hotel, the beach, and said that our son had gone to a disco.

I looked at the man I had once loved, and all I wanted was for him to leave us in peace. He made my son feel like a stranger. But he continued to talk about how good our son was getting at swimming, how we would have to buy new trunks for him and about how they had shared a double bed at the hotel. He said that last part just to reiterate that they had been alone on their trip. Why ever that was important for him to put out there. He asked how I had been and I said that I'd missed my son, that I'd done the washing and ironing, relaxed and taken it easy. Not that I had been to the cemetery, fought with a bunch of flowers, thought about death, drunk champagne and prank called an old man.

'Do you have *La Vache Qui Rit*, Monsieur?'

'What?'

'The cheese.'

'Aha, I should do.'

Mancebo scans through the cheeses in his refrigerated section. The two girls wait patiently by the counter. He would guess they were about ten.

'Yes, here we are. One pack?'

The two girls nod shyly.

'Do you know the fun thing about the packaging?'

The girls look at one another and then shake their heads. Mancebo is in a great mood this morning. He half sang all the way to Rungis, and the traffic flowed smoothly. Having two sweet girls in knee-length dresses asking to buy cheese as his first customers of the day just puts him in an even better mood.

Mancebo immediately thought of his daughter, Nadia, when he saw the two girls approaching the shop. Hadn't she worn a similar dress when she was younger? I need to call her, Mancebo thinks, maybe tonight, if I have the energy and if she's home. London's nightlife usually tempted her out several times a week. That worries Fatima. Mancebo doesn't know why.

'If you look closely at the cow's earrings, you can see the entire picture in them.'

Mancebo isn't sure they understand.

'The cow's earrings have a picture of the entire packet on them, the one you're holding in your hand.'

Even now, he isn't convinced they follow. They look at the cow on the packet and then at one another. One of the girls bites her lip. The other places the right change onto the counter.

'We're having a picnic today, but we didn't have anything to put in the sandwiches.'

'Aha, I see.'

Mancebo puts the cheese into a white plastic bag, but he stops before he hands it over to them. He looks at the girls, and without knowing where the idea has come from, he grabs one of the Chinese notebooks and drops it into the bag.

'Here's a little present, too. No, two,' he says, adding another one.

The girls' faces light up, one of them even curtsies, and Mancebo blushes. They run out of the shop, and he watches as they stop outside the patisserie to look into the bag. Mancebo smiles, he feels proud. What does he need sixty-nine notebooks for? If they can make someone happy, why not?

Someone else who is cheery today is Tariq, who comes charging into the shop. This time, he doesn't startle Mancebo.

'Morning, brother. Everything OK?'

'All fine,' Mancebo says.

'Yeah, couldn't be otherwise. Richer, and a relatively cool morning.'

'Yes, but I heard the weather forecast before . . .'

'No, stop, I don't want to hear it. Don't ruin my good mood. But you know what, if it gets warmer, do you know what your cousin's going to do? Get some air conditioning. And not a day too late. Yes, brother! We can sleep over in the cobbler's,' Tariq says, heading off to his abode, his territory.

*

Something is happening over on the other side of the boulevard. Mancebo pushes back his coat sleeve, glances at his watch and gets up. He grabs the window-cleaning fluid and an old rag, and calmly goes out onto the pavement. This is what he has learnt, to behave sensibly, to act ice-cold, even if, deep down, he wants to rush around so that he doesn't miss a thing. The writer locks the front door and then pauses, not for long, just a few seconds, maybe not even that, but long enough for Mancebo to detect a slight hesitation, a reluctance to leave the apartment. Maybe I'm wrong, Mancebo thinks, since he can't quite explain what gives him that feeling. But suddenly, the writer jogs down the stairs as breezily as usual, maybe even more so. It's almost as if he's compensating for the pause he took at the top of the stairs by picking up the pace on his way down. But when he reaches the pavement, his hesitation is back. He slows down, as though he would otherwise be too early to a meeting and therefore wants to cut the pace.

Mancebo forces himself to turn his back on the action. To his joy, he can still see the outline of the writer reflected in the shop window. Mancebo sprays some cleaner onto the pane of glass and starts rubbing it with the old rag. The writer pauses with his face turned to the cobbler's shop. Maybe he's reading the sign for the opening hours. A lorry stops right in front of the shop, and Mancebo's heart starts beating more quickly. A traffic jam will stop him from being able to do his job. He glances around in desperation. If he wants to see anything, he'll have to move away from the shop, go maybe twenty metres or so. He doesn't dare.

If the writer spots me, it'll be obvious that I'm spying on him, Mancebo thinks, scratching his head and studying the traffic further down the boulevard. He can't see an accident, but the traffic is at a complete standstill. It might take time to clear, and time isn't something he has to spare right now. He has no choice. Mancebo peers around and then squats down. It's not enough. He gets down onto all fours and tries to spot the writer's feet beneath the lorry. He can see shoes of all colours, a lot of flip-flops, moving like a shoal of bright fish on the other side of the road. But in the middle, like two brown rocks, one pair of feet is standing still. The lorry starts to move. Mancebo is brushing himself off as the writer steps into the cobbler's shop. He rushes inside to grab the binoculars and gets himself into his safe position behind the till. Two girls come into the shop and peer at Mancebo, who is squashed in behind the counter.

'Hello,' he says, unable to hide his disappointment at having customers.

'Hi,' the girls say in unison.

The taller of the two gives the other a shove.

'Do you have any notebooks for us, Monsieur?'

At first, Mancebo doesn't understand, and his eyes flit between the girls and the cobbler's shop. Then the penny drops.

'They're just for people who buy something,' he hisses, but he immediately regrets his ill-tempered outburst.

That was stupid. It would have been easier just to give them each a notebook. Now their visit is being drawn out. The girls seem disappointed, but they head deeper into the shop just as the writer comes out of the cobbler's with a box beneath his arm. He climbs the stairs to his apartment, unlocks the door and drops the box inside, then quickly heads back down again.

Mancebo never normally turns his back on his customers, and he is convinced that the girls have their pockets full of sweets. Though not so long ago he read an article which claimed it was pensioners who did the most shoplifting. He doesn't know whether to believe it or not. A bottle of Coca-Cola has appeared on the counter, and next to it the correct change. Two sweetly fascinating girls are waiting for a present.

'Aha, are you going on a trip?'

Mancebo feels guilty about his behaviour. It isn't their fault that they came in at the exact moment the writer decided to visit the cobbler's. They run off happily with their drink and two notebooks.

One child after another comes into the shop that afternoon. Business is brisk, and Mancebo hands out lots of notebooks. The children mostly buy soft drinks and sweets, but he also sells the occasional packet of biscuits. Mancebo doesn't have time to document the day.

After he brings in the fruit and vegetable stands for the evening, and after Tariq rushes through the shop up to his apartment, Mancebo sits down behind the counter, takes off his watch and pulls out his notebook. It takes him a few minutes to jot down everything that happened during the course of the day. He is careful to be objective and wonders whether he should mention the moment of hesitation he thought he saw. After writing and rubbing out his words a number of times, Mancebo eventually decides to add his observation to the report. You never know what might be of interest, and if it isn't, then it won't do any harm, he thinks. Before he shuts up shop for the day, Mancebo counts how many notebooks he has left. Fifty-three.

That evening after dinner, once Mancebo has smoked his one and only cigarette of the day, Nadia calls. She knows that they always eat in the apartment below. It's Amir who picks up the phone, because Fatima tells him to. They exchange a few words. A handful of brief remarks about the weather, the family's health, how the shop is doing. Then there's silence. At both ends. There are fifteen years between the two siblings; they barely even grew up together, considering Nadia was in such a rush to leave her family home and Paris. After a few trips to London, she decided to put down roots there. 'London is more international,' she liked to say in defence of her decision to live in a different country to her parents. Amir had been six when she left.

Three years ago, Mancebo and Fatima had gone to visit their only daughter. They took the train under the sea and, just two hours later, arrived in the country where they drive on the wrong side of the road. That was Mancebo's first thought. The second was that Nadia was right. London was, in many ways, more international than Paris. Mancebo had liked the place.

After his brief conversation, Amir hands the receiver to Fatima. If he hadn't, she probably would have snatched it from him anyway.

'My child!'

They exchange more words than Nadia and her brother had. The conversation is mostly about Nadia's new job. She has found herself a position as a town planner in the county just outside of London where they live. A good, well-paid job. Fatima is proud. Their conversation is coming to a close, Mancebo can hear it in Fatima's voice. She's getting breathless, as though she had been running. Adèle yawns and raises her hand to show that she says hello.

'Wait! I want to talk to her.'

Fatima's heavily made-up eyes stare at her husband in surprise. It's the first time he has asked to talk to his daughter over the phone. They've occasionally exchanged a few words, if he happened to pick up when she called, but that's all. Mancebo gets the information he needs through Fatima. She hands him the receiver and everyone falls silent to hear what Mancebo has to say. Even Adèle seems to perk up to follow the approaching conversation.

'My daughter!' Mancebo starts, but those words don't feel like his. In his uncertainty, he is making use of Fatima's vocabulary.

'Hi, Dad.'

Mancebo doesn't quite know what he wants to say. In truth, he doesn't have anything particular to talk about. But he had been thinking about calling her today, and then she rang. Funny coincidence, he thinks, considering she doesn't ring very often, just a few times a month.

'Is everything OK, Dad?'

She sounds worried. Maybe she suspects something is wrong, given that her father wants to talk to her.

'All fine, better than usual actually.'

'Glad to hear it. Was there anything particular?'

For the first time since the day Madame Cat set foot in his shop, Mancebo has to struggle not to tell everything. The words are on the tip of his tongue, demanding to stretch their wings and make a break for freedom. Of course he has something special to say. It's thanks to his new job that he feels better than he has in a long time. Mancebo doesn't know why he has such an urge to tell Nadia everything, but not the others. Maybe it's because she lives so far away, which provides a certain security. Nadia is quicker than Mancebo at leading a phone call. Something she inherited from her mother.

'Have you won the lotto too?'

Nadia laughs. Mancebo hadn't thought she knew about that, and her words come as a surprise, a shock even.

'Aha, so you know about that?'

'Yeah, of course. Mum called after work yesterday, right after Adèle checked the ticket.'

'Aha,' Mancebo says.

'It's good to hear you're doing well. And the shop?'

Mancebo wants to hang up. Something else is weighing on his mind right now, he just isn't quite sure what.

'Yeah, yeah, it's going.'

'Good.'

'Is it warm in London too?'

Mancebo tries to round things off. Eventually, he hangs up and heads into the bathroom, mostly so that he can have a few minutes to himself before the tea and biscuits. He needs to work out what it was about his call with Nadia which ruined his good mood. Emptying his bladder, splashing a little water onto his face and sitting on the edge of the bath for a few minutes is enough. The revelation that Fatima talks to Nadia without his knowledge is proof that the world might not be quite as he imagined.

He has always taken it for granted that Fatima told him every time she spoke to Nadia, but clearly that isn't the case. That, in turn, suggests that there are probably other things that Fatima doesn't necessarily lie about, but which he never hears of because no one ever tells him. Like the fact that she goes out and about in the mornings when he's in Rungis, and that she visits the tobacconist.

Mancebo looks down at the cracked bar of soap in his hand. Is it cracked because no one uses it? Though if no one uses it, it must still come into contact with water on the edge of the bath? In which case, how can it be so dry that it's cracked? Adèle and Tariq shower, don't they? He thinks about that for a while, and then scratches his head. These questions about the soap are manageable, and that makes him feel a little better.

After dropping the key twice out of sheer stress at being a few minutes late, I reminded myself that if any messages had arrived, they would still be there when I got in. Surely it wouldn't matter if I didn't forward them immediately. I unpacked my own laptop before I turned on the desktop computer in my office. I felt rested after a good night's sleep. No emails. I dialled the number for Monsieur Caro in Marais again, mostly so that I could avoid thinking about him.

'Hello.'

The greeting was hissed, precisely what I had expected to hear from the man when he answered the phone.

'Good morning. I'm looking for Monsieur Caro.'

'Why?'

I recognised his voice.

'I just wanted to know how he was doing.'

'To whom am I talking?'

The simplest thing would have been to tell him who I was, but something held me back. I couldn't even bring myself to make up a name.

'Is this Monsieur Caro I'm speaking to?'

'Yes,' the man replied.

'It was me who . . . met you in the cemetery. And then we spoke in the hospital, if you remember.'

'Of course I do! What do you want?'

'As I said, I just wanted to see how you were doing.'

There was silence on the other end of the line. I was sure he was about to hang up, and I couldn't think of anything good to say to prevent it.

'12 Rue des Rosiers. The first door code is 12A90, the second is 223B,' he eventually said.

'Are you inviting me over?'

'Call it whatever you want. I never got any answers to my questions at the hospital.'

'I'm working now, but I could come by for a while after four. Is that OK?'

There was another moment's silence.

'Yes, I suppose so.'

I heard a *pling* at the same moment I hung up. The fact I would be going to Monsieur Caro's apartment felt surreal.

'One has to put one's foot down sometimes, but she never did. The opposite. Why the flowers?'

'The fact I put flowers on your mother's grave was a pure coincidence, it could just have easily been . . .'

'I don't believe in any bloody coincidences!'

I laughed. I was no longer afraid. He was angry, but he wasn't going to hurt me. He wouldn't be slapping me again. Monsieur Caro was like a great big nuclear meltdown. Dangerous fallout was constantly seeping out of him, things that he had been carrying for a very long time.

His apartment was dark, despite the big window looking out onto the inner courtyard. It was the furniture, the books and paintings which gave the apartment a subdued feeling, though it wasn't gloomy. When I rang the bell, he had opened the door and then turned his back on me, walked into the living room and sat down in an armchair. It was as though I had come to serve him, like the home help had arrived. He immediately launched into the conversation about his mother.

I sat down in an armchair on the opposite side of the coffee table.

'So, no coincidence. Why the flowers on my mother's grave?'

Why, of all the graves, had I chosen Judith Goldenberg's? And why had I gone back there?

'Don't know. Maybe I'll be able to answer that one day, but right now I don't know.'

'That's a better answer. Not good, but better. Coincidence . . . there are no coincidences. One has to put one's foot down, and she never did, my mother, who you've been honouring.'

'What?'

And with that, he started to explain:

Judith had been very young when she qualified as a doctor. Too young to be wise. On graduation day, the cheers mixed with the shrill voice of the Führer, the voice which cut through everything – walls, graves, understanding. Perhaps it was because of the cheers that she didn't see what was in her own and others' best interests. I don't know, and it makes no difference.

Shortly after she graduated, she opened a practice just outside of Munich. A pretty young woman, a Jewess, with her own doctor's surgery. Well, you can work it out for yourself . . . She was so caught up in her own success, in her own happiness, that she didn't notice the tanks passing by outside. Even when patients came to her with injuries from attacks on the street, she waved it away, said they were exaggerating. Said that half of them had probably fallen down drunk or been brawling with a rival. Even when they asked her to wear the notorious Star of David she adopted it with a certain sense of pride. She wore it next to her doctor's badge. The red cross shared space with the swastika. I think she thought of it as nothing more than one star among others. What stupidity.

Her patients were both Jews and Germans. She was a fantastic doctor, and word of the unmarried young woman who cured the majority quickly spread. She was open to alternative therapies but never overstepped the boundary of what was considered proper for a doctor. She would write prescriptions for tried-and-tested homeopathic medicines and holy cures, but she kept away from the laying on of hands . . . and faith in God, I might add. But she was a good doctor, I won't deny that.

Monsieur Caro stretched out his feet, pulled at one trouser leg and then fixed his eyes on the wall behind me. He continued:

Perhaps she understood the gravity of the situation, what was about to happen, when the neighbouring family was taken away. She had long ignored the black eyes and broken arms, but when an entire family disappears it becomes so obvious, an empty room which couldn't be filled with explanations or excuses. She had helped to repaint the neighbours' kitchen. She knew how fond they were of their home. They would never have left voluntarily. She knew that, despite her ugly denials. And then it was her turn. They came to her practice. One of them was a patient of hers. She had, in her foolishness, thought he was interested in her. Ha ha . . . well. As I said, she was unmarried, but she dreamt of a husband and children, so long as her career still took off. And it would, take off that is, but not as she had hoped.

The men told her to pack her things. She grabbed her coat and was about to shut up the practice as usual. What she hadn't understood was that the men were asking her to pack up and close the entire practice for good. They had with them a list of things she would need. Aside from bandages and antiseptic, she should also bring scalpels, needles and thread, and morphine. She packed everything into her big leather bag. Turned off the lights in her practice for the very last time, and headed out towards what she believed was if not a voluntary task, then at least a worthy one. She had taken the Hippocratic oath. She would treat anyone who needed it.

Her final destination was Dachau. She arrived there on an ordinary passenger train with a handful of Germans on board. They let her travel

in German class! The passengers were spread out between the different
carriages. She was given food, and able to use the bathroom. The remark-
able thing was that the restaurant car was open, and that behind the coffee
and the pastries, there was a soldier trying to work out how to use the cash
register. That might have been one of the most remarkable things of all.
The Germans take over Europe, take a train straight towards Hell, and
demand payment from themselves in the restaurant car.

On a number of occasions after the war, she returned to that journey,
and it was the restaurant car which was on her mind when she died.
Remarkable, truly remarkable.

'I'm tired,' Monsieur Caro suddenly said, looking up.

Maybe the episode in the restaurant car had worn him out. But
he couldn't stop now. I tried to come up with a way of making him
return to the story. I even took the liberty of turning off the radio.
But Monsieur Caro remained silent, and I realised it was probably
time to pick up my son. On the metro, my thoughts turned to the
restaurant car. I couldn't forget that that was where he had ended.
He had asked me to go back tomorrow, at the same time. I looked at
myself in the window of the metro car. I looked innocent and young,
but I felt old, tired and sinful.

Mancebo is bored. For twenty-eight years, he's sat in the same spot without ever getting tired of it. But now that he's been given this new task, his days feel long and uneventful. A few children stopped by to buy biscuits and collect their free notebooks, but otherwise the day has been quiet.

Mancebo is on his stool as usual, studying the boulevard. He can't for the life of him remember how he used to pass the time before he was given the task by Madame Cat. And as though the writer can hear Mancebo's complaints about his uneventful existence, he suddenly appears on the street, carrying a laptop bag and a book. Just as he passes the pink flashing light above the cobbler's shop, he stops and shakes hands with a woman.

Mancebo practically skids inside to grab his binoculars. He can't afford to miss a thing. He casts a glance in both directions, mostly because doing so feels professional, and then he raises the binoculars to his eyes. He shudders and wonders whether he will ever get used to seeing the world enlarged, whether scientists feel startled every time they look at a virus through a microscope. The writer is still chatting to the woman. She's much older than he is.

Without warning, two men stop right in front of the writer. As though they are deliberately trying to sabotage any detective work. Mancebo doesn't want to lose track of the writer, and he keeps the binoculars trained on the same position until the two men move off. The writer and the woman shake hands again, and then they part ways. That's the last thing Mancebo sees before everything goes black.

At first, all he can see is a light. A terrible, piercing white light. Mancebo chooses to close his eyes again. There's something reassuring about the darkness.

'Answer me then!' he hears someone shout.

He opens his eyes. In the centre of the light, in the doorway, he sees an enormous man who seems to be trying to make himself look even bigger. Mancebo automatically thinks of an animal, he can't remember which, one which inflates itself to scare off predators. Somehow, he has trouble believing that the voice he heard came from the man in front of him. His body doesn't look like it would house that kind of voice. A toad, Mancebo thinks, it's toads that inflate themselves when faced with danger. Someone grabs his jaw and turns his face towards them. Now, for the first time, Mancebo feels scared. Terrified. Before, there was no reason to be afraid, because he had no idea what was going on. But now he is starting to understand. He's in his shop. Someone must have covered his eyes with something and dragged him in from the pavement. There are two people keeping him prisoner, telling him to answer something. It's a robbery. Mancebo is sure of it.

'The money . . .' Mancebo mumbles.

He's sure that's what they're after.

'What bloody money?' the man next to him hisses.

'The money . . . it's in the till.'

'I didn't ask about any bloody money!'

The man grabs Mancebo by his coat, causing one of the buttons to fly off, and he dearly hopes it's the only one which will whizz through the air. The man throws Mancebo onto the stool, which is now inside the shop. Mancebo has no idea how it got there, and he doesn't have time to think about it. The fat man suddenly turns his head towards the street, but his body doesn't move. Maybe he's driving off a customer. For the first time, Mancebo looks at the man who dragged him onto the stool. He is the polar opposite of the one blocking the door. Tall and thin, with unnatural, dark muttonchops. Mancebo clutches his forehead.

'So, you little worm, what exactly were you staring at?'

'Staring?' Mancebo manages to splutter.

'Yeah, what the hell do you stare at through those bloody binoculars of yours?'

Mancebo glances up at the fat man in the doorway, and then back to the one with the muttonchops, but neither is the writer. He could have partners, friends who are looking out for him. But isn't this a bit much to keep an extramarital affair quiet? Mancebo tries to think clearly. The two men might not have anything to do with the writer. They could be drug pushers who do their business on the boulevard. The man with the muttonchops takes a step towards Mancebo, who automatically raises his hands, and he realises he can't stay quiet any longer.

'I was trying out my new binoculars.'

'Trying out your new binoculars? On a busy street? What the hell do you need binoculars for?'

'Horses.'

The last time anyone mentioned binoculars, it was Tariq, when he said he couldn't forget to take a pair to the races on Sunday.

'Horses?'

Mancebo nods.

'Auteuil, Sunday. Big race. Win some dough.'

He regrets that last part. Completely unnecessary information. The two men glance at one another. The man with the muttonchops yanks Mancebo from his stool and starts searching his pockets, throwing everything he finds to the floor: a damp handkerchief, a piece of chalk and a couple of keys. He pushes Mancebo back onto the stool and moves over to the till. Drug pushers can also be thieves, Mancebo thinks, the two go hand in hand. But the man with the muttonchops doesn't seem the least bit interested in the money, and he starts rifling around on the shelves instead. Mancebo swallows. The man is going through his receipt book, shaking it as though to make sure there's nothing hidden inside. Then he leafs through a couple of empty notebooks and gives Mancebo a questioning look. Eventually, he grabs the notebook Mancebo has been using for his reports. The man stops, leafs back a few pages, and says something to the toad in the doorway. Mancebo doesn't know whether it's just that he can't make out what they're saying or whether they're speaking another language. The man with the muttonchops smiles.

'You writing a book? Guess you need something to do while you're sitting here all day. Or are you spying on someone? Wasn't me who ran down some bloody fire escape with a bag, anyway. Know what? I don't give a shit if you're playing hobby detective, but you should be bloody careful.'

The man with the muttonchops leafs forward a few pages. After reading through Mancebo's notes, his body language changes. Though he keeps searching beneath the till, he no longer does it with the same intensity. He says something to the big man, and Mancebo is now sure that they aren't speaking French. It's not Arabic or English either. That's as far as Mancebo's linguistic skills stretch.

'You should be careful who you point your binoculars at. No more binoculars on this boulevard, mate! Understand?'

Mancebo reacts to the word 'mate'. It doesn't work on someone you've just assaulted. He nods. No more binoculars on the boulevard. The man with the muttonchops grabs everything he took from beneath the till and throws it back. He nods to the huge man in the doorway, who is still keeping watch. Both men nod and then vanish out onto the boulevard. Mancebo stays where he is on the stool. He becomes aware of a warm sensation between his legs, and realises that a small pool has formed on the floor.

Other than the small puddle on the floor and the button lying over by the canned goods, there's nothing to suggest that Mancebo has had any visitors. Real thugs, Mancebo thinks as he picks up the button and drops it into his pocket. He pushes the door closed but leaves it unlocked, it would just draw attention otherwise. Still, it might stop any spontaneous customers from coming in. He can do without those right now.

He holds his forehead as he makes his way over to the till. First, he organises the notebooks into neat piles and then he opens a pack of toilet roll and starts to wipe the floor. He could get the mop from the apartment above, but he doesn't have the energy. Never before has he felt so humiliated. He tosses the wad of wet paper into the bin and heads over to the refrigerator. His hands shake as he opens a can of Coca-Cola and gulps it down.

'Where was I? Ah yes, the restaurant car. That's where I usually stop.'

There had been a smile on Monsieur Caro's lips when he opened the door, but then he turned serious, as though he regretted inviting me over.

In the restaurant car, she was served coffee with sugar and a vanilla bun. I've never seen her take sugar in her coffee, nor eat a vanilla bun for that matter. It was still light when she arrived in Dachau. It was a foggy day, and the cold was biting. She was dressed for the journey between her house and the doctor's surgery, not for a long train ride. A group of soldiers came to meet her, and it was only then that she realised how few passengers there had been on the train. Other than the German soldiers, there was only an elderly man and two couples. On an entire train. She was the only young woman to be travelling alone. And she was the only one with a bag. The others had arrived empty-handed.

Judith was taken into a room which had previously been used as a ticket hall. There were benches pushed up against the walls, but she never had time to sit down; she was the first to be called for. She smiled warmly at the others and followed the man. They crossed a muddy field, and she stumbled several times in her low heels. She automatically reached out for the man to help her up, but he kept walking. Convinced he hadn't realised she had fallen, she shouted out to him. Hearing her own voice came as a surprise. It was a long time since anyone had spoken to her, and she hadn't dared talk to anyone else. The man turned around, peered down at her, and then kept walking. There and then, she lost not only her self-respect but also her title: doctor. Which she considered worst is up for discussion. Nonetheless, she was a clear-thinking woman, and so, despite the cold, she took off her shoes and walked in stockinged feet through the chilly mud behind the man who had robbed her of her human worth.

'Please could you turn off the radio?'

Monsieur Caro cleared his throat and took a sip of water. He was behaving as though he was giving a speech. As though reading from some internal script.

In a building separate from the others, she was told to sit down and wait. She wiggled her toes to stop them from freezing, and wondered whether she had anything in her bag that might be of use to her. Perhaps the gauze bandages could work. The man who had robbed her of her human worth out in the field was leaning against the door, but when he heard a noise in the adjacent room, he stood to attention. The door opened and he made the now-famous Nazi salute. The man who came in was small and stout, with thin hair. He looked down at Judith and her feet, and ordered the soldier to fetch something for her to wear. The soldier turned and left. The corpulent man returned to his desk in the next room, but he left the door open. Not a word to Judith.

The soldier came back with what looked like a pair of thick, white football socks, and he handed them to her. She took off her black nylon stockings and pulled on the white socks. She even tried to put on her shoes, but she couldn't, the socks were too thick. In stockinged feet, she was called in to see the man behind the desk. It was only then that she found out why they had brought her there. To serve her country. She was there as a doctor. She had been the best in town, and now that the town had been emptied of both Germans and Jews, she was needed in Dachau. She would be responsible for taking care of any ailments in the camp. Any ailments caused by the dirty Jews, that was. She wouldn't be allowed to treat her own people, she was informed, but rather the Germans infected by them. And it wasn't just because she was one of the best doctors that she had been brought to the camp, it was also because she was a charming woman, someone the German soldiers could fantasise about. Only the best was good enough for them. And she didn't put her foot down. She never did.

Monsieur Caro fell silent, and I wondered where I had heard that line about putting a foot down before, but my thoughts were interrupted when he continued:

They wanted to know what she needed to run a doctor's surgery, and she quickly drew up a list of medicines and instruments. In all the stress of leaving, she had even forgotten her stethoscope. It usually hung around her neck, but she had taken it off as she pulled on her coat. That was what she always did when she was leaving for the day. The corpulent man glanced at the list and then quickly handed it back to her. He asked her to note down all of the furniture she would need in the surgery. Other than scales, a measuring stick, an examination table, a chair, paper sheets and a few good lights, she couldn't think of anything else. She tried to remember what there had been in her own surgery, but her memory failed her. A defence mechanism, perhaps. Or maybe she realised, right there and then, that she would never see her own practice again, that she may as well forget it as quickly as possible.

Monsieur Caro rubbed his eyes.

She spent her first two days in Dachau alone in a small room with a bunk bed without sheets. Twice they came in with food and coffee. No one spoke to her. Countless times, she opened and closed her doctor's bag. But she kept her head high. If I had allowed myself to cry at everything

I saw, I wouldn't be alive today, she always said. Yes, yes . . . On the third day, a man came in with a pair of black boots. He asked her to put them on and follow him. They crossed the muddy field. She had put her old shoes into her bag. The barracks spread across the field didn't look how she remembered them from her arrival. Some looked like old containers, but others were more like neat, modern houses. The man stepped into one of them, over by a small cluster of trees, and she followed him in. She immediately realised that she had just set foot in her new doctor's surgery, and without uttering a word the man showed her round. Over by the door there was a small space which, with a bit of imagination, could function as a waiting room. The surgery itself was big and airy. There was an examination table, a chair, a desk, and everything else she had added to her list. The bulb hanging from the ceiling cast an unrelenting glow. Behind a partial wall there was a simple shower and a toilet, no more than a hole in the floor.

In the midst of her misery, and despite the fact they had taken both her freedom and her self-respect, she had now regained some of her working honour. It was that tiny glimmer of light which gave her the strength to begin unpacking her possessions. She placed the morphine into a small metal cabinet on the wall. Several of the medicines she had requested were already inside. She studied one of the bottles to determine the strength, opened another and sniffed it, to double-check that it really was the medicine she had requested. She placed the nail scissors with the bandages. The last thing she unpacked were her shoes. She dampened a little cotton wool and tried to clean off the dried mud. Then she placed them in the shower area to dry off. Suddenly, she heard the sound of a child shouting, and she glanced out of the window. But all she could see was the cluster of trees, and that was probably her salvation. Not long after that, she heard a woman's cry. She tried to open the door and discovered to her surprise, naive as she was, that it was locked. She went back into the room and peered out at the trees.

After just a few hours in her new doctor's surgery, her first patient arrived. It was the stout man. For the first time, he introduced himself. She noted down his name, Fritz Erk, in one of the notepads that would serve as both her register of patients and her prescription book. Erk was a diabetic, and now that he was away from home, his condition had worsened. On that first day, she saw just two patients: Erk and a soldier who had sprained his arm. Each patient had the key to her surgery. They unlocked the door, stepped inside, were treated and then left. The doctor was locked in, and the patients had the key. What a farce!

Monsieur Caro started to laugh and cough. I couldn't understand the humour in what he had just told me. It was as though he had suddenly forgotten his internal script, and once it had happened, he couldn't hold back. His feelings took over.

So, where was I? Yes, Judith took care of Erk and another soldier, and that evening, the dinner tray arrived. After she finished eating, she waited to be taken back to her bunk, but no one came. She even started to long for her spartan room. As evening turned into night, she eventually lay down on the examination table and slept. What she didn't know was that she would do the same for over a year. The room was no longer just her doctor's surgery, it was also her home. Judith got her doctor's surgery and her patients, but perhaps not in the sense she had been expecting.

Erk stopped by several times a week, and was probably the only person she had any personal interaction with. It was Erk she dared ask for newspapers; she was going crazy without anything to do between patients. He promised to see what he could do. The next day, he came back with bad news. It wasn't possible. But she wasn't stupid, my mother. Many less flattering words could be applied to her, should be applied to her, but she wasn't stupid. The next day, after she had injected insulin into his German veins, she asked whether she couldn't at least be given the medical journal Ärzteblatt. It was for their own good, she insisted. The field of medicine was making such rapid advances, and she needed to stay à jour. Particularly when they were living so close together. She needed to know what kinds of bacteria and viruses were running riot out there in society. Erk looked pleased, but he was slightly concerned he hadn't thought of it himself. He wanted to help Judith. But not because he was good, remember that! Because he was a man.

The very next week, he returned with a copy of Ärzteblatt. *The cluster of trees and those journals were what kept Judith going. She must have read every copy at least ten times.*

Judith didn't talk much about what she experienced in Dachau. She said she didn't see anything. Just heard it. Shots and cries. Cries like she had never heard before, shrill cries, she called them pig cries. I suppose they sounded something like when you cut off a pig's head, however she knew how that sounded. It makes no difference. But one incident she often returned to was how one day, after his injection, Erk handed her a rolled-up package. It was a pair of nylon stockings. By then, she had been in Dachau for a month or two. The clothes she had arrived in were all she had. She washed them in the shower every other day, and then hung them to dry above the radiator. Which meant that every other night, she was forced to sleep in her doctor's coat. The nylon stockings looked used, there was even a ladder in one of them, but she washed them, dried them, and pulled them on. And here comes the inexplicable part.

Monsieur Caro swallowed.

The thought that another woman must have worn them struck Judith. She wasn't stupid, after all. She knew that this woman was probably dead, that, in all likelihood, she had fallen victim to Erk and his men. How could she wear a murdered woman's stockings! Which she had been given by the murderer! Even as a child, I questioned my mother on that point. I was eight then. Can you understand that? Eight!

*

The room suddenly felt very small. Monsieur Caro's face was flushed and blotchy. I wondered whether I should say something to distract him, to turn his mind to something else, but I wanted to know what had happened.

'What did she say to that?'

'That it was important for her to wear her own shoes. To avoid the boots. And then she told that old story about not knowing how you'll react in an extreme situation until you find yourself in one. Drivel! Drivel! Drivel!'

Despite everything, I felt a certain responsibility for Monsieur Caro's health, and so although it might have meant the end of his story, I asked him if he wanted to take a break. I told him I could come back tomorrow. Monsieur Caro glared at me angrily.

'We may as well get to the end of this shameful tale. So we can draw a line under it.'

I was more than happy to be taken back in time.

After the stocking affair, she had asked for a change of clothes. Erk arranged it all. She was given a pair of white socks, two pairs of black trousers, two pairs of white underwear, two white shirts and a grey cardigan. All men's sizes.

She took care of her surgery. Laid out the latest issue of Ärzteblatt *in the waiting room. She even asked one of the soldiers to bring in a sprig of pine, which she placed in a test tube on the waiting room table. It's for all this that I blame her. What the hell was she thinking?*

'Did you ever ask her?'

'She said it was her way of surviving. But she could hear the screams! Though actually, do you know what I find worst? That she had the stomach to talk about it. That she was, in some way, proud of it!'

'But she was just telling the truth.'

'To hell with the truth!'

'She was a proud woman.'

'Like hell!'

This was the Monsieur Caro I recognised. But he quickly returned to his more restrained behaviour. As though he had made up his mind to tell this story to the end. His way of expressing the past was as though he wanted to pass it on, so that it would be preserved after his death.

She fell ill herself. Though I say ill, she became weaker. But as the camp doctor, she could order whatever she needed. She took care of herself with iron tablets and vitamins A and D, all while her countrymen and women were dying just a stone's throw away. She lived like that for a little over a year.

She never set foot outside her doctor's surgery until the day she left Dachau. Without warning, a soldier appeared and told her to pack up her things. She asked what she needed, because she was convinced she was being sent to tend to someone who was seriously injured, a patient who couldn't make it to the surgery themselves. The soldier thought for a moment and then turned on his heel and left. He returned after a few minutes. 'Whatever Monsieur Erk might need,' was the answer. And so she dutifully packed the insulin, the needles and various painkillers into her huge doctor's bag. It was summer outside. The birds were singing. The first things that struck her were the scents of the outdoors. For over a year now, she had lived in a relatively scentless environment. Sweat, damp, cigarette smoke, the occasional cigar, vomit, acetone, chlorine and food were all she had come into contact with.

There was a train waiting in the station. A couple of men with Stars of David on their arms hurried past, a guard barking at them to speed up. She smiled at them. They stared back at her in terror. She couldn't under-stand their reaction. She wasn't wearing a Star of David. There was a huge black car parked alongside the train. The soldier gestured for her to get in, and she became scared. Her doctor's surgery had become her only source

of security. Had her time come? The door opened, and she looked inside.
Erk was sitting in the back seat, and he asked her to climb in. A driver in
a Nazi uniform started the engine.

'Where were they going?'

I had been drawn so deep into the story that I could no longer
hold back my questions.

'To Paris.'

'Why Paris?'

'German troops had occupied the city, Erk had been ordered to go
there. He had requested that Judith go with him, since he couldn't
control his diabetes. And since her mother was French, she knew the
language; in fact, it was her mother tongue. Practical, having that
woman with him.'

'But maybe Erk liked her, maybe it was a way to get her out of
there?'

'He was a swine! Let's not try to dress this up.'

They drove to southern Germany, and from there they took the train to the
Gare de Lyon in Paris. Once there, they checked into a hotel – and not just
any hotel, but the Hôtel Ritz by the Place Vendôme. My mother was given
a sum of money for new clothing. An absurd gesture. Keeping a woman
locked up for over a year, with access to only a shower and toilet, and then
suddenly taking her to a luxury hotel in Paris and giving her spending
money. She went straight to one of the most exclusive boutiques by the
Place Vendôme and was quickly seen to by the shop assistant. Erk had told
her that if anyone asked her name, she was Mademoiselle Dörner and she
was his fiancée. Idiot German. It would have been more believable that
she was his daughter.

'Did she have to live up to that?'

Monsieur Caro's eyes darkened.

'Do you mean me?'

'Do I mean you?'

'Never mind. No, she didn't have to live up to that. If she had, she would have likely bragged about it too, like she had with the nylon stockings.'

He sighed deeply.

'I'm tired. But we need to draw a line under this.'

Back at the hotel, she examined him and administered his injection, and then she returned to her own room. Yes, he did at least have the decency to book two rooms. Erk let her know that she was a free woman, so long as she came to his room at eight every morning to check his health.

That night was the first in over a year that she had slept in a bed. But her body was stiff. She lay in the middle of it so as not to fall out. That was how she had slept on the examination table in Dachau. And that was when the anxiety came. She sweated, paced back and forth across her room. She heard the shots and the cries, and she saw the eyes of those emaciated men when she smiled at them. She tried to remember her father's phone number. She rifled through her bag in the hope of finding something to calm herself down. On the table next to the bed, she found a brochure about the Moulin Rouge. Eventually, she pulled her coat on top of her nightgown and went down to reception to ask to use the phone. She fumbled with the numbers and was given help calling the switchboard, which could connect her to Germany, but the line went dead. She went to the hotel bar and got so drunk that a man had to help her back to her room. She lay down on the floor to sleep. The bed was too soft.

At seven the next morning, she was already outside Erk's hotel room. At eight, she knocked on the door. He opened it, seemed stressed, but asked her to come in. Her hand shook after the previous night's drinking, and she fumbled with the needle. He slapped her, hard, and that brought her back to her senses. She did her job. In a way, that was his farewell.

'What do you mean?'

'They never saw one another again after that. He left. It was the 22nd of April, 1945. It'd make a good book, no? *The Treasonous Mother.*'

I wanted to protest at the word 'treasonous', but I stopped myself.

'What happened next?'

'Everything and nothing. She landed on her feet, I suppose you could say. Met my father in Paris. A sensible man. Without him, things never would have worked out.'

'And he was Jewish?'

'Yes, thank goodness for that!'

'Did she continue to practise medicine?'

'No. She was done fixing people. She had five children instead.'

'Five. So you have four siblings? Are they still alive?'

'Yes, they're all alive, I'm the eldest. They're all fine, all but one, my little brother, he suffers from schizophrenia. Odd that we didn't all develop it, considering our mother.'

'How do your siblings feel about your mother? The same as you?'

'I don't know, and it doesn't interest me.'

'Why are you so hard on her? As far as I can see, she hasn't committed any crime. I might have done the same.'

'You, yes! I can understand that! You even put flowers on her grave, without any explanation.'

Yes. He was right.

'In any case, she's been harshly punished. None of her children leave flowers on her grave.'

'Not true. She got off lightly, considering her crimes.'

'What crimes?'

'Taking care of those terrified butchers. Those butchers who took the lives of millions of people! What worse crime could a person commit? She got off lightly. Only one person has ever dared judge her, and that was me! I forbade my siblings from honouring her, and they've kept their promise. Do you realise what you've done?'

I was scared. Not that he would hurt me, but that he might die.

His face was red, and his lips had started to turn pale. His hate would be the death of him.

'You said yourself that your mother's fate would be a good book. Could I write it?'

He had calmed down now. Staring at the TV like it was on.

'Please, could you turn on the TV.'

I realised he wanted to divert his thoughts, but I couldn't find the remote. I realised there wasn't one. A debate programme was on.

'So that she could be glorified in a book? No, thank you.'

'No, not at all. Not if the story is told objectively. No beautification, but no judgement either. That way, your view of your mother might even be confirmed.'

He looked at me and I realised he didn't follow.

'I mean that the readers could decide for themselves. They might take your side. Surely that would be punishment enough for her?'

His eyes glimmered. The spoils of revenge. Once and for all, he would see his own mother judged, and thereby gain justification for his own behaviour. The thought that others would cast aspersions on Judith would, in some strange way, purify him. It would be his trump card. Not just for his own enjoyment, but also as proof to his siblings that he had done the right thing in keeping them away from their mother's grave. If Judith could hear us, I hoped she would understand my ulterior motive.

'When did you get your tattoo?' I asked.

'A long time ago.'

'Who by?'

'I don't know. Some madman with a ring in his nose here in Marais.'

'You went to a tattoo parlour?'

I couldn't help but laugh.

'But you've had a number tattooed on yourself, the kind the Jews were given in the concentration camps?'

'Correct.'

'Why?'

'She should have had one. Someone from the family has to carry the burden.'

I studied him, watching TV with that dogged look on his face.

'Your visit can end now,' he said, pointing to the door.

Mancebo stares straight ahead into blank nothingness. Is this the end, he wonders. How will I ever dare set foot outside the door again? I lost. I had a good story in my hands, and they took it away from me, whoever they were.

After an hour or so, Mancebo makes his way over to the door on shaking legs. He pushes it open with his foot and then hurries back to his safe place behind the counter. He doesn't dare look over to the writer's building, but he knows that if he doesn't open the door now, he never will. It's like falling off a horse, Mancebo thinks. You have to quickly get back in the saddle, otherwise you'll never dare. 'Horses,' Mancebo mumbles to himself. Lucky I managed to come up with that story about the binoculars and the races.

He debates whether he should go to see a doctor. His head is pounding. The two men didn't hit him, but he's probably suffering from shock. He opens another can of Cola, and remembers that his mother always used to say that the American drink should be used as medicine and nothing else. It feels good to drink a little medicine right now. The thought of his mother makes Mancebo feel like crying, but he manages to hold back the tears. No sense mixing things up.

Mancebo's head starts to clear, and he summarises the situation: two madmen paid a visit to his shop. The way the man with the muttonchops reacted when he found and read through the notes about the writer suggests they had nothing to do with him. Strange things are happening on this seemingly peaceful boulevard, that much is clear. It's not just unfaithful writers running wild, other dodgy dealings are also going on. All I promised was not to point my binoculars out at the boulevard, Mancebo thinks. I'm sure I can probably keep that promise.

There are now four empty Cola cans on the counter. The smell of dinner has started to make its way down to the shop, and after everything he's drunk, Mancebo has to struggle not to wet himself again. He starts pulling the vegetable stand inside, his eyes fixed on a couple of carrots. He still isn't ready to see what's going on outside, on the boulevard. Tariq comes over and pats him on the back before he disappears into the shop.

'Party?' Mancebo hears him say before he trots up the stairs.

At first, Mancebo doesn't understand what he means. Then he realises that Tariq is talking about the four Cola cans lined up on the counter. He pulls down the grille and locks the door, making a decision as he does. 'The show must go on,' he mumbles to himself, though he isn't one hundred per cent convinced. He turns off the light in the shop.

He replays the entire scene to himself, over and over again. The way he was dragged into the shop, and everything that followed. Mancebo is barely aware of what he puts into his mouth during dinner. He twists and turns the day's events in his mind, and realises that he's starting to lose the plot. He can't bring himself to look at it objectively, and blames that on his new friend, imagination. It's playing tricks on him. He has two versions of events, and both could be taken as the truth. One tells him that two pushers, both in a drug-fuelled state, mistook him for a plain-clothes officer spying on them. They made a mistake, to put it bluntly, but they regretted it. And they'll probably change the spot where they either drop off or buy their drugs. That version calms Mancebo. The other doesn't. In that version, he was attacked and abused by two madmen who have something to do with his task. Which means they'll be back.

'Well?'

Fatima elbows him.

'Do you want more rice?'

She talks slowly, articulating each word, as though she is trying to get someone with learning difficulties to understand what she is saying. The others laugh, and Fatima gets up and carries the rice away before Mancebo has time to reply. Tariq's fingers drum nervously on the table, and Mancebo quickly retreats into himself again.

Mancebo carefully runs his hand over the spines of the books. He knows that Amir reads a lot, but he wonders whether he has really read all these books on the shelf. None of the books are by an author named Cat.

'Are you looking for something?'

Mancebo jumps, as though he was doing something forbidden. Amir seems puzzled. Mancebo knows that the attack, or whatever he should call it, has left its mark. He overreacts to sudden sounds. Amir can't remember having seen his father in his room since he was young, when Mancebo carried him up to bed after he fell asleep on the sofa.

'No, not really. I was just looking at the books. Have you read all of these?'

Amir nods. The same urge that he felt while on the phone to Nadia washes over him, he feels like talking about his detective work. Mancebo glances around the room, as though it was the first time he had ever set foot in it.

'Do you remember how I used to carry you up to bed when you fell asleep on the sofa?'

Amir nods and smiles.

'That was a while ago. How are things?'

'Good.'

'I have a question for you, I know you read a lot.'

Mancebo is about to do something spontaneous. He is about to hand a piece of the puzzle to an outsider. He would never have expected it to be Amir, but he can't stop himself. The case needs to move forward, because right now he isn't getting anywhere, and the need for results is breathing down his neck.

'Sit down.' Mancebo gestures to the bed, but he instantly regrets the hand movement, it feels like he's giving a command to a dog.

Amir cautiously sits down next to his father, and Mancebo notices how slender his son's arms are.

'Do you know of any writers living here . . . in the neighbourhood?'

Amir purses his lips and thinks, as though it's an important question, which it is after all. He shakes his head, and Mancebo realises how stupid his question was. Madame Cat's husband is probably just an amateur. If he's even a writer at all. Maybe Madame Cat just made something up. He could just as easily spend his days writing academic texts, diaries, anything really.

'You mean Ted Baker?'

Mancebo jumps. The blood starts pumping more quickly in his veins, and he attempts to control himself.

'Where does he live?'

Amir points to the building on the other side of the boulevard. Bingo. The fact that Mancebo now has a name for the man he has been watching for a week gets him excited. It wouldn't really have made any difference what name Amir had said. Mancebo knew he had a name, of course, just like everyone else, but everything feels so much more exciting and real now that he knows what the man is actually called. But in his agitation, Mancebo reminds himself not to reveal any more details.

'Do you have any of his books?'

Amir shakes his head.

'Have you read any of them?'

Amir shakes his head.

'No, they're not really my style.'

'Style?'

'Yeah, he mostly writes crime novels.'

'Crime novels?'

'Yeah, about private detectives, murders, stuff like that.'

Mancebo's heart practically comes to a stop, and he waits for it to return to normal before he continues.

'Private detectives . . . ?'

'He's English. Why do you want to know?'

'He . . . he came into the shop. We talked . . . and I was just curious about who he is.'

Amir studies his father with his big brown eyes, and he pulls at the bedcover with his fingers.

'What are you going to do now?'

Stupid question, Mancebo thinks.

'Go to bed.'

Mancebo gets up. He feels sweaty and cold at the same time.

'Night then.'

'Night,' Amir says expectantly. 'I'm going to the library tomorrow, do you want me to borrow one of his books? I mean, if you want something to read.'

'The library? They have his books there?'

'Of course.' Amir laughs. It's a fond laugh. 'Dad, you need to get out into the world, not just sit in your shop all day.'

'I'd like that, thanks.'

'What? To get out into the world?'

'No, or yes, I'd like you to borrow one of Ted's books. I can give you money if you need it.'

'It's free. I've got a library card.'

'Aha . . . Goodnight, my son.'

'Sleep well, Dad.'

He knows he won't.

Mancebo is afraid. Afraid that his body will give up one day, and soon, that it will simply stop working because it was never allowed to sleep or even rest. That kind of thing can happen. Mancebo has heard about studies which prove it. Stopping people from sleeping was one of the methods of torture used by the Nazis. Maybe there's no comparing it with my situation, but still, I'm exposing myself to the risk, Mancebo thinks.

Oddly enough, he doesn't seem to be affected by any extreme weariness during the day. That isn't necessarily a good sign, though. In fact, it could be the opposite. Maybe the human body stops feeling tired after a while, before it gives up completely.

Mancebo spends the night awake, listening to the sounds all around him. The low hum of the dustbin lorry, the police sirens, the sound of the toilet on the floor below, the buzz of the refrigerator. After all of his sleepless nights, Mancebo has learnt Fatima's sleeping patterns. It doesn't take more than a few minutes after they say goodnight until she's asleep. Then, roughly an hour and a half later, before she moves into a deeper sleep, she turns over and clears her throat.

During his first few sleepless nights, Mancebo had been convinced she was about to wake up. But now he knows she's just clearing her throat, nothing more. Sometimes, she even stops breathing. Once, so long seemed to pass between breaths that Mancebo thought she was dead. And after that, he had been worried about himself, because he hadn't felt as upset as he should.

The new information that the writer has a name, Ted Baker, scares Mancebo slightly, and he isn't sure why he didn't find it out before now. The writer is no longer an object, he's a person. The nameless has been given a name. The anonymous has become known. Even Amir knows about him. Mancebo realises that he has certain limitations as a private detective, certain gaps in his general education, but they aren't so big as to be insurmountable. It'll take time and hard work, but he isn't afraid of that. Mancebo has never been scared of working.

He wonders whether Madame Cat and Ted Baker might be messing with him. Could Monsieur Baker be working on a new book, one about a small man with a grocer's shop, and about a lady who comes in one day to make him a decidedly unusual proposal? Then they send two madmen into the shop to see how he reacts.

Mancebo lies there in bed, getting himself worked up, wondering whether perhaps Monsieur Baker spends all day watching him. He feels tricked. What could be better for a writer than having a story play out right in front of him? It's a bit like an artist being given a life model. All they need to do is write. Imagine if that's the case. That one day, he'll be able to read all about himself.

Before I went home, I scanned through an article about the world's most beautiful cities. Paris was in thirtieth place. Vienna first. Hard to believe there was a more beautiful city, I thought as I looked out at the Sacré-Cœur, the pointed white basilica rising up like an iceberg in the sun. I heard a *pling*. By that point, I had learnt how to carry out my peculiar task even while my mind was elsewhere. When I looked up, I noticed that the cleaner was standing in the doorway. I wondered how long she had been there.

'I'm just going,' I said, starting to gather my things.

Usually, she just charged in, so the fact that she was just waiting in the doorway gave me an uneasy feeling. Why did she even come to clean the office? The bin was empty. I had just been sitting in a chair for a few hours, no one else ever came by. She, too, was carrying out a pointless task. She moved as I approached the door.

'There's not really anything to clean here, the bin doesn't even need emptying.'

'I'm just doing my job,' she said flatly.

Why was she so brusque? What had I done to her? Her black headscarf was tied tightly at the back of her head. What was she going to clean in an already clean room? The cord to the vacuum cleaner was knotted, and she patiently started untangling it. It seemed like she was trying to kill time, as though she wanted me to leave before she started her Sisyphean task. But I didn't move. Maybe her overalls were a disguise just like my sales manager pass was. Maybe she was turning on the computer after I left. Maybe she did the night shift.

'If you ask me, there's no need to clean the room. As far as I know, I'm the only one who ever uses it.'

I knew I was close to overstepping a line. I wasn't meant to talk to anyone in the building. But the woman didn't reply, she didn't even look up.

Without waiting to be called, I decided to challenge them and headed straight to the reception desk. It was as though the receptionist had just been sitting there, waiting for someone to come. Maybe that someone was me. She seemed so happy to see me, and though the exchange I had with her was as meaningless as most other things in my life, she did at least smile, and I was grateful for that.

'Oh, so pretty! How nice to be given flowers today!'

I couldn't help it. The sarcasm was born out of the pointlessness of it all. It was a way of surviving. I thought of Judith. We all have our coping strategies. The receptionist laughed, and I wanted to believe that it was an honest laugh, that she realised I was being sarcastic. My plan was to quickly get rid of the flowers and head straight home.

'Hello!' I heard someone shout.

I turned around and the revolving door slammed mercilessly into my back. Someone behind me sighed. They had lost a few precious seconds of their life in the time it took for the doors to start turning again. Christophe and another man were hurrying out behind me. Safely outside, I took a deep breath. The performance could begin.

'Are you OK? Sorry, I didn't mean to startle you.'

Christophe ran his hand through his hair.

'Fine . . . thanks.'

The two men exchanged a few words before they said goodbye, and the other man held out his hand to me. I conducted myself in line with all of the rules. The man hurried away over the street.

'So, what's the flower girl up to now?'

'The flower girl's going home.'

'A coffee before you go?'

'No, thanks.'

'Do you work at Areva?'

'Yes.'

'What do you do?'

'Sales manager.'

'OK . . .'

'You work here too?'

Christophe shook his head.

'No, but directly opposite, at Capgemini.'

I nodded.

'You like flowers, then?'

I couldn't help but laugh. His sense of humour was a good match for my new-found irony.

'Yep, a lot.'

'What do you do with them all?'

'Leave them on graves. Unless I've given them to statues of dead authors.'

He laughed warmly in the belief that I was joking, and I laughed because it was all true.

'Unless you've given them to me, that is. So you're some kind of messenger of death? That sounds fun. Though now I don't know whether I dare to cross the street, a car might come along and bring my world to an end.'

The oppressive heat was doing all it could to bring our conversation to an end.

'What about a glass of something cold instead of a coffee?'

'Here,' I said, holding out the flowers.

This time, he showed firmly that he didn't want them.

'If you take them home, put them in some water and enjoy them for a while, maybe we can go for a coffee next time we run into one another. OK?' I said.

My suggestion wasn't just an excuse to get rid of the flowers. I hoped we would run into one another again, and then it would be practical if we'd already agreed to go for a coffee. Plus, I was scared of giving the flowers to strangers, because that had already shown it could have unexpected consequences. It felt safer giving them to someone who had already been initiated.

'Is that a promise?'

I nodded, turned my back to him and walked away. Christophe ran after me.

'I don't believe you. Monday? Lunch?'

'Coffee, we said.'

'OK. When?'

'Monday? Twelve?'

'Meet here.'

I nodded.

'Good evening, madame!'

The cheery florist waved to me. My route home was lined with people who, in one way or another, were all mixed up in my task. I can understand why he's happy, I thought. He might be the only one gaining anything from this whole tale. The metro came as a relief. I had never appreciated its long, dark tunnels as much as I did right then. But in the darkness, my phone rang, and it took a minute or two of rifling through my bag before I found it.

'Would you be able to come and turn on the TV for me on Saturday? Sabbath.'

'Sorry, to whom am I talking?'

'Why the sudden bloody politeness?'

It was Monsieur Caro. I had known immediately, but I wanted to tease him a little. I had left my phone number beneath his beautiful marble lamp the last time I was there, but I hadn't thought he would call.

'Aren't I always meant to be polite? To whom do I have the honour of speaking?'

I realised I was smiling as I talked to Monsieur Caro. An infatuated, ridiculous smile.

'Honour and honour, it's Monsieur Caro here. Could you come over on Saturday at 12.30? 12.25, actually? Yes or no?'

My smile refused to fade. On the way to my son's summer club, I debated whether I should ask my ex-husband to look after him on Saturday, but then decided I would take him with me. Maybe we could do something fun after our visit to Monsieur Caro's apartment. And by doing so, that would give us a natural way of spending the day together.

But the closer I got to his summer club, the more surreal it all felt – Areva, Bellivier, Christophe . . . The mother of one of my son's friends came over and started making small talk. It felt like I was floating away during our conversation. An unpleasant feeling. But then, to my delight, I saw my son coming towards me with a smile, and I excused myself and said I had to go.

Damned sun, what are you playing at, Mancebo thinks, pulling out a small hand fan which has been gathering dust beneath the till for years. Anything to defend ourselves against the sun's weapon: the heat. The little hand fan is going flat out, but to no avail.

'It'll be the end of us all,' Monsieur Cannava warns, pointing up to the sun as he passes by on his way to work.

'Yes, this heat really saps your strength,' Mancebo replies from his seat behind the till.

Other than the necessary trips outside with the fruit and vegetable stands, he still hasn't ventured onto the street. His fear and sadness have now transformed into anger, but Mancebo still isn't ready to take up his surveillance of the boulevard. Anger, sleeplessness and heat are not a good combination. Before Monsieur Cannava has time to pass the shop, Mancebo spots Amir moving off on his scooter, not wearing a helmet. Mancebo shakes his head and sighs deeply.

No one will stop me from doing my job, he thinks, placing the stool where it has always stood outside the shop. He angrily looks up at the window opposite. 'Bastard writer, don't think you can mess with me,' he mumbles quietly. Mancebo almost feels like shutting up shop, crossing the boulevard and making his way up the fire escape. Knocking on the door and telling that word-loving jerk that he knows full well what is going on; that he, Mancebo, has been drawn into some stupid crime novel, and that he doesn't give a damn. If the writer didn't have any ideas of his own, then he should go for it. Let yourself take inspiration from a poor grocer, you miserable Englishman. He might not even speak French, but that doesn't matter. He deserves to stand there like a fool, and even if he has no idea what Mancebo is saying, he'll surely understand that the little grocer has managed to work it all out. And that would be the end of his new book.

Two boys come into the shop. Mancebo gets up from his stool and shuffles over to the counter. They're quick, the boys, and have already managed to grab two Coca-Colas.

'Was that all?'

'Yep.'

'Three euros, please.'

Mancebo places the drinks in a plastic bag, and politely hands it over. The boys look up at him.

'Did they run out?'

'What?'

Mancebo doesn't know what they mean.

'The Chinese notebooks?'

Mancebo sighs and feels the urge to throw them out. Not because he's tired of children coming in and asking for notebooks, but because he has more of an urge to cross the road and strangle Ted Baker than he does to play the kind uncle figure who gives out presents. But Mancebo manages to pull himself together, and he drops two notebooks into the white bag without a word.

'Thank you, monsieur.'

'No problem.'

Just then, Amir comes into the shop, and the two boys leave.

'Hi, Dad.'

'Why did you drive off without . . .'

But Mancebo immediately regrets the fact that he can't even greet his son without giving him a telling-off.

'I wanted to get to the library before it got too busy.'

'Aha.'

'I only managed to get one of them, the others were already on loan. If you want, I can join the waiting list. But maybe you can start with this one and see whether you like it. You know, sometimes you might not like the actual language the author uses.'

Mancebo's anger quickly subsides, replaced by curiosity. But his fear is still there. He doesn't want any information that could strengthen his suspicion that he's being used as the inspiration for a book.

'Thanks, Amir. Wear your helmet next time you go on the scooter. He's probably not worth dying for.'

Mancebo points to the photograph of Ted Baker on the back of the book.

During the day, Mancebo tries to read the first chapter of Ted Baker's *The Rat Catcher*, but he finds himself being constantly interrupted by customers. Mostly children looking for notebooks. Mancebo has no idea how many he has handed out. When the time comes for his afternoon break, he decides not even to attempt to start the book again today. He feels like he might need a break from Monsieur Baker and his fantasy world. Imagine that there are people who get paid for using their imagination, Mancebo thinks as he starts to close up the fruit stand. Tariq quickly locks up his cobbler's and is soon over at Mancebo's shop.

'You've had a heck of a lot of customers today! Every time I looked over, you were busy. Hope they start running to your place so much that they wear out their shoes, then maybe I can get some customers too.'

Tariq laughs. Mancebo doesn't. Though his mood has improved slightly over the course of the day – once he decided to give up his attempts to read the book – he is still far from laughter. They walk slowly along the boulevard and leave the centre of commerce, Mancebo's world, to make their way towards the periphery, Le Soleil. The world beyond the bar is somewhere they prefer not to, and rarely do, make their way out into. They say nothing and shake hands with François, who quickly pours them both a pastis.

'Any ice?'

Mancebo shakes his head. It might be warm, but ice in the pastis doesn't appeal to him.

'So how's business in this heat? Things've been at a near standstill here.'

François gestures with one hand over the empty bar.

'Mancebo hasn't had a quiet minute,' Tariq explains. 'Don't ask me why. Mostly schoolkids.'

'Schoolkids? Aren't they on holiday?'

'Yes, most of them,' Mancebo replies, 'but they go on trips, picnics.'

'What do they buy, then?' François sounds genuinely interested.

'Juice, mostly.'

'I was just about to say that you've taken my customers, but no, not schoolkids, I've never had those here.'

Mancebo tries to find somewhere he can rest his gaze, because he's bubbling inside. It's all starting to get too much for a lone green-grocer to handle. Too much to keep to himself. And it's not just that he's keeping the task quiet, that he has two jobs to do, has been threatened in his shop and hasn't had a good night's sleep in a long time. On top of that, he also has a book to read and a constant stream of children coming in to ask for notebooks.

His eyes dart around the bar, and drops of sweat glisten on his already damp forehead. He takes off his hat. A clear sign that something isn't right. Tariq and François are talking, but Mancebo can't make out what they're saying. He's out of it. He has departed reality, it's given him too much to handle in too short a time. For a few seconds, Mancebo doesn't know what he is doing in the bar. His head feels like a ticking bomb, and it feels like his tongue is swelling in his mouth. Too many words have been stored up by that fleshy part of his body. Eventually, to put an end to the febrile activity in his mind, to stop his tongue from splitting at the seams, he shouts:

'Bloody madmen!'

François and Tariq fall silent. The bar owner quickly goes to fetch a glass of water, which he places in front of Mancebo.

I knew it, Mancebo thinks. I'm going mad. Maybe I should go to the doctor. But what would I say to him? The truth, perhaps. Doctors are sworn to confidentiality, after all. Maybe I need to go and talk to someone. A psychologist? A psychiatrist? For the first time, Mancebo thanks God for the heat, which might lead Tariq and François to think that he's simply suffering from an innocent bout of heatstroke. It can happen to the best of us.

Mancebo looks down at the glass of water in front of him, but he doesn't seem to be able to lift it up. His hand fumbles for it, but the glass seems to move every time he tries to get close. Suddenly, he can see two glasses. He's seeing double. Two of Tariq, two of François. But Mancebo isn't afraid, he's already thrown in the towel, he can't do it any more. He doesn't even have the energy to be afraid. He needs to get help. He's sure of that now. He sees the two Tariqs say something to him, but he can't make it out. Mancebo now sees the four men glance at one another and exchange a few words. His head is pounding as though someone has hit him with a club.

Mancebo closes his eyes and feels himself being carried away. The next minute, he realises he's in his own van. Tariq is behind the wheel, his eyes darting between the road and his cousin.

'Can you hear me? You'll be OK soon. We're on the way to the hospital. You don't feel any pain in your chest?'

Tariq is speaking with an unusually calm voice, but then he practically screams:

'All we need now is for this boneshaker to stop working!'

'It won't. That was a lie. It's always run smoothly,' Mancebo says before he vomits onto the atlases between the front seats.

'Shit! Shit! Shit!' Tariq shouts, almost driving into the back of the car in front.

He slams on the brakes, takes a deep breath and then holds up a hand in apology to the other drivers.

'OK, OK, it doesn't matter, doesn't matter at all, we're almost there, stay with me, brother, we'll sort you out, whatever the hell's wrong with you.'

Tariq doesn't sound confident, and the sweat is running down his forehead as he pulls up outside A&E. There are two ambulances by the entrance, and once Tariq parks the van, it looks like three. Mancebo can't make out anything but light and shadow at the moment. But in the midst of his suffering, he feels a certain relief. He's given up. Someone else can take over. He needs help.

Mancebo is lying on a bed. The strip lights on the ceiling are like long, bright dashes as he is rolled forward. He discovers that his upper body is bare and that there are some kind of suction cups on his chest. He notices people coming and going. Someone holds a pen in front of him and tells him to follow it with his eyes. Mancebo tries, but his headache is like a monster. It's handicapping him.

He looks straight past everyone in the room. Someone shines a light into his eyes and someone else quickly holds out two white tablets and a glass of water. He takes the glass and swallows the tablets with his eyes closed. The light is his worst enemy right now, but someone doesn't want him to defend himself against it. A doctor asks him to sit up and open his eyes. But he can't.

'Could you tell me your name, monsieur?'

Mancebo wants to be helpful. He is, by nature, a helpful man, but his mouth refuses to co-operate. He knows what his name is, but he can't get it out.

'When were you born?'

'Second . . .'

'What is the name of our president?'

Sorry, sorry, Mancebo thinks, sorry for all the trouble I've caused. I'm just a burden, I'm being a burden, I'm no good. Mancebo feels his bed start to move, and he hears someone tell him to close his eyes. He is moved onto a trolley and then pushed into an enormous tube. They're going to take a closer look at his brain.

He still has a headache, but the worst of the pain is gone. Mancebo glances around. He is alone in a relatively small room. He has been given a drip. There's a glass of water on the table, and he wishes he could reach it. He's wearing a yellow hospital gown, but he has no idea how he got that on. He hears voices and footsteps outside the door. Wonder if I can talk now, he asks himself, making an attempt:

'My name is Mancebo. I was born on the second of May, our president is François Hollande . . .'

The door opens. Fatima stares at her husband. She just heard him mutter the president's name. The doctors have shared Mancebo's diagnosis with her, but now she questions whether they're right. She gently closes the door and moves over to her husband. She pulls out the chair, sits down and catches her breath.

'How are you feeling?'

What should I answer, Mancebo wonders. He scratches his head and realises that his hat is missing.

'Have you seen my hat?'

'Have I seen your hat?'

Fatima casts a quick glance around the room. She notices that there is a plastic bag over by the wardrobe, and that Mancebo's black coat is at the top of the pile.

'It could be in the bag with your clothes?'

'Can you get it for me?'

Fatima peers at the bag, braces herself against Mancebo's bed, and then heaves herself up, huffing and puffing as she does. She shuffles over to the bag. She returns, out of breath, with the black cap in her hand. Mancebo quickly pulls it on. Immediately, things feel a little better.

'What's wrong with me? Stroke? Brain tumour?'

'Migraine.'

Fatima sounds slightly disappointed when she says it, as though all the trouble they've gone through was worth more than a simple migraine.

'Can you just suddenly develop those?' Mancebo asks, sounding like a small child.

He is neither relieved nor worried. His reaction would probably have been the same regardless of the diagnosis.

'Apparently. They asked whether you'd been stressed lately, or sleeping badly, but you haven't. Maybe you can develop them without any real reason.'

Mancebo nods and thinks that considering everything he has been through lately, it might have been more surprising, a medical mystery even, if he hadn't developed a migraine. The door opens and a young, male doctor comes in with a few sheets of paper in his hand.

'How are you feeling?'

'He . . . when I came in, he . . .' Fatima begins.

'I'm feeling better,' Mancebo interrupts her.

And it's the truth. Just the fact that Mancebo manages to stop Fatima speaking on his behalf makes him feel better. A few weeks earlier, he would never have even realised that she often spoke for him. Maybe that was how he had wanted it, but not any more. And people have the right to change their minds.

A pair of clean underpants is probably the only thing Mancebo is missing.

Freshly showered, he is sitting in bed watching one of the many game shows on TV. Since he would normally be working at this time of day, it's the first time he has ever watched that type of programme. Fatima is watching it too, but she already knows that the blue team will win. It's a repeat. As Mancebo follows the games on TV, he busies himself with the tiny plastic cutlery and small pots of jam. He feels great, sitting there in his yellow gown and black hat. A nurse even offered Fatima a tray of food, but she said no.

Just as the blue team is about to be given their knock-out questions, there's a knock at the door. Mancebo takes a sip of his coffee and loudly and clearly asks whoever it is to come in.

'Is it OK if Madame Flouriante stops by in a few minutes?'

'Yes,' Mancebo replies. 'That's fine.'

'Then I'll have to ask madame to leave the room,' the nurse says with a smile, nodding at Fatima.

'Yes, she will,' Mancebo replies.

Fatima gets up and leaves before Madame Flouriante even arrives. Madame Flouriante doesn't look like a psychologist, but Mancebo has no idea what she could be otherwise. On the other hand, Mancebo doesn't know if he's ever met a psychologist before. The only one he can think of is the woman in *The Sopranos.*

'How are you feeling, monsieur?'

'Yes, fine, thanks.'

'That's good. Could you tell me a little about yourself?'

Mancebo thinks for a moment, and imagines that the psychologist will interpret any pauses as something unusual.

'I'm still working. In the service sector. Owner of a grocer's shop, to be specific,' Mancebo explains with his customer-service voice.

'Aha, and where is that?'

'At the foot of Montmartre.'

'Ah. That sounds cosy.'

Mancebo smiles. The word 'cosy' is probably the last one he would choose given the events of the past few days.

'You're smiling, what are you thinking about?'

Mancebo is starting to dislike this entire situation. Typical psychologist, barging onto private property, into my head, asking seemingly innocent questions which don't have any answers, Mancebo thinks, licking the jam from the corner of his mouth.

'I don't know.'

Madame Flouriante nods and jots something down. I've done it now, Mancebo thinks. Now they're never going to let me out. Maybe they'll move me to a different ward. He had seen the arrows for the psychiatric ward when they rolled him through the hospital. Staying in could be nice for a day or two, of course, but no longer than that. He has a job to do, after all. He wonders whether it would be worth telling Madame Cat about the attack in his next report. It could have something to do with the case, after all, and it would also help to explain why he has been absent all day.

The psychologist interrupts his thoughts.

'How has your life been lately?'

If only you knew, madame, Mancebo thinks. I've become a private detective, earned some money and been attacked by two madmen.

'Chugging along.'

'Chugging along like normal, or perhaps a little faster?'

Now he almost wishes that Fatima would come in and speak on his behalf. Maybe I do need her after all, Mancebo thinks, though he quickly brushes the thought to one side.

'Yes, I've had a lot on the go, if I may say so.'

'Have you felt under pressure?'

Mancebo feels like laughing. Under pressure? That would be putting it mildly.

'Yes, business has to go on.'

'As you perhaps already know, you suffered a migraine, and possibly also a mental breakdown. The two often go hand in hand, and I'm trying to understand whether you have any sense of what may have caused it. Do you have any idea?'

Mancebo shakes his head.

'Not the foggiest.'

'I can drive,' Mancebo says, holding out his hand for the keys to his van.

'No, thank you. Tariq will drive,' Fatima hisses.

She jumps into the front seat next to Tariq. The van doesn't have a back seat, so Mancebo opens the back doors and climbs into the roomy storage area. He sits cross-legged on the floor where he usually stacks the fruit and vegetables. The white van pulls away from A&E, and Tariq has to give way to an incoming ambulance with its blue lights flashing.

'Now it's some other poor soul's turn to be taken care of,' Mancebo says, following the events with excitement from the back.

'Yeah, but as long as the sirens are going, there's hope. It'd be worse if the ambulance was creeping along without any,' Tariq explains.

'Like we are,' Fatima says with a laugh.

Tariq agrees with his bullish laugh, and it strikes Mancebo that his cousin and his wife have something in common.

The rest of the journey takes place in silence. Mancebo looks out of the window and remembers the way he often used to ride backwards in a horse-drawn cart as a child.

Tariq is heading back towards the neighbourhood where everything happens. Mancebo can see Sacré-Cœur rising up in the distance, and despite everything that has happened, he feels an inexplicable happiness. It's as though the collapse has put an end to the after-effects of the attack. Mancebo is back to normal and feels, if not stronger, then at least slightly calmer than before.

The entire Marais district smelled like falafel. We pushed our way through the hungry queues of people. There might not have been many Parisians around, but there were plenty of tourists interested in experiencing the multifaceted neighbourhood. And through them all, I walked hand in hand with my son, struck by a feeling of sorrow, of being on the outside.

For the first time, I realised how absent I had been lately. Now that I was holding my son's hand, it seemed especially obvious. He had grown, I could see it from his shorts. To him, these past few weeks had been like any other, full of summer club and football practice. He wouldn't have any lasting memories of them, other than the time he and his father had gone to A&E to pick up his mother after she saw an old man collapse in a cemetery. I squeezed his hand. He seemed sad. Had he looked that way for long?

'Has something happened, darling?'

He shook his head.

'Is everything OK otherwise? Summer club? Have you been playing with David?'

He nodded. It felt good to walk, and my sadness at having lost out on time with my son was replaced by an unbecoming self-pity at having to deal with everything myself. Having to watch a neighbour fade away, having to keep secrets, constantly being worried about what I had got myself into.

Though it was, to a certain extent, something I had chosen, I still needed to feel sorry for myself. We pushed our way forward through the falafel-eating crowds.

'Can I do it?' my son asked.

I picked him up and his eyes shone as he punched in the door code I whispered into his ear. He made a mistake twice, but it didn't matter, I was just enjoying having him in my arms, feeling his body, the smell of the back of his neck. The door buzzed open, and he glanced at me to make sure it was a good idea to go in. I smiled and stepped over the wide threshold which led into the inner courtyard. He took my hand and we crossed it.

'It looks like the gardener's.'

He was right. There were plants and flowers everywhere. Someone had even planted some in the basket of an old bike leaning against the drainpipe. My son pointed over to it. The door into the stairwell was ajar, meaning, to my son's disappointment, that we didn't need to use the second code. We went in and climbed the stairs. At first, I thought the woman's voice we could hear in the stairwell was coming from Monsieur Caro's apartment, and that threw me off balance, but then the door of the apartment opposite flew open, and a woman in a green silk dress came out, laughing. She was clutching a bottle of wine, and said hello to us before she disappeared upstairs.

'She wasn't wearing any shoes,' my son pointed out.

I knocked firmly on the door and glanced at my watch to make sure we were on time, something I assumed was important to Monsieur Caro. I heard a cough, the rattling of the safety chain, and then the door was flung open. Monsieur Caro looked at me in surprise, as though he hadn't been expecting to see me, and then pointed at my son. He didn't look at him.

'What's he doing here?'

Had it been our first meeting, I probably would have been angry and turned on my heel. But by now I knew there was no point. Once you had joined the game, you had to accept the consequences. My son hadn't interpreted Monsieur Caro's comments as anything unfriendly, and if I had given the old man a telling-off he would have realised that it meant he wasn't welcome.

'This is Monsieur Caro. He's the one who was ill and had to go to the hospital.'

I realised my son knew who he was, but I said it to put Monsieur Caro in his place. And his reaction was exactly as I had expected.

'Ill! And who was it that made me ill?'

Suddenly, he had forgotten all about the fact I had brought my son with me. I was the problem for Monsieur Caro now, and I could take it. Without waiting for him to invite us in, we stepped inside. I straightened my son's T-shirt, pushed a strand of hair from his face and hung up my bag. Everything took its time, and I did it all with a certain conscientiousness.

Once I was finished, I was able to observe two people staring awkwardly at one another. One of them, my son, was peering all around. Occasionally, he smiled at the old man, probably so that he wouldn't be told he had been impolite later. Monsieur Caro's eyes didn't wander, he stared straight at my son with a mixture of fear and uncertainty.

'What does it eat?' he asked, looking over to me with wide eyes.

I had never seen him so animated before, and I couldn't help but laugh.

'*It* eats the same as you and me. And it can also go without being fed for an hour or two.'

Monsieur Caro disappeared into the kitchen. My son and I glanced at one another and shrugged before we continued into the apartment.

Now that my son was there, the apartment felt different. From the way he moved, I could tell that he was scared of breaking something in the living room. I sat down in my usual armchair and gestured for him to sit in my lap. He turned down my offer, even though a part of him probably wanted to take it up. Six-year-olds always want to show that they're big boys, even though it would still feel comforting to sit in Mum's lap, particularly in an unfamiliar place with an unpredictable man.

Monsieur Caro strode into the room, and my son quickly sat down in the big armchair. The old man was about to say something, but he stopped himself when he saw that the boy had taken his place. He looked over to me, and I pretended not to know what was bothering him. Rather than comment on the situation, Monsieur Caro held out a bowl of pine nuts. I nodded and he put it down on the table.

A clock started to chime. Monsieur Caro went over to the bookcase and turned off the small, red alarm clock.

'You can turn on the TV now, please.'

'Do you want to turn the TV on for Monsieur Caro?' I asked my son, who seemed relieved to have been given something to do.

He went over and switched on the old TV. Monsieur Caro vanished into the kitchen, and this time came back with a pretty silver pot of coffee, which he also put down on the table. He stared at my son and then went back to the kitchen to fetch a glass of juice.

'Blackcurrant,' he mumbled, glancing around to see where he could sit.

Eventually, he sat down opposite me and poured the coffee, first for himself and then for me. He didn't ask whether I wanted sugar or milk, probably because he was so absorbed by the programme he wanted to watch. My son took a sip of juice, glanced at the TV and then at me. I smiled. The programme was about the history of the Silk Road.

'You can help yourself if you want. They're nuts.'

I pointed to the bowl.

'Quiet,' Monsieur Caro hissed, glaring at me.

We drank our coffee and juice. It didn't take long. My son twisted in his seat.

'Sorry to interrupt, monsieur, but when does the programme finish?' I asked, winking at my son.

'13.55.'

'In that case, I think we'll say thanks for the coffee. I hope you have a nice weekend. You have my number, so feel free to call.'

My son quickly got to his feet, he seemed relieved.

'But you need to turn the TV off.'

'OK, then let's do this. We'll go out for a while and buy some new clothes for my son, then we'll come back and turn off the TV, OK?'

It felt like I had two children.

'And then you'll leave?'

'Yes, then we need to go to football practice.'

Monsieur Caro's face was expressionless, and he continued watching the programme.

'OK, we'll be back later,' I said, gesturing to my son that we were leaving.

'You play football?' Monsieur Caro suddenly asked, looking over to my son, who nodded shyly.

'What position? Forward?'

'I'm goalkeeper.'

Monsieur Caro nodded slowly and poured himself more coffee.

'Goalkeeper. That's good. Someone who defends. Someone who is looking for results, not glory. Someone who takes responsibility, who's solitary, and strong in that role; someone who knows their place, who has to do it all on their own.'

I had never heard someone dwell so deeply on the role of the goalkeeper before. My son didn't quite seem to know what to say, but that didn't matter, because Monsieur Caro was on a roll.

'So you're not like your mother. She'd probably be a midfielder, someone who wants it all, who pokes her nose in everywhere, who doesn't understand the difference between your territory and mine, who'd barge in, barge about, who'd help herself, but who'd fight . . .'

I laughed.

'I'll take that last part as a compliment.'

'You should, because it's the only one you'll get.'

Somehow, I felt incredibly amused by Monsieur Caro's behaviour. There was an ounce of truth in what he had said. And surprisingly enough, it was also amusing my son. He thought it was funny that the old man was pretending to argue with his mother. The programme on TV no longer had Monsieur Caro's attention. Philosophising about football seemed to be far more entertaining. I winked at my son, as though to say that we should tease the old man a little.

'Which position would you hold on the team, monsieur?'

'Defender. Not quite as brave as keeper, but defending what I believe in, holding my own. I don't need any glory. I see the people in front of me, the people running around like idiots, but I'm still enough of a coward to need someone behind me. Too much to completely put my foot down . . . too much to tell certain truths. That's probably some damn inherited gene from my mother.'

'I think you're pretty good at telling truths,' I butted in.

'I could be better.'

Monsieur Caro's face had taken on a healthy colour during our football discussion.

'Sit down here,' Monsieur Caro said to my son.

He disappeared out of the room and returned with a big brown box which he put down on the table.

'Do you know what this is?'

My son peered into the box.

'A chess set.'

'Bravo! And do you know how to play chess?'

My son shook his head.

'Chess is superior to every other game, even football. Do you know why?'

My son bit his lip.

'Because in chess, it's black and white that matters. As in life. There's only ever one winner. Either the black or the white. As in life. Which will win is determined by the sum of their moves, tiny steps, as in life. You get many chances. It's natural to make mistakes. It's human to make bad judgements, once, maybe twice . . . but if you do it again and again, you lose.'

As he launched into the rules of chess, Monsieur Caro got himself worked up again. It struck me that he had his mother on his mind. In everything he said. To Monsieur Caro, life was black or white. Good or bad. In his view, his mother had chosen the bad side, time and time again. I curled up on the sofa and studied the two boys in front of me, huddled up together. Maybe Monsieur Caro was interested in me because he didn't know where to place me. I was in the grey zone.

He took piece after piece from the box, said their names and explained how they could move. My son seemed genuinely interested in learning the rules. Monsieur Caro set out the pieces to begin the game, and I got up and went over to the window which looked out onto the courtyard. There wasn't a soul outside. It looked warm. I moved over to the bookshelf and studied the photos of the young and the old, children and newborns. All the men wore kippah, and even the boys seemed to be wearing them, made from some kind of softer material. How could such a lonely person have such a huge family? Maybe he had decided they were all on the dark side. That was bound to be lonely.

He had a lot of books, from many different genres. The German dictionary seemed slightly out of place in his collection, but that might only have been because I knew about his history. Otherwise, the majority of the books were by French Nobel Prize winners. I found a book about the Silk Road next to one on the history of Paris. I pulled it out and sat down in the armchair, and my son asked Monsieur Caro why it was always the white pieces which started in chess. Most of the pages in the book had been folded down at the corner, which bothered me greatly. A good deal of text had also been underlined in pencil, and I decided to read only that, to see what Monsieur Caro had deemed important and interesting.

I closed the book. The underlining had been done by someone who wasn't interested in the importance of the economic exchange between countries, only in how different religions and syncretic philosophies had been spread by that medieval network of trade routes. I studied Monsieur Caro. He was probably a well-read man with an interest in mankind, despite often suggesting otherwise. A man who chased people away when all he really wanted was to understand them. I glanced at the clock and realised it was time for us to leave.

'Darling, it's time to go if we want to make it to football practice.'

Monsieur Caro glared at me, as though to make me understand that I was a traitor. Someone who came along and ruined a nice moment. He really did have an ability to shine a light on my negative sides. He was probably doing all he could to place me on the bad side. The chess pieces were carefully returned to the box, and I was pleased to see my son help even though I hadn't asked him to. Despite everything, he probably did respect the old man. We went out into the hallway and Monsieur Caro undid the security chain. I kissed his cheeks. He was surprised but accepted it, and we went out into the stairwell.

'The TV!' he suddenly shouted.

It took me a moment to realise that he wanted us to turn it off.

'You can go in and turn the TV off if you like,' I said to my son.

But then I suddenly worried that Monsieur Caro would slam the door shut, put on the chain and take my son captive. I didn't really know the man, and I didn't think he was the most level-headed of people. In fact, he was unpredictable and had a twisted view of the world. I quickly went back into the hallway. Monsieur Caro glared at me again. It was his way of behaving when he didn't understand something. My son came back, I took his hand and we left.

'Why can't he turn the TV on and off himself? It's really easy.'

'For Monsieur Caro, Saturday is a day of rest, and that means he doesn't want to turn on the TV himself. He thinks he'll do something stupid if he does.'

My son looked bewildered.

On the way back to the metro, my son's hand no longer felt strange, and his too-small shorts no longer made me feel guilty. Now, they actually gave me a certain sense of comfort. Maybe he could keep wearing them all summer after all. I studied him as we moved between the tourists. He was whistling. His face no longer seemed sad, and he looked relaxed and lively.

'Are you looking forward to football?'

'Chess was fun.'

The night after the collapse, Mancebo is sitting in the armchair by the window, his eyes fixed on the writer's apartment. For once, Tariq and Adèle have come up to the apartment he shares with Fatima. Maybe they don't want to leave Fatima alone with him. Everyone is pussyfooting around Mancebo, constantly casting anxious glances in his direction, as though to reassure themselves that he isn't about to suffer another migraine attack. If it even was a migraine. Not everyone is completely convinced about that. Adèle has announced that she also suffers from migraines once a month, when she gets her period. Tariq and Fatima laughed and said that probably wasn't the same kind of migraine.

Mancebo enjoyed being the centre of attention, being taken care of. They never stopped asking whether he needed anything. They thought that he was getting some rest in his seat by the window, but what they didn't realise was that he was actually hard at work. Not that anything of interest was happening on the other side of the boulevard.

Even Amir, who never normally had opinions or advice for others, questioned why his father should be working that Sunday. Wouldn't it be better if he stayed at home and rested after his collapse? Mancebo himself had wondered whether it was worth going down to the shop, he could do one of his jobs from the apartment, after all. But when he put his hand into his pocket and found the button which had flown off when the madman yanked him from his stool, any doubts he had about going down to the shop that day vanished. Back in the saddle, Mancebo thought, wondering how many times you had to haul yourself up onto the gee-gee before you were finally allowed to admit that maybe horse riding wasn't the sport for you after all.

The fruit stands seem to have grown wings overnight. They glide over the threshold onto the pavement, where they tempt customers with their contents. A visit to A&E seems to have done some good. Everything is moving more quickly than usual, and Mancebo enjoys feeling good again. He sits down on the stool outside the shop with his eyes fixed in the direction of Monsieur Baker's office. Thin clouds pass overhead, and the people on the street move as though they were several kilos lighter. Mancebo notices this as he sits on his stool, thinking about everything.

Before it's time to close up for the day, Mancebo takes a Coca-Cola from the refrigerator and guzzles it down. My mother was right, he thinks, medicine can be addictive. He's drunk more Coca-Cola over the past few days than he has in all the years leading up to that point.

At closing time, the fruit and vegetable stands seem to have lost their wings, they feel much heavier to haul in than they were to pull out. Mancebo stretches and prepares to write the week's report.

But just as he adds the final full stop to his report, the writer's window opens. Mancebo can see a woman's arm sticking out of it. He carefully puts down everything he is holding and makes his way from the stool out onto the pavement as quietly as he can. He practically tiptoes through the shop, and it's as though the city is helping him along by creating the right atmosphere. A pretty pink evening light is illuminating the boulevard, and the people passing by no longer seem to be in as much of a rush. They're hardly walking on eggshells, but a calm has descended over the Parisians as they try to make the most of the last few hours of the weekend.

It's a slender, white arm and it places a box on the windowsill. Mancebo debates going to get his binoculars, but just the thought of that makes him feel like he needs to empty his bladder. His jaw drops. This is the closest he's ever come to the writer's lover. It can't be Madame Cat's arm. There's no way he could have missed her arrival, he's sure of it. Mancebo tries to make out the woman's face, but it's difficult. She struggles with the box, but eventually manages to get it into the right spot. The arm curls back inside like a white snake. And then Mancebo catches sight of the writer as he carefully closes the window. His jaw drops again. He closes his mouth and rushes into his shop. No more tiptoeing about now. He's far too excited for that.

The lover has to come out. At some point, she has to come out. If the lover has a family, then she'll have to go home to them sooner or later. And if she doesn't have a family, she'll still need to leave before Madame Cat gets home. I'll wait her out. I've got you cornered now, Mancebo thinks, slumping down onto the stool behind the till. He glances at his watch. This is probably the latest he has ever stayed in the shop on a Sunday. There's no sign of anyone in the window. Mancebo glances at his watch again, though he doesn't take in the time. The scent of dinner is making its way into the shop, and this stresses Mancebo out. Ordinarily, he closes much earlier on Sundays. He should already have shut up shop. The food he can smell tells him as much. He glances at his watch again. And again. If he doesn't make his way up to the apartment soon, the others will wonder where he is. He's sure of that, even though no one would miss him especially much if he wasn't there. He's also sure of that.

Maybe I could follow her? Mancebo's imagination runs away with him. But the smell of dinner challenges it, and drags him back to reality. The scent of bean stew transforms into poisonous gas. Mancebo looks at his watch.

After a moment of panicked deliberation, Mancebo realises that he needs to go over to the writer's apartment before anyone comes down to look for him. He knows he has just minutes before Fatima sends someone down; she won't have the energy to come herself. Mancebo isn't that important.

He needs to go to the apartment over the road, but how? I could pretend to be selling something, he thinks. And then he catches sight of the remaining notebooks. Just last week, a man had knocked on the door selling calendars full of pictures of half-naked firemen. Fatima had said that maybe they should buy one for Adèle, to get her in the mood for making a baby. Mancebo is a desperate man. He has so many of the notebooks that it could seem plausible that he really is going around the neighbourhood trying to sell them.

The smell of dinner is almost suffocating now, and he grabs the notebooks and hurries out of the shop without a thought for locking up or even closing the door. His journey over to the other side has begun. I'll knock on the door and introduce myself, he thinks as he hurries across the boulevard. It'll probably be the writer who answers. But maybe his lover will be standing behind him, wrapped up in a white sheet. At least I'd get a look at her. Maybe the writer will invite me in, or maybe it'll be the lover who answers the door, and then . . .

A car honks its horn. Mancebo drops a couple of notebooks. He quickly grabs them again. Another car slams on its brakes. Mancebo continues to hurry across the street. He makes it to the other side. Now it's time for the climb, but to be able to hold on to the handrail, he has to carry one of the notebooks in his mouth. He finds himself surprised at how steep the staircase actually is.

'What are you doing, man!'

Mancebo spins around, he's on the verge of falling. He sees Fatima rushing across the street in her pink slippers. Mancebo registers everything as though in slow motion; it's the first time he's ever seen Fatima run. He's seen her hurry in the past, but never run.

He didn't know she could. Mancebo is motionless on the staircase, the notebooks under his arm and in his mouth. The game is up. He glances towards the writer's door. The answer is just beyond it. The end. The purpose of his entire task.

Fatima's eyes flash as she grabs her husband's arm and drags him down the fire escape and across the boulevard. Mancebo clutches his notebooks. A couple of cars sound their horns. Two young men lean out of their car to watch the spectacle. A small man with a notepad in his mouth being dragged over the boulevard by a much larger woman.

Fatima pushes Mancebo onto the stool in his shop, and he has the feeling that it isn't the first time someone has done that to him. She closes the door and then pauses with her back to him. When she finally turns around, it's as though all her energy is gone. Her eyes have lost their fire.

'Do you want me to call them?' she asks, trying to sound considerate.

She pulls the notebook from her husband's mouth.

'Call them?'

'Yes, so you can get help.'

Mancebo realises that she thinks he's mad, which is understandable. Forty-eight hours earlier he had a mental breakdown, and now she spots him running around with an armful of notebooks, in the belief that he's some kind of reseller. In a sense, Mancebo is relieved that she thinks he's gone crazy, but he also doesn't want to go into hospital. He has no desire to talk to Madame Flouriante again. Above all, he just wants to finish his work. He can't do that anywhere but here, on Boulevard des Batignolles. Mancebo hears footsteps on the stairs behind him, and immediately knows who they belong to.

'What's going on?'

Tariq is in the doorway, with a bewildered look on his face.

'He was running around to the neighbours with books.'

Tariq stares at Mancebo as though he wants an explanation. Mancebo shrugs.

'Where did you get all of those?'

His cousin points at the notebooks, which are lying in a heap on the floor. Fatima shrugs.

'He had one in his mouth, too.'

'What?'

'I'm saying he had a notebook in his mouth, too!'

Mancebo is sitting on his stool.

'I thought he was OK now,' Tariq whispers, seemingly in the belief that Mancebo won't hear him.

Fatima pulls Tariq over towards the till.

'There's something I didn't tell you. When I went to see him in hospital, he sat up in bed and said he was President Hollande.'

'What the hell are you saying?' Tariq exclaims.

Mancebo realises that madmen have to listen to a lot about themselves. But just because a person is mad doesn't mean they've lost their sense of hearing.

'You mean he thinks he's someone else?'

Fatima shrugs, but she doesn't reply.

'Oh God. What do we do now?'

'Eat,' says Fatima. 'I'll have to call up and make an appointment tomorrow.'

She disappears upstairs. The shuffling sound of her slippers seems to last for a long time. Tariq hesitantly approaches his cousin.

'We'll sort this out. But just between us, why were you running about with books for the neighbours?'

In a way, Mancebo feels a certain gratitude towards Tariq for treating him with some degree of respect. He deserves a straight answer, but not the truth, Mancebo thinks.

'I got them from a customer. Chinese. But what am I going to do with them? Business hasn't been good lately, so I thought that if I could flog a few of them it'd be good.'

Mancebo, with his new-found ability to observe and interpret people's behaviour, can see that Tariq is coming round to his side. That's just what he needs. If both Tariq and Fatima think he has a personality disorder, then he'll be locked up in a straitjacket in no time, or else he'll be so heavily medicated that he'll never finish his task. They're strong, efficient people, Fatima and Tariq, and he doesn't want them against him. Mancebo knows what he needs to do to bring Tariq completely round to his side.

'When you won that money, I just felt even more poor. I thought that if I sold a few notebooks, I'd at least have a bit of change in the till. Every little helps . . . I'm fine. You don't need to worry about me, brother. I know who I am.'

Tariq now has one foot on Mancebo's side and the other on Fatima's. It will only take one more thing to bring him over completely.

'I suppose I just need something new to do, too. I just sit here all day. You've got your plans for the skydiving school, your dreams, but I . . . Nothing happens here.'

Tariq pats Mancebo on the shoulder.

'Do you need help tidying up?'

Mancebo shakes his head.

'OK, then let's do this. I'll go up and talk to Fatima. Calm her down. You have to understand that she's worried.'

Mancebo smiles.

'Thanks.'

'Of course, brother. And listen, this money thing, you just need to ask and you can borrow however much you need. I've got money.'

So do I, Mancebo thinks. Tariq gives him a jokey punch on the shoulder and disappears up the stairs. Mancebo grabs the notebooks from the floor, and wonders which was worse: tussling with the two madmen who paid a visit to his shop, or with these two. He takes out the weekly report, and just as he is about to add the latest development to it, he sees Madame Cat in the apartment opposite. She puts an arm around her husband, who is sitting at his desk. Suddenly, he has nothing else to add to the report.

There was no way it could have been there before. I had walked that way for years and never noticed it.

'Built in 1998,' Christophe suddenly said, as though he had read my mind.

It looked like a small, square glass tent. Not that it was really all that small, but in comparison to the buildings surrounding it, that was the impression you got. A high red cross revealed that it was no ordinary office block.

Christophe opened the door and allowed me to go in first. He gestured for me to climb a set of stairs. A man came forward and shook Christophe's hand, and I realised he must be a regular churchgoer. We went up into the main church hall. It was hard to believe that we were in the middle of one of Europe's biggest business districts. Christophe studied me as I looked around the room, taking in the unknown. I was cautiously looking for a sign that this really was a church.

'What do you usually do here?' I asked quietly.

'What do I do? When I come to church?'

I nodded. Christophe shrugged, took his hands from his pockets and went over to the altar, where he knelt down and prayed. He looked so fragile. Not just because he was sharing his faith in such an intimate manner, but also because his position gave off a sense of vulnerability. I was struck by the thought that it looked like he was waiting for the guillotine. Once he finished praying, he crossed himself and then got up to go and sit on one of the pale, shiny wooden benches. There was a tense silence over the hall. If we were brave, we stayed within it; if we were weak, we broke it, and it should be simple. A cough or a clearing of the throat would be enough. I sat down. We glanced at one another, and then I realised what the tension was. It wasn't the church, or the silence itself, it wasn't me or him. It had been something in his prayer. I cleared my throat. He was brave. I was weak. He sighed.

'I've asked before, and I'm going to do it again. Why did you give me the flowers?'

'The first time?'

He nodded.

'I didn't want them. They weren't meant for me.'

'You don't like flowers?'

'Not any more.'

The stairs creaked and a man in a suit came in. He ignored us. He knelt in front of the altar, crossed himself, and then calmly went on his way.

'Coffee break,' Christophe said, nodding towards the man. 'Why did you give them to me?'

The stairs creaked again, and an older woman in a brown shawl came in. She said hello and sat down on one of the benches at the very front.

'You must have God on your side. Every time I ask the question, someone comes in and takes the focus away from you.'

He was whispering, and somehow that made me feel young. We were like two obstinate teenagers at the very back of the church, whispering to one another while the adults prayed. Maybe it was because we were in a church, but I wasn't in the mood for lies.

'There was something in your eyes which made me want to give them to you.'

I looked down at his hands, which were resting in his lap.

'What did you see in them?'

'A deep sadness . . . but maybe also a gratitude.'

I didn't look at him as I spoke, my eyes were focused on the old woman, as though to reassure myself that I wasn't bothering her. But from the corner of my eye, I could see Christophe had closed his eyes.

'Do you believe in the truth?'

'Is there any alternative?' I asked, and the older lady left the church.

'I mean . . . do you believe in the truth? In all respects.'

'Yes. But I guess it can be withheld sometimes.'

'Do you believe in forgiveness?'

'Yes, I think so, from an egotistical point of view if nothing else.'

My thoughts returned to Judith Goldenberg, and I debated whether I should tell Christophe her story, to see how he took it. But I had the feeling there was another story ahead of it in the queue, and there was.

'My wife cheated on me with another man.'

He said it with emphasis.

'I found out the night before you gave me the flowers. She just came out and told me. She hadn't been able to keep it to herself any longer. My first impulse was to push her away, but despite everything, we managed to talk. We sat up all night, and by the time the sun came up I had forgiven her. Truly. I forgave her. It wasn't easy, but I managed . . .'

I realised Judith would have to wait.

'On the way home from work that day, I was full of everything you saw. Sorrow and gratitude. Impressive interpretation. Grateful to have such a wonderful family, and to have the ability to forgive.

And just as I was thinking about that, you shoved a bouquet into my hands and disappeared from the metro. Do you know what bothered me most?'

I shook my head.

'That I didn't have time to say thank you. But then . . .'

He fell silent.

'I don't know if I should tell you this.'

He looked at me and smiled. His eyes were glossy with tears.

'Me neither, but do it anyway.'

'When I got home with the flowers, my wife thought they were for her. She took them and put them into a vase and thanked me for buying them even though she . . . She was grateful I had forgiven her and that I was showing it by buying her flowers. But then I told her I hadn't bought them at all, that a woman on the metro had given them to me.'

You stupid man, I thought, looking up at him.

'What are you thinking about?' he asked.

'That we're allowed to be really stupid sometimes . . .'

Our laughter echoed through the church, a laugh which relieved the tension. He raised a finger to show me we needed to be quiet.

'Aha, so now your wife thinks you're seeing someone else?'

'No, not at all. Worse. She thinks I bought the flowers and then claimed another woman had given them to me. That I'm doing it to torment her, to make her feel bad. She doesn't believe I've forgiven her at all. She thinks I've decided to belittle her and torment her as some kind of punishment.'

He sighed and continued:

'I guess it was the final straw . . . the flowers. That evening, she decided to leave me. She said she couldn't cope with constantly being reminded of her guilt. And that I didn't deserve to have her as my wife.'

'All that because of the flowers?'

'I guess she thought they were the tip of the iceberg.'

'What do you want me to say? Sorry?'

'Only if you really mean it.'

'I don't.'

'And you don't need to, either.'

My head was spinning as I went down the stairs. Christophe was still up in the church, but I stepped outside into reality again. Thousands of people all gasping for air during their lunch breaks, but inside the church everything went on as normal. Christophe was thinking about forgiveness, the door creaked, someone came and left.

It was only when I heard her shuffling footsteps that I realised it was time to leave. Oddly enough, I hadn't even heard the lift arrive.

'Good afternoon,' I said.

'Good afternoon,' the woman replied, giving me the evil eye as she started pulling at the vacuum cleaner cable.

'You're a Muslim, no?' I asked.

The cleaner looked at me with a weary expression.

'I was thinking . . . I was wondering, what's your view on forgiveness?'

She muttered something and wiped her nose with her hand.

'Why were you wondering that?'

'I'm . . . going to a debate tomorrow . . . on forgiveness, not at Areva, it's a private lecture, and wanted to get some input . . .'

'Input?'

'Just thought it would be good to get another viewpoint . . .'

'Allah says that those of us who enjoy a privileged position and live in comfort may never refuse to help those closest to us, those in need, nor anyone who has abandoned the kingdom of evil for Allah's cause. If they have done wrong, we should forgive and forget. Allah is always forgiving, always merciful.'

'OK. And how do you view the truth?'

'You ask a lot of questions, madame.'

The vacuum cleaner roared to life. She was free. The on switch was her stop button. I put on my sunglasses. The cleaner glanced at me. I packed away my computer, though I took my time doing it. It was almost like I was challenging her, attempting to prove, perhaps mostly to myself, that this was my office. If I hadn't had this strange contract which told me to go home at a specific time, I would have stayed behind. I left without saying goodbye. It felt like we had already done that through our conversation.

He was dead. I was sure of it. It was almost like I could smell that corpse scent in the stairwell. And if he was still alive, he would surely be in hospital somewhere, on morphine and awaiting the end. I was convinced he was dead, or at least dying, but I doubted whether I could do it.

I was aware that my everyday had become extremely unusual, which meant I could easily carry out peculiar tasks. Imagine if he wasn't dead and came home in a tracksuit with needle marks all over his arms, only to be met by a bouquet of flowers hanging from his door handle. Maybe he would take it as a sign that someone wanted to welcome him home. If he didn't have any relatives, he might just assume it was a neighbour, or why not the concierge who had hung them there. And if he was dead . . . well, then it didn't matter.

The flowers were a mix of every cheery colour possible. You're worth it, I thought as I tied the bouquet to the handle. I had a sudden feeling that the door was about to fly open, and there he would be, healthy and strong. Like he had never been unwell. And I would stutter some odd explanation. I even imagined I could hear footsteps behind the door. I stood there for a while, just to make sure no one would open up. But the door remained closed. And without really thinking, I knocked. I didn't hear any footsteps. A closed door meant a dead neighbour, which meant I was still in possession of my wits. So far, anyway.

Everything goes as planned. Mancebo pulls on his blue coat and his black cap, tiptoes out of the apartment and down the first set of stairs. He passes Tariq and Adèle's door. Just like always. He goes down the next set of stairs and unlocks the door to the shop, but he doesn't turn on the lights, only the little reading lamp. Things aren't like usual. Mancebo isn't going to Rungis today. The case needs to move forward; he needs to change his routines without anyone suspecting as much. Hence his decision to skip Rungis.

He sits down on the little stool behind the counter. No one would suspect that there was anyone in the shop. Nor would anyone be able to see the small beam of light casting its cold glow onto Ted Baker's book, *The Rat Catcher*. Odd name, Mancebo thinks, turning to the first page.

It's unusually quiet. Mancebo can't remember the shop ever having been this quiet before. I should have arrived in Rungis by now, he thinks, glancing at his wristwatch. Though he's been doing business there for years, he is still relatively anonymous at the huge market. He changes traders quite often, and there are always new staff. Everyone who goes to Rungis is in a hurry to find the best goods they can before they rush back to their shops, restaurants, cafés or wherever else they work.

It's true there are some people there that Mancebo usually exchanges a few words with, but if he doesn't turn up one morning, there's nothing strange about that. They probably just assume that their goods didn't live up to the grocer's high demands. It's important that Mancebo keeps an eye on the time so that he knows when he should be heading to Le Soleil. François will be waiting for him, he knows that. If he doesn't turn up, the bar owner will think that something is very wrong, particularly after his collapse.

Mancebo jumps. Just as the tough journalist in Ted Baker's book finds himself in a fix in a dark garage, Mancebo suddenly hears a noise behind him. It's the front door slamming shut. Usually, that wouldn't scare him, but he was so engrossed in *The Rat Catcher*. He spots Fatima hurrying over the road, or hurrying as fast as she can in her slippers and with her hulking great shape.

Mancebo glances at his watch. What is she doing up so early? Before he has time to wonder any further, he watches his wife go into the bakery. It doesn't take long before she's back out again, recrossing the boulevard with a paper bag in her hand. Mancebo returns to his seat behind the counter, waiting and listening. The door creaks open and swings shut with a thud. He hears her shuffling footsteps on the stairs, and then silence. How can an iceberg disappear so quietly?

Without thinking about it, he turns off the reading lamp and carefully opens the door to the stairwell. It's dark and empty. He goes out through the front door, closing it gently behind him, and then heads for the bakery, sticking close to the building. After a quick glance at his watch, he grabs the door handle and goes in. A wonderful smell greets him.

'Good morning, Monsieur Mancebo!'

'Good morning.'

'How can I help you?'

'My wife was just here . . . a few minutes ago . . .'

'Yes?'

The red-cheeked baker is looking at Mancebo in bewilderment.

'I just wanted to know what she was doing . . . what she bought.'

Maybe he should have thought about how he would explain his visit.

'What did she buy? She bought the same as always.'

'The same as always?' Mancebo says in surprise.

'Yes, every morning.'

'My wife, Fatima, she comes here every morning?'

'Yes. And she always buys three pains au chocolat.'

Mancebo looks like he has just found out that Fatima is involved in some kind of organised crime.

'Aha. Could I ask you a favour? Don't tell my wife I was here.'

The baker seems confused, but then he laughs.

'Is she on a diet or something, cheating with the odd treat?'

Mancebo smiles. Let the baker believe that.

'No, I won't say a word, even if I don't understand a thing. Won't you take a warm croissant?'

The entire situation is absurd. In truth, there's nothing odd about Fatima buying breakfast pastries every morning, but she has never mentioned eating breakfast with anyone. In fact, she always says that she has so much to do that breakfast is nothing but a coffee on the go. Why lie about it?

The chocolate pastries raise a number of questions. Seemingly innocent ones, but Mancebo is starting to feel like more and more of an outsider in his own family, detached from the people he thought he knew. And it's not like he can just ask Fatima about her breakfast routine. If he did that, she would wonder why he hadn't been to Rungis. An absurd situation. Mancebo comes close to bumping into a badly parked car, and he has to do an extra lap around the block to approach Le Soleil from the same side as usual. He parks his van in the disabled space.

Though the temperature climbs above twenty-five degrees that day, the majority of Parisians have pulled on a cardigan or chosen a long-sleeved sweater. Some are doing it to convince themselves that the heatwave is finally over. Others are wearing that extra layer in the belief that they actually need it. They're used to temperatures above thirty now.

For Mancebo, the slightly cooler temperature doesn't change a thing, he always wears the same clothes. The fruit and vegetable stands are outside and open. The apples and strawberries have kept well overnight. The same can't be said of the plums, but Mancebo still doesn't regret his decision not to go to the market. He sprays a little extra water onto the fruit and vegetables. He's wearing his watch, high up on his wrist, and he has counted the notebooks. Thirty-one left. He doesn't know why he did that. Some kind of countdown, perhaps. But to what?

He opens *The Rat Catcher* and starts reading where he left off. The main character, Stéphane, a journalist in his thirties, is waiting on an enormous amount of money from a drug smuggler who calls himself The Rat, hence the title of the book. Stéphane is blackmailing The Rat in exchange for putting a stop to an article on the Paris drug trade. As he reads, Mancebo is surprised by how much he can recognise Ted Baker in his words. He feels like he can make out the writer's light, lively walk between the lines. There are no slow, heavy sections to the book, everything flows easily, perhaps too easily at times. It actually annoys Mancebo slightly, and the section in which the drug dealer is meant to hand over the bag of money to the journalist is a good example. Everything happens smoothly and quickly. No unforeseen events hindering or even prolonging the scene. No, the drug baron simply hands over the bag, Stéphane takes it and leaves. Mancebo can practically see the journalist skipping out of the garage, and he recalls Amir's words about Ted Baker not being one of the greats. Is this the kind of thing they call pulp fiction, Mancebo wonders, shutting the book as his first customer of the day comes in.

The temperature continues to climb during the course of the day, and the Parisians take off their cardigans. The homeless crowd around the Picard chain, which sells nothing but frozen goods. The company's air vents save lives. And never before have so many people made their way to the city's libraries. Inside, the homeless have pulled out books at random and are now resting their heads on them. The guards know they aren't there for the sake of literature, but they leave them to sleep with the books as pillows. And not because they feel a sense of compassion for these unfortunate Parisians, they just don't have the energy to do anything about them. Everything they have is going towards coping themselves. Out on the boulevards, the victims of the heatwave are also visible. More drivers are crashing. Some shops have already closed for the day, and people are hauling so much mineral water that their hands turn pale.

Tariq is out on the pavement, and Mancebo wonders why he hasn't installed the air conditioning he has been talking about for so long. He gestures to his cousin that it's time to head to Le Soleil.

The dirty money is false. Worthless. He has lost.

The heat has given Mancebo more time to read during the afternoon, he doesn't have the energy for anything else. Hidden away behind the counter, he swallows and raises his hand to his mouth. The thought that the money from Madame Cat could be fake had never occurred to him before. Up until that point, he had seen the money as evidence that she wasn't using or deceiving him as part of some kind of writing project.

The thought is dizzying. Not just that he might find himself drawn into a book, but also that he might have received fake money. He has to read on. *The Rat Catcher* has captivated Mancebo. The book he was reading so reluctantly at first now has him completely hooked. Ted Baker has gone from being a zero to an average writer in Mancebo's eyes. But at the same time, if you're working for that writer's wife, and have received money in a similar way to the lead character in the book, it's obvious that a text like that would drag you in. It's nothing to do with the quality of the writing, Mancebo thinks, not at all fond of the idea that he might appreciate anything created by Ted Baker. And yet he spends the rest of the day with the novel in hand, on the edge of his seat.

The story of the deceived journalist continues in the same monotonous way, but in Mancebo's mind, a completely different tale is playing out. This one is about a grocer who has been drawn into a dirty affair. When a couple of girls come to the shop to collect their notebooks, the grocer is being interviewed by the police; they've had reports that he is in possession of a large number of fake 50 euro notes. What really happens in the book is lost on Mancebo, because his imagination has run away with him. One of the girls asks whether the book is good, but he doesn't hear her.

The book has come to an end, and with it, the day. The evening air has already begun its laborious task of cooling the city. Tariq's cobbler's shop has been closed for some time now, and he is sitting in the office with his well-polished shoes on the desk, reading the newspaper. Mancebo studies his younger cousin. Before Tariq turns off the lights for the day, he picks up his phone. Does he normally ring someone before he locks up? Or did he get a call?

Mancebo is standing with a couple of half-rotten tomatoes in his hand, waiting for the answer to his question. He has never really cared about what Tariq gets up to at this time of day, given that he is usually up to his ears trying to ward off his hunger pangs so that he can finish shutting up. But today his hunger has given way to other feelings. Mancebo lost his appetite the moment he read about the fake notes in Ted Baker's book. Tariq slams down the phone after a short conversation. Mancebo watches him grab a shoebox and throw it straight across the office.

It's not long before Mancebo feels a familiar hand on his shoulder.

'Everything OK, brother?'

'All fine.'

'It's been the quietest day in a long time.'

'Yeah, it's been quiet here too.'

'Maybe today's the day we can finally say that our wives have worked harder than we have.'

Tariq laughs and heads towards the door and the staircase with his usual boorish gait.

'Was it something particular?' Mancebo asks.

Tariq turns around and gives his little cousin, the man he calls brother, a questioning look. Mancebo doesn't know whether he should go on. He stays silent for a moment, mostly to give himself a bit of thinking time.

'I saw you got a phone call which seemed to . . . upset you.'

Tariq is completely motionless. Then he lets go of the door handle and moves right in front of Mancebo, as though he were preparing to attack. His eyes darken, and Mancebo suddenly feels panic-stricken. He doesn't recognise his cousin. But as quickly as the darkness in his eyes appeared, it disappears again, and Tariq smiles. The fact is, however, that Mancebo prefers the dark eyes to the smile. He tries to tell himself that he should probably stop reading crime novels. They just put ideas into his head, and he starts reimagining reality.

'What? A phone call?'

Mancebo tries an easy-going nod, but it comes out more like an apology for ever having raised the subject.

'I was on the phone? I don't remember that.'

'No, you weren't on the phone.'

A completely joyless laugh comes out of Tariq's mouth. Mancebo doesn't want to know where it has come from.

'I wasn't talking on the phone? You just said I was. Listen, brother, is the heat getting to you again?'

Tariq shakes his head and leaves the shop.

He leaves behind a chill, the likes of which has never been felt in the shop before. It gives Mancebo goosebumps. Something worrying has crawled in beneath his skin. There's something I'm not seeing here, something right in front of me, he thinks, and swallows.

Mancebo hears a laugh, then a bang, and after that another howl of laughter. As Mancebo opens the door, he sees the cause of the commotion, and with it the laughter. Adèle is on the floor, holding her stomach and laughing. A wooden chair is in pieces next to her. Mancebo can't work out whether the mood in the apartment is unusually cheerful or whether it's just that he has his frequency set to a lower level, meaning that his surroundings seem oddly easy-going. Things don't improve when Fatima pats him on the cheek.

Memories of that morning come flooding back, and he finds himself being drawn deeper into his already thick bubble. From the inside, he peers out at the world around him, a world which is acting oddly. Fatima's hand feels surreal on his cheek, and he imagines that it smells like butter pastry and greasy chocolate. Lying on the floor, Adèle's cheeks are rosy. Mancebo can't remember ever having seen her look so healthy before.

'Has someone won the lotto again?'

Mancebo is pleased that he came up with the lotto win as his opening line. It'll make them believe he's with them, at least for a while. Now he just has to come up with more of the kind of thing he would usually say. The fact that it won't have any basis in what he is really thinking and feeling isn't something his family will notice, because they're too exhilarated.

'No lotto wins today, but my wife just managed to sit down on Fatima's bread, which was proving under a tea towel.'

Tariq points to a baking tin on top of a small green stool.

'And then she moved on to the wooden chair and took its life.'

Adèle creeps into her husband's arms, and Tariq holds her as though he never wanted her to leave him.

'And I think I laughed more at that than the lotto win. But I've already won the jackpot with my wife!'

Tariq laughs again and nibbles at Adèle's neck. Suddenly, she pulls away and her smile is transformed into her usual cramped expression. Gone is the Adèle Mancebo saw just a few minutes earlier.

Mancebo studies Tariq as though attempting to work out where he has him, as though he was a tame wild animal. You're in control, you know the animal, but you can never forget its true nature. The Tariq he caught a glimpse of down in the shop just a while earlier is gone without a trace. Left behind is the version Mancebo has known since he was a boy, the simple, boorish, normal Tariq who likes the modest but good things in life: good food, the woman he loves and his cigarettes. As long as he has those, he's happy. If he doesn't, he'll be furious, but in a manageable and almost comic way. The Tariq who is happy to step up and help out, particularly with practical problems, is also back. And even Fatima, the same Fatima who potters about all day, is back. The Fatima who is always grumpy, but never quite angry. The woman who brutally spits out amusing remarks and comments no matter where she goes. The Fatima who thinks that Adèle should pull her weight as far as the housework goes.

As Mancebo studies his wife, he doesn't see the woman who hurried across the boulevard like an overfed polecat just to get her hands on a few pastries. Or the one who apparently spends time behind the curtain at the tobacconist's.

'Where's my son?' Mancebo asks.

'He's at the library, Georges Pompidou,' Fatima replies, pouring the tea.

'This late?'

'It's open until quarter to eleven,' Adèle says, her cheeks now back to their characteristic pale shade.

Mancebo is about to check his watch, but he quickly pulls down his shirtsleeve and pretends to be brushing something away. No one saw his gesture, and he hasn't forgotten to take off his watch. It's back beneath the till.

'What time is it? Shouldn't he be home soon?'

As the words leave his mouth, Amir closes the door behind him. Mancebo's face lights up and he feels relieved to see his son. He's the only person in the room who feels genuine. Amir smiles at his father and goes into the kitchen to wash his hands. Mancebo stretches. He feels so proud of his son.

He never needs to tell Amir to do his schoolwork, because he's an exemplary student, and at every parents' evening the teachers shower him with praise. He's particularly good at French and history. Once, one of the teachers said that it was unusual for a 'Beur', a second-generation immigrant from North Africa, to have such an excellent command of the French language. Mancebo is a proud father, but an uncertain husband.

The light is on in the room. The door is half open. A small shard of light is visible on the dark brown carpet in the hallway. Fatima is getting ready for bed, and Mancebo can hear her gurgling her green mint mouthwash. There's a strange smell in the hallway, a mixture of heat, food and petrol fumes.

Amir went straight to his room once they got back to their apartment after dinner. Now, Mancebo knocks cautiously on his half-open door. No reply. He pauses and knocks again.

Fatima is wheezing in the bathroom. The confusion Mancebo has felt all day has temporarily subsided. A certain peace has descended with the arrival of night. Ordinarily, it's the other way around, and the darkness brings with it anxiety. But Mancebo has seen his day unfold as though it was a film, full of unpleasant and unexpected surprises. Night means turning off the projector, giving Mancebo time to breathe out and gather himself before the next one begins. He knocks gently on the door. Amir opens it and gives his father a questioning look.

'Sorry to bother you.'

'Don't worry.'

'Are you reading?'

'Nah, not really.'

Mancebo isn't really sure why he is so keen to talk to his son, but the minute Amir opens the door, the important things he has on his chest start to fade. Or, at least, nothing feels quite so urgent any more, which makes it harder to bring up.

'What about you, Dad? Have you been reading?'

It's as though Amir has already heard the unspoken question, and that helps him to get going.

'Yes, I've . . . Can I come in?'

Amir opens the door wide and then goes back over to his bed, where he sits with his legs crossed. Mancebo follows his example, but decides to keep his feet on the floor.

'Yes, like I said, I've been reading. Actually, I've finished it.'

Mancebo feels childishly proud, sitting there in the moonlight, and every now and then he casts a glance towards Madame Cat's apartment. The light is on in the bedroom over the boulevard.

'So you've finished the book I gave you?'

'Yes. But can I keep it for a while longer?'

You never know. Maybe I'll have to go back to study a chapter or two, Mancebo thinks.

'Sure, I think you can keep it for a month.'

'A month? That's generous.'

'What did you think of it, then?'

Amir suddenly seems to have more energy, and he even looks slightly excited that his father has read a crime novel.

Mancebo wants to say something intelligent so that Amir can feel proud of him, and he chooses his words carefully.

'It was protracted . . . monotonous, that's what it was, monotonous.'

'But you liked it?'

'No, it was monotonous.'

'Yeah, but a book can be good even if it's monotonous. Last week, I read a book that didn't really go anywhere, the same thing, nothing much happened. You could say it was monotonous, but it was beautiful. I loved it.'

Mancebo had been happy with his choice of 'monotonous', but now he feels slightly disappointed because Amir isn't happy with it as a description of a book.

'But this book wasn't good literature, the language didn't grab me.'

Mancebo suddenly feels irritated, not at his son, but because Ted Baker can't write better books. He doesn't do anything but write, he has all the time in the world to sit there, crafting words and scenes all day. And then the result is still a wishy-washy story about an idiotic journalist who'll go along with anything? Amir laughs and that pulls Mancebo back from his thoughts about Monsieur Baker's authorship.

'You're funny, Dad. I didn't know you liked reading.'

Mancebo scratches his stubble. If Amir thinks Mancebo is funny based on what he just heard, that's nothing compared to how he'll feel when he finds out what Mancebo really has on his mind this late evening.

'It wasn't just because of that watered-down story that I wanted to talk to you.'

Amir yawns, but he covers his mouth with his hand to hide it. He doesn't want his father to think that he's boring him, because that isn't the case.

Mancebo pretends not to notice the yawn. A little yawn can't stop Amir from hearing the truth.

'In the mornings, once I've left for Rungis, what happens here?'

Amir's big brown eyes grow even larger, and he questioningly raises an eyebrow.

'I mean, how long have I had the shop now, over twenty-five years. I have no idea what you lot get up to here during the day, so I just want to know what goes on in my home when I'm not here.'

His voice has turned authoritarian, about as far from the ordinary Mancebo as it can get. But tone is one way of coming closer to the truth, and one way of having slightly more control over his family. Mancebo knows that there are men who want absolute power at home, maybe they always sound this authoritarian when they speak.

'Do you mean anything specific? If I go to school on time, or . . . ?'

'No, I know you behave, it's not about you, it's everyone else.'

Amir gives him a suspicious look.

'Tell me about this morning, for example.'

Amir thinks for a moment.

'I slept in quite late because I stayed up reading, then . . . well, I woke up when Adèle and Tariq got here.'

'Adèle and Tariq?'

'Yeah.'

'Do they come often?'

'For breakfast every morning.'

Amir is looking at his father with uncertainty, as though he can't quite work out where he stands with him. Mancebo can't, either.

'What do they have for breakfast?'

'Pain au chocolat . . . Why do you want to know all this?'

'OK, then what happens?'

'Tariq goes to work and Adèle stays here. Then I don't know. I normally leave after that.'

Mancebo kisses his son on the forehead, says goodnight and gently closes the door. This new information about their morning routine has made him stronger, though it would be no exaggeration to say that he is also in a slight state of shock. The fact that his wife goes to buy breakfast for herself, Tariq and Adèle every morning might seem innocent. But if it really is, why didn't he know about it?

Mancebo passes the bedroom where Fatima is reading in bed. He continues into the bathroom, locks the door and sits down on the toilet. He remembers an occasion not long ago. It was a Sunday, and Raphaël had invited them over for breakfast. Fatima had sat down on his white leather sofa and claimed that she wasn't used to breakfast, that for her it was never more than a quick coffee before she got to work on the day's jobs.

Mancebo is deep in thought, he wants to remember every detail of that particular occasion at Raphaël's. There is something more to this breakfast story that Mancebo can't work out. The way Fatima hurried over the street made it look like she was doing something forbidden. Why did she want to keep her morning routine secret? How many times has Mancebo heard her say that she can't bear to see Adèle other than at dinner? Why say it if it isn't true?

It's a determined Mancebo who washes his hands after using the toilet, dries them carefully and walks confidently towards the bedroom. Fatima doesn't even look up from her book when he comes into the room. He nonchalantly pulls back the covers and crawls into bed.

'Well, that's another day over,' he says with emphasis.

Fatima doesn't reply. What is there to say?

'And tomorrow a new one begins,' he continues.

'Yes, and all the toiling that goes with it.'

Toiling, he thinks; you, who munch on pastries all morning long. Fatima puts down her book, pats his cheek and turns off the lamp at the same moment the long-awaited thunderstorm lights up their room.

'Give me some dough, I'll buy beer with it!'

The honesty of the beggar made people smile as he shouted his message. And many of the passers-by did actually hand him a couple of euros for something cool to drink. The red cross on the church reminded me of my meeting later that day. I felt like a teenager who was about to break up with a boy I wasn't quite sure was actually my boyfriend.

Somehow, I wanted Christophe to realise that we couldn't go on seeing one another for much longer. I didn't know why it was so important to me that he understood. Maybe it was because the truth became so important in his company. And the truth was that we wouldn't go on seeing one another. He was just part of the experiment, and it was all going to come to an end.

The paranoia that, for a time, had remained relatively passive, flared up as I forwarded combinations of numbers all beginning with 0033 – the dialling code for France. For a while, I debated whether to try calling any of them. But why should I try to work out who these possible phone numbers belonged to? It was too late to play private detective. I tried one of them anyway. The number was unknown. I shut my computer and got ready to leave for church.

*

216

'Allah is forgiving and compassionate, unlike the Christian God.'

'When did you convert to Islam?'

'Friday.'

We laughed.

'I think you're probably a little religious, despite everything.'

'No, I'm about as much a sales manager as I am a believer.'

Christophe gave me a questioning look. How was he meant to understand the joke?

'Why an atheist?'

'Because I don't like going behind my own back.'

'What an outlook on life.'

He sounded dejected and disappointed.

'Exactly, that's precisely what I mean. If you're one of the people who can convince yourself, you're lucky, and that gives you a slightly condescending view of us poor sods who'll never find the way.'

I regretted it. Maybe I had been too harsh, but Christophe didn't seem to take it badly.

'But what harm can religion do?' he asked instead.

'You want me to say war, because you've got a counterargument for that and you'll say it's not religion that goes to war, it's people. But I won't do it. I'm going to say that the harm in most religions lies in the belief in a higher power. It takes away a person's natural ability to act. We take our own happiness away from ourselves, and give the honour to something or someone outside of us. Religion makes us smaller. Everything is already inside us, plus a little more. I'll never associate that power with anything but mankind itself. I'm a spiritual atheist who doesn't *believe*, I know.'

Christophe looked at me with a certain joy in his eyes. But he remained silent. It was never the right time to end things. I knew that. But now was as good a time as any.

'How are things with your family, your wife and kids?'

I had thought, truly, that I was about to say it, to get it over and done with, but I had veered off.

'How are things? My wife is fine. She's a strong woman, with a strong faith, even if you want to claim that she's being deceived. And my kids . . . I'm going to see them this weekend.'

It wasn't enough that I had failed to draw a line under things, I had started poking at an open wound just as I was about to leave him.

'See them this weekend? You're not living at home any more?'

He shook his head. The room was silent like only a church can be.

'I'm living here in La Défense, at the Hilton. You've already been for a run up there.'

He smiled.

'It's a temporary solution, work's paying. They're happy to do it, because they know I'll stay late and come in early . . . so it's not just out of compassion. I'm going to take the kids to my parents in Brittany during the holiday, and by the time summer's over I'll probably have an apartment sorted, somewhere near my wife.'

I took a deep breath.

'I'm not going to be here after the summer.'

'New job?' he asked gravely.

'Yes, but I can't say any more.'

'It's something to do with Areva, isn't it? Your role there? You're not really a sales manager, are you? Obviously a company like Areva must have its secrets. And now with the kidnapping of their staff in Nigeria . . . my word. You're being careful, aren't you? You're not going abroad?'

I shook my head. Everything felt much better now. In a way, he knew the truth. I was working on something secret at Areva. I wasn't a sales manager, and I was going to change roles. There was just one thing which bothered me: his thoughtfulness.

The concierge ran after me, but she slowed down once she realised she would catch me before I got into the lift.

'Good evening, madame.'

'Good evening.'

'I just wanted to say, since we were talking about him the other day . . . Monsieur Cannava has died. Just so you know.'

'I think I knew it. His apartment has been dark day and night.'

'Yes, dark is the right word. He had a cat, did you know that?'

'No,' I replied. I didn't have the energy or the desire to mention that I was aware of the poor cat.

'Yes, well, he had a cat and that was why I went up to the apartment, to take care of it and give it some food. And when I got to his door, do you know what I found?'

I shook my head.

'A bouquet of flowers!'

I was surprised by how shocked she seemed.

'Can you imagine? Who could have done such a thing? It's awful!'

I couldn't understand why she thought that, but I honestly wanted to know what was so shocking.

'What's so awful about that?'

She looked at me in surprise, as though she was wondering whether I was pulling her leg.

'Who wants to celebrate, who wants to poke fun at a dead man? It's like tipping a gravestone!'

She started to cry. I put down my two shopping bags and wrapped my arms around her. Her slender body was shaking.

'But, madame, who said they were poking fun at him? Maybe it was to honour him?'

I realised that I sounded like Monsieur Caro. She looked up at me with her big eyes.

'It was a colourful bouquet, with a thick red ribbon around it. It would've been fine for a wedding, but not for a death!'

She shouted that last part. I hadn't given a single thought to the fact that my symbolic gesture might be interpreted as a desecration. And I was sure that Monsieur Cannava wouldn't see it that way. But then again, it wasn't the first time that a bouquet for a dead person had been misinterpreted.

The sight of the banknotes in the olive jar evokes mixed emotions in Mancebo. The same had happened the first time he saw them, but now that he has doubts about whether they're really genuine, he handles them more cautiously. Like ticking bombs. The shop doors are already open, the fruit and vegetables in place, the canned goods brought in and unpacked.

Mancebo had decided to get everything in order before he counted the money. He's done its now, three times, and each time he found himself filled with new emotions. He has no words for these unfamiliar feelings. When he received the first payment, he had even felt slightly guilty. He received the money though he hadn't really worked, more entertained himself. But this time, now that he's endured both a visit from two madmen and a physical collapse, he no longer feels that way. He might even ask for a pay rise.

At the same time, he can't imagine life without this second job. Mancebo remembers he had similar thoughts when Nadia was born. He found himself unable to remember what life had been like before, when he didn't have a child, and there was nothing he wanted less than to go back to that time. Even if having children is hard work. But his new job will come to an end, he knows that. Sooner or later, the writer's lover will turn up, and if she doesn't then Madame Cat will probably call the whole thing off. Neither of those options appeals to Mancebo. But he knows that once it does come to an end, something else will take over.

He hides the money beneath the till and places the olive jar next to the binoculars. Both items feel loaded. He takes out his notebook, and for the first time realises that he can make out a huge dragon amid all the patterns on its red cover. He casts a quick glance at the other books and notices that they're all different. One has a small rabbit on it, another a dog, another a monkey.

Even if Mancebo is a man who is fundamentally indifferent to detail, he feels pleased that he chose the one with the dragon for his reports. He writes down the date and then carefully hides the book. Over the course of the morning, he regularly glances over to the building opposite.

Tariq shows no sign of being offended by the telephone saga, or by anything else for that matter, when he charges into the shop. In fact, he's in a great mood.

'Have you heard about the church clock the storm brought down?' he asks, helping Mancebo to unload a box of wine bottles.

'Yes, François told me. Have they found the hand yet?'

'Yeah, and do you know what, it made it all the way to Porte de Clichy. It landed in someone's backyard. What bloody luck, it could've speared someone like a kebab.'

'How do you know all this?'

'What do you mean?'

Tariq's voice changed.

'Do you have time to read the paper in the morning?'

Tariq puts down the box of wine.

'There are other news outlets.'

'Do you watch TV in the morning?'

'What's up with you?' Tariq attempts to laugh. 'Am I your son now? I saw it online. You know, that invention you should learn to use, brother. You can't keep resisting. It's the exact same thing as refusing to recognise the phone as a revolutionary device. You can't stop progress. I don't know how your kids are so enlightened with a father like you.'

That last part cuts Mancebo deep, and once Tariq leaves he sits for a while with his head in his hands. If there is anyone he loves and wants the absolute best for, it's his children. They're the reason he works so hard every day. They're the reason he gets up at five in the morning. They're the reason he decided to leave Tunisia, even though they hadn't even been planned back then. And he had wanted to have more, but fate had other plans.

Fortune had smiled on them when Nadia came along, but they had later gone through difficult periods. The shop barely broke even for the first few years, and they didn't have time to try for any more children. But after a handful of years, Fatima did get pregnant again, and she organised a huge party to welcome the child. The very next day, she had a miscarriage. It took a few years, but she fell pregnant again. And this time, there was no party. There was, however, another miscarriage. After another couple of years, it was time again. And this time, everything went according to plan. Amir came into the world one Sunday afternoon, just as Mancebo was shutting up his shop.

Mancebo fills the shelf with wine bottles.

'Good morning, Mademoiselle Lopez.'

'Good morning, Monsieur Mancebo. How are you?'

'Fine, thanks. And how are you, Mademoiselle Lopez?'

Mademoiselle Lopez's dog energetically sniffs around the shop as the old lady picks up the usual: parsley, a bottle of red wine, mustard and some pasta. She places it all on the counter and starts rifling through her bag for her purse. Mancebo begins ringing the items through the till.

'And I'd love one of those cute books too.'

At first, Mancebo doesn't understand what she means, and he frowns.

'One with a rabbit on it if you have one. I'm a rabbit in the Chinese zodiac.'

Mancebo understands, but he doesn't move.

'Maybe the little one was wrong. But Carine, you know, my granddaughter, she said she'd been given such a beautiful book by monsieur, one with the Chinese zodiac on it, that you were giving them out for free. She must have meant another grocer. And here I am, telling you I'm a rabbit. Forgive me!'

She laughs heartily.

'Of course mademoiselle shall have a rabbit.'

Mancebo bends down and quickly hunts out the right cover.

'Oh, thank you, they're so pretty. Why do you have so many?'

'Ah, mademoiselle, it's a long story.'

'And life is too short for those. But thank you anyway.'

She pulls on the lead and the dog vanishes from the shop ahead of her.

Mancebo is sweating. It's not because the air is close. In fact, the thunderstorm has cooled the city down. Mancebo is sweating because he is thinking about the book, or more accurately about the chapter in which the journalist finds out that the money he's been given is fake. Mancebo is waiting his turn on the bench. He's going to deposit this week's income at the bank. Tariq had to go to Le Soleil alone.

Mancebo has taken some of the money out of the weekly float and replaced it with the money from Madame Cat, so that his incomings and outgoings add up. Maybe he's being too careful. Surely no one would have the energy to look too closely into a difference of a thousand euros. But every time he hears the *pling* for a new queue number, his heart jumps in his chest.

To hide his nerves, he has his hands in his lap, but the fact is that Mancebo does look a little odd, sitting there on one of the only chairs in the bank, his back straight and his hands clasped on his knee.

It's his turn. Madame Grados welcomes him from behind a brown screen. Almost all of the shop owners in the area come to her to change money and to make transactions and transfers. Madame Grados has worked at the bank, behind the brown screen, for almost fifteen years now, and she knows Mancebo's business well. She is a strict woman who doesn't tend to smile, and any jokes from Mancebo often fall flat. In the beginning, he always tried to make small talk with her in an attempt to improve the mood, but he eventually realised it was better to say only the necessary. Today, however, he has no choice but to say a little more. Madame Grados gives him a quick handshake and invites him to sit down opposite her. He takes out a thick wad of notes.

'Yes, the usual. Weekly float to be deposited.'

The sweat is working its way out from beneath his cap, and he starts to feel ill. What will happen if the money is fake? Will I go to prison? No, how could I help being given fake money in the shop? He carries out his plan.

'I'd be grateful if madame could check the money carefully, whether it's genuine or not, particularly the 50 euro notes. I heard a couple of businessmen talking this morning, and one of them said he'd been handed a fake one.'

It's better to play honest and anxious if the money does turn out to be fake. Madame Grados looks up from behind her small glasses. She doesn't like to be interrupted while she's counting.

'How unusual. But that's why you should always check all high denomination notes carefully. In the end, you're the one who will lose out if you accept a fake note.'

She turns on her magic lamp. The first of the 50 euro notes are from Madame Cat. Mancebo has it all planned out. The phone rings, and Madame Grados replies without apologising, she sees it as nothing more than doing her job. What's to say that the person on the other end of the line is any less important than the customer in front of her? That's her philosophy. After making a few notes, she hangs up, takes the bundle of cash from the table, and sorts out all the 50 euro notes. To Mancebo's horror, he realises that the possible fake notes are now at the bottom of the pile. It won't have any impact on the final result, but it does mean that his wait will be longer.

Madame Grados passes one note after another through her lie detector. Mancebo keeps count, and as she picks up the first of Madame Cat's notes, he can't keep it in any longer. It's as though he already knows they will turn out to be fake and wants to quickly mount his defence.

'Yes, as I said, I think I know who it was going about with the fake notes. Those Americans. They bought the strangest things, and all with 50 euro notes.'

He chooses Americans for the simple reason that there's an entire ocean between him and them, July is the month when they tend to go on holiday, and the city is crawling with them. In truth, Mancebo likes Americans. Madame Grados looks up again and pulls the first of Madame Cat's notes through the machine. Everything has a price, Mancebo thinks, casting a quick glance out of the window. Sink or swim. The first note passes the test. The second, too. As do the third and the fourth, and then the rest. A huge weight lifts from Mancebo's chest.

The decision to skip the usual drink at Le Soleil and go to the bank instead suits Mancebo perfectly, because he has no desire to see Tariq for any longer than necessary today. His cousin's remark about him somehow having neglected his children is still niggling at him, like a thorn in his heart. He's also pretty tired of François and the way he goes on about Tariq's childlessness. And thirdly, changing routines is good. It's happened before, of course, that Mancebo has gone to the bank rather than the normal afternoon drink at Le Soleil, so the act in itself isn't completely unheard of, even if it isn't a common occurrence. Mancebo spends the afternoon on his stool outside the shop. The scent of dinner makes its way down to him like invisible smoke. It curls beneath the door and fills the shop. Mancebo can't quite work out what it is. It's a sweet scent.

Fatima seems annoyed during the whole of dinner. When they get back up to their own apartment, she kicks off her slippers and goes to take a bath. She returns after half an hour, wearing her nightdress and with a pink towel wound tightly around her head.

'That Adèle,' she says, shaking her turban-clad head.

It's as though she hadn't planned to share what was annoying her with her husband, but she can't hold back any longer. But the fact that she feels the need to get a weight off her chest where Adèle is concerned is nothing new, it's something she allows herself to vent roughly once a month.

Fatima slumps down into the armchair by the window, next to Mancebo, who has been sitting there twiddling his thumbs. Every now and then, he casts a glance over to the building opposite. Without warning, Fatima swings her feet up into his lap, and he knows that means it's time for a foot massage. It always is whenever Fatima needs to get something off her chest. As though every application of pressure makes her let go of the words.

'She needs a good thrashing.'

Mancebo starts to massage her big toe.

'Who?'

The question is unnecessary, Mancebo knows Fatima means Adèle, but pretending not to know is all part of the routine.

'Adèle of course!

Mancebo nods. That's another part of it.

'She's so spoilt. Here I am, slaving away from dawn until dusk. And what does she do? Sits around with her books, complaining.

No, what a woman he's got himself, poor, poor Tariq. He's worth someone better, don't you agree?'

'Yes, maybe.'

By changing foot, Fatima demonstrates that the first half of her complaint is over. They're often short halves. Short but intense.

'No "maybe" about it, Tariq deserves a better woman. She's not a good person, that Adèle. Not good at all.'

'And yet you eat breakfast with her every morning.'

Mancebo can't stop himself. The words just come out of his mouth, and without the need for a single foot massage.

Fatima pulls her foot away and stares at Mancebo. She rolls her eyes oddly.

'Why do you say that? Who told you that? It's happened before, but it's hardly a regular occurrence.'

For a few seconds, Mancebo doesn't know what to believe. But it doesn't seem likely that Amir would lie. Nor the baker. And if he adds to that the fact that he has seen her running to the bakery twice now, the evidence against her is strong.

Why on earth is she reacting like this, Mancebo thinks, not knowing what he should say or do.

'Do you honestly believe that I have the time, the inclination, or the energy for that matter, to spend time with her in the morning? I've got better things to be doing. Do you think your clothes wash themselves? Maybe you think I spend my days like Adèle? Well?'

Fatima is scaring Mancebo in the same way Tariq scared him after his brief phone call. What am I getting myself into, he wonders.

The metro came to a halt in the middle of a tunnel. Some kind of announcement was barked through the fuzzy loudspeakers, and everyone in the carriage looked at one another as though searching for an explanation. It was probably just an abandoned bag in a station which needed investigating, technical problems or someone who had jumped in front of a train . . . But I was going to be late, and I started to feel anxious. I lost my Parisian nerve, the very thing you need to be able to survive in this city. The nerve which reminded you that there was nothing you could do, nothing at all, and that it wouldn't make the least bit of difference if you got yourself worked up about it.

Two emails had already arrived by the time I got to the office. Odd, considering I was only half an hour late. That made me wonder whether someone was keeping track of my movements after all. I didn't forward them on straight away, mostly to see whether any more messages would suddenly come raining in, but nothing happened.

I managed to finish an article about wine-growing in Paris and was just about to start on another when I heard someone clear their throat. I swung around in my chair but I couldn't see anyone on the other side of the blinds. I calmly switched off the computer and moved slowly towards the door. I remembered to have a smile on my lips, as though I was on my way to greet someone, when all I really wanted was to scare off whoever it was.

There was no one by the lifts, and I started making my way down the corridor. The floor seemed enormous as I paced around it. After I had done one lap, I saw that the door to my office was wide open, which wasn't how I had left it. I stopped. My heart was pounding. There was a man inside my office. He must have been going in the opposite direction. He caught sight of me and I took a step out into the corridor.

'Hello,' he said, coming towards me.

'Can I help you, monsieur?'

My welcoming smile was gone.

'Yes, maybe you can. I have a meeting with a man named Monsieur Toussaint. I called him, they were in a meeting and the call got cut off, but he said he was at the very top . . . So I took the lift up here, but the place seems deserted . . . other than you, that is. Odd that an entire floor is empty considering how high the rents are round here.'

'It's a big company, I don't know any Monsieur Toussaint. This space doesn't get used.'

'Other than by you. What a luxury!'

'No, it's not used by me. I had a document to finish and just needed a bit of peace and quiet.'

I was in control of the situation, and if I could just get the man into the lift then it would all be over.

'I guess I should go down, but I'll be damned if I can't find out where they are.'

'Ask the receptionist. She'll help you.'

The man nodded silently and headed off towards the lift. I watched him as he feverishly started punching numbers into his phone.

The chair squeaked when I sat down. All the air had gone out of me.

I quickly checked my inbox and started to write an article for a tabloid which had offered too high a fee for me to say no. It was then that the flickers started, in the corner of my eye at first, like always, quickly spreading across my entire field of vision. It had been just over four months since my last migraine.

Whenever a migraine comes on, it's always accompanied by a certain sense of panic. Losing some of your ability to see makes a person weak, exposed, something which isn't helped by the knowledge that it's just the first stage. The pain monster has only sent out its fluttering messenger birds to let you know what's coming. Instinctively, I knew that I had to get home as quickly as possible. I tried to call my ex-husband, but he didn't pick up. There were just over two hours of my working day left, but I couldn't stay there. I was afraid for myself: the pain, the vomiting, the blindness.

I don't remember much of the journey home. My ex-husband called while I was outside our son's summer club. He was in Normandy and couldn't help. This time, he didn't tell me who he was sharing a double bed with.

The darkness came as a relief, but the pillow felt hard against my head. There was so much that was bothering me: the noises from my son's computer games, the light seeping in through the crack in the door, the sirens outside. The bucket next to my bed was still empty, and I hoped it would stay that way. My son snuck past the door. I could sense his anxiety, and I managed to shout that I'd be back on my feet soon enough. It was true. Migraines are like an intense stomach bug: they pass as quickly as they arrive. You feel drained afterwards, but you can get back on your feet.

I must have fallen asleep. The light from my alarm clock made me feel sick. My head felt heavy, but I knew the worst was over. A relatively manageable attack. It could have been worse. I went into the kitchen, drank a glass of water, sat down at the table and peered out across the courtyard into the dark, empty apartment. I looked down at the table again.

I had to be kind to myself. It was hard to handle the stress of possibly being active in a terror network, or the anxiety of getting rid of a bunch of flowers every day. Suddenly, I realised that I couldn't remember whether I had brought any flowers home with me yesterday. I glanced around the kitchen and then went out into the hallway to reassure myself that there weren't any terrifying, dying bouquets anywhere. No flowers to be seen. On the way back to my bedroom, I looked in on my son. He was sound asleep, his pyjamas twisted around his slim body. I lay down again. I would probably manage to make it up to the top of the skyscraper in a few hours' time.

I said goodbye to my son just as the gate into his summer club was about to close. For a while, I debated taking a taxi to the business district, but then I pushed on my sunglasses, wound my scarf around my pounding head and started to make my way towards the metro. The thought of the missing flowers suddenly came flooding back, but it was interrupted by a car slamming on its brakes right next to me. I jumped. I had been centimetres from being run over.

The receptionist smiled at me. The office felt particularly clean and tidy. I logged in. Two emails had arrived after I left yesterday. Before I even had time to open the first of them, the second email grabbed my attention. It wasn't from laposte.92800@free.fr. It was from Monsieur Bellivier. The subject line held a question mark.

My heart was racing as I opened the email. 'Where are you?' it said. No hello or signature of any kind. I took a deep breath. I knew I had to reply quickly to show I was there. Should I be detailed or brief, apologetic or . . . ? Maybe it was enough to simply forward the message I had missed yesterday, to show Monsieur Bellivier I was back? I replied: 'Migraine yesterday, sorry.' I tried to calm myself down by looking out over Paris. Was it because I hadn't forwarded the email that Monsieur Bellivier knew I wasn't in the office, or was it because I hadn't taken the flowers?

*

Maybe he was waiting in the church. Maybe he was eating lunch with colleagues, maybe he was travelling. Thoughts of Christophe appeared one after another over the course of the morning. Lunchtime arrived, but hunger hadn't dared return to my body yet. I went downstairs, to foreign territory one floor below, to buy a coffee from the machine, but I drank it back in my office. The sun was shining brutally through the windows, and I kept my sunglasses on. There were only a few days of the experiment left. The question was how it would end. Would Monsieur Bellivier himself come up to thank me on the last day? If I was going to be paid, how would the money reach me? And would I ever find out why I had been forwarding these messages?

I thought of Christophe again. Maybe he would be worried if I didn't turn up? No, why would he?

By chance, my leg bumped against the box beneath the desk. Since there was no reason to start working before my lunch break was over, I pulled it out to look at the books. I opened the lid, which was just folded over, and found myself face to face with a huge number of bright white polystyrene chips. Their whiteness stung my eyes. I dug as deep as I could, causing the sugar-lump-shaped contents to overflow onto the brown carpet. There wasn't a single book inside. I tried to think calmly and logically. What did I know about the box?

The man had said it was full of books I could read if I got bored. But hadn't I opened the box and seen the books before? Or was that a false memory, nothing but a fantasy? I closed my eyes. There had been a number of well-thumbed paperbacks inside, hadn't there?

I heard a *pling*. I read the string of letters and numbers and forwarded the message. The man had said that the box beneath the desk was full of books. I was sure of that now. Either he was lying or someone had stolen the books and filled the box with polystyrene. There was no point trying to work for that last half-hour, because those polystyrene chips had taken up all the free space in my mind and sucked the air out of the room. I decided that the man must have thought there were books in the box. That theory seemed manageable. Time moved slowly, and for the first time, I wished I had a good book to read.

The sound of the phone interrupted my polystyrene thoughts. I looked down at my mobile. It wasn't a number I recognised, and I hoped my son wasn't ill or hurt.

'Hello?'

'Is that the journalist?'

'Yes . . . I'm a journalist.'

'Hello, I'd like you meet you.'

The voice belonged to a woman. She sounded older.

'Who is this?'

'My name is Edith Prévost.'

'And why do you want to meet me?'

'I'd rather not get into that on here, but I think I've got a . . . project, an idea for you, madame.'

It sounded as though she had only just realised that she really did have something for me.

'I work during the day, and can't meet in the evenings. Could you tell me any more about your idea? Is it a suggestion for an article? Could you email it to me?'

'No, I'm afraid not.'

'But who are you? How did you get my number?'

'I'm a pensioner. I got your number from a friend of yours.'

'Who?'

'I would rather not reveal that until I've told you about my idea.'

I couldn't take any unnecessary risks.

'I could meet you at lunchtime. Twelve o'clock tomorrow? But I'm in La Défense, so you would have to come here.'

'La Défense, OK . . .' She laughed. 'It's been a few years since I last went there, but I can get the metro. It's line one, isn't it?'

'Yes, I'll meet you by La Grande Arche.'

'OK, thank you, madame.'
'Thanks, see you tomorrow.'

There was another *pling*. It had to be the last message of the day. Time to pick up my son and then head home to bed. I pulled on my scarf. I'd been wearing the sunglasses all day. A few women gave me odd looks as I made my way out of the lift. Suddenly, I stopped dead. I was already outside. Empty-handed. No flowers. Should I just continue without them? But it felt like part of my task.

I bit my lip and cursed the fact that I couldn't make quick, rational decisions. The receptionist must simply have missed me, probably because I was wearing a scarf and sunglasses. If she was in cahoots with Monsieur Bellivier, she would probably tell him that I hadn't picked up the flowers for two days in a row. I didn't have the courage to leave the building without them and so I went back inside. Would she give me yesterday's bouquet too? The receptionist was gazing towards the lifts. I took off my sunglasses and waited like any other visitor. She caught sight of me.

'Oh, I thought I'd missed you again today.'

She smiled and handed me three lilies.

'Winter whites,' she said with another smile.

Like polystyrene, I thought.

The early bird gets the worm, Mancebo thinks, wondering why that particular expression has come to him today. It's slightly ironic, considering how tired he feels after last night's dispute with Fatima. He hears a scraping sound in the kitchen and goes out to see what Amir is doing up so early. There, in the middle of the little kitchen, he is calmly buttering a piece of bread in his underpants.

'Are you up already, my son?'

'No, I haven't been to bed yet. We've got the oral exam today, Khaled and I, to see if we can apply for a year abroad. It's at eleven, so I'm going to bed now.'

Mancebo remembers Fatima mentioning something about Amir wanting to study abroad. He takes in his son's young body. He looks like a baby bird, standing there, almost naked, with a piece of buttered bread in his hand.

'You know how proud of you I am, my son. I always have been. You're so intelligent, you do everything so well. I just want you to know that no matter how the test goes today, I love you.'

Amir is embarrassed and looks down at the floor.

'It should go fine, Dad. But . . . thanks.'

Amir pours a glass of milk and takes it and the piece of bread to his room. Mancebo watches him close the door and feels pleased with himself, almost grateful to Tariq. After all, it's his comment about Mancebo's relationship with his children which made him tell Amir he loves him. Maybe the early bird really does catch the worm, he thinks, heading into the bathroom.

Mancebo stretches his neck. His working position that afternoon has made it stiff. He's had a lot of paperwork to do, goods to order, invoices to check, and a couple of insurance forms to fill in.

In order to stay alert and aware of whatever might be going on in the apartment opposite, he has been using the drinks shelf as a desk, albeit a sticky one. But it also means that every time he looks up towards Madame Cat's apartment, which he has done countless times now, he's had to turn his head, which has resulted in a dull ache in his neck. Nothing noteworthy has happened in the apartment over the road, or not until now, as Mancebo stretches his aching neck.

The door opens and Madame Cat comes out onto the fire escape in a pretty, tight, navy skirt, a fitted jacket made from the same material, and a white blouse. She is carrying a small suitcase and seems slightly stressed. Her eyes sweep the boulevard as though she is searching for someone. Not long afterwards, a blue car pulls up alongside her and she opens the boot for her bag. She jumps into the car. The driver seems to be a middle-aged man. Mancebo gets up and goes calmly out onto the pavement, pretending to be doing something with the plastic bags for the fruit.

The four black spots on the tarmac stare up at him. They have done every day for years. For a moment or two, a few times a day, they get the chance to look him straight in the eye. But Mancebo has never noticed them before. Round, black impressions in the tarmac, left by the legs of his stool, they glare up at him today. For the first time, he notices them, and for the first time, he picks up the stool to work out how it can be possible for a green wooden stool to make black marks on the ground.

He shakes his head and places the stool perfectly on top of its markings. But then he picks it up again and pauses with it in his hand. He studies the black grooves, then the stool and then the marks once more. Eventually, he places the stool a few centimetres away from the marks. He stands there for a moment, and then he picks up the stool, places it on the other side of the entrance and sits back down.

A strange feeling comes over him. It starts in his stomach and slowly spreads through his entire body. It's almost dizzying to be on the other side of the door. For almost thirty years now, he has always sat to the left of it, he has no idea why. And why today, of all days, he decided to move the stool isn't something he knows either. Suddenly, he feels as though everyone is staring at him, but why should they be?

Maybe it's to do with feng shui, Mancebo thinks, before he gets up to help two girls who have come into the shop.

'I'm a rabbit.'

'And I'm a horse.'

Mancebo bends down to see whether there are any horses or rabbits left.

Once he's back on his stool, Mancebo gets back to work, that is he looks up at the apartment opposite. To begin with, he shudders. He suddenly feels like he has come too close. In truth, he's no closer to the object than before, but everything seems different when viewed from another angle, unfamiliar somehow. From his new vantage point, he can see one of the side walls in the writer's office. There's a portrait on it. He can't make out who the portrait is of, but he has the feeling that it's someone famous. He has no idea why. Nothing really suggests that. But nothing suggests otherwise, either. The wallpaper is greenish, or maybe greyish, and it features some kind of busy pattern, perhaps flowers.

Everything feels so unfamiliar. Mancebo thinks about how well he would be able to see with his binoculars, but he leaves it as a thought. If he could sit in the exact same spot watching his surroundings all these years, he can manage a few hours in his new position without any help.

Mancebo's new spot on the pavement amuses him so much that he finds it irritating when two boys go into the shop. He knows what they want.

'Afternoon, do you know which animals you are?'

'Monkeys.'

'Both of you?'

The boys nod. Mancebo rifles among the twelve remaining notebooks. This time, he doesn't bother encouraging them to buy anything. All he wants is for the notebooks to run out so that he can get back to his important work.

'There's only one monkey. One of you'll have to convert to a horse or a rooster.'

The boys quietly confer.

'We'll take a monkey and a rooster. Thank you, monsieur,' they say in unison.

Mancebo can't help but laugh; their conversation sounds more suited to a pet shop than a greengrocer's. He is just about to sit down again, but then he changes his mind. He picks up the stool and takes a few steps towards the right of the entrance, then a few more. He sets the stool down. Once you've made one change, it's all about continuing, he thinks.

He is now so far from the entrance to the shop that one of the awnings is blocking his view of the door, but he'll still be able to see if anyone goes in. He can see why passers-by might find it odd that the owner of the shop is sitting so far from his business. It must look like the shop and I have had an argument and now we're sulking on our own, Mancebo thinks. And in a way, it's true.

Mancebo isn't fond of his shop today. Rather than being the base for his surveillance, it has now become a hindrance, a prison. He doesn't know if it's because he has grown away from it or just

239

because the case now demands more flexibility. Suddenly, he feels a burning sensation on his hand. But Mancebo is so lost in his own fantasies that his brain doesn't do anything but register the pain. It doesn't send any follow-up questions so that he can work out what could have caused the pain. His sense of smell takes over instead. Cigarette smoke, his brain notes. Mancebo's sense of smell is always engaged, there's no off button for that. That's how he knows when dinner is ready every day. Mancebo is sitting perfectly still. He feels a sudden burning sensation on his other hand, and he pulls it back without moving the rest of his body. As though in slow motion, he looks up. A few metres above him, he spots Fatima's fat, gold-clad hand clutching a cigarette. He doesn't need binoculars to see that.

For the rest of the afternoon, it's as though he's in a haze. Customers come and go, but afterwards he barely knows who has been in nor what they bought. Mancebo is in shock. Despite that, he manages to stay cool, until his brain has time to process the shocking reality that has just emerged. His wife smokes. A revolutionary fact for Mancebo, who, for almost forty years, has been living with a woman who complains when he smokes and claims to be allergic to nicotine.

The private anti-smoking campaign that she has been waging rushes through his head at high speed. Occasionally, the memories crash into one another, mix together, weaken, strengthen, and he doesn't know how to organise, calm or give structure to them. He has no control. He remembers one occasion when they had to change restaurants because they didn't have any non-smoking tables, and he remembers how Fatima had applauded from the sofa when she learnt that there would be a smoking ban in bars and restaurants on the news.

He also remembers countless occasions when she hit his fingers as he tried to smoke a cigarette over his daily allowance. Memories of the evening when they celebrated Tariq's lotto win overtake and mow down all the others. Fatima slamming the lid of the cigar box onto his fingers. Mancebo really doesn't need to go looking for these memories. Some come crashing in like steamrollers, others like small, irritating flies.

A young woman leaves the shop with a smile, and Mancebo finds himself standing with money in his hand. He doesn't know whether it's the change he has forgotten to give her or if it's the money she gave him. But if she's paid, then why hasn't he put the money into the till? Mancebo pants, his heart starts beating more quickly, and he feels anxious. Imagine if Fatima's smoking gives him a heart attack. That would be too ironic. Mancebo takes a couple of deep breaths. The memories are coming to him more slowly now, and he knows that in just a few hours it'll be time to face his wife.

He picks up the stool from behind the counter, though he has no memory of putting it there. He goes outside and consciously places it back on top of the four black impressions on the tarmac. That'll have to be enough for the day. He doesn't want to discover anything else, or not today anyway. He has no desire to spend yet another night in hospital.

Being back in his safe place just to the left of the door does him good. It lulls him, if not into a sense of security, which would be an exaggeration, then at least into a certain state of calm. The evening air rolling in over the city helps to cool his overheating brain, and his heart starts beating more normally. But then he notices the scent of dinner and his pulse picks up again. He knows he is going to have to face his wife. How long has Fatima been smoking? Why has she kept it secret? Why does she claim to be allergic to cigarette smoke? How much does she smoke? And the last, and most important question: what else doesn't he know about?

His questions head off down the boulevard. He doesn't know whether anyone will answer them. Sitting outside his shop, on his green wooden stool, Mancebo feels incredibly lonely.

*

Mancebo gets up and reluctantly starts packing away the fruit and vegetable stands. He does it slowly. As though he is attempting to gain some time before he has to see his wife, who now feels like a stranger to him. All the same, part of him wants to rush up to their apartment to find the evidence. Maybe she has a box of cigarettes stashed away somewhere, maybe she smells of smoke? Tariq closed up his shop early today, and he's now sitting in his office as usual. Every now and then he gets up to light a cigarette, but he quickly returns to his paper. He seems restless. Mancebo registers that fact, but he has things other than his cousin on his mind.

Tariq drums his fingers on the table in irritation. Fatima huffs and puffs as she brings the food to the table. Amir pulls at his lip as he reads a book about blue whales. Adèle is filing her nails with a smile on her lips. Mancebo's eyes flit between the members of his family. It's as though he has come across a body, and now his job is to work out who the murderer is. The culprit is in the room. It could be the person he least suspects.

'My old friend Ali called today. Good man, that one,' Tariq says, stopping his drumming.

Mancebo casts a glance at his cousin. When no one comments on the news that his friend called, Tariq starts drumming his fingers again. Mancebo's eyes pan over the dinner guests.

'Think we're going to the races in Auteuil tomorrow. Ali's probably keen to win after my jackpot.'

Adèle suddenly comes to life.

'So you're going to the races tomorrow. Fatima and I are going to the hammam.'

She says it as though Tariq would try to force her to go to the racing with him. He surely doesn't want her to come, and he doesn't reply. The room is silent. Mancebo wonders how many of the people around the table know that Fatima smokes. His eyes focus on Adèle. She looks up and meets his gaze with a smile. She knows. Mancebo can see it in her eyes. Adèle resumes her filing. Mancebo turns his attention to Amir, but he is so engrossed in his book that he doesn't notice his father studying him.

'Amir, my son, why are you reading about blue whales?'

Amir shrugs.

'Why not? They're interesting animals.'

Mancebo is convinced that Amir doesn't know a thing. Tariq's turn. He's more difficult. Mancebo doesn't know where he stands with his cousin, whose eyes reveal nothing. Tariq must feel Mancebo watching him, because he suddenly says:

'How's it going, brother?'

A musty smell hits them as they open the door to the apartment. Mancebo notices Fatima's hand as she coaxes the key from the lock. It's the same hand which, just a few hours earlier, was clutching a cigarette. The same one which, time and again, has pulled cigarettes from his own hand and wagged a finger at smokers. But it's also the hand which has caressed him.

They step into the apartment. Amir quickly heads off to his room. Mancebo hangs up his coat and Fatima starts taking off her jewellery. He isn't sure how to take the next step, and he stays where he is in the hallway instead. Then he goes towards Amir's room and is just on the verge of knocking when he changes his mind. He needs a day to develop his plan before he drags his son into it. Mancebo has big things brewing.

The morning at home was one long torment, a wait. All I wanted and could think about was opening the box and confirming that again, today, it was full of polystyrene. The thought of it being full of books filled me with panic. Though the metro was running smoothly, the journey to La Défense felt twice as long as usual.

I hurried past the florist and half ran the last part of the way to Areva, slipping in through the revolving doors, pulling out my pass and making it into the lift at the last moment before the doors closed. With the keys in my hand, I quickly made my way to my office.

I dropped to my knees and pulled out the box, tore back the flaps and shoved both hands inside. My fingers groped through the smooth polystyrene pieces, right down to the bottom. There were no books, what a relief. Not a single paperback. Maybe there never had been. Maybe I had just imagined seeing them there. Relieved, I remained on my knees for a few seconds and found myself thinking of Christophe as he prayed in church. I got up and turned on the computer.

The way Areva towered up against the grey sky made it look terrifying. Maybe there was a storm on the way. I left the plaza and climbed the stairs. I didn't know quite who I was looking for, only that it was a woman. The place I had suggested to meet might not have been the best, but it meant I could slip away if I didn't want to follow through on the meeting. Thoughts of the polystyrene chips had been weighing so heavily on my mind over the past day that I hadn't given the meeting much thought. And as I stood there waiting, it suddenly struck me that it might have been Christophe's wife who contacted me, to find out whether I was the one who had given him the flowers on the metro. Or maybe it had something to do with my real job and the revelations about the HSBC affair.

She was late, but the minute I saw her coming up from the escalator, I knew she was the woman I was waiting for. Somehow, she seemed to belong to a different day and age, and in the ultra-modern business quarter, the contrast was striking. She was a small woman in her sixties, wearing a brown skirt and a black polo shirt. She had a beige shawl with red flowers covering her head, and she was carrying an old canvas bag in one hand. She stopped and looked dejectedly up at La Grande Arche, as though she was going to be forced to climb it. I felt a sudden urge to rescue her from the trendy, overwhelming surroundings, and I suppose I did in a way; I jogged over to her, all to shorten her suffering.

'You must be Madame Prévost?'

Her face lit up.

'How did you know?'

I smiled and she linked her arm through mine. A natural gesture for her, perhaps, and oddly enough it didn't feel unnatural to me, despite the fact we had never met before.

'Where should we go?'

'There', I said, pointing up at La Grande Arche.

It was a long time since I had last been to the top of the huge marble arch. There was a nice café at the very top.

'Are you sure, madame?' she asked gravely.

Without replying, I steered her towards the lifts and bought tickets. The roomy glass box began its journey up to the top of the modern triumphal arch.

'Did you know it was a Danish architect who designed this? Sadly he died before it was finished,' I informed the woman.

That was my anecdote for the lift journey, and I remembered that the man who showed me into Areva had told me something similar.

'So, now I want to know what you want from me, how you got hold of my phone number,' I said once we were sitting down in the café.

She clutched her canvas bag.

'My name is Madame Prévost. I'm Monsieur Caro's sister.'

The whole situation was starting to amuse me. I thought about how odd it was that she called her own brother monsieur, but considering his personality maybe that was natural. To begin with, I assumed she had contacted me because she was worried about her brother's health, maybe she thought we were closer than we really were. Her fingers played with the canvas bag.

'And I . . .'

I had the sense she wasn't feeling well. It was as though she disappeared elsewhere every now and then.

'What do you want from me?' I repeated, to get her back on the right track.

'Monsieur Caro talks about you, how you're a journalist, and I found your number next to his phone. I . . . I wanted to give you something.'

Initially, I planned to tell her how I knew her brother, but I changed my mind out of fear that she would vanish again. She opened her canvas bag, which had a Velcro fastening. She pulled out a thick brown envelope and placed it on the table. Then she quickly closed the bag again, as though she was worried something might jump out. She licked her lips, took a worn green book out of the envelope and handed it to me.

I wiped my hands on the napkin, mostly out of respect for the woman.

'You want me to look inside?'

She nodded. I opened it at random. The pages were thin, like greaseproof paper, and on the verge of falling out. They were covered in hard-to-read handwriting.

'What is this?' I asked with the same page still open.

'It's my mother's diary.'

'Judith Goldenberg's diary?'

Madame Prévost nodded.

'Why do you want me to have it?'

'Monsieur Caro said you wanted to write a book about her. He thinks it's an awful idea, but I think it's a good one.'

I smiled.

'It's from when she was the doctor in the German concentration camp. Everything is documented.'

'How could she have this? I mean, how was she allowed to keep a diary?'

Madame Prévost gave me a questioning look.

'Can't you see?'

I leafed forward a few pages and saw the stamps on almost every side. After reading a few complicated words and dosages, I finally understood.

'Incredible. This was her prescription book.'

'It contains information which never came out.'

She opened her bag and took out two more brown envelopes.

'Here's another one from her time in the concentration camp, and this one is from Paris, post-war.'

She put the books down on the table. I didn't know what to say. I picked them up and leafed through them, mostly to give myself time to think.

'Writing a book is an enormous undertaking. I know I said I wanted to do it, and I still do, but I'd like the chance to go through everything before I make any promises. All the same, it's an honour . . . I'd be very happy to read them.'

Something was scaring her, and I didn't want to leave before I knew what it was, whether I could help her.

'Does your brother know you called me, that we're meeting?'

'No.'

So that was it.

'And you don't want him to know? I can understand that. I know what a temper that man has. I won't say anything. You have my number.'

My departure felt abrupt, but there was no more time, I had to get back to work. Madame Prévost held out her canvas bag.

'Oh great, can I borrow it?'

'Yes, I sewed Velcro into it this morning because it looked like rain.'

She took my arm and we walked to the lift in silence. I had something valuable on either side of me, Madame Prévost and the canvas bag.

'Why do you have the diaries?'

'Monsieur Caro was going to burn them. I begged and pleaded for him to let me keep them. He agreed as long as I promised never to show them to anyone.'

I nodded and could see that she was fighting back tears. Her fear had vanished.

Since I had both a computer and a canvas bag full of one of the most significant events in world history, I had to hold the flowers in my mouth as I knocked on the concierge's door. She was quick to answer, and I caught a whiff of food.

'Good evening, madame. I don't want to bother you. I just wanted to wish you a good holiday. I saw the note in the stairwell that you're just working the rest of this week.'

I handed over the flowers.

'You can enjoy them for a few days, at least.'

'Oh, thank you, they're beautiful. They're asters, aren't they?'

'Yes . . . perhaps they are.'

'Did you know that Monsieur Seguin, the one two floors up, is selling? Imagine, they've got three kids and . . .'

'No, I didn't know, I'm sorry to hear that, really. But I don't want to bother you.'

'You never do.'

Back up in my apartment, I placed the canvas bag at the very top of my wardrobe, quickly got changed and headed back out to pick up my son.

Mancebo is reluctant to haul himself out of bed that bank holiday. On the national day, no less, he has permitted himself to lie in until nine, and he is in no rush to get ready. He feels like a small child who doesn't want to go to school and who hopes that Mum will write a sick note so that he doesn't have to. Though who his mother could be by this point in time is something he has trouble imagining. Fatima hasn't exactly been showing her most maternal side lately – loyal, honest and sage. Mancebo feels like a stranger around her. The radio is on in the kitchen, and Amir is moving around the apartment as though he's looking for something. Fatima has already left for the hammam. Mancebo heard her shout goodbye.

As Mancebo is brushing his teeth, the child, or at least the teenager in him, comes out. He spits the toothpaste into the sink, rinses his mouth and goes to grab his blue jacket from the hallway. He feels to check that the button is still there, grabs his packet of cigarettes, shakes one out and lights it. It's the first time he's ever smoked in the apartment. He even leaves the window closed and slumps down into an armchair, takes a few deep drags and studies the apartment opposite. The lights are off, and as a result he can't work out whether anyone is home or if they're just sleeping.

For some reason, he takes it for granted that Monsieur Baker is still lying alone in bed. Writers probably take all the liberties they can, and Mancebo can't imagine they work bank holidays. He takes a deep puff on his cigarette, which has never tasted so good. He would like a little fresh air inside, but his new-found obstinacy stops him. Instead, he allows the cigarette smoke to work its way into everything that might belong to Fatima: the clothes, sheets, hand towels. He blows a cloud of smoke straight at her pink bird, whose glittery wings change colour with the temperature. Not that the smoke seems to have any impact on it. It looks as pink as ever.

'What're you doing, Dad! Mum's going to go crazy if she finds out you're smoking at home! You know that! Put it out!'

In all his teenage obstinacy, Mancebo had forgotten that Amir was at home. It's easy to forget him, since everything he does is so discreet.

'No, she's not going to go crazy, she already is.'

He regrets what he just said. He can't allow his obstinacy to cross over onto his innocent son. But at the same time, something tells him that it's not right to protect Amir from what is happening. His son is old enough to know the truth, what's really going on around here. No son of his will live a life that's not based on the truth. Even if it turns his view of his mother upside down. Amir is staring at the cigarette with wide eyes, as though it was a wild animal his father was playing with.

'Sit down, Amir.'

But Amir doesn't move. Mancebo weighs up whether to let his son remain on his feet.

'Please, sit down.'

He taps the ash into one of the flowerpots and lets the butt lie. Amir is staring at his father as though he's mad, and maybe he is. Amir's powerful reaction confirms Mancebo's suspicions – that he has no idea about Fatima's smoking. But no more.

'Please, Amir, my son, sit down and I'll explain what's going on. It's not so bad, you've seen me smoke a thousand times. Never here, but still. Please sit down.'

Amir sits down on the tired old armchair and stares at the cigarette butt in the flowerpot, as though it might suddenly launch an attack.

'You know it was a surprise to me that your mother . . . my wife often calls your sister, that she buys pains au chocolat every morning, and that she runs . . .'

Amir's expression makes it clear that the things he has just mentioned are nothing compared to smoking in the apartment.

'I know you don't think it's the same thing, but I'm trying to explain something very, very complicated so that you can understand everything that's going on here.'

Amir looks worried.

'For almost thirty years, we, your mother and I, have lived here. That's longer than you've even been alive. Can you imagine that? And for all these years, she's complained that she doesn't get a chance to sit down all day. When she talks about her day, she's never mentioned that she goes to the bakery to buy breakfast. Isn't that odd? After thirty years? But the strangest thing is that she has breakfast with Adèle. The woman she has done nothing but moan about for ten years. Every day for ten years, I've had to listen to her complain that dinner is a torment because she has to spend time with Adèle and hear about all of her aches and pains and so on. And if we ever stayed a minute longer than planned in their apartment, she would complain about that extra time she had to spend with Adèle. For ten years now, I've had to listen to it!'

The teenage obstinacy has now taken full control of Mancebo's body, and he does nothing to stop it. In fact, it helps him relay everything to Amir in the right way.

'So when I found out that she runs over to the bakery every morning to buy pastries for herself and Adèle, of course I was surprised. And here comes the interesting part. When I confronted her with this truth, she denied it! If she's been hiding that for ten years, what isn't she capable of hiding? And what else is she lying about?

I'll spare you the other things she does during the day.'

Amir's expression has changed, and his eyes leave the cigarette butt and move to his father, as though he wants him to continue. Something he's more than happy to do.

'What I'm about to tell you is something I need you to believe. Yesterday, by changing my routine, I discovered that Fatima smokes.'

Mancebo can see that the information in itself isn't enough for Amir.

'Due to various circumstances, I moved a short distance away from the shop, and when I looked up I saw Fatima, my wife, smoking a cigarette on the balcony. She tapped the ash straight down onto the pavement. This was in the afternoon, when Tariq and I were at our respective jobs and you're usually in school. Where were you yesterday afternoon?'

'At Khaled's.'

'That's when Fatima smokes. She's probably been carrying out this ritual at a different time every day, all depending on the circumstances.'

Mancebo is pleased with that last sentence. The room is silent.

'Are you sure?'

'More than sure.'

For a moment, Amir seems to be thinking, and then he starts acting as though he were Fatima's defence lawyer. A desperate one.

'Are you sure she was the one smoking? She might've been helping someone else tap the ash from the cigarette . . .'

Amir immediately realises how his attempt at a defence sounds. Bad.

'So why does she say she's allergic to cigarette smoke?' Amir asks, going back to his pondering.

Mancebo shrugs.

'She didn't even come to my poetry reading at the bar. She said there was too much cigarette smoke and . . .'

Amir falls silent, and Mancebo suddenly feels a great deal of sympathy for his boy. He would never have imagined that this information about Fatima's cigarette habit could hurt Amir so much.

'My son. We'll have to take it for what it is. We don't know why she does what she does.'

'Haven't you asked her?' Amir wonders, sounding surprised.

So far, Mancebo has forgotten to say that no one else must find out that they know about Fatima's smoking habit. He bites his lip, attempting to gain enough time to find a reasonable explanation as to why they shouldn't confront Fatima with what they know. If they do, Mancebo is worried she will just become more cautious and that any other habits she has will never come out. He can't tell Amir about his surveillance on Monsieur Baker, either. His son isn't ready for that, and nor is he. The case isn't mature enough to be released yet.

'No, I haven't asked her. I want her to tell me herself. You know, if you've discovered something that has been kept secret, you really want to hear it from the person involved. I'll see what I can do to make her tell me herself. I think that would be best for all of us. You'll have to give me some time. Until then, we'll keep quiet about this. OK?'

Amir seems to buy his explanation without protest, which does surprise Mancebo, but he feels relieved all the same.

Amir packs up his notebook and pens. He's going to the library. Out on the streets, the Parisians have started making their way to weekend brunch. The queue outside the bakery grows, people rush by with bouquets of flowers, and a few take the dog out before they leave to see their relatives. Mancebo glances at the clock in the kitchen and realises that he's late, then he lights a new cigarette and blows more smoke at the little pink bird which might soon turn a shade of grey.

He feels strong and calm, and is looking forward to the coming days. By telling Amir, he also managed to clarify the situation for himself, which was a very good move. Recent events have lined up like beads on a string, one after another, and all the information he receives from now on will simply lengthen and improve his string of pearls. Cigarette smoke is hanging over the living room like a blanket. The annual military parade down the Champs-Élysées is being shown on TV. Tanks driving up towards the Arc de Triomphe is the last thing Mancebo sees before he leaves the apartment, heading out to war himself.

Mancebo obstinately rocks back on the stool. With his new-found teenage hormones, the bank holiday is boring, there's nothing interesting going on. The apartment opposite seems to be empty. Mancebo doesn't even have Tariq to spy on, because he's spending the day at the races. He goes into the shop and opens a pack of toothpicks, returns to his stool and nonchalantly pushes one into his mouth. In the distance, further down the boulevard, he spots Fatima.

'Hello,' she says as she reaches her husband, who is sitting on his stool like always. 'What do you say about going out for lunch today? It'll probably just be you and me. Adèle's at her pottery class, Tariq's at the races and Amir said he wouldn't be eating at home. There's no point cooking just for two. We could go to the Pakistani place.'

The Pakistani place isn't actually Pakistani, the owner is from India and opened a restaurant with his family not far from Le Soleil. Mancebo swallows, his tough teenage lingo has suddenly vanished. A one-on-one lunch with his wife wasn't something he had planned, and nor is it something he is looking forward to.

Reluctantly, Mancebo closes up his shop. Fatima has gone up to the apartment to drop off her things, but she quickly returns.

'Did the window open itself up there? Or did you open it? I think it's better if we try to keep the heat out.'

Mancebo immediately knows what she's talking about. Amir

must have decided to air the apartment out of fear that Fatima would notice someone had been smoking.

'No, I haven't opened any windows. Ask Amir.'

'Why on earth would he suddenly start opening windows?'

'I don't know.'

They begin to make their way down the boulevard, and before they turn the corner Mancebo casts one last glance back towards the writer and Madame Cat's apartment.

He is eagerly awaiting Fatima's remarks about how good it is that the smoking ban now applies to restaurants. Mancebo knows she'll say it any minute now, but what he doesn't know is how he'll react. He doesn't quite trust himself. He might start laughing, but he could just as easily smash his fist against the table and spit out some truths. He could even start crying. He just doesn't know, he's unsure of himself in this situation.

They sit down at a table close to the window. There is only one other couple in the restaurant, a young pair, plus an old man who is getting ready to leave. Fatima is quiet and starts absent-mindedly reading through the menu, though she quickly puts it down again. She seems to know what she wants. She probably knew before she even suggested they go there. Mancebo doesn't know what he should order, but he knows exactly what Fatima will choose. He knows his wife in that regard, at least, if not in many others. She looks around the room and Mancebo starts to tremble with fear at how he will react when she brings up the smoking ban. He might be just seconds from surprising himself.

'It's so nice that people aren't allowed to smoke wherever they want any more!'

Her words come at him like a cannonball, smashing into everything in their path. Though Mancebo was expecting it, her words still surprise him; it's like waiting for the pop of the champagne cork flying into the air. But the content is far from champagne. Mancebo gives himself some time. It's over now, calm, he tries to tell himself.

'It's good to get out like this and avoid cooking,' Fatima says when the waiter brings their food.

Mancebo helps himself to the warm bread. He tries to forget that he has company and simply enjoy the food. But things take a difficult turn. The fat tobacconist comes into the restaurant. Mancebo reaches for his glass of water and wonders whether he should say something to his wife, who is sitting with her back to the door. The restaurant owner shakes the tobacconist's hand and gives him the food he pre-ordered in two white plastic bags. Mancebo waits until after the tobacconist has vanished onto the pavement to remark on his visit.

'The tobacconist from Rue de Chéroy just left.'

Fatima stares at her husband.

'And?' she eventually says.

'You might have wanted to say hello to him?'

'Why would I want to do that? And if I had, you should've bloody said before he left.'

She has a point there, Mancebo thinks, emptying his glass.

'It smells like Christmas!' Adèle shouts as she settles down at the dinner table.

Raphaël has stayed behind for dinner after fixing Adèle's hairdryer. Tariq is talking about a horse which ran in the wrong direction at the racetrack. Everyone laughs.

'It's the saffron in the stew,' Fatima interrupts as an explanation for Adèle's Christmas feeling.

The three men, Mancebo, Tariq and Raphaël, are smoking.

Fatima doesn't say anything, but she energetically flaps her hand in front of her face. Every time she puts something down on the table in particular. One person in the room is quiet, but his eyes speak volumes. Amir glances nervously at his father. Is he going to smoke more than he's allowed?

The morning's cigarette demonstration has affected him more

powerfully than Mancebo could ever have imagined. And now that Mancebo's teenage hormones have left his body, he does regret having drawn his son into things in the way he did. It's purely down to Raphaël's presence that dinner is bearable. The evening's guest helps to lighten the tense mood of lies and unspoken truths. Raphaël is a breath of fresh air that enables them all to breathe.

The two women are chatting in the kitchen. Amir stares at his father. Raphaël lights a new cigarette and Tariq goes through the race programme again, to memorise the winners for next time.

France's national day is almost over, and everything will soon be back to normal, whatever that means. To Raphaël, it might mean getting a broken toaster to toast bread again. To Tariq, it means shoes to reheel, and to Fatima . . . Mancebo stops wondering and breaks off a piece of baguette to soak up the sauce on his plate.

'Are you starting the washing-up at the table, Mancebo?' Tariq asks, and everyone laughs.

The first thing I did when I got to the office was to open the box and check, once more, that it still wasn't filled with anything but polystyrene. It wasn't. There were no books to be seen.

My morning consisted of three *plings* and Judith's fate. What struck me was the pride with which she carried out her duties and daily tasks. There wasn't a hint of self-pity or complaint.

Against my better judgement, I had to admit that it did actually feel slightly provocative. The woman hadn't just tended to the worst monsters of our age, she had done it with a certain amount of love. Matter-of-factly, she gave an account of life in the surgery. And even when she described the terrible conditions, she never placed the blame with those who had taken her freedom. I was starting to understand where Monsieur Caro's hatred came from.

It was the absence of *plings* which made me realise I should take my lunch break. I was fifteen minutes late and placed the diaries back into the canvas bag, I didn't dare leave them unguarded. I hurried towards the lift. I didn't want to think about why I was in such a rush.

The door of the church was stiff, and I clung tightly to the canvas bag. Here I come, with a Jewess who took care of the Nazis during the war, I thought as I ran up the stairs. I was out of breath as I came into the main hall. He was sitting inside, and he was worryingly pleased to see me. As usual, we didn't say much to begin with.

'I'm reading a book about the Second World War. It was written by someone who survived the concentration camps,' I said.

'Ah, what's the author's name?'

'I can't remember.'

'People are funny. It's the same for books and wine. People can drink a good wine and then forget to memorise the name. They'll remember the colour of the label, though. It's the same with books, people remember the covers but not the name of the author.'

Since I was neither of those people, his comments bothered me.

'Her name is Judith. She lived in terrible conditions in one of the concentration camps, but when she writes about it it's as though she's defending the Germans. Or maybe not defending them, but she doesn't blame them. She doesn't seem to hate them.'

Christophe was silent. I hadn't been planning to share any more, but I was confident he would know how to treat sensitive information.

'She wrote it inside the concentration camp. It's her diary,' I continued.

Christophe looked up at me, and it was hard to read his expression.

'Well then,' he replied.

'What do you mean?'

'She did it to survive. The simple explanation would be that she did it out of fear they would find what she wrote. The more complicated explanation, but maybe also the true one, is that she likely did it to survive. It was probably too difficult to acknowledge the situation she found herself in. Maybe she wrote it for herself, to distort her view of reality and therefore survive.'

It felt like he knew more about Judith than anyone else. I wanted to give him more information so that he could help me understand.

'She was a doctor and was forced to work for the Germans in one of the camps.'

Christophe looked up at me again.

'Interesting.'

Sadness overwhelmed me. I wanted to believe it was because of Judith's tragic fate that I started to cry, but it wasn't. It was the knowledge that I was close to the end which made me so sad. Judith was just an excuse. I couldn't remember when I had last cried, but I did so now. In a church. With a man I didn't even know.

'Was she a relative of yours?'

I was crying even harder now, and I think he interpreted that as a yes.

'These will be your last flowers, Judith,' I said, placing the yellow bouquet onto the grave.

Now I've even started talking to the dead, I thought, spotting a man in a blue tracksuit approaching.

'Madame, madame, don't do that.'

The memory of meeting Monsieur Caro reared its head, and I stepped back, away from him.

'Madame, I beg you, please remove those flowers, right now.'

There was nothing threatening in his voice, only afraid. He stayed at a safe distance, and at first, I thought it was me he was afraid of, but then I realised it was Judith's grave which was scaring him. His eyes were fixed on the headstone, as if it were a living creature that might attack at any moment.

'Good evening, monsieur. Why don't you want me to put flowers on this grave?'

'My brother forbade it.'

The man started to hit himself on the head, and then he raised his hands to his face.

'My brother has forbidden anyone to leave flowers on this grave. You should watch out for my brother. He isn't evil, but he's just. That's my mother lying there, under all that earth, under the stones, and we shouldn't honour her because then the world will split. The universe.'

I realised who he was. Monsieur Caro's schizophrenic brother.

'I know your brother. He knows I'm putting flowers on your mother's grave. He's not angry.'

The man looked at me.

'You don't need to say you've seen me if you're afraid your brother will be angry,' I continued.

'You need to take the flowers.'

'I'll do it if you leave.'

'Promise?'

He nervously ran his hands over his face and then wandered away. I broke my promise, shoved my empty hands into my trouser pockets, and looked down at the pretty flowers before I left the churchyard.

To begin with, I had said that the invitation was a bit last-minute, but then I said yes anyway, without really knowing what I was getting myself into. My son was happy when I told him we were going to see Monsieur Caro again.

We were early, and so we snuck into a café. It was raining, and the city finally felt a little cooler.

'How did the rook move again, Mum?'

'I don't know, but you can ask Monsieur Caro.'

My son sipped his juice.

'Why do they have those hats on their heads?' he asked, pointing to a boy in a kippah passing the café.

'Because they're Jewish, their religion is called Judaism. They believe in Jesus, but not that he's God's son. The hat they wear is called a kippah. They wear it to show that they're Jewish and that they have respect for God.'

'Judaism?'

I nodded. My son took another big sip of juice and I looked into his curious brown child's eyes.

*

I automatically entered the door code. The door buzzed open and we stepped inside and crossed the courtyard. Monsieur Caro's window was open, and we could hear laughter and voices up above. I smiled to my son, who didn't seem the least bit bothered that apparently there were a number of people inside Monsieur Caro's apartment.

'Imagine if we see that green lady with no shoes again, Mum.'

Since Monsieur Caro had explained he was inviting a few other friends over, I thought I had prepared myself for all eventualities, but now it felt like absolutely anything could happen. The front door was half open, and a small boy around my son's age was busy putting on his shoes.

'Kippah,' my son whispered, discreetly pointing to the boy.

The boy greeted us politely and then rushed downstairs. Since the door was open, I paused for a moment and didn't know whether we should knock or just go straight in. My son had already gone ahead, and so I followed him.

He seemed to feel much more comfortable than I did, and he led me down the hallway and into the living room. But then he stopped. He probably hadn't expected to see so many people. A few were standing, others sitting, but they were all engaged in various discussions. The apartment smelled of food and cigarette smoke. There was no sign of Monsieur Caro. My son looked up at me and I knew it was my responsibility to try to make him feel comfortable. I took his hand.

'Let's see if we can find your chess mentor. He might be hiding in the kitchen.'

We pushed our way through the room. Most people paid no notice to us, but those that did smiled warmly. A few placed their hands on my son's head as we passed.

'There she is!' a man suddenly roared.

The room grew hushed, and everyone looked first at the man who had shouted and then at me. The man had a glass of water in one hand and he was pointing straight at me. I recognised him immediately. It was the man from the graveyard. Monsieur Caro's brother. Though the room was full of people, I felt vulnerable.

'Don't mind him!' I heard Monsieur Caro roar from the kitchen. 'He's not right in the head!'

Monsieur Caro hurried over and guided his brother away; the man didn't put up any resistance.

'Monsieur Caro didn't have the option of taking psychology at school,' one of the men closest to me joked, and a few of the others laughed.

He quickly returned.

'Welcome,' he said, wiping his brow. 'Please, sit down.'

'Where did your brother go?'

'I locked him in the bathroom.'

I started to doubt it was a good idea to have brought my son here.

'I'm joking. You've got no sense of humour, woman. I sat him down with his favourite puzzle in the bedroom. I hear you had a nice meeting in the graveyard.'

Monsieur Caro smiled.

'Yes, you like the dramatics in your family.'

'Yes, yes, yes . . . Come on, let's have a game. I've set up the chessboard in the kitchen, so we can skip that,' Monsieur Caro said, putting an arm around my son.

My security blanket, my son, was suddenly gone, and I was left alone in the living room. No one had reacted badly to the brother's outburst. Maybe it was a common occurrence. I moved over to the window and looked out as though it was the first time I had been to the apartment.

'Good evening, madame. I had no idea Monsieur Caro knew such beautiful women.'

The man who had come over was in his fifties, and he was wearing a black hat from beneath which his long side locks stuck out. We shook hands.

'Can I get you anything?'

I hadn't noticed what the others were drinking, so I didn't know how to reply. He seemed to detect my nerves, and he asked me to wait while he went to fetch something nice from the kitchen. He quickly returned with a small glass.

'How do you know Monsieur Caro?'

It struck me that I didn't know what Monsieur Caro had chosen to say about how we had met.

'I bumped into him outside, by coincidence. He wasn't well, so I helped him get to the hospital.'

'That was sweet of you. And I'm sure you never got as much as a thank you for it. He has a big heart, however hard that might be to believe at times. I'm an old friend of his. We've lived in the same building for almost twenty-five years. We often play chess or go for a stroll together. Or else we go to the synagogue here in the neighbourhood. Would you like me to introduce you to my wife?'

'Yes, please, that would be nice. I don't know anyone here.'

'I think she's preparing the food in the kitchen.'

I suddenly realised that I should have brought something with me, and I sipped the drink I had been given. The man and I pushed our way over to the kitchen. There were three women inside, all brushing egg wash onto dumplings. My son and Monsieur Caro were sitting at the little kitchen table. It felt good to see my son, but he hadn't noticed me.

'Anne,' the man shouted, and one of the women wiped her hands on her apron as though she knew she was about to meet someone.

Anne was pretty, and at least ten years younger than her husband. She had lively, warm eyes.

'Nice to meet you,' she said, holding out a hand.

'She's the one who saved Monsieur Caro's life.'

Maybe most of them knew what had happened in the graveyard that day. Maybe they all knew who I was.

'Can I help you with anything?' I asked Anne.

'I think everything is ready, we can start taking the food out to the big table.'

There were five large plates with various small dumplings on them. Another woman smiled at me, and a third handed me one of the plates.

'Just put it down out there. It's not too hot, so you can put it straight on the table.'

Once I had carried the plates out, I sat down on the sofa and got into a discussion with a man who had plenty to say about the Marais district. Suddenly, I had the sense that someone was watching me, and I glanced to one side. There was Edith Prévost. I was happy to see her, and I may have smiled a little too much. She gave me a startled look and I decided to pretend I hadn't seen her unless she made contact herself. My conversation partner changed frequently. The sun had started to set outside, and my son came back from the kitchen and glanced around the room. I waved him over and he crept up onto my knee on the sofa.

'Who won?' I asked.

'Monsieur Caro.'

'Couldn't you let a little boy win?' a man said to Monsieur Caro, who was now sitting in his armchair.

'Why would I do that? It's a nonsense to give in to kids. If you want to create a weakling, you'll let him win.'

'What is that, Mum?' my son asked, pointing to the dumplings.

'It's bread with meat inside. Chicken, I think, and the others are sweet, full of apricots and almond paste. We can go if you like.'

'Soon,' he said, taking one of the chicken dumplings.

Huge bowls of salad appeared, paper plates were handed out, and I realised that the dumplings had only been a snack.

'I want to go now,' said my son.

We got up to say goodbye to Monsieur Caro at the very moment his brother came out of the bedroom.

'We just wanted to say goodbye and thanks so much for everything. You'll have to come over to our apartment next time.'

'Are you leaving just because Daniel is here? I can send him back,' Monsieur Caro replied from his seat of honour.

'No, no, we were going anyway.'

The brother paused next to us.

'She's the one who put flowers on Mother's grave,' he said listlessly.

'I know. Nothing to worry about, we can't keep track of what all the madmen and women get up to in this city,' Monsieur Caro replied with a wink at my son.

I gave Monsieur Caro two kisses on the cheek and we removed ourselves from the murmur, the laughter, the food and the madness. Suddenly, I felt a hand on my shoulder.

'Thank you,' Edith whispered before she disappeared back into the room.

The telephone rings a couple of times. It's Mancebo's suppliers, wanting the week's payment. Three children come into the shop to ask for Chinese notebooks. Mancebo thinks he recognises them and suspects that they've been in for them before, but he wouldn't dare swear on it. There's so much going on in his head right now. Before the children leave, he counts the notebooks: there are seven left. He's handed out sixty-two of them, so it's probably not so strange that a few children might be back for a second helping.

Tariq rushes in.

'Hello, brother, time to get started then. Tough life.'

Mancebo doesn't reply. Tariq crosses the boulevard and unlocks his cobbler's shop while he exchanges a few words with the baker. Everything is just like normal. Mancebo glances at his watch and writes down his latest observations, then he carefully stashes everything back beneath the till.

Tariq is cutting a key and Mancebo is rocking on his stool. It's back in its new position, and he peers up towards the balcony to see whether he can see Fatima, or at least her hand. To his horror, when his eyes return to the street, he sees the two men who attacked him approaching. Before he has time to really panic, they go into the cobbler's shop. Mancebo watches Tariq put down whatever he was holding and welcome the two men into his office.

Mancebo gets up from his stool and gets ready to run, if necessary. But just as quickly as the men arrived, they're back out on the street, and they disappear in the direction of the metro. Each is carrying a shoebox beneath his arm. Tariq never usually invites customers into his office. My cousin knows the men who attacked me, Mancebo suddenly realises, and he wipes the sweat from his forehead. He'll have to have the conversation with Amir tonight. It can't wait any longer.

'I'm just going to sell the lot and move soon.'

'Where? Saudi Arabia?'

François seems genuinely interested in where Tariq might go.

'Yeah, why not? This is no good, shoes and keys, no way.'

Mancebo studies his cousin and swallows a sip of pastis. He knows Tariq. Something is bothering him.

'I should just bloody do it now. Sell all the crap here and take off. Live on the money as long as I can and hope more starts coming in soon.'

'What about Adèle?'

'Well, what does she do here that she couldn't in Saudi Arabia?'

That last point is true.

'Maybe you'll end up having to send money to your cousin, Mancebo?'

Mancebo hasn't been part of the discussion so far, but François draws him in and Mancebo shudders at the thought of having to share his money with Tariq and Adèle. It's something he feels slightly ashamed of. Family should always be there for one another.

'Yeah, but business will have to get a bit better first. Have you heard the story about the scorpion who wanted to cross the river?'

Both men, Tariq and François, shake their heads and seem genuinely interested in what Mancebo has to say, or maybe they're just happy to move on from the discussion about skydiving schools in Saudi Arabia.

'Once upon a time, there was a scorpion who wanted to cross a river, but, of course, he couldn't swim. So he asked a frog if it couldn't carry him across on its back. "You'll just sting me," the frog replied. "I'd never do that," said the scorpion, "I'd drown too. I'm not that stupid." So the frog buys the scorpion's argument and starts swimming out into the river with the insect on its back. But as they reach the middle, the scorpion stings the frog. Just as they're both about to drown, the frog asks: "Why did you do that? Now you're going to die too." And the scorpion replies: "Sorry, but it's in my nature."'

Tariq nods.

'You're saying I don't have any choice in the matter, that I might just be going on a whim, but that it's in my nature to take off, even if I'll drag someone else down with me. Damn good story.'

Mancebo doesn't understand Tariq's interpretation of the tale about the scorpion. He mostly told it for himself. He needs to get into the cobbler's shop to find out what's really going on there. It's in his nature, as a private detective, to investigate and get to the truth, even if it involves risk. Even if it sinks his cousin. He has no choice. Mancebo makes up his mind to talk to Amir that evening.

It falls like dirty snow, ash floating down through the air. The gold-clad hand taps the cigarette up on the balcony. Mancebo could catch her red-handed. He wouldn't even need to go up to the apartment to surprise her. Shouting would be enough. She would hear him from where she's sitting above him. But something tells him he should keep this to himself. Amir knows, but that's where it'll have to stop.

Rather than stay in his seat beneath the degrading shower of ash, Mancebo goes into the shop and starts pricing some bottles of ketchup which arrived earlier that day. He sees Tariq raise his hand in greeting. It can't be aimed at anyone but Fatima. So, he knows too. Mancebo starts to feel weak, he wishes the day was over already.

Everyone knows, but no one knows that he knows. That gives him the advantage, but it's difficult to run at the head of the pack. It's hard work seeing reality as clearly as Mancebo does.

Mancebo knocks on Amir's door, though he feels a little hesitant. He doesn't really want to draw his son any further into this mess, but he has no choice.

'Yeah?'

Mancebo notes that Amir doesn't say 'come in', and as a result he remains outside.

'What is it?'

'Can I come in?'

It takes a while before Amir appears in the doorway, and Mancebo notices that his son's face is slightly flushed. He wonders why.

'Do you have a minute? There's just something I wanted to ask you about.'

Amir shrugs. Mancebo doesn't just start to doubt his plans, but the whole of humanity. What on earth am I about to do, he wonders.

Eventually, he sits down on the bed without waiting for Amir's invitation. A couple of fire engines pass by outside, hurling their deafening sirens into the room where father and son are sitting at opposite ends of the bed. Words will soon start flying over the blue bedding, words which form the start of the end of one story and the beginning of a completely different one. They hear Fatima open the window to let in some cool air. I lear her pacing back and forth, puffing and panting. She does it every evening, but they've never noticed it as intensely as they do now. Amir's cheeks start to return to their normal colour, and the honking of the fire engines disappears into the darkness. Maybe they've reached their destination, somewhere in the Paris night.

'OK, what is it?'

Amir sounds tired, and Mancebo thinks about how that isn't a good basis for an important conversation. The task he wants to propose to Amir will require the utmost in energy and commitment, everything depends on him.

Suddenly, the door flies open. Both men jump. Fatima takes the liberty of coming into the room without knocking. She holds out a couple of freshly ironed shirts. Amir gets up and takes them with outstretched arms, as though Fatima was handing him a baby.

'What are you sitting in here for?'

Mancebo looks up at his big wife and then at his son. It's hard to believe that little Amir is this woman's child.

'Dad wanted to know how the English test for studying abroad went.'

Fatima looks at Mancebo, who stares straight back at her. For a few seconds, their eyes are locked in battle. But what is it they're fighting for? Fatima closes the door.

'Thanks.'

'Thanks for what?' Amir asks, sounding resigned.

'The English test.'

Amir shrugs.

'How did it go then?'

Amir shrugs again.

'We get the results tomorrow.'

Mancebo knows that Amir is tired and wants to sleep. The last thing he wants is for his father to come into his room and ask about obscure authors and deliver information about Fatima's breakfast and smoking habits. But Mancebo has no choice. It's just a matter of starting.

'OK, I wanted to ask you for a favour. I need certain information from Tariq's computer.'

Amir's tired eyes widen.

'And I think, or I'm afraid, that you're the only one who can help me.'

'Why?'

Mancebo wonders whether he should answer any questions as he goes along, or whether he should just continue his exposition.

'I suspect, or rather I know, that Tariq is involved in some kind of dodgy dealings. It's not really my problem, but you know, he's still my cousin, we work and live so close to one another. And I'm worried that if he gets into trouble with . . . the police, the law, then it might also affect us. I just want to find out what's going on, so I can work out what I need to do to help him.'

'And you think you can find the answers on his computer? What are we talking about here? Cheating on his taxes? I doubt I'll be able to see that kind of thing.'

Now it's Mancebo's time to shrug.

'I don't know. And maybe I'm wrong.'

Amir looks at his father. 'Just think, Mum smokes,' he suddenly says.

Fatima is sleeping when Mancebo returns from Amir's room. It strikes Mancebo that she might have hung around outside his door and eavesdropped on them. But when he catches sight of her looking like a beached walrus in the bed, he realises she must have been asleep for some time. She probably went straight to bed after handing over the clean, freshly ironed shirts. And the idea that she might be pretending to sleep is out of the question. No one pretending to sleep could look so grotesque.

Mancebo rests his head on the pillow and runs his hand through his beard. He's set the ball rolling. In a few hours' time, the operation will start, and it'll be over in less than a day.

I could feel that it was the last day in every inch of my body. Strange, since such charged days tend to lose all sense of what makes them remarkable when they finally roll around. Never before had the water in the shower felt so purifying. Never before had the colour of the shower gel been so bright, never had it smelled so good, never had I made a coffee with so much attention. I chose my clothes carefully. The same clothes as the first day. I was ready to draw a line under things. I was well prepared for something you couldn't prepare for.

When I come to pick you up, I thought as I kissed my son's soft cheek, it'll all be over. The next time I put my key into the lock, I might know who Monsieur Bellivier is, and maybe I'll understand what I've been doing these past few weeks. Maybe I'll be surprised, tired, happy, sad, afraid, disappointed ... I'll feel something, anyway. How many days, weeks, months has it been since I last felt a thing as I unlocked this door?

The neighbour's dog barked goodbye as I pressed the button for the lift.

The metro quickly came thundering into the station, and I managed to find a seat. I could see my face in the windowpane. I looked tired. Final stop. Several hundred people left the train together. Some half ran, maybe they were late for a meeting, stressed about tasks of more or less importance. I took it easy and politely greeted the florist as I passed, but then turned back after a few steps to ask him a question.

'It's the last bouquet today, isn't it?'

He looked thoughtful, as though he was wondering whether that was information he could give out or not.

'That's right,' he eventually replied.

I smiled. It felt good to know. That was coming to an end, at the very least. I started walking towards Areva.

'Madame!'

I turned around.

'If I were you, I would be . . . careful.'

'Careful?'

'Yes, though maybe discreet is a better word.'

'Discreet?'

The florist looked embarrassed and self-conscious.

'I mean, if you've got a devoted admirer, there might be others who don't like it.'

A customer appeared, wanting to look at some of the flowers, and the florist seemed relieved that he wouldn't have to explain what he had just said. I hesitated for a moment. Why had he said that? Was it just that he thought the entire situation was insane, anonymously delivering flowers to someone every day, and therefore took it for granted that Monsieur Bellivier must be crazy?

I had to leave to avoid being late.

I stared up at the huge Areva tower. It looked dark up at the top. The woman in reception greeted me politely. Nothing about her suggested it was going to be a special day. As I stepped into the office, horizontal rain began to thud against the window, and it made me happy. It was raining on my last day. That was fitting. Good reading weather, I told myself, double-checking that the box was still full of polystyrene chips before I turned on the computer and opened Judith's last diary from captivity. 'She's writing to survive,' ran through my mind. There was a *pling*. I read the string of numbers carefully to make sure I wasn't missing any message about what might happen today, but the numbers revealed nothing about the end.

I had made it halfway through the diary. Judith still wasn't free, but judging by the date, it wouldn't be long. I wasn't all that familiar with the literature of the time, which meant I had no real idea whether I was in possession of unique material or not. Many of the Germans were mentioned by name, so maybe there was some value in that? And after reading a paragraph in which one of Judith's patients told her in detail how he had tortured three Jews, I looked up and watched the rain drumming against the window. As Judith wrote about the car pulling up in the yard and the way she left the camp, I closed the book. Odd that Monsieur Caro had been able to tell the story with such clarity. He must have read the diaries a number of times.

It was time for lunch. Despite the rain, I wanted to get out. I had to go to the church. I shut down the computer, packed Judith's diaries into the canvas bag and left the office.

The rain whipped at my face as I ran into the church and bumped into the priest, who was just on his way up to the main hall. It was the first time I had ever seen him there. We said hello and I hoped he wasn't on his way to a funeral or Mass. But the church was empty. No ceremony, no one praying, and no Christophe. I sat down at the very back, and clasped my hands for the first time, mostly to see how it felt. But it felt completely wrong, and I gently lowered my hands to my lap and looked down at them. It was empty without him.

Just a few hours of this strange story left. I was sitting with my eyes closed, feeling proud of myself, of everything I had done and managed these past few weeks. His laughter shattered the magical atmosphere. Christophe seemed to be in a great mood. We greeted one another with two kisses on the cheek.

'Has something happened? You seem so happy.'

'I'm happy to see you here. In church. Imagine, you find your own way here now.'

'But I have to leave soon.'

'Oh God, you always have to see everything from the dark side.'

I felt ashamed. We'd had discussions about ourselves in the past, but the sentences we had just exchanged were probably the most personal thing we'd ever said. They meant so much more. I had rushed there in the rain to make the most of every second with Christophe. He had been happy when he arrived, and I made him sad.

'Do you think I see everything as black because I don't have any faith?' I asked honestly.

Christophe didn't reply.

'Speaking of faith, do you know where I've been? At a Jewish party.'

'Does it have anything to do with Judith?'

'Why should it?'

'Last time we met you talked about the book Judith had written, and then you go to a Jewish party. There could be a link.'

'Yes, in a way, but not quite . . .'

'Is there anyone who understands you?'

I mustered what little strength I could, looked him in the eye and shook my head. We sat in silence, we grew closer. I got up and said I had to go.

The rain continued to drum against the window. The sound felt uncomfortable now. What would I do if no more emails arrived? If no one got in touch before the end of the day? What would I do if I didn't get my money? Nothing. And what would I do on Monday? The money hadn't been the driving force behind everything, but it would feel slightly sad if I wasn't going to be paid after all. I heard a *pling*. The largest of Pavlov's dogs woke up. A string of numbers. Possibly the last. The rain stopped suddenly. It went from sounding like a machine gun pointed at the window to complete silence. The end. Loneliness. Sacré-Cœur was bathed in a grey haze. Paris looked more like a battlefield beneath my feet than a romantic big city. I headed towards the lift, turned off and passed the other offices. All equally empty. Why did no one use this floor, when every square metre in the business district was so fiercely sought after?

As I finished my lap of the floor and approached my door, I heard another *pling*. The emails didn't usually arrive so close to one another. My heart was pounding. This time, there was no string of numbers. 'Are you waiting for Monsieur Bellivier? Let's say four o'clock by reception. Just leave the computer, lock the door and bring the key.' So, all I had to do was lock up and go. That was it. In forty-seven minutes, I would be meeting someone. Monsieur Bellivier, perhaps. Or maybe someone else. There would be an ending.

The choice of location, by reception, managed to calm me down despite everything. In my imagination, it had always been in completely different places. At a bar in Paris, somewhere I wasn't familiar with, sometimes even in different countries.

I packed up my own computer and moved around the room like a prisoner during exercise hour.

Though I'd had almost an hour to prepare my exit, I realised that I was already four minutes late. I started to shiver, which was a clear sign that I was nervous. I locked the door and double-checked that Judith's books were in the canvas bag. The lift seemed to take forever. Six minutes late. Reception was unusually busy. Maybe because it was Friday, some people left earlier, others treated themselves to an afternoon coffee. I suddenly worried that my pass wouldn't work. That it might have a best-before date, which had expired six minutes earlier. But it beeped like always and the green light came on. I immediately felt like I was being watched, but I couldn't tell from which direction.

I sat down on one of the benches by the window. Whoever had

sent the email would be able to see me without me having to make an effort to be seen.

'Xavier Rossi,' a man said politely.

The man who had come into the café a few weeks earlier smiled as we shook hands.

I got up.

'Helena Folasadu.'

'How does it feel?'

I didn't quite understand the question, and I gave him a quizzical look.

'How does it feel to be free?'

I didn't know what to say. Since I still hadn't been given any explanation, I wasn't free. And he seemed to understand that.

'Maybe we should start with the most important thing.'

He opened a black plastic folder and took out a cheque for the amount which had been written in the contract.

'This is for you. And this, too.'

He took out another cheque, but then changed his mind and put both back into the folder.

'I should probably explain first. The first cheque is your payment. It's all yours. Just needs to be cashed. You'll also be given another one, but you need to use that one, or use the money, more accurately.'

He sighed.

'I'm not very good at explaining, even though I did practise at home.'

In his uncertainty, he was simply tightening the noose he was trying to loosen. I'd been expecting answers to my big questions first.

'OK, I've had the exact same task as you. It's like . . . a chain letter, I suppose you could say. And now it's your job to find your successor. The first cheque is your payment. But you'll also be given a second one, and you need to use it. Your successor needs to have something delivered to them every day.'

'The flowers?'

He nodded.

'But it can be anything.'

'What did you get?'

I don't really know why I asked. There were probably more relevant questions, but in a way I was trying to make the mystery more manageable.

'Bottles of wine.'

'Flowers are healthier, then.'

'Yes, and let me tell you, I'm tired of red wine from Bordeaux.'

We laughed. It was as though we were playing some kind of party game. Taking turns to roll the dice and being drawn deeper and deeper into a game with unusual rules.

'So you can choose who your successor is, and what he or she will receive after each day's work.'

I noticed that the cheques had been made out by a Monsieur Bellivier, and that the line for the recipient's name was empty.

'And then there's this.'

He took out an envelope and handed it to me.

'In this envelope, there's an extra key which you need to keep, plus the contract. It contains the start and end date for whoever you choose. When you bring the new person here, there'll be a pass for him or her at reception. You keep your pass. On the last day, you come back at 16.00, like I did, and you collect a plastic pouch from reception. Inside it, there'll be two cheques and a new contract. And now you've got everything you need. All the information. You just need to find someone new. You know how I did it. You do it however you want.'

Monsieur Rossi fell silent.

'Who is Monsieur Bellivier?'

He shrugged.

'I know as much as you.'

'But his address is on the cheques.'

'I know. I went there, but I couldn't find anyone by that name.'

'Who knows?'

'What do you mean?' he asked, sounding surprised.

'The woman at reception?'

'I don't know. What do you think?'

'She must know. How else could she go along with delivering things? And what about the cleaner?'

'I think we're all doing things where we don't know, or understand, what they'll lead to. I think we're all just carrying out meaningless tasks. We're probably all employees of Monsieur Bellivier.'

I hadn't seen it like that. But I knew that he'd had more time to think over his time at Areva. I was still in it.

'What do you think of it all? Now that you've had time to reflect on it,' I asked.

'Don't know. Maybe I've realised that we have a real bloody duty to make the most of our experiences. You don't need to have gone through anything dramatic to be able to utilise them. You don't need to have come close to death to appreciate life. I'm leaving for Chile tonight. A long trip. The idea took root while I was forwarding those meaningless messages. I know I need to go. My biological father lives there.'

'Yeah, I don't know what I've learnt or how I should make use of this odd experience,' I said.

'Write a book.'

We headed towards the revolving doors.

'Madame!'

The receptionist smiled as I took the bouquet.

Monsieur Rossi and I walked out into the rain.

'I'm going that way,' he said, pointing towards the taxi rank.

'Here,' I said, holding out the flowers.

'No, it would be a shame. I'm going away.'

'We all are.'

In the end, he took the flowers and hopped into a taxi.

Before I left Areva, I cast a glance back towards reception and saw the cleaner emptying a bin. She looked up, but I don't know if she saw me, her eyes were so crossed. I decided I had to say goodbye to her.

'Afternoon, I just wanted to say goodbye. I won't be coming to the top floor any more.'

She glanced up and gave me a look which said that I shouldn't poke my little nose into other people's business.

Tariq charges down into the shop. If only he knew what the day would have in store, Mancebo thinks, stashing the day's post beneath the till.

'Wait, brother, before you run off, I need to ask you a favour.'

Tariq pauses, places a hand on the counter and waits impatiently for the question.

'Amir needs to borrow your computer today. I don't know why exactly, but I think it's to check some kind of exam result, for studying abroad, and there's such a long wait for computers at the library. Is it OK if he stops by sometime before lunch?'

Tariq seems relieved, as though he had been expecting something completely different, less agreeable.

'Sure, I'm always happy to help the boy, you know that.'

'Thanks.'

'But listen, when're you going to get yourself a computer? You know Raphaël can help with that kind of thing. It'd be good for the boy to have the Internet at home.'

'Yes, there'll be a time for that,' Mancebo says with a smile.

Tariq waves goodbye, and Mancebo takes out a knife and opens the day's post.

It's approaching lunchtime when Amir appears. Everything happens very quickly. Too quickly for Mancebo to keep up. He is busy serving an old woman when Amir waves to him from the other side of the boulevard. As Mancebo listens to the old lady's ailments, he tries to see how his son is getting on, and by the time she leaves the shop, he sees that Amir has already positioned himself behind the computer in the office. Tariq is in the room with him, keeping himself busy. Every now and then, he positions himself behind Amir and points at the screen. Both laugh. Mancebo is nervous. If Amir doesn't find out the password, the whole plan will fail. Mancebo knows that he has set a huge ball rolling.

The scent of cooking makes its way down to the shop, time for lunch. Amir gets up and moves away from the computer. He and Tariq exchange a few words, and then Amir comes out onto the street. Mancebo starts to despair. But then Amir bends down and ties his shoelace. That's the sign. The task was a success. And with that, the plan moves into its second phase. Mancebo closes up the fruit and vegetable stands, and Tariq casts a quick glance at his cousin. He realises it's time for lunch.

Everyone is already at the table by the time Mancebo makes it upstairs. Amir ignores his father, out of fear that someone might see they have something on the go. But in reality, there still isn't anything to reveal. The game has only just begun. Fatima waves away a couple of flies which have landed on the table.

'We need to go and buy food today.'

Her words are directed at Adèle. Once a week, the two women take their trolley bags up to Franprix to buy everything Mancebo can't get hold of at Rungis. It's the only thing the two women do together other than visiting the hammam on Sundays. And their breakfasts, of course.

Amir casts a glance at his father. Mancebo knows why. He's worried that Fatima and Adèle's chores will hinder their plan. But over the past few weeks, Mancebo has developed the ability to think on his feet, and before Fatima even has time to finish her sentence,

Mancebo realises that this new information doesn't change a thing. In fact, it could be good for Fatima and Adèle to disappear for an hour or two. At worst, they'll leave or come back while Amir is in the cobbler's shop. But even that scenario wouldn't be a disaster.

Their plan also accounts for the worst, and slightly unlikely, prospect of Tariq deciding to leave Le Soleil early. If that happens, Mancebo will have his mobile phone with him, and he'll call the cobbler's shop. Mancebo nods calmly and hopes Amir will understand the gesture and feel less stressed. Amir breathes out and helps himself to a piece of freshly baked bread.

Lunch passes relatively painlessly for Mancebo. Though he has plenty on his mind, he manages to enjoy the food. But when the oranges appear at the table, his pleasant calm is disrupted.

'No pastries today?' Tariq asks when he spots the fruit.

'No, because someone in this house has to think of our health. There's enough smoking and eating pastries as it is. You need to look after yourselves a bit better, you're not spring chickens any more. Fewer cigarettes and a bit more fruit won't do any harm.'

Fatima cuts the oranges into slices, puts them back onto the plate and then offers it around as though she was distributing medicine. Mancebo suddenly feels a lump in his throat. All the times Fatima has rapped his fingers when he tried to light one cigarette over his daily allowance now feel like a slap in the face. Why on earth is she doing this to me? Why does my family have so many secrets? Tariq smirks as the plate reaches him, and he takes a handful.

The plate approaches Mancebo. The orange-coloured slices look like sneering mouths. Mouths laughing at the way he is being kept in the dark. Mouths whispering secrets he isn't allowed to hear. Mouths screaming that he's being deceived. Everyone knows Fatima's secrets. And the conversation they recently had was solely to make fun of Mancebo's ignorance. He knows that. Mancebo takes the plate from Fatima, who can't move around the table with it herself, and he passes it on to Adèle without taking any orange. Adèle takes the plate with bewildered eyes. She seems to be wondering why he hasn't taken any, but she doesn't say anything. Mancebo is grateful for that. No one else has noticed that he isn't eating dessert.

A girl and a boy come into the shop. Mancebo says hello to both of them, he knows exactly what they want. He's learnt to recognise the look that those who want the Chinese notebooks have. The phone rings and Mancebo picks up. It's someone trying to sell a new card machine.

'No, thanks, I have one which works. But you don't sell those devices for checking notes, do you?'

Silence on the other end of the line.

'You know, for checking whether they're genuine or not,' Mancebo continues.

'No, I'm calling from Cebex, we make card machines.'

'You don't know where I can turn, do you? If I want one of the machines for checking notes, one of those lamps?'

'No, monsieur, I can't help you with that.'

'Thanks anyway, and have a good afternoon.'

Mancebo turns to the children.

'You want two notebooks? Am I right?'

They nod. Mancebo searches beneath the counter. There aren't many left now. He finds a dragon and a tiger, and places them into a bag along with the pack of chewing gum they want to buy. They hand him the right change and then run out of the shop. They practically crash into Fatima and Adèle, who are standing just outside ready to go to Franprix. Adèle waves and Fatima smiles at Mancebo, and then they head off to do their shopping. Mancebo sees his chance. Tariq has come out onto the street to wave to his wife on the other side of the boulevard.

'What do you say, brother, should we follow our wives' example and fly the nest?'

Mancebo doesn't normally shout straight across the boulevard, but he has no choice. It might be a little too early for a drink, but he can't let this opportunity go to waste. This way, Amir can carry out his task in peace and quiet.

Before they turn off the boulevard on their way to Le Soleil, Mancebo casts a glance back towards his apartment, but there's no sign of Amir. He feels a pang of anxiety. Could he have missed Tariq leaving? Or has he already noticed, and now he's getting ready to carry out his task, making sure that not even a second goes to waste? Once they get to Le Soleil, Mancebo tries to gain some time by starting a meaningless discussion about the new pension reforms with François.

'It doesn't bloody affect us, we don't drive buses or trains, do we?' Tariq grunts, hinting that it's time to go back.

The two men thank François and head out into the heat.

During the afternoon, Tariq closes up shop twice to sit down at the computer in his office. Mancebo consciously stops himself from devoting any effort to working out what he is doing. Whatever it is, he'll find out that evening, so why waste energy on guesswork? His work has to come first now. No one is paying him to spy on his cousin.

The thought that Tariq might suspect someone has been inside his shop that afternoon strikes Mancebo, but he decides not to worry about that either. It makes no difference whether he suspects anything. Amir could just say he had forgotten a book in the office and gone back to pick it up. They keep a spare key for the cobbler's in the apartment. No one would suspect a thing. Just like no one would suspect an old man outside a grocer's shop of spying. People aren't always who we think they are.

It's always the same at dinner whenever the two women have been out shopping. The table is groaning beneath the fresh goods. The usual stew is replaced by salad, the rich sauces by light yoghurt dressings, and, in honour of the day, fresh tuna steaks which don't seem to bear any relation to the usual chunks out of cans.

'This is the opposite of fireworks,' Tariq says after studying one delicious thing after another.

Adèle looks up at him as though she doesn't quite understand what he is talking about.

'I mean that with fireworks, you start gently and then have a crescendo at the end. But you two do the opposite. The day you've been shopping, you go big straight away and then we end with simplicity.'

Adèle is looking for Fatima's support, which comes quickly.

'What does the man mean by that? Isn't he happy with the food? He can cook his own dinner if he'd rather.'

Fatima sounds angry as she tries to give Tariq a telling-off. But you never know with her, she can sound furious even when she's joking. Tariq glances at Mancebo for support, but he gets none. The men at the table don't stick together like the women do. And one of the men, Amir, doesn't even seem to be in agreement with himself. Pale and silent, he helps himself to some avocado salad.

The sight of Amir gives Mancebo mixed feelings. First, relief that he knows the plan was a success. It seems as though Amir has found something. But Mancebo is also slightly anxious about what he will find out later, and how Amir will take it.

Suddenly, Amir gets up and thanks the women for the food, despite the fact that both Adèle and Fatima are still eating.

'I feel a bit rough. I think I'm going to go up and get some sleep, if you don't mind.'

Amir's words go relatively unnoticed. Fatima mumbles something about the English exam having taken it out of him, and Adèle says goodnight as he leaves the room and the apartment. At first, Mancebo thinks that leaving the table early is a conscious move on Amir's part. Though they never agreed on it, he might want Mancebo to follow him up so that they have time to talk. But the more he thinks about it, the more convinced he is that Amir genuinely doesn't feel well. Whether that has anything to do with his task, Mancebo isn't sure.

Mancebo stays for a while, and then gets up and excuses himself, saying he's going to check on his son. No one raises an eyebrow, and he leaves them during a heated discussion about recycling.

The apartment is dark. Mancebo closes the door, and before he goes over to Amir's room he pauses in the living room and looks out towards the dark apartment opposite.

'Black, black, black like the cat,' he whispers to himself without really knowing why.

He peers down at the small, pink, glittery bird on the chest of drawers and then confidently moves over to Amir's closed door. He knocks. No answer. Mancebo is convinced that Amir is sleeping, maybe he really is ill. That, in turn, may mean he wasn't able to complete the task after all.

Mancebo can't blame his son, not under any circumstances. He's already asked too much of him, he knows that. He has placed too big a burden on Amir's slender shoulders. Mancebo knocks again. No answer. Worried about his son, he takes hold of the door handle and discovers, to his surprise, that it's locked. He can't remember Amir ever having locked his door before. No one locks doors in this apartment. They don't even lock the toilet door, something their guests have often complained about. Mancebo knocks again.

'Amir? Are you there?'

No answer. He knocks and pulls at the door handle. He listens. Silence. All he can hear is Adèle's laughter from the floor below.

'Amir, please, open the door, I'm worried.'

Just as he is about to head to the kitchen to grab something to open the door, it swings open and Mancebo sees Amir making his way back to bed.

His son lies down on his back and stares up at the ceiling. Mancebo has forgotten all about the task, he's just happy to see his son. He sits down on the bed, hesitates for a few seconds and then strokes Amir's cheek. He was worried that Amir would flinch, but he actually seems to appreciate it.

'How are you?'

Amir doesn't react. His cheeks have regained some of their usual colour, and Mancebo can detect a hint of anger in his eyes.

'Why did you lock the door?'

Amir sits up and gives his father an accusatory look.

'Maybe we all should.'

Amir gets up from the bed and walks over to the window. Mancebo is silent, because he knows that Amir needs time to gather himself. After a while, he turns around and comes back to sit on the bed next to Mancebo, who attempts a smile. It's not too successful. Amir is about to start talking, but he stops himself and moves over to the desk instead. He reaches as far as he can underneath it and pulls out one of the Chinese notebooks. At first, Mancebo doesn't react, he's used to seeing them everywhere, every day. But then he freezes. Amir realises what it is immediately.

'Oh, sorry. I saw a few of these under the till and took one to use. Is that OK?'

Mancebo quickly comes back to his senses and looks up at his son with pride. Of course a person needs a notebook for an important job. The murmur of the discussion below calms them both. It means they can talk without being disturbed. Amir opens the notebook and then snaps it shut again.

'First of all, everything went to plan. I went over there this morning and Tariq was happy to help me. I pretended to be reading the school website, the test results and that kind of thing. He had a few customers, and since I didn't have time to catch the password – he was the one who logged in – I turned the computer off and told him

I'd accidentally shut it down. He whispered that the password was under the keyboard. Not very smart.'

Amir falls silent, but Mancebo nods to show that he is keeping up and that his son can go on.

'Anyway, it was there. He changes his password pretty often, he crosses out the old one and writes down the new one. Weird to change so often . . .'

'What's the password?'

Amir leafs through the notebook. He has written down thirty or so words.

'Here are all the ones he's had.'

Mancebo licks his lips and nods again, proud of his little companion who has clearly managed to keep a cool head in a difficult situation. Mancebo reads through the words, scratching his head as he does. Doha, Al-Qahira, Bamako, Ouagadougou, Dubai, Riyadh, Penza . . . He scratches his head again. Amir knows that his father isn't exactly a geography buff and gives him a helping hand.

'The majority are cities in the Arab world, but there are also a few in Africa and even some in Russia.'

Though the names fascinate Mancebo, he's well aware that he shouldn't come to any hasty conclusions. Maybe his cousin has just been picking them from a map he has lying somewhere.

'When I was leaving, I deliberately left a book behind. So I waited here,' Amir points to his desk, 'until Mum and Adèle went to the supermarket. Then I opened the window and heard you shout to Tariq that it was time to go to Le Soleil. We got lucky.'

Amir's face lights up with a childish, slightly excited smile.

'And once you left, I went back over to the cobbler's.'

He falls silent, as though he is afraid to remember.

'Getting into the computer was no problem. And Tariq is sloppy with his documents, no passwords or anything.'

'Documents?'

'Yeah, papers, information, the things on his computer. It was a bit like doing a puzzle, but I think I have everything you need to know. The key for the cabinet was hanging there too . . . there were two shoeboxes at the very bottom, and . . .'

The front door opens.

'My little chicken, how are you feeling?'

It's Fatima's voice, and Amir quickly hands the notebook to his father.

'It's all in here. I wrote down everything first, then a summary. You'll understand.'

Fatima's head appears around the edge of the door. Her gold earrings swing as she speaks.

'My little chicken, how are you? We're just washing up downstairs, but if you're feeling ill I can ask Adèle to do it herself. Do you need anything? A cup of tea?'

Amir shakes his head.

'I just need to sleep, it's been a long day.'

Mancebo closes the notebook he has been reading in the armchair by the window. It was an unparalleled read. Amir's report towers above any crime novel. And all that information just from looking at Tariq's computer. The last few notes were the most shocking thing he has ever read. Amir's description of how he opened one of the shoeboxes in Tariq's cabinet could be the start of a thriller.

Mancebo swallows, he now knows why Amir locked the door to his room. Mancebo knows that he might only have a few minutes, perhaps even seconds, to gather himself before his wife makes her entry. A similar state of shock to the one Amir was in earlier has now dug its claws into Mancebo. He's heard far too many uncomfortable truths about close relatives lately. Dear God, I'm related to that man, Mancebo thinks, staring out towards the cobbler's shop. Thanks to Amir's notes, the place now looks completely different. And he doesn't even want to think about how he'll view his cousin from now on.

Before the door is flung open and Fatima comes in with a couple of pans beneath her arm, Mancebo decides that it's best to try to get to bed as soon as possible. It's the only way he can give himself time to think before the curtain comes up on yet another performance. Because a performance is exactly what it is. Everyone is playing some kind of role. Fatima: the hard-working woman who never has time for breakfast, who's allergic to cigarette smoke and who could never be with another man, not least the tobacconist. But offstage, she's completely different. And Tariq, he's been playing the role of the cheery cobbler who fixes shoes and makes copies of keys, but he is, in fact, an arms dealer. He also has hundreds of cartons of cigarettes stashed away in his office. Those shoeboxes of his contain something very different to shoes.

'That's all I know for now, but I'm not done yet,' Mancebo mumbles quietly to himself.

I won't give up before the truth to this rotten story is out, Mancebo thinks, staring up at the ceiling. Fatima is snoring away next to him. Occasionally, he hears Amir go out into the kitchen to get a glass of water. He doesn't know whether his son is doing it just to convince Fatima that he's ill, or whether he really can't sleep. The last wouldn't be surprising, given the day's events.

Before the sun starts to rise, Mancebo has time to think back to his childhood and how Tariq could have ended up the way he has. Tariq's parents ran a dairy with several hundred goats in Tunisia. They were honourable people. But what do I know, Mancebo thinks, with his hands beneath the pillow. The goats might've been full of smuggled goods.

The district was unfamiliar to me. All Parisians have areas they don't know too well, places they rarely go. The city grows over time. Sacré-Cœur towered up on the horizon. The white church was in a different and, to me, alien neighbourhood: Montmartre.

For many tourists, the area is synonymous with Paris. It's a historic part of the city, but to me, everything there seemed as though it was built for and by our age; it's as though the quarter was made up entirely of backdrops meant to depict the turn of the century, La Belle Époque, a time when the can-can dancers raised their dresses in front of an absinthe-drinking Toulouse-Lautrec as he sat there, discovering the art of the poster.

Cars thundered past along the boulevard. I didn't know what I had expected, but it was probably something more intimate. The idea that Bellivier lived on such a wide boulevard just didn't seem to fit. I realised I was walking around with the cheque in my hand as though it was a GPS. I knew the address by heart, I had been staring at it for hours, so I could have easily stashed the cheque safely in my bag. But I kept it in my hand anyway.

I realised that I was on the wrong side of the boulevard and crossed over to the even numbers. A pink sign bearing a shoe acted as my pole star. Sure enough, it turned out to be number 78, and it was a cobbler's shop. The door was closed.

I cautiously peered in through the window. There was someone towards the back of the shop. Maybe Monsieur Bellivier was a cobbler?

I knocked on the door. The man inside shifted, but he paid no attention to the fact that someone had knocked. I tried again, more firmly this time. A well-built man came to the door. Though he only opened it a fraction, I caught a waft of chemicals, leather and cigarette smoke. The cobbler didn't say anything, he just stared at me. I shoved the cheque into my bag.

'Good morning. I'm looking for a Monsieur Bellivier at this address, I was wondering if you knew who he was?'

The cobbler peered at me with a look that was hard to read. Then he smiled an odd smile, but he still didn't speak.

'Are you Monsieur Bellivier?'

The man wiped the sweat from his brow.

'No, I'm not, and I don't know anyone by that name. But you're not the first person to come here asking. Maybe I should put up a sign saying: "No Monsieur Belliviers here."'

'Yes, maybe you should, because there's a chance there'll be more of us.'

'Who is this Monsieur Bellivier? Why all this chasing after him? Actually, don't tell me, I don't want to be dragged into any of this madness.'

'Who lives above the shop?'

'No one. The apartment's empty. The pharmacy has been using it as a storeroom.'

'What about the apartment above that?'

'No idea. A couple, I think.'

I tried to make out what was behind the cobbler's back. Whether there was anything to suggest he was lying, that he was, in fact, the man I was looking for. But everything looked normal for a cobbler's shop.

'You are Monsieur Bellivier, aren't you?'

It was my last chance. I had nothing to lose by trying. His eyes narrowed.

'Look, madame. I don't know what your problem is, but I'm not open yet and I can't help you. OK?'

'OK. Thanks anyway.'

The man flashed me a fake smile and then closed the door. There was one more possibility – the apartment at the top of the building. I noticed a fire escape to one side of the cobbler's shop, and I took out the cheque as though to justify my behaviour. The stairs were rusty, but there was something charming about them. Maybe because it was something different in the overall picture of the city. Fire escapes like these were common in American cities, but they were unusual in Paris. In some strange way, as I climbed the stairs, I had the feeling I had found the right place.

Here, above the boulevard, I finally experienced the intimate feeling I had been missing since I came up out of the metro. This was somewhere Monsieur Bellivier could live. I was standing in front of a door without a nameplate. Was he just behind it? I glanced down at the boulevard before I knocked. With each knock, my heart started beating harder. Maybe this was how he got hold of his victims? The empty apartment below could be used for all kinds of things. Maybe the pharmacy had left behind some less popular drugs. My imagination ran wild. The cobbler might have a direct staircase up here. I took a step back, with one hand on the railing, the other clutching the cheque like a white flag I could wave in the air. But no one came to the door. That didn't help my nerves.

I knocked once more and then went down to the floor below. Something about the door suggested it hadn't welcomed anyone in a long time. I knocked anyway. Empty apartments were unusual in Paris, which made it all the more interesting.

Above the cobbler's shop, there was a narrow metal roof. Now that I was here, I had to take all the chances I could. If I climbed out onto the roof, I would be able to see into the empty apartment. And without really thinking it through, I ducked beneath the handrail and out onto the roof. The whole time, I was waiting for someone to shout at me and wonder what I was up to. I saw an old lady staring at me, but she chose to continue down the boulevard. She was probably afraid she would have to catch me if I fell. One look through the first window was enough to get a good overview of the entire apartment. It was completely empty. Not a trace of anyone or anything. I carefully made my way back to the fire escape, and with it, safety. I decided not to look down at the boulevard until I was back onto the stairs. My hands were damp with sweat, and that made me happy. It meant I didn't have a death wish.

Once I made it back to the stairs, I turned towards the boulevard as though nothing had happened. Happily, the scenario I had imagined, in which a group of people had gathered beneath my feet, hadn't materialised. But outside a grocer's shop on the other side of the boulevard, I noticed a man in a blue coat studying me through a pair of binoculars.

The man who, just a few seconds earlier, had been standing on the pavement with a pair of binoculars pointed straight at me had his back turned as I came into the greengrocer's. The shop smelled like an unidentifiable herb.

'Hello.'

The man turned around.

'How can I help you in this heat?' he asked.

'Well . . . I was just wondering if you knew who lived in the building opposite, monsieur?'

'Opposite . . . ?'

'Yes, number 78.'

'No, sorry.'

'OK . . . It's just I saw you watching me . . . you were using a pair of binoculars.'

I realised that I had never been closer to the truth than I was now. The little man stared at me with raised eyebrows.

'Are you Monsieur Bellivier?'

'No.'

He said the word no clearly and firmly, as though he was in court and it was of the utmost importance that everyone knew that he was not, under any circumstances, Monsieur Bellivier. His denial felt too firm for me to be able to strike him off the list of suspects.

'Do you know anyone by that name?'

Again, the man said no, this time slightly too confidently to be convincing.

'OK, but you were watching me through your binoculars. Do you often do that to people?'

He seemed to be thinking.

'My name is Monsieur Mancebo.'

I didn't tell him my own name.

'Why is it so important for you to know who lives opposite?' he asked gravely.

I had no choice. If I wanted to find out any more, this was my chance, but it would mean I had to give him something. He was behaving like someone who had something he wanted to say. Suddenly, he was standing with a stool in each hand.

'Let's sit down out here and talk.'

He put down one of the stools and then picked it up and moved it. He did so three times. Obsessive behaviour, I thought, putting on my sunglasses and taking a seat next to him. It felt strange to be sitting next to a strange man, looking at what might be Monsieur Bellivier's home.

'We're discreet,' he said.

I smiled. The entire situation was anything but. Two people sitting on the pavement in the burning heat, staring at a carefully chosen building.

'I'll tell you what I know about the people who live straight across the boulevard if you, madame, let me know why you're interested in knowing. OK?'

And with that, he started to talk.

'The cobbler's name is Tariq. He's my cousin. The apartment above his shop is empty, as I'm sure you saw. The pharmacy further down the street used to use it as a storeroom.'

He paused.

'A certain Ted Baker lives above the empty apartment. He's an English writer, and he lives there with his wife.'

He paused again and I realised that it was my turn to give him something.

'Well, it's a bit complicated . . . For a few weeks, I've been working for someone called Monsieur Bellivier. I've never met him, but he gives this address as his, and . . . I'd like to get in touch with him.'

We sat in silence for a while, but then I took the chance to draw a little more out of him.

'Could your cousin be working on anything you don't know about in secret?'

Monsieur Mancebo remained silent and looked down.

'I don't know. Maybe. We've drifted apart lately.'

'What do you know about Ted Baker?'

'Not much.'

'Why did you say no to the question about knowing who lives there at first?'

'Because I'm working for Ted Baker's wife, it's quite sensitive.'

'What's her name?'

'Madame Cat.'

'Cat? That sounds strange.'

'Why?'

'I mean that if you're married, you usually have the same surname. Ted Baker could be a pseudonym if he's a writer . . . but Cat just sounds weird.'

'Psedadym?'

'Pseudonym. Authors can write under a different name. It's quite common. So you're working for Madame Cat? Doing what?'

There was no doubt that Monsieur Mancebo was debating whether to tell me the truth or not.

'How long have you had your shop?'

The question wasn't really relevant, it was more an attempt to gain his trust, an effort to get closer to him. He chose to answer my previous question instead.

'Madame Cat asked me to spy on her husband. She suspects he is having an affair.'

Though the information wasn't particularly spectacular, I was surprised. Somehow, the man's task sounded closely related to mine. It couldn't be a coincidence that Monsieur Bellivier claimed to live at an address where things like that went on. I was convinced that Madame Cat was the person I was looking for. And as a result, the man by my side became important to me. Suddenly, he jumped and positioned himself right in front of me, blocking out the sun.

'There's Ted Baker going up the stairs,' he whispered

Monsieur Mancebo disappeared into the shop and returned with a spray bottle. He began to spritz the fruit, looking very unnatural as he did it. I watched Monsieur Baker as he went into his apartment. What should I do now? Go and knock? Monsieur Mancebo stopped spraying the fruit and came and sat back down on the stool.

'How are you spying on him?'

'I keep track of when he comes and goes.'

'You've never followed him?'

'Once, in the van.'

I decided to wait a while before I went to knock on the door. But it wasn't long before it opened and Ted Baker was back on the fire escape. I got to my feet and smiled at Mancebo, who looked up at me with wide eyes.

'What are you going to do, madame?'

'I'm going to follow him. He could be going to meet his wife, and I'd like to do that too. I think she's the one I'm looking for.'

'You're going to shadow him?'

'No, I'm just going to see where he goes, and then I'll ask him if he knows who Monsieur Bellivier is.'

Monsieur Mancebo gave me a confused look, but I didn't have time to find out what was behind it. Monsieur Baker was already on the pavement, and I left the little grocer's shop and quickly crossed the boulevard.

Paris wakes reluctantly. The only people who are alert are the tourists, despite the heat. They want to cram in everything before they leave. Go up the Eiffel Tower, shop at Galeries Lafayette, take pictures of Notre Dame, and also find time to eat snails at a restaurant somewhere, though which restaurant they choose is less important. They don't have time to wait for the city to wake. They don't notice the smell of bread drifting from the bakeries. They don't see the taxi drivers yawning in unison after they finish the night shift. They don't manage to study the skill of the binman standing on the back of the truck, grabbing one bin after another with just one hand as the van drives on. They don't have time to take in the morning calm on a boulevard in one of Europe's biggest cities. They simply don't take the time to experience the city they have come to discover.

Mancebo is someone who has neither the time nor the inclination to discover the city. He doesn't want to do any more searching, not for a good while. He is sitting on his stool on the pavement, watching a strange woman take up pursuit of Ted Baker. Mancebo glances at the empty stool beside him. Just a moment earlier, she was sitting there next to him, asking what he knew about Madame Cat, Ted Baker and Tariq. And, before that, she had knocked on Madame Cat's door, and when no one answered she had madly climbed out onto the roof to peer into the apartment below. It was the first time Mancebo had used his binoculars since the attack.

Mancebo takes a deep breath. He remembers what happened last time he felt so overwhelmed. He can't allow it to happen again. No migraines or collapse. And so he goes inside to sit behind the counter. A copy of the newspaper *Le Parisien* is lying beneath a couple of invoices, and he starts leafing through it, mostly to bring himself back to reality, or away from his own reality. For a long time, he stares at an old weather report. At least that won't give him any surprises or do anything unexpected. More of this kind of thing, Mancebo thinks, leafing forward to the page with the horoscopes. 'Taurus: A week of speed and action which will offer many pleasant surprises. Finances: An unexpected bonus will perk up your finances. Career: Perhaps it's time to change tack? Love: If you have a partner, you'll discover a new side to them.'

Mancebo has never believed in horoscopes, but he does now. He continues to leaf through the paper. Even an old horoscope has the ability to scare him these days.

There's no sign of Amir at lunch, and to begin with Mancebo doesn't know whether he should ask where he is. Eventually, he plucks up the courage. He's responsible for what he has set in motion, after all.

'Isn't Amir coming for lunch?'

The question is aimed at Fatima. She's the one who should know.

'He'll be here soon. He went to meet Khaled. I suppose they'll probably both be here soon.'

'So he's feeling better?'

'Yes, I think so, he's been on his feet all day anyway.'

Just then, the door opens and Amir comes in with a football beneath his arm. He carefully sets it down on the rug in the hallway. Khaled closes the door behind him and comes in to greet everyone already sitting around the table. It's a while since Khaled last came over, but Mancebo can understand Amir's decision to invite a friend round for lunch. Mancebo would like a friendly face by his side too, someone from outside of the family. The problem is that he can't work out who it should be, and that brings him down a little. He doesn't know who he can trust any more. Raphaël, perhaps, but on the other hand he's too close to Tariq. What about François? He feels relatively innocent, but you never know. The two boys sit down. Amir takes the seat at the end of the table, next to Fatima. There's a reason for that, too. As far from the arms dealer as he can get. Tariq jokes with Khaled, and starts playing the spoons.

'Save some energy for tonight,' Fatima snorts at Tariq. 'We need to plan the holiday this evening. When we're going, who we're staying with and so on. I don't want it to be like last year, with me ringing around to find beds for all of us a few days before we leave.'

Adèle nods. Mancebo comes back to his senses and realises that he has forgotten one crucial thing. In a week's time, he's meant to be shutting up shop to go to Tunisia for a month. I'm not going, he thinks. Not under any circumstances. He starts to sweat.

After lunch, Mancebo gives the second-to-last notebook to a girl in a pleated skirt who comes in to buy two bananas. She curtseys in thanks and then hurries out. She was a rabbit, she said, but since there weren't any rabbits left, she took a dragon. Mancebo doesn't even have time to put the money into the till before he, Ted Baker, the writer, his object, Madame Cat's husband, comes into the shop. Mancebo grabs the feather duster, mostly so that he has something to hold on to, turns his back to his customer and begins dusting the canned champignons. The thought that the writer might come into the shop had never struck him before. Mancebo knows it was stupid never to consider it. He does live just over the road, after all.

Mancebo can sense that Monsieur Baker is standing right behind him, but he hasn't heard him put anything down on the counter. Not a good sign, Mancebo thinks. It might mean he's come in for some other reason than to buy something. He starts to imagine that the writer's visit might have something to do with an earlier visit that day; the woman who shadowed the writer must have squealed. This is what happens when I let out a few words about the job to an outsider. I'm in a fix now, Mancebo thinks.

Ted Baker, the writer, the object, suddenly clears his throat.

'Excuse me, monsieur.'

Mancebo swallows, stares at the colourful feather duster and makes a silent prayer. He turns around.

'How can I help, monsieur?'

It's as though Mancebo's heart is trying to leap out of his chest, and he's sure it must be obvious.

'I'd like to buy a bottle of champagne.'

'Of course, not a problem. Which would you like?'

Mancebo points to a few dusty champagne bottles high on a shelf behind the till. Some of them must have been standing there for over a year. It isn't often that someone comes in to buy champagne. He does get the occasional American wanting to spend their last few euros on a bottle before they head home, but usually it's something people buy elsewhere.

Ted Baker peers up at his four options.

'It'll be served as an aperitif.'

Unfortunately, Mancebo can't help; he's a good deal shorter than the writer and he can barely distinguish the bottles from one another.

'Could I have a closer look?'

Ted Baker gestures with his hand, as though to ask whether he can move behind the counter and study the bottles. It's somewhere Mancebo would rather he didn't go. Behind the counter is where he keeps the reports for Madame Cat, the binoculars and Ted Baker's own book, *The Rat Catcher*.

But Monsieur Baker is already behind the till. His blue T-shirt is just a few centimetres away from this week's report, which documents and explains what he has been up to lately.

'I'll take the François Giraux Brut, please,' he eventually says, though he makes no attempt to lift it down from the shelf.

Mancebo has the feeling that Ted Baker is holding back out of respect for him, as the shopkeeper, but it also means that he must now climb up onto the stool to get it down. Mancebo fetches the stool and takes down the bottle. It's the most expensive of the four.

'Celebrating something?'

Mancebo is proud of himself. He's back, this time with smart questions.

'Yes, I suppose you could say that. I've just finished a . . . project.'

'Aha, well that's always something worth celebrating. I'm afraid I don't have anything to wrap the bottle in.'

'It doesn't matter, I just live across the boulevard.'

'You do? I don't remember seeing you before.'

Mancebo doesn't know if the last sentence was too much. It's as though Monsieur Baker disappears for a few seconds. He bites his lip, turns the champagne bottle, and brings his hands to his face.

'Are you OK, monsieur?'

'Sorry . . . it's the heat.'

'Yes, it's taking it out of all of us,' Mancebo replies, puffing slightly.

'I'll take this too.'

The writer places a jar of black olives on the counter. The sound of the glass against the wooden surface is one Mancebo has heard before, and he stares down at the jar.

'Do you think these will go with champagne, monsieur?'

'I'm sure they will. They go with most things,' Mancebo replies.

Mancebo hands him a bag containing the champagne, the olives and the last of the notebooks.

Mancebo has eyes like a hawk. No one buys champagne for themselves. He must be planning to share it with someone. Mancebo almost starts to feel sorry for the writer. He seemed so out of it. He said he had finished a project, and Mancebo wonders whether that might mean he has ended a love affair. There's just one thing

I should be focusing on, Mancebo thinks. Who will Ted Baker be sharing the champagne with? Even if it requires different surveillance methods, he's determined to find out. He swings back on the stool and brings the useless fan to his face.

Tariq raises his hand to show that it's time for a drink. Mancebo hurries to shut up shop, and is ready by the time Tariq makes it over the road. The plan is clear. They start making their way down the boulevard, the afternoon sun lighting their way. But as they turn the corner by the last building, Mancebo suddenly says:

'No, damn it! I forgot to drop off a bag of food at Monsieur Beton's.'

A few times a month, an old veteran by the name of Jean Beton calls Mancebo to place an order, cans mostly, because he is convinced that war is approaching. Usually, it's Amir who drops off the goods.

Monsieur Beton lives in an apartment above the bakery, but Mancebo hasn't heard from him for two months now. Madame Cannava told Mancebo that Monsieur Beton is probably dead, but he doesn't care about that now, and he hopes Tariq hasn't heard about any deaths.

'Can't the man wait an hour?'

'I promised it before four, and you know what he's like. The food's all packed and ready, I just need to take it up. You go ahead, I'll come along if I have time.'

'Can't Amir do it?'

Tariq offers Mancebo his mobile phone, because he knows his cousin rarely brings his own.

'No, I don't want to bother him, he's playing football with Khaled.'

Tariq shoves his phone back into its case, which Mancebo suddenly realises looks like a pistol holster. He trots back to the shop, and gets there just in time to see the door close. Ted Baker has company.

Mancebo positions himself at the corner of Boulevard des Batignolles and Rue Clapeyron. Strategically, it's a good location.

He has a good view of the fire escape, and if Tariq decides to come back early, Mancebo will spot him relatively quickly, perhaps even quickly enough to hide. Fatima, Adèle and Amir won't be able to see him from the apartment and wonder what he's doing there. Purely in terms of surveillance, it isn't the smartest of places to wait, since he can't actually see into the writer's apartment, meaning he also can't see which room the man is in. But Mancebo isn't so dumb that he can't guess.

Despite the exceptional circumstances Mancebo finds himself in, he manages to maintain a calm that any other private detective would be impressed by. His cool state is based on the fact that, for once, he is in control, but also because he knows that this is the start of the end. The thought brings with it a slight sense of melancholy, which in turn results in yet more calm. He glances at his watch and guesses that the visit will soon have been going on for twenty minutes. What will I do if she never comes out? Though she has to at some point. He won't make the same mistake he did last time he caught sight of the woman's arm. This time, he'll keep his cool.

Mancebo decides not to leave his spot on the corner before Tariq comes back. Monsieur Beton must have wanted a long chat. I'll have you soon, Mancebo thinks. You marriage wrecker, people like you should be nailed to the wall.

His pulse picks up. What should he do if the woman leaves the apartment alone? Mancebo starts to feel unsure, he knows that this situation could lead to any number of surprises, which is precisely what he wants to avoid. But he has no choice. He quickly debates it with himself, but he can't come up with any other solution than to follow the woman if she comes out alone. He needs to see who she is, where she lives, maybe even talk to her.

Madame Cat didn't explicitly say that she wanted to know who her husband was having an affair with, but maybe it's obvious that she does. If Fatima was unfaithful, wouldn't he want to know who the man was? The thought of Fatima with someone else still seems unlikely, despite her secrets. He glances at his watch. He feels like a racehorse seconds before the start, shut up in a box waiting to give it his all. Horses usually drool, but Mancebo's mouth is bone dry. Not an ounce of his melancholy is left. This isn't the end. It may be the end of the writer's double life, the end of Ted Baker and Madame Cat's marriage, the end of his notes and the money in the olive jar. It may even be the end of the entire story, but Mancebo's new life has just begun. His right eye begins to twitch.

Suddenly, Mancebo catches sight of a white van pulling up outside the bakery. He recognises it. He recognises the stickers on the side of it. Bad timing for Raphaël to turn up right now, Mancebo thinks. If he's in luck, he'll just be going to repair something in the bakery and hasn't given a thought to visiting Mancebo or Tariq. Mancebo stands still and allows his eyes to roam between Raphaël's van and the fire escape. He can see a woman in the seat next to Raphaël. Mancebo assumes it must be his wife, Camille, and he's even more convinced when he sees them kiss. But everything happens very quickly after that. Suddenly, the woman jumps out of the van and Raphaël starts the engine and drives away. The woman wraps a black shawl around her head and cautiously glances around, then hurries over the boulevard and slips into the doorway beside the grocer's shop. Mancebo is just a few metres away from his cousin's wife as she carefully closes the door behind her.

It's as though Paris falls silent. Mancebo's organs start working more slowly. But there's no time for him to recover, because suddenly the door to the writer's apartment opens and the married couple step outside. Madame Cat is laughing. Ted Baker is holding his wife's hand and carrying a picnic basket in his other hand. Mancebo can see a bottle of François Giraux Brut sticking up out of it. He leans back against the wall, as though attempting to melt into it. A couple of passers-by look at the strange man pressing himself against the brick wall like a timid ghost. Mancebo is afraid. How is he meant to deal with all this information? He can't allow himself to break down again. He doesn't want to see Madame Flouriante. He has to try to save himself.

The day must go on. The fact that life in general would also have to go on is, right now, too much for Mancebo to process. Just the thought that the day has to go on feels overwhelming. His longing for night, when everything is calm, when everyone is in their own bed, is enormous. But the day goes on. Mancebo has heard that people gain unexpected strength in difficult situations, but now he has also experienced how they are actually able to act, to all appearances, like normal when really they are in shock. The ingrained pattern continues, despite the fact that a great deal of brainpower has been knocked out. His reserve engine kicks in, the autopilot takes over and, while waiting for relief – in this case night – everything continues to work pretty much as normal, despite chaos reigning.

After spotting Raphaël and Adèle, everything went black. Mancebo can't remember what he did, but in the end he found himself outside Le Soleil. He can't remember if he waited for Tariq to come out, or if he appeared just as Mancebo arrived. Mancebo has no idea what they talked about on the way back. But they must have come back, because he is now sitting on the stool behind the counter in his shop. It's the only place he dares to be. He no longer knows where he stands in relation to the world outside. Ideally, he would like to be curled up in the foetal position in bed. He glances at his watch and guesses that around two hours must have passed since the revelation.

Mancebo thinks about how many things Raphaël has fixed for Adèle and what Tariq would do if he caught them. That last part causes Mancebo to shudder.

He jumps every time someone comes into the shop, not to mention when the phone rings. At that moment, two boys literally fall into the shop. They seem to have been racing one another, and when one stumbles on the doorstep, they both fall. Mancebo pretends not to notice them until they pick out two packs of biscuits, which they place on the counter. Mancebo takes their money and hands them the right change. His autopilot is working overtime.

'Do you have any notebooks left, monsieur?'

'No, they're finished. And so am I.'

Monsieur Baker hurried along the pavement with light steps. I felt more expectant than nervous as I followed him. In fact, this was the exact kind of thing I had been longing for for so long. Being the active person, the one who thinks they're in control. Having a person, rather than a string of numbers, to focus on for a change. The big yellow metro sign loomed up fifty or so metres ahead, and I managed to find my ticket without slowing down. Monsieur Baker took the stairs below ground.

We weren't sitting far from one another in the carriage. The majority of our fellow passengers were staring at their phones, a few were engrossed in books. One woman was talking quietly to herself while she filed her nails. A young Asian couple were frantically leafing through a dog-eared guidebook. It struck me that the writer and I were the only ones without something in our hands. Monsieur Baker's eyes were fixed on the black tunnel wall. Occasionally, he glanced down at his neighbour's book. I studied the metro map on the roof and tried to work out where he could be going. Maybe he would change lines? If that was the case, his only choice was Charles de Gaulle Étoile.

The metro barely had time to leave the dull grey station of Ternes before it was time to slow down again. And it was as though I had sensed it, because I got up before him. Monsieur Baker was changing lines. Charles de Gaulle Étoile had to be one of Paris's worst stations if you wanted to shadow someone. Its underground corridors snaked off like a crowded family tree, meaning that the people in your field of vision changed rapidly. Just as I became convinced I had lost Monsieur Baker, I spotted him again. He was on an escalator. I tried to remember which exits were at the top, which metro lines he could choose from. If he had a meeting on the Champs-Élysées then he would probably take the first exit on the right after the barriers. I started climbing the escalator and bumped into a big woman who mumbled something behind me.

Monsieur Baker had already made it through the barriers by the time I got to the top. He turned left, which meant he was going to take another train. I started to jog after him. There was nothing un-usual about that, plenty of people were rushing about. Not because they were shadowing someone, but because they were late for work or wanted to catch the next train out to the suburbs.

The corridor Monsieur Baker had chosen led to line number 1. La Défense was the end of the line. He was standing in the middle of the platform when I came out of the corridor, and I chose to wait right behind him. The train quickly thundered into the station. The doors opened and people poured out. Before everyone had managed to get off, those waiting to get on began to push their way forward. I didn't want to get too close to Monsieur Baker, but nor did I want to run the risk of not making it onto the train. In some strange way, he seemed completely indifferent to all of the pushing and shoving. He just calmly positioned himself in the middle of the carriage and firmly gripped the handrail. I pushed my way in behind him and stood by the doors.

The train left Charles de Gaulle Étoile with a jolt, and a middle-aged woman in a red dress almost fell. Luckily, she managed to grab a man's arm at the last minute. She apologised, but the man seemed more pleased that he had been able to help. They started talking about transportation in the city and why the new trains were taking so long. Monsieur Baker seemed interested in following their conversation. There were five stations before La Défense that he could get off at. At each stop, I readied myself to leave the train. But he stayed where he was, listening to the man and the woman, who had now realised they didn't live at all far from one another. When the metro stopped at Porte Maillot, a family with small children attempted to get off with all of their luggage. They apologised to everyone at the receiving end of the sharp corners of their suitcases. In all likelihood, they would be taking one of the Ryanair buses to Beauvais airport.

The metro continued, drawing closer and closer to its final destination. At Les Sablons, an old woman pushed her way on board. Her hands were full of carrier bags, which probably contained everything she owned. She was barefoot but dressed warmly. I watched her struggle to transfer all of the bags to one hand so that she could use the other to beg for change. With her entire life in one hand, she now moved around the slightly emptier carriage. A few people shook their heads. Others pretended not to see her. She didn't seem to care what reaction her outstretched hand caused. Monsieur Baker studied the woman's face, and as she moved in front of him he placed a couple of euros in her dirty palm. She nodded in thanks.

The woman in the red dress and the man who had unintentionally saved her from a fall seemed relieved when the beggar left the carriage. When the metro pulled into Pont de Neuilly, they both stepped out onto the platform. Would they see one another again, I managed to wonder before the doors closed. As we pulled out of the station, Monsieur Baker turned around as though to catch one last glimpse of the couple who had just found one another. Maybe he was also thinking about their future. Two stations left.

The metro pulled into Esplanade de La Défense. I realised that Monsieur Baker had no intention of getting off there, either. His only option now was the final station, La Défense. I wondered what he could be doing in the business district at this time of day. And, as though on cue, everyone shoved whatever they had been holding – their phones, books, nail files – into their bags. It was time to get off. I was back where it had all begun. Then, like now, I didn't take any risks, just one thing at a time.

I accidentally came too close to Monsieur Baker. His blue T-shirt rubbed up against my bag. He was only a few centimetres away from the cheque inside it. Was it his handwriting on it? Or his wife's? I gave him a head start. He took the escalator up to the plaza out-side the shopping centre. He didn't look up at Areva, he continued straight towards the Cnit building instead. I picked up the pace. He had a meeting. I was convinced of it as I stepped into the huge complex. The glass lifts shot up and down, but he continued past them towards the lifts at the back of the building.

I quickly ran into an interior-decoration shop to let him take the lift before me. For the first time, I felt nervous. Once Monsieur Baker had stepped into the lift, I left my spot behind the huge vases. The lifts had only one destination: the Hilton restaurant.

Though the restaurant spread across the entire floor, I immediately spotted Monsieur Baker at one of the window tables. There was a blonde woman sitting opposite him, with her back to me. I could have gone straight over, but I decided to head to the bar, have a coffee and gather my thoughts for a few minutes.

Monsieur Baker took the woman's hands without saying anything to her. They kissed, and that was the starting shot for me to act. I walked over to their table. The woman looked familiar. To begin with, I couldn't place her, but then I realised who she was. Monsieur Baker had just kissed the receptionist from Areva.

'Excuse me.'

He looked up at me with kind eyes. The receptionist, on the other hand, seemed terrified. Neither of them said anything.

'We've met before,' I said, holding my hand out to the receptionist.

315

She had a weak handshake.

'Nice to meet you,' I said, looking Monsieur Baker straight in the eye.

He glanced at the receptionist, as though searching for an explanation.

'It's her,' the woman said, squeezing her lover's hand.

The writer looked disappointed. I sat down and he started talking. He had no choice. If he explained, there was a chance everything could go ahead as planned.

After yesterday's discovery, Mancebo had followed his son's example and pretended to be ill, going to lie down immediately after dinner. Nothing strange about that. He could have caught it from Amir. That night, he got up and packed a bag. He now has it stashed in the broom cupboard in his shop. The entire day has been spent behind the counter; he doesn't want to see anything else.

Dusk is approaching, and Mancebo is in Tariq's office. His cousin is helping him with his accounts and his tax return. Tariq thinks that Mancebo is eager to get all of the paperwork done because he's going on holiday soon, but that's not the reason. Mancebo feels ill as he sits there, surrounded by shoeboxes. In one sense, it's pure madness to keep weapon parts and cigarettes in the open like that, but in another it's a stroke of genius. No one ever suspects what's right in front of them. Tariq eventually stacks the papers into a pile and shoves them into a folder which he hands to his cousin.

'That's everything, brother. You can go on holiday with a clear conscience now.'

The minute Mancebo steps out of the cobbler's and sees who is waiting outside his own shop, he hurries across the boulevard without checking for traffic. A car horn honks. The woman who followed Ted Baker smiles when she spots him. All Mancebo wants is to get her inside as quickly as possible, and once he has her sitting on one of the stools, he thanks God that she gets straight to the point. He has no interest in hearing anything other than the necessary.

'Well, I just came back to tell you what happened when I followed Monsieur Baker, I thought it might be of interest to you, too.'

Indeed it might, Mancebo thinks.

'Anyway, I followed him all the way to a café in La Défense, and waiting for him there was . . .'

The woman's mobile phone beeps and she falls silent and looks down at it. Mancebo feels like he is sitting next to an ill-mannered teenager, someone who sees no problem in giving all of their attention to their phone, even in the company of others. Please, Mancebo thinks, I can't handle any more. It's already over, I've capitulated, just tell me what you know and then leave me in peace.

'Sorry, the writer had a meeting in a café, with another male author.'

Was that it, Mancebo wonders.

'I didn't see any sign of a lover. But what do I know?'

Mancebo is trying to think straight.

'Did you find the answers you were looking for?'

'Yes, Monsieur Baker is Monsieur Bellivier.'

'So that Ted Baker is just a sedonym?'

'A pseudonym, yes. It seems like we've both been waiting for Monsieur Bellivier.'

For the second time, Mancebo watches as the woman disappears down the boulevard. His mouth is wide open. He feels completely empty. Finished.

'Am I interrupting?' Amir asks, though he doesn't come into the shop.

Mancebo turns around, closes his mouth, and looks blankly at his son. Just a few weeks earlier, he would never have asked, he would have just come straight in. But now that Amir knows what Mancebo has to deal with every day, he has a new-found respect for his father. Mancebo hasn't quite made it back to reality yet, and he's staring into space.

'Is everything OK, Dad?'

Mancebo nods.

'It's just that Mum's on the way out . . . I thought you might want to know.'

'Let her go.'

'Yeah, but after everything that's happened . . . She got a phone call and suddenly everything was a rush . . . I asked where she was going and she said "sort out the money". I don't know if she was joking, but after everything that's happened . . .'

Amir steps into the shop and then pauses, with his eyes fixed out on the boulevard.

'Anyway, she seems to be in a hurry,' he says with a nod.

Mancebo looks out towards the boulevard and sees Fatima rush past with a white box beneath her arm. OK, Mancebo thinks, I'll do it for my son. Even if it's the last thing I do.

'I'll go. Can you look after the shop for a few minutes?'

Amir nods. Mancebo thinks, or perhaps he's just imagining it, that he can see both excitement and admiration in his son's eyes. Why would he have come down to the shop to tell Mancebo that Fatima was heading out unless he wanted to see his father chase after her?

'You can trust me, Dad,' Amir says, squinting in the afternoon sun.

'And you can trust me, my son,' Mancebo says, throwing himself out onto the boulevard with his coat-tails flapping behind him.

Fatima slows down as she turns onto Rue de Rome, and Mancebo also drops the pace. He knows where she's going. Behind the curtain. He'll catch them red-handed, he thinks. But what does that mean? That the huge tobacconist will be standing with his pants around his ankles and Fatima . . . ? The image is grotesque, and Mancebo is worried that he will be the one to feel most guilty when he sees it. Mancebo is sweating and he slows down, though he knows there's a risk he will lose her. But he knows where she's going. He can't get there too early, either. It must surely take a few minutes before they really get down to business. Not too early, but not too late either, Mancebo thinks, wondering how the tobacconist goes about it, from a purely practical point of view. Does he shut up shop?

He can't see Fatima any longer. Mancebo has made it to the tobacconist's shop and he glances at his watch. I'll give them ten minutes, no, five, he thinks. I'll give them five minutes, and not a second more. But after just one, he can't contain himself any longer and tries, from his position on the pavement, to work out what's going on inside. He can make out some kind of movement behind the curtain. He gives them exactly one minute and thirty-six seconds before he goes in.

He carefully opens the door so that the bell makes only the slightest of sounds. Mancebo now knows why the tobacconist's shop has a warning bell. He wipes the sweat from his brow. The curtain is moving rhythmically.

He supports himself on the counter so that he can move as quietly as possible, and luckily there are a couple of tabloids lying on the floor. Like a predator preparing to attack, he pauses. He spends a moment weighing up whether to pull the curtain to the left or the right. He can't remember which he eventually chooses, because in the heat of the moment it's just about getting rid of the curtain. And he does it with such force that, suddenly, he finds himself standing there with a piece of brown fabric in his hands.

Mancebo's wife and the tobacconist look up at the intruder in terror. Fatima, who is usually so talkative, is completely speechless. Mancebo, who is usually so awkward and aimless, has just a few seconds to take charge of the situation. On the table behind what used to be the curtain, he can see shoebox after shoebox full of cartons of cigarettes. There's no doubt that the boxes have come from Tariq's cobbler's shop. After all these years, Mancebo would recognise those boxes anywhere; they're such bad quality that even the slightest hint of moisture makes them fall to pieces. Tariq buys them cheaply from a removals firm in a suburb to the north of Paris. Everything now makes sense. Fatima shakes her head and her eyes flash. The tobacconist puts the lid back onto one of the boxes and scratches his broad neck.

'Well, the game's over now,' Mancebo says theatrically.

It takes a second or two for Fatima to spot her chance to regain control.

'The game? There's no need to be so dramatic.'

She even tries a smile.

'Yes, the game's over. I know everything.'

Fatima stares at her husband, astounded.

They couldn't agree on who first came up with the idea. It had started when the receptionist mentioned to her lover that the top floor of the building where she worked was completely empty. One night, after they checked in to the Hilton, Monsieur Baker had reluctantly admitted that his writing wasn't going as he'd hoped. His publisher back in England was putting pressure on him, and he needed to come up with something new.

On another occasion, also at the Hilton, the writer had revealed that he'd lost his enthusiasm for sitting alone all day, writing. Every morning, he would watch other people as they headed to work. He wanted to be one of them. He'd read about cyber nomads, the people who moved from café to café with their work, a modern way of working for those in solitary jobs like his. Maybe he could become one of them.

During a sleepless night, the writer's lover had come up with an idea, and she had presented it to him the very next morning. To begin with, Monsieur Baker had been wildly enthusiastic. The experiment would give him if not the entire story, then the inspiration for something new at the very least. And then he had lost his nerve; it would be too complicated to pull off. But the lover managed to convince him by saying she would take care of all of the details, that the concept was simple. The whole thing was self-sufficient.

Like a human chain letter. By using the cashed cheques, Monsieur Bellivier, aka Ted Baker, would be able to find out the identities of his test subjects, and after the experiment was over, the plan was to gather them all together one evening so that they could share their experiences. It was a unique idea, and the book would be completely different to anything he had written before.

The experiment required a lot of money, which the writer had; what he lacked was inspiration. And inspiration was precisely what he would find by watching how these creative cyber nomads managed to work, in complete isolation, on a boring, verging on pointless, task. At the end of each day, they would be given a randomly chosen gift. All to see how they reacted and what the consequences would be. Were they happy to just sit there doing as they were told, or did they take on the task of trying to work out who Monsieur Bellivier was and why they were carrying out this peculiar job?

But now I had found them out. Neither the writer nor the receptionist asked anything of me, but they led me to understand that though I now knew everything, they would prefer it if I didn't break the chain. Before I left, I had one last question for them: how many more people would there be after me? Two more, they said, and then the experiment would end. I didn't need to make up my mind immediately. If I cashed the second cheque, Areva would welcome a new guest. I had time to think.

I couldn't remember when I had last been out at night. And for the first time ever, I had a babysitter. I glanced up at the fire escape, but I couldn't quite picture how it must have looked as I was balancing up there on the narrow roof section. The pink shoe was illuminated, meaning that the cobbler's shop was open. But the grocer's was closed. Maybe Monsieur Mancebo was away on some kind of job. I decided to wait a few minutes. I wasn't in any hurry. And if he didn't turn up, I could come back another day. I was free and it wasn't urgent. Or so I thought.

'Good evening, madame.'

I hadn't needed to wait long. Monsieur Mancebo had a dogged look on his face as he unlocked the door and stepped inside. I followed him in. Somehow, in some strange way, I felt at home in the shop, despite the fact I had only ever been there once before.

'Quiet?' I asked.

'Yes, a lot of people are on holiday, and . . . or did you mean quiet across the street?'

He nodded discreetly in the direction of Monsieur Bellivier's building. I didn't know quite what I had meant.

'Well, I just came back to tell you what happened when I followed Monsieur Baker, I thought it might be of interest to you, too.'

I had come here to tell the truth. He had helped me, so it was obvious that I should help him in return. That was how the world worked. Monsieur Mancebo grabbed the two stools, but this time he set them down inside the shop, and I sat down beneath a shelf of jars of olives.

'Anyway, I followed him all the way to a café in La Défense, and waiting for him there was . . .'

I heard a beep. I apologised and looked down at the phone I was clutching in my hand. It was the first time I'd left my son with a babysitter, after all. I'd received a photograph, taken by Monsieur Caro as he and my son sat by the chessboard. Only half of my son's face was visible in my picture, and I guessed it was probably Monsieur Caro's first selfie. 'Everything's fine. He's still alive,' he had written. I smiled. For a second, my weeks at Areva flashed through my head.

Dusk had started to fall. A small bird was hopping around outside the door, and I suddenly realised what I was about to do. If I told Monsieur Mancebo the truth, I would be the one who had drawn a line under the whole thing. I would prevent other people from experiencing what I had experienced. I had solved my mystery, surely it was up to Monsieur Mancebo to solve his own. And if he couldn't, then maybe it was meant to stay a secret. For everyone's sake. I looked at the photo again. It hadn't been difficult to convince Monsieur Caro to be my babysitter.

'Sorry, the writer had a meeting in a café, with another male author.'

Monsieur Mancebo gave me a quizzical look.

'I didn't see any sign of a lover. But what do I know?'

'Did you find the answers you were looking for?' he asked, unconsciously giving me an explanation as to why I had come back when I didn't actually have anything to reveal.

'Yes, Monsieur Baker is Monsieur Bellivier.'

'So that Ted Baker is just a sedonym?'

'A pseudonym, yes. It seems like we've both been waiting for Monsieur Bellivier.'

I left Boulevard des Batignolles and headed in the direction of Place de Clichy. It felt as though I was going against the flow. As though the pavement was one way. People passed me by, but no one walked alongside me. I saw a couple of prostitutes getting themselves ready for the Paris night in a stairwell. They would probably walk over to Rue Saint-Denis or take a taxi to Bois de Boulogne.

In the late-night pharmacies, addicts crowded for space alongside the parents of small children wanting to collect their prescriptions in the hope of a good night's sleep. They all looked exhausted. The restaurants were welcoming their first guests of the evening, and though it was still quiet, the waiters seemed stressed. They always did. It went with the job. A couple of West African women held up bags of food to one another, and it seemed as though they were swapping vegetables between themselves. A few older men were playing boules on the little strip of sand in the middle of the avenue. A group of teenagers were pretending to fight while their friends cheered them on. A young man next to them, high on drugs, was seeing things no one else could. The police passed by without even noticing him.

One person after another passed me by, each making an impression on me. Then I arrived. And there he was. He didn't walk past me, he was more of an obstacle in my way. And it was as though he had been able to feel my approach from behind, because he turned around.

'It's my turn to give you flowers,' Christophe said, holding out a bouquet.

I realised that I could still appreciate flowers after all.

There's no doubt about it, Fatima has had time to tell Tariq what happened. That Mancebo found her at the tobacconist's. Equally certain is the fact that Tariq will have come up with a more or less believable explanation for it all. Mancebo continues to process the situation in his head. Tariq knows that Fatima smokes. Fatima knows about Tariq's arms dealing and Adèle's infidelity. She must.

But what does Adèle know? Mancebo isn't at all sure about that. She must know that Fatima smokes, but is that all? Her nerves might not be up to caring about the rest, or maybe it's her knowledge of the weapons dealing that ruined her nerves. Mancebo feels like he has the power structures in his family clear in his mind as he locks the door to his shop and climbs the stairs towards dinner, towards the end of the drama, whistling as he goes.

When he makes it upstairs, he is greeted by silence. Fatima smiles at him. Something she never normally does. There's no sign of anyone else.

'Where is everyone?' he asks.

Fatima seems relieved, as though the question shows that her husband will continue to act as normal, as though nothing has happened, as though he won't bring up the events of the day. But she is wrong.

'Adèle's drying her hair and Tariq's picking up Raphaël, he's eating with us tonight.'

Fitting, Mancebo thinks, very fitting. Couldn't be better.

'Which is good, because Amir's not eating with us tonight,' Fatima informs her husband before she vanishes into the kitchen.

Fitting, Mancebo thinks, very fitting. The conditions seem ideal. Amir is smart, Mancebo thinks. My son, he'll go on to do great things. Adèle comes into the room and wraps her headscarf around her hair, but she deliberately leaves one strand loose. Mancebo knows why, and he sits down at the table and lights a cigarette. Adèle stares at him with wide eyes and then starts to giggle hysterically.

'What next? Have you been given permission to smoke before dinner?'

If Fatima hears Adèle's words, she doesn't come out of the kitchen. Mancebo is sure she'll stay there until Raphaël and Tariq arrive. He draws the smoke deep into his lungs. It tastes good. It's the best damn cigarette I've ever smoked, Mancebo thinks, looking out at the boulevard. Adèle peers at him in amusement and then they hear the sound of the door downstairs. The last few are on their way up. Mancebo stubs out his cigarette, though it isn't finished, and lights a new one. Tariq and Raphaël come into the room. Tariq produces a strained smile for Mancebo. The same kind of smile Fatima recently flashed at him. They're alike, those two, Mancebo thinks. You would almost think they were related.

'Have you seen this, he's smoking before dinner!' Adèle laughs.

'Yeah, what are we going to do with this one,' Tariq jokes.

Fatima appears from the kitchen. Adèle eagerly waits to see what she will do or say when she sees her husband smoking before they eat.

'Can't you see?' Adèle blurts out.

Fatima looks nonplussed.

'Your husband's smoking before dinner! It's his second cigarette!'

'Yes, what are we going to do with him,' Fatima mumbles before she heads back into the kitchen.

Adèle seems bewildered by Fatima's cool reaction. Raphaël shakes Mancebo's hand and greets Adèle with kisses on the cheek. Hypocrite, Mancebo thinks, taking a long drag on his cigarette. Fatima returns with bowl after bowl of food and places them all on the table.

'Well, dig in,' she says as she sits down.

It's time for Mancebo to do it. But because he is enjoying the situation so much, he feels a slight reluctance. He wants to draw it out a little, but he knows that he risks losing the perfect moment if he does. Amir could come home, Raphaël has an uncanny ability to suddenly run off to fix something, Adèle might decide to go and lie down . . . He has to seize his chance now.

Mancebo picks up the heavy rice spoon and wipes it with his napkin. He has never clinked a glass to get everyone's attention before, and he does it a bit too hard. The gentle clinking he'd planned sounds more like an attempt to break the glass. But it has the desired effect all the same. Everyone stops talking and pauses, other than Adèle, who continues chewing and smiles in amusement.

'Yes, I'd just like to say a few words. It won't take long.'

Tariq and Fatima try, despite their nerves, to look as cool and peaceful as they can. Adèle and Raphaël are calm, albeit slightly confused.

'We all have our secrets, or so I've learnt. Secrets can cause damage. Your secrets have hurt me, and I would like to share what I have learnt so they don't do any more damage. We're all grown adults here, and that means we can take responsibility for our actions.'

'Darling, can't we do this later, we have a guest this evening.'

Fatima nods in the direction of Raphaël. I was right, Mancebo thinks, Raphaël was only invited as a kind of buffer, a shield, a way of keeping the evening nice and calm.

'No, it's an excellent opportunity precisely because we have Raphaël here.'

Adèle casts a quick glance at Raphaël, who takes a deep breath before he meets his lover's eye.

'It's always difficult to know where to begin, but I'll start with the parts which affect me directly. My wife smuggles cigarettes to the fat tobacconist on Rue de Chéroy. She gets the cigarettes from Tariq, who runs an extensive cigarette-smuggling ring.'

Mancebo looks out at the people around the table and realises that this information was news only to Raphaël. He knows them so well that he can tell precisely what they know, even though they all react differently.

'You're exaggerating,' says Fatima. 'I sold a few packets left over after Tariq was given them by a friend. I told you as much already. So, can we eat now?'

'No, not yet. Tariq has a cobbler's shop, we all know that, but in actual fact, on the side of the cigarettes, his business is in dealing weapons.'

'No, enough now, man!' Fatima shouts.

Tariq glances at Fatima, as though looking for an explanation as to how his cousin could have found that out. Did she squeal in an attempt to exonerate herself from what happened earlier?

Mancebo looks at everyone around the table. This was news to Adèle and Raphaël.

'Don't listen to what he says,' Tariq whispers to Adèle, taking her hand. 'He's gone mad.'

Adèle seems terrified.

'Yes, and that brings me to Adèle and Raphaël.'

Mancebo has reached the part he was most looking forward to. He turns to Tariq.

'Your wife is having an affair with your friend Raphaël.'

Everyone but Tariq knew about this, Mancebo quickly determines. Tariq drops his wife's hand. Adèle raises both hands to her face.

'Do you know what you're accusing us of?' Raphaël snaps.

'Yes,' Mancebo says, loud and clear. 'And finally, being a greengrocer isn't my primary job. I'm a private detective now. So, time to eat.'

It didn't take me long to work out what I needed to do to hand over the baton. I'd done some preparation. I didn't really know whether that was allowed, maybe there were rules about the victim needing to be a complete stranger, someone you had never had any contact with. But I had felt compelled to soften up my chosen person a few days earlier, by smiling at him as he worked in a café.

A newspaper article had given me an idea of what I should use the second cheque for. The article was about a study which had shown that the French preferred *l'éclair* above all other baked goods. That was what would be awaiting him at the end of every day. I had ample budget for three weeks' worth of éclairs.

I went to the biggest bakery in the business district. The assistant gave me a strange look and asked me to wait. After a while, an older woman came forward and asked what I wanted, despite the fact that she had probably already been told. I suppose she wanted to make sure someone really was asking for éclairs to be delivered to an office every day for a few weeks.

The woman shook her head and said that they didn't do that kind of thing. I could have turned on my heel, I could have come up with something else or gone to another bakery, but I just wanted to get it over and done with. I explained how much I was willing to pay. The older woman studied me and asked me to wait. By now, practically every member of staff knew about my request. They looked at one another and then smiled at me. Their smiles were quite hard to read. Maybe they felt sorry for me, maybe they thought I was mad. The woman came back.

'We have an apprentice who could deliver them, but we'll need to know the exact address and the relevant days.'

I felt quite proud of myself, pulled out the contract and wrote out everything necessary.

But reality caught up with me. What was I about to do? If the man was going to accept the task, there were so many obstacles in the way. For the first time, I became convinced that the strange chain letters were going to end with me. It would be a shame. My eyes scanned the people in the café. The man was sitting where he usually did. Now or never. I felt ill. He wore a gold signet ring on his chubby ring finger. I hate signet rings. I slowly moved over to his table. He snatched the newspaper out of the way. I smiled.

'Are you waiting for . . . Monsieur Bellivier?'

Monsieur Rossi hadn't said that I had to start with that question, but it felt as though it was part of the game. If you took that away, maybe the rest of it would collapse. I did, however, modify the question by adding an unnaturally long pause before uttering Monsieur Bellivier's name. In doing so, it was clear that there was no Monsieur Bellivier and that it was just an excuse to start a conversation.

'Am I waiting for Monsieur Bellivier?' he asked, sounding slightly amused.

He didn't want to seem unsure. Not to me, in any case. A scared man was good. This was all just a game. I fished out the key to the office and started playing with it in my fingers. I had been planning to save that gesture for later, but I didn't know what I would do otherwise. I nodded in reply to his question. Bit my lip, but quickly realised that my improvisation was starting to turn into some kind of parody. The newspaper on the table saved me.

'He picked the wrong woman,' I said.

There was a picture of Dominique Strauss-Kahn, the former head of the International Monetary Fund, splashed across the cover. The man who had sexually assaulted a woman in a New York hotel.

There was no doubt about it. He was convinced I was trying to chat him up.

'And you'd be the right woman?' he asked with a nervous laugh.

He seemed pleased with his comment. I held out my hand.

'It's not far from here. Just there.'

I pointed over to Areva. The Hilton was right next to it.

Only a few weeks earlier, I had been worried about being mistaken for an escort, but now I was trying to do just that. The man was convinced we would be going to a hotel room together. A day-use room which could be booked by tired or horny businessmen for a few hours.

Maybe he would change his mind once he realised we were on the way into a skyscraper. Maybe not. Maybe he was so horny that it would take him a while to cool down. The man closed the lid of his computer and grabbed his coat. I could see in his eyes that he was trying to think rationally, to think through his horniness. He glanced around and then followed me in the belief that I was a woman who wanted him.

It was time to cool him down, to plant the seed of doubt.

'It's the very top floor. Did you know that Giovanni Agnelli, the CEO of Fiat, used to have the entire top floor as his apartment?'

We headed towards reception, and I started to feel slightly sorry for him. I was calm. The receptionist looked up and caught sight of me. She did all she could to avoid a smile, but it was no good. She got up and came back with a pass.

'Thank you, madame,' I said.

She looked at me. She was part of the game. The man was sweating. He took the pass and looked down at it. I suspected he was debating with himself, maybe he would decide to put a stop to things there and then.

The lift plinged and we reached the very top. I realised I had to act quickly and therefore handed him the key. It wasn't enough. He was neither horny nor interested in playing along any more. The thought that I could grab his crotch ran through my mind. I was desperate, he couldn't pull out now, not now we'd come so far. We stepped out of the lift and I grabbed the contract.

'Monsieur Bellivier would like you to read this carefully and check that the amount is correct. That you approve the payment.'

With the mention of money, I managed to pique his interest again. He read as we walked down the corridor. I stopped in front of the door. He already had the key.

'This is your office.'

He started searching his pockets, and I thought about how much of a turn-off it would have been if we had actually been going up there for sex and he started emptying his pockets to look for a key. He unlocked the door and immediately entered the room as though it was his. A feeling of anger washed over me; the room was still mine. How many hours had I spent looking out at the Sacré-Cœur from that window?

'Sit down and read through the contract, I'll fetch some coffee.'

I didn't know if I was doing the right thing by leaving him alone, and so I hurried downstairs and quickly returned with two coffees. He was sitting in my chair, behind my desk, at my computer. The imposter. I would probably never get another opportunity to see Paris the way I had these past few weeks. He would get to live my life, a life which wasn't really mine. I'd borrowed it from Monsieur Rossi, who had borrowed it from someone else. The man turned around as though he'd been able to read my thoughts behind his back.

'Have you had time to read the contract?'

He ran his hand over his chin. It was as though he had become uglier once he realised this didn't have anything to do with sex. Not that he had been attractive before, but his entire body language had changed.

'Yes, yes,' he eventually said. 'And this sum of money at the end of the . . . project, or whatever it is?'

'Yes, didn't you know?'

I needed to put him in his place, I needed to make him so unsure of himself that I could row this thing ashore. And I got my way. It was as though he became aware that the question might be his downfall, that he would never get a glimpse of the payment.

'Yes, yeah, but you just want to be certain before you sign, you know?'

'Of course,' I said, placing the mug of coffee beside him.

He got up and moved over to the window. He stood there like that for some time. I wasn't worried, I knew he would sign the contract. It was as though he was saying goodbye to something. A trip, a friend, a job.

I held out the pen. He signed. His signature gave me one last chance to make him doubt himself. I studied the scrawl at the bottom of the contract and heard him swallow. He quickly held out his hand. This was a man who was used to acting. It had been the prospect of sex which made him follow me up here, but it was the money which had made him stay. Those weren't good motives in the long run.

'Excuse me,' I said quickly, pretending that I had received a phone call.

I left the room and walked over to the lift. I prayed a silent prayer before I returned.

'That was Monsieur Bellivier.'

The man smiled and sat down.

'He wanted me to say that he's thrilled you've accepted to do this as compensation. He also said that he knows you like American authors, so if you get bored there are some books in the box beneath the desk.'

The man didn't say anything. Even if he was only doing it for the money, I had, at least, given him something to think about.

'And the agreed fee, I get that from you?'

You money-hungry pig, I thought, reminding myself that he had only followed me up there for sex.

'It's all in the contract. Oh, one more thing, though you may already know. It's best if you try not to mix with the other employees here.'

We took the lift back down to reception in silence. A group of men in suits were laughing, a corpulent secretary was running after a young man with a document, a few women were chatting. A man was playing with his cufflinks as he talked on the phone. The receptionist pretended not to see me.

I held out my hand and said goodbye to the man.

What a damn circus, Mancebo thinks, looking out at the room. Adèle's hairdryer is in three pieces on the floor. 'Try to fix it now!' Tariq had shouted as he smashed it in front of Raphaël. There's rice all over the red Persian rug, and Raphaël, in his rush to leave the apartment as quickly as possible, has forgotten his phone. The same phone on which Tariq found proof that what Mancebo accused him of was true.

To begin with, Raphaël had flatly denied the accusations. He would never do that to his best friend. Tariq had then calmly asked to borrow Raphaël's phone. He hadn't stayed calm for long after that.

Once Raphaël left the apartment, Tariq had taken his wife over to the cobbler's shop. From the window, Mancebo had watched him practically drag her across the boulevard. What they are talking about now, in the brightly lit shop, Mancebo has no idea. At Tariq's request, Fatima has gone up to her own apartment.

Mancebo is alone at the table. There's enough food for five people, and he takes turns eating and smoking. He hears a knock at the door downstairs, gets up and glances over to the cobbler's shop. Tariq is sitting in the armchair in his office, and Adèle is opposite him with her face buried in her hands. There's another knock. It must be the shop door. Mancebo stubs out his cigarette and immediately lights a new one, then he heads downstairs.

He leaves the door to Tariq and Adèle's apartment open, because he doesn't know whether they took any keys with them when they fled. Maybe Raphaël will come back to pick up his phone, or maybe Mancebo will feel like eating again in a while. If any burglars happen to pass by, the place is in such a state that they would probably turn around in the doorway thinking that one of their colleagues had beaten them to it. Mancebo hears another knock. This time, it's harder.

'Yes, yes, yes, I'm coming,' he mutters as he walks down the stairs.

Her green eyes glow in the darkness. Mancebo lets Madame Cat into the shop. She looks tired, and she is holding a white shoebox in one hand, something which makes Mancebo freeze. He's had enough of those boxes.

For the last time, Mancebo takes out the two stools and places them in the middle of the shop. He can see Tariq shouting at Adèle on the other side of the road, gesturing wildly with his arms as he does it. What a bloody boulevard, Mancebo thinks, just as Madame Cat suddenly bursts into tears.

After a few awkward attempts to provide some comfort by patting her on the shoulder and reassuring her that everything will be OK, Mancebo decides not to do any more and to let her finish crying instead. When Madame Cat leans against Mancebo's shoulder, the lid on the box shifts slightly and he catches a glimpse of a dead body – a bird. It's the one which flew into his window. He has no idea how he can be so sure. And as though by reflex, he pushes Madame Cat away. She has a body under her arm, that could mean something. In mafia circles, they use dead animals as a warning that a close friend or relative is going to be executed. He can't allow himself to forget that she is, after all, a stranger.

'Madame Bellivier, what do you have in your box?'

Mancebo feels proud. If she's going to try to kill him, he has, at least, elegantly shown that he knows her real name.

'Oh, sorry. It's a bird. I found it on the pavement outside a while ago. I kept it on the windowsill to begin with, but it bothered my husband when he was working and I put it into the freezer. But that's no place to be left lying. I haven't had the chance to bury it yet, but I wanted to do it tonight. Maybe it would be symbolic, burying this whole story with it.'

Mancebo feels slightly calmer with regards to his mafia theory, but he is also disappointed that she didn't react to him knowing her real name.

'I got your reports and wanted to come and say thanks. You've done a good job.'

'I don't know if I've been any help . . .'

'Yes, you've done everything I asked. And I know, at least, that the woman doesn't come to our house. Maybe he does have some respect for me, after all.'

'So you still think your husband is having an affair?'

Madame Bellivier gives Mancebo a resigned look.

'I don't think. I know.'

Mancebo is convinced she's about to bring up female intuition, or use her husband acting strangely as proof. The kind of thing which would never stand up in a court of law. But instead, she shoves a hand into the pocket of her sleeveless black dress.

'Could you hold this a minute?' she says, handing Mancebo the shoebox.

Mancebo reluctantly takes it from her, but he holds it at arm's length. It smells like death. Madame Bellivier takes out two scraps of paper.

'Here are two receipts. I found them among my husband's papers. He bought a case of wine to share with his lover. And he's also been buying flowers. Every day for three weeks, he's had a bouquet delivered to her. I'd call that courting someone.'

Madame Bellivier's slender finger points to the total for the deliveries.

'I even went to the florist to see if there was any explanation, but it's so obvious . . .'

I'll be damned, Mancebo thinks.

'What are you going to do now, madame?'

Madame Bellivier is staring straight ahead, but then she shrugs.

'I don't know. All I know is I can't stay here. But I don't know where to go or what to do.'

Like me, Mancebo thinks, but he doesn't say anything, despite his desire to tell her his story.

'I can take that now.'

Mancebo is so surprised by the evidence she has managed to uncover that he completely forgot he was holding a bird coffin.

'Well, I'll go and bury this.'

Madame Bellivier attempts a smile.

'I'll join you,' says Mancebo.

He grabs his suitcase from the cupboard and locks up his shop for the last time. Mancebo and Madame Bellivier wander down the boulevard together. He can see Sacré-Cœur on the horizon. For the first time, Mancebo admits to himself that his grocer's shop isn't at the foot of Montmartre.

I read the last sentence in Judith's diary twice. It's as though I don't want things to come to an end. I now know that what I have in my hands is unique material. I carefully close the first diary and look out across the café. I've been looking forward to this day. Now that everything is like it was before. Only now, everything just feels empty and sad. But then I think of my neighbour, the man who had no say in where the line was drawn, and I pack up my things and leave the café.

A homeless man is curled up on the air vent above the metro's ventilation system. His mattress is nothing but a couple of blankets, and I can see a wine bottle sticking out from between them. Like a maladjusted Princess and the Pea. His feet are shoved into a pair of shoes far too big for him, and a string of saliva is trickling down his cheek from his open mouth. There's a dog's lead on the ground next to him, but I can't see any sign of a dog. And it's while I'm searching for the dog that I see it: a white, half-open box with gold writing on the lid. Inside, there's a fresh *l'éclair au chocolat*. Melancholy courses through me. Everything continues.

The ashtray is smoking. It almost always is, since Mancebo leaves the cigarettes to burn out on their own. He likes to watch the smoke curl up towards the ceiling in the stuffy room.

Three huge, brown leather armchairs surround a heavy marble table. The blinds are closed, but angled so that the sun's merciless light can still force its way in.

Through the window, the Sacré-Cœur is visible. Next to the ashtray, on the marble table, there's a small black device which could easily be mistaken for a modern mini calculator. But it's no help with additions and subtractions, it checks the authenticity of banknotes. Its red light blinks away, ever-ready to test the worth of those thin but valuable slips of paper. Beside the device, a pair of binoculars.

The phone rings. Someone out there needs his help. Mancebo wants to launch himself at the phone, but he allows it to ring a few times to give his prospective client the impression that he's extremely busy. He wonders whether the job might be to do with suspected illegal activity, suspected infidelity, a missing person . . .